Sarah Challis has lived in Scotland and California. She now lives in a Dorset village and is married with four sons.

Praise for Sarah Challis:

'A well-spun, charming tale'   *Scottish Daily Record*

'Brilliant, stunning local description, captivating story'
                                        Bournemouth Daily Echo

'An immensely enjoyable read, with a twist in the tale that makes this better than the usual. A great setting, well-formed characters and a happy ending – what more could you ask?'   *Dorset Echo*

'A novel with a romantic element, and even a mystery, held together in the web of family emotions' *Writing Magazine*, Leeds

'A sense of heightened emotions and drama and this novel should more than enhance Challis's reputation as an author of literary substance'   *Lancashire Evening Post*

'[Her] attention to detail and wonderful use of words help to paint an intricate picture in the mind'   *Western Morning News*

'A gem of a novel, a real sparkling jewel' *Newbury Weekly News*

'Contains her unique style of drama, humour and warmth'
                                        Huddersfield Daily Examiner

That Summer Affair

Sarah Challis

headline
review

First published in Great Britain in 2007
by HEADLINE REVIEW
An imprint of HEADLINE PUBLISHING GROUP

First published in paperback in 2007 by
HEADLINE REVIEW

1

Cataloguing in Publication Data is available from the British Library

ISBN 978 0 7553 3086 7 (B format)
ISBN 978 0 7553 4423 9 (A format)

Typeset in Bembo by Palimpsest Book Production Limited,
Grangemouth, Stirlingshire

Printed and bound in Great Britain by
Mackays of Chatham plc, Chatham, Kent

Headline's policy is to use papers that are natural, renewable and recyclable
products and made from wood grown in sustainable forests. The logging
and manufacturing processes are expected to conform to the
environmental regulations of the country of origin.

HEADLINE PUBLISHING GROUP
An Hachette Livre UK Company
338 Euston Road
London NW1 3BH

www.headline.co.uk

For Adam and Darunee, with much love

Chapter One

LATER ON THAT summer, when Rachel Turner thought back to the events which were to change her life, she found that she could remember every detail of the evening she heard that Jodie Foot was missing, even the exact time she learned the news. It was seven twenty-six on the second Friday in June. She saw herself standing at the sink while the thick golden evening light lay across the grass at the back of the house and spread like syrup on the kitchen floor. She remembered hearing the back gate clang and she glanced up at the clock, thinking that it would be Dave, her husband, who had telephoned to say that he was working late. For a moment she felt mildly satisfied that she had already put the new potatoes on to cook, before the heavily pregnant figure of Cathy, her neighbour, blocked off the sun as she crossed the window on her way to the back door.

Surprised, because an evening visit was unusual, and picking up a tea towel to dry her hands, Rachel moved across the kitchen and met Cathy in the open doorway. Her friend's face looked both troubled and excited by the weight of whatever news she had come to impart and Rachel had a memory of putting out a hand to touch the outside wall and finding it was warm from the hours of sunshine and how the sharp little points of cream-painted render dug into her palm.

Cathy stood there with the evening sun bright behind her, shining through the cotton top that covered her nine months' pregnant belly. She'd had her hair permed and it had taken on a strange woolly texture, thick and crinkly, so that it stood out in stiff waves on either side of her long face. She looked a bit like a gentle, mildly surprised cow peering through a hedge.

'Here,' she said confidentially, breathing hard and glancing towards the gate as if to check that she hadn't been followed by an eavesdropper, 'Jodie Foot has done a runner. She got off the school bus with the other kids but she's not been seen since. No one knows where she's to.' She used the Dorset pattern of speech that still sounded strange to Rachel's ear. 'Marion's going right mad.'

Rachel shrugged. Jodie was not a child she would worry about. There were so many possible explanations for her not having come home and she knew that Cathy liked a bit of drama. Hardly anything happened in the village that Cathy didn't find worthy of intensely coloured speculation. Even when old Mrs Bagshaw lost a chicken, Cathy had come up with some theory that it had been stolen by travellers camped on the other side of the village. She was in her element when passing on a snippet of information with a nod and a knowing look.

Rachel wasn't that concerned. Jodie could have gone home with a number of other kids from outside the village. She wasn't exactly overwhelmed by parental supervision. Marion, her plump, chain-smoking mother, had children by three different men and Jodie came somewhere in the middle and was more or less left to her own devices. She was often out on the street after dark, hanging around with the older girls, yelling challenges at the boys. Rachel had seen her smoking and some of the mothers of younger children said that she was a bully. She was not a likeable child, not one you took to. She'd turn up all right. She wasn't a kid you'd be fearful for. She was too knowing, too worldly, a right little smart arse. 'The boys never said anything,' she said to Cathy, 'not when they were in for their tea.' Her two sons, Pete and Jamie, went to the same school as Jodie and came home on the lumbering bus that threaded its way along the lanes from the local comprehensive to the outlying villages. 'They've gone somewhere on their bikes. Has Marion asked the other kids?'

'Haven't you heard her hollering? She's been yelling blue murder to find where they're all at. It seems like Jodie's vanished. Disappeared. No one's seen her.'

'Not since she got off the bus?' Rachel frowned, working it out in her mind.

Marion nodded. 'That's nearly four hours past. Oh, I'd be worried sick if she was mine.'

'That's not so long. I'm surprised Marion's even missed her.' Rachel couldn't keep the note of criticism out of her voice. She disapproved of the Foots en masse. A feckless, troublesome lot they were, one and all.

'She's waiting to go out. She's wanting Jodie home to babysit the little one.'

At the bottom end of the line of Marion's children was an unattractive, lumpen toddler with a potato face and small, close-together, squinting eyes. Rachel had seen Jodie pushing him around in a stroller. His body was often contorted with rage at being restrained by the harness, his back arched, his legs braced, his fat, red dimpled hands clutching at the sides of the chair. She'd seen Jodie park the stroller and abandon him, bawling, while she went off to sit on a swing in the village playground with some of the other girls, swivelling round so that the chain wound tightly into a spiral, her thighs spreading to fill the scuffed black plastic seat, her clumpy fashion shoes treading in the scoop of dirt where the grass had been worn away beneath.

'Where did she get to the last time?' she asked, deliberately reducing the importance of the news Cathy had brought her with a reminder that Jodie had pulled this trick before.

'Bournemouth. She walked up to the main road and hitched a lift.'

'There you are then. She'll turn up all right. Like she did before.'

Cathy sighed and nodded reluctantly. She had to acknowledge the truth of what Rachel said.

'Still,' she added. 'You never know, do you? Not these days. Not with a girl like that. Anything could have happened.' Her face was solemn with dreadful implication but she was already moving towards the gate. She'd seen an unknown car pull up outside Jodie's house, further down the road, and she didn't want to miss anything. Alert to the prospect of new developments, she waved at Rachel over her shoulder as she lumbered away, one hand beneath her enormous belly.

Rachel glanced at the clock again. It was a shame they asked Dave to stay late so often, she thought, as she went back to tidying the kitchen. That was the trouble with him being foreman at the electrical contractors for whom he worked. He was always having to put in extra time when they had a rushed job on. It would have been nice to have had him home so that they could all have had supper together and then maybe gone for a walk. It was such a beautiful evening. The late sunshine flooded over the window sill and she could smell the warm, dusty scent of the scarlet geraniums she had growing there in a coil pot one of the boys had made years ago in primary school.

She drained the potatoes and as she rinsed the saucepan under the hot tap, she looked out of the window at the neat back garden. Dave had just finished replacing the fence along the bottom, beyond the vegetable plot. The palings were a raw red against the pale green of the new lettuces under the darker green netting used to deter the pigeons.

The garden was such a pleasure to Rachel, so well cared for and tidy, the square of lawn as smooth and bright green as a boiled sweet. The narrow flower beds, set on either side, glowed with the jewel colours of her bedding plants. Outside the back door was the paved area Dave had put down to stop the boys spoiling the grass when they scuffed about with a football and he'd put a basketball hoop up on the side of the shed. Not that they used it much these days. This summer they'd just wanted to be out on their mountain bikes or hanging around outside the pub with their friends, sitting on the wall drinking from cans of Coke, laughing, teasing, mucking about. Sometimes the publican let them into the skittle alley, or allowed them to practise shots on the snooker table. It was like that in the village. A close community where people felt they had a responsibility to keep an eye on the kids.

Any other evening, Jodie Foot would have been there with them.

Jodie. Rachel reckoned she'd be twelve or thirteen years old, because she was in the same school year as

Jamie. Her face was round with puppy fat and she still had the complexion of a child, smooth and pink and fine. Her hair was lately streaked with magenta and orange, scraped off her face and held back with a row of sparkly slides, which she kept taking out and replacing as she talked. She was a gobby sort of girl, always giving someone lip. She was foul-mouthed, too. Rachel had heard her swearing into her mobile, every other word an effing this or that.

This summer she had taken to wearing tight, low-cut jeans that forced a roll of pale belly and soft, roly-poly back to spill over the waistband. She wasn't blessed with the languid grace of some teenage girls. An image of her loitering down the road in the morning to catch the school bus came into Rachel's mind, solid-legged in her short skirt, trailing her bag by its strap.

Of course, you should feel sorry for a kid like that. She came from a nuisance family, for a start. The two older boys had a loutish air that was almost threatening now that they were adults. They screamed about on motorbikes, ignoring the speed limit through the village, or drove cars with the windows rolled down, pop music blasting, and fitted with exhaust systems that roared and stuttered. No one complained because

Marion had a reputation for having an evil temper. Rachel had heard of the flaming rows and feuds that dominated the Foots' end of the road and she was grateful that when she and Dave bought their house ten years ago, it was at the further end, with six or seven houses in between.

The garden was a disgrace too. You only had to look at it to see the sort of family they were. The patch of grass at the front was long and matted and littered with discarded plastic toys, a broken slide, an old carpet, last year's Christmas tree now a brown, dry skeleton, keeled over on its side. A large, unloved Alsatian-cross dog barked from behind the side gate.

But the real difference between the Foots and Rachel was that the things that she had strived for all her adult life – tidiness, respectability, well-brought-up children, a nice home – they treated with contempt, sneered at, raised a finger to. Yet, even so, she admitted, as she sat down to wait for Dave and have a look at the newspaper, there was something about them that she envied. They belonged here in the village; a proper Dorset family, with cousins and aunts and uncles by the dozen. The names of three Foot family members were on the war memorial on the green, and dozens of them were on the gravestones in the churchyard. Someone had told her they had been quite an important family years back. Once they had owned Mill Farm at the end of the village, but between the wars things had been hard for them and they had lost their own land and ended up working for other people as farm labourers and herdsmen, lorry drivers and shop assistants. Yet they didn't have about them the air of the downwardly mobile – the hopeless slope of the shoulder, or a defeated, lifeless expression. They were the opposite, Rachel thought; pleased with themselves, throwing their weight around, behaving as if they owned the place.

Marion, who according to Cathy had never married or bothered to take on any man's name, was just like that. She was a loud, confident woman, always comfortably at ease whenever Rachel saw her chatting to people on the street or leaning on the bar in the pub. She gave the impression that being born and bred in the village put her in a position to judge everyone else. Her watermelon breasts massively rounded out the front of her T-shirt, her short plump arms jangled with bracelets, her ready laugh rippled around her. Her snouty face was mostly agreeable and good-natured, and Rachel had never witnessed one of her legendary rages, but she could imagine how Marion could turn. She could imagine the slashing of her tongue, the shouted insults, the physical threat of her stout body and meaty arms.

Rachel had to admit that she couldn't stand the woman, and she guessed that the feeling was mutual. She was sure that at some point Marion had cast a look in her direction and didn't care for what she saw. Rachel knew that in Marion's eyes she was stand-offish and snooty even, with her well-behaved sons and her rotary washing line and her nesting box on the beech tree in her garden. And there was Dave. Marion liked to run men down, taking the view that they were more trouble than they were worth, while at the same time going out of her way to receive their attention, and Rachel was certain that she would have noticed Dave. She must have seen what a good husband he was, reliable, hardworking, never loud-mouthed or loutish, or roaring home late from the pub. Marion would be jealous, thought Rachel. It was only natural that she would be.

She was thinking of Dave when she heard his van pulling up outside and then the door slam. He came round to the back door and Rachel looked up to see him pass the window in his pale blue denim workshirt, open-necked with the sleeves rolled up. She loved that shirt and every time she ironed it she was reminded of the colour of his eyes, which had been the first thing she noticed about him. He wore his fair hair very short and his face was tanned but this evening he seemed preoccupied and weary and walked without his usual jaunty step. He's worn out, she thought, and no wonder, with the hours he put in. It was seven forty now and he had left the house before eight o'clock that morning. It was too long a day for any man.

Further up the village street, on the same evening that Jodie Foot disappeared, Juliet Fairweather was unpacking her hire car and moving her bags into Jasmine Cottage. Of course, she had no idea that anything had happened out of the ordinary because she was a stranger, newly arrived in the village. She was vaguely aware of a group of teenagers wheeling back and forth on bicycles, and wondered how they could possibly find enough to occupy themselves in a place that was so off the beaten track it had neither pavements nor street lights.

With the front door standing open she ferried stuff between the car and the cottage until the bags of groceries, her books, her suitcase and her laptop stood in the little white-painted hall that was really hardly more than a passage. These cottages were built for stunted medieval peasants, she thought, as she opened the door into the beamed sitting room. Looking in, she was pleasantly surprised to discover it was quite spacious and light, maybe two rooms knocked into one, with windows on both sides, straight onto the village street on one, and to the green seclusion of the rear garden on the other. It was attractively furnished in plain, bright colours, not the dreary floral chintz she might have expected, and someone had thoughtfully left a vase of yellow roses on a little cream-painted table that stood between the windows

The kitchen, she discovered, was tacked on at the back and looked perfectly adequate and well-equipped, large enough for a small round dining table and four mismatched chairs and with French windows to the garden. Well, it's charming, she thought, her spirits lifting, and taken unseen, better than she could have hoped. Somewhere in her bag she had the email message from Dr Hector Ballantyne, the owner, explaining the idiosyncrasies of the place, but for the moment it was enough to go round the ground floor and open the windows to the lovely evening air.

Then, mounting the narrow stairs which rose steeply

from the hall, she found two bedrooms, one with a double bed, and the other with twin beds, and a small bathroom over the kitchen. No shower, she noticed, but a nice old china bath on clawed feet, and, relief, it was unstained and sparkly clean.

This was it then, she thought. This was to be her home for the next six months while Dr Ballantyne, a man she had never met, would shortly move into her two-roomed apartment in Charles Street, Greenwich Village in New York City. This arrangement was a sort of sublet which was actually forbidden in the deeds of her apartment, but since no money was involved and she had vetted him very carefully she had taken the risk. For his part, he was being equally trusting in allowing a stranger to move into this lovely cottage and even use his car which was waiting for her in the little wooden garage at the side of the house.

So here she was, looking about her and wondering what it was going to be like, this unexpected alteration in her life. It wasn't as if there had been any dramatic event to trigger this change of location, unless she counted turning fifty and finding herself unmarried, unattached, childless, and with an empty summer ahead of her.

She had lived in America for the last five years since moving from London to work at New York University, as a professor of social and economic history. Apart from the usual pressures connected with this type of job, the lack of tenure, the pitifully low salary, the irritating departmental strictures, she enjoyed her work enormously and as far as her personal life went, liked to think that she had reached a point where she was happy and settled. She had a lot of friends, both here in England and in America, and was a fond sister to her two brothers and a dutiful daughter and niece to her ancient mother and aunt, all of whom lived in London. But if you had told her at twenty, Juliet often thought, that this was to be her future, the sum of her life, she would have been horrified. At that age, it was not what you wanted for yourself and for years and years, as a young and then a middle-aged woman, she had gone on expecting that at any moment she would meet the man who would change her life for ever, with whom she would live and mate and produce a lot of brilliant, beautiful children and with whom she would grow old.

It didn't happen and the years went by and gradually she stopped expecting it to. She fell in love easily and had enjoyed various affairs of differing lengths and intensity, including one that had taken up ten years of her life when she had been mistress to a married man, and she did not regret any of them, not for one moment, but none had amounted to what she had been waiting for.

Then lately, with her fiftieth birthday behind her, she had felt suddenly rootless and unsettled and wondered whether it was time for a summer's change. She had come to the end of a very busy academic year in New York and had gained a term free of teaching in the fall. Her two graduate students were able to keep in touch with her by email and she found herself at liberty to go anywhere for a few months.

England suddenly seemed a good idea, especially as she would anyway have come over for a few weeks to see her family, and there was some research that she wanted to do in the library of a grand Dorset house whose owner had issued her an open invitation. One of his nineteenth-century ancestors, an Admiral Thomas, had been a naval reformer of some note, and she was hoping there might be enough material to consider a biography. She should get an academic paper out of him, at least.

Finding the cottage had been a piece of luck. Gavin,

her long-time ex-lover, a professor at Oxford and still a good friend, had suggested that she might consider a house-swap with a colleague who was looking for accommodation in New York for a sabbatical term. After a series of emails and the exchange of references, Juliet and Dr Hector Ballantyne had clinched the deal.

So here she was, hauling her suitcase up the narrow stairs and trying to decide which room to sleep in. The cottage was only one room wide and therefore both bedrooms shared the same view, back and front, with identical small casement windows that she had thrown open to the delicious summer evening.

It was rather a weird feeling to be poking around someone else's home. She opened a white-painted wardrobe which had been neatly fitted under the eaves on the landing and found one half of it occupied by men's clothes, pushed together and covered by a sheet as if to protect them from her prying. As if I'd be interested, she thought, but all the same pulled the sheet back and had a look. The shirts were OK, the expected M&S and a few more expensive, in not very thrilling colours, collar size 16. There were two tweed jackets and three or four suits of a traditional sort. Dr Ballantyne was clearly a stodgy old thing, but this was reassuring more than anything else. It suggested that the beds wouldn't have seen any exotic action, which was a relief. Imagine if she had found black rubber trousers and a whip collection.

She opened the drawers of a chest in one of the bedrooms and found that they had been thoughtfully emptied to take her own clothes, and were clean and lined with fresh white paper. She stopped to wonder whether fussy, careful Dr Ballantyne would find her own apartment clean enough; she hadn't spent long scrubbing and polishing before she left. She had bundled her own stuff in boxes and shoved them into storage in the basement of the building, because at the time, rushed as she was, she had guessed that a man wouldn't be too particular about whether the shelves were dusted and the paintwork washed.

But then, of course, Dr Ballantyne had a cleaner – a 'help' he called her in his emails. Her name was Rachel Turner and she lived somewhere in the village and she would come in once a week to 'do' for her. Juliet imagined a round, rosy-faced country woman, unlike the sullen, exhausted East European girls who were sent by the agency to bang a Hoover round the flat her mother and aunt shared in North London.

She sat on the double bed and tested it for comfort and lifted the candlewick bedspread and found it unmade, with a folded feather duvet on the top. She supposed this was the room used by Dr Ballantyne, and maybe his wife, although she hadn't got the impression that he had one. He had never referred to sharing her own apartment with anyone, and now she came to think about it, perhaps at some time she had warned him that it was too small for two persons to live comfortably, and he had written back to say that he would be on his own. She was aware of resisting a self-imposed pressure to take the other, twin-bedded room, as if she were a guest but, sod it, she thought, he'll be sleeping in my bed, and she liked a wide space where she could read and work and spread papers out on the unoccupied side.

There was an airing cupboard on the landing, rather empty and tidily organised, and she checked the sheets and duvet covers and pillowcases – all OK in terms of colour and design, thank goodness. She realised that it was dangerously old-maidish to care about such things, but she couldn't bear sleeping in anything but cotton or linen sheets, and she really minded if they were in sludge colours or the hideous patterns that men seemed to veer towards choosing if left to their own devices.

She spent the next ten minutes making up the bed and enjoying the smell and smooth feel of clean linen. Then she dragged her case in from the landing and opened it on the floor. Her familiar stuff spread out and she dug out a nightdress and threw it on the pillow. She was pleased to see that on one of the bedside tables there was a small radio. Lying in bed and listening to Radio 4 was one of her chief pleasures in being back in England. That, proper tea, digestive biscuits and the sex that she occasionally indulged in with Gavin, her Oxford ex-lover, if he managed to cook up a good enough alibi to escape his gimlet-eyed wife.

Gavin was a professor of architecture, charming, good-looking and kept very much on pin-down by Sonia, his clever, plain wife; rather wisely, Juliet had to admit. In fact, given the chance, Sonia would have had him tagged with one of those electronic things worn by young offenders; strapped to his ankle, it would bleep a warning alarm if he strayed.

So here I am, she thought again, looking about her and sitting back on her heels beside the suitcase, amongst the shoes and jumbled clothes. The carpet was pale seagrass, or another of those prickly natural fibres, and extended over the whole top floor of the cottage, and the uneven old walls were white. This gave the rooms a light, airy feeling and, now that she had the windows open, the curtains stirred slightly with the breath of a breeze. The heat that had collected up here throughout the day would soon disperse.

She felt restless and unsettled and did not want to continue unpacking, not on such a lovely evening, and she moved to the window that overlooked the little strip of garden. Immediately outside the back door was a square of paving on which there was a table and chairs and a collection of pots. Lovely, thought Juliet, imagining sitting there in the morning with a cup of coffee, or in the evening with a glass of wine. Beyond, there were three steps up to a length of lawn, with some unambitious flower beds and an apple tree at the end.

She thrust her head and shoulders out and leaned her elbows on the sill. The air smelled of hay and beyond the green crown of the apple tree she could see fields rising to meet a distant wood. A tractor and trailer burdened with huge round bales moved slowly across them. The sound of the engine drifted towards her and then she became aware of the ringing cries of sheep. Now she had identified the sound, it seemed to grow in volume until the air trembled with their voices.

Then quite suddenly she heard the sound of a woman screaming, in rage or alarm, she could not tell.

Pete Turner had seen Jodie Foot get off the bus. In fact she had got off immediately in front of him, because, as usual, he and Gary Russell had been slouching on the very back seat and he was the last one off at the stop in the village. Later on, when he was asked again and again to go over what he could remember of what was the last sighting anyone had had of Jodie, he was able to say with complete confidence that she had got off in front of him, swinging her school bag by its long strap and carrying her blazer. He could describe that she was wearing a dark school skirt and a white shirt and that she had undone her tie so that it hung loose.

Gary, a heavy lad with the height and bulk of a man and a fleshy, surly face, was not exactly a friend but the fact that they were in the same year and lived a mile or two apart and shared the same journey to and from school had thrown them together. He stayed on for one more stop, and had laughed and waved at Pete out of the window as the bus drew away towards the next village, and Jodie was there in front of him on the main

village street. She was walking slowly and so he over-
took her to catch up with his brother who was with a
group of younger kids further on. He thought that Jodie
was probably making a telephone call from her mobile,
or texting, maybe, because she was dawdling along,
preoccupied with something, and that was the last he,
or anyone else, saw of her.

It had been a completely normal journey home, he
told everyone that evening when it was discovered that
Jodie was missing. Nothing happened out of the ordinary. That was what he had told his mum and dad and
what he told Jodie's mum when she was going mad at
everyone. After all, it was the truth, wasn't it?

After tea, and of course his dad was working late so
it was just the three of them, he and Jamie had gone
out on their bikes and mooched around with some of
the other kids. It was such a warm evening that most
of them had been turned out of their bedrooms, away
from their televisions and computers, to spend the end
of the day out of doors. They gathered down by the
old war memorial where they could sit together on the
low wall and where the entrance to the farm opposite
meant that the lane was wide enough to try stunts on
their bikes. That's where they were when Mrs Foot

came past in her car and yelled at them about where the bloody hell was Jodie, as if they should know. They had all looked at her and shrugged. One of the girls had said maybe she was at Karen's house, but she wasn't, Mrs Foot had already checked. Karen was ill with a sore throat and hadn't been at school. So they had all just sat there and looked at one another.

He'd piped up then, about seeing Jodie get off the bus, and from then on wished he'd kept his mouth shut, because it became like he was the Jodie expert, or something. It was he who had to answer all the questions and Jodie's mum treated him as if he should know where she was. It wasn't as if the kids were that bothered anyway. Jodie was always doing something stupid to draw attention to herself. She was like that, so after her mum had driven off, they carried on as before, laughing, mucking about. When he and Jamie got home, it was only just getting a bit darker – after nine o'clock. His mum was in the kitchen, making the sandwiches for the next day, and his dad was through in the sitting room watching the television and drinking from a can of beer. Neither of them said anything about Jodie. They weren't that bothered either.

'Do you want tuna?' his mum asked.

'Yes,' and 'No,' he and Jamie said in chorus.

His dad chipped in without looking up.

'Did I hear "please"?'

'Fish breath,' he said to Jamie and they'd scuffed at each other before he went off to have a bath. He'd only just discovered the bathroom, his mum said, and it was true. Lately he loved going in there and locking the door. It was the only place in the whole house where you could do that – slide a bolt and shut the rest of them out. He liked undressing slowly, revealing his long white body which had changed so much over the last six months that he could hardly believe it belonged to him, sprouting hair and growing knobbly. His chest was white and narrow and the skin so fine looking that it clung to his ribs like a piece of wet silk. He could see every one of his ribs and if he breathed in and held his breath and tried to inflate his chest to manly proportions he looked even punier. His arms were long and thin but he was surprised at their new strength. He could tense his upper arms and watch muscles jump out like tight balls and sinews like thick ropes reached down into his bony wrists.

He liked to stand sideways in front of the bathroom mirror and tense these muscles and look at the slender lines of his long waist and his small high buttocks, just as long as he didn't look at his face, which always spoiled things. Over the last few months as his body had shot up, something had happened to his face. His features suddenly seemed to be those of a stranger, his eyes glowering under new heavier brows, his nose grown out of proportion, while his mouth was still pink and boyish over slabs of teeth, and the whole thing looking long and thin and surly where it had once been round and smiling. He had to shave now, every other day, and secretly at first as if it was his own dirty secret, and his skin had become full of new pits and craters and angry bumps of threatening spots which only in the privacy of the bathroom could he explore and squeeze and anoint with tea tree oil his mum kept in the cupboard.

He would lock the door and stare in the mirror at the stranger he had become and then try out different angles and expressions but he looked crap whatever he did and sometimes it made him feel unbearably sad that this was what he had become and that there was nothing he could do about it.

He would run a long bath and lie in it, his feet hooked up over the taps, his head full of the steamy heat and close his eyes and let his thoughts drift away from his body, and on the night that Jodie Foot disappeared this is what he did as usual. He lay back and felt the hot water lapping at his sides and swaying the fronds of his pubic hair, but however hard he tried, he couldn't stop thinking about her.

With Karen, her mate, off sick, she'd been on her own on the bus, plonking down in the girls' usual seat in front of him and Gary. It wasn't that they picked on her exactly but they'd made a remark or two and she'd seemed funny about it. Her face had got red. He'd watched the pink flush right across the back of her neck. She'd yelled, 'Shut up, will yer?' and that had egged them on, like it always did when someone got in a strop. You just got at them worse. If Karen had been there, the two of them would have giggled together and said something back and the boys wouldn't have bothered and that would have been that, but without Karen something different had happened. Pete didn't want to think about it as he closed his eyes and felt the warm water wetting the back of his hair, but he couldn't shut it out, or forget that odd feeling of exhilaration as he and Gary wound Jodie up. Gary was better at it than him because he was quicker witted, sharper

27

tongued, and he'd got an older brother who was cool and a 'bad boy' and knew stuff that Pete had never heard of.

Anyway, that's all it was, just saying stuff and watching Jodie go hot and red and then stare out of the window with her face all twisted and funny and they'd kept on a bit, and then she'd got up in a flurry and moved to sit further down the bus away from them and they'd laughed and that had been that. It had only been a bit of fun and he didn't know why he kept thinking about it now.

He had been relieved when none of the other kids had mentioned it tonight, not even amongst themselves – perhaps they hadn't noticed what was going on, the bus was that rowdy on the way home. The trouble was that thinking about it now made him feel miserable and sick and he wished that he could go back to when things were simple – when he was just a little kid. In a sudden movement he plunged his head and face backwards under the bath water and held his breath until his lungs were burning.

Henry Streeter was working in his allotment on the evening of Jodie's disappearance. He'd been there since

four o'clock; later, when the police began asking questions, that fact was to become important. He'd crossed
the road twice to go to his cottage, walking up the
narrow gravel path that went along the side to the back
and taking the key from where he hid it underneath
the water butt, opening the kitchen door and going
inside. Once he'd gone across to make a cup of strong
tea, deep orange in colour, in the mug he'd won at the
funfair in Weymouth in 1968. He drank it standing by
the curtainless window in the kitchen, looking out at
the small square of back yard which he had gravelled
over years before. Henry didn't see the point of flower
beds and now the neatness of the area comforted him
as it always did, just the clipped privet hedge which ran
along one side and the shed set at the back, facing the
rear of the semi-detached cottage.

The second time he crossed the road was to cut
himself a square sandwich filled with a cold sausage and
thick yellow mustard. He ate it at the kitchen table, off
a folded newspaper, methodically and without much
pleasure, tearing off the soft white bread with his strong,
yellow teeth, and chewing in the same way that he dug
the allotment, as if it was a job to be done properly.

Henry was still a tall man at over seventy, with a crest

of thick grey hair and a bony, stern face which appeared to have set in one expression – or rather lack of it. There was a stoniness about his features which was reflected in the austerity of the room, the grey dish-cloth dried to a stiff square folded over the tap, the old-fashioned kitchen units whose Formica tops were empty of any clutter, the ugly green linoleum on the floor worn to a scuffed grey between sink and stove. At a glance it would be obvious to anyone that there was no woman in this house.

There had been Fred, though, the younger brother whom Henry had always had to keep an eye on because he wasn't all there in the head, not the full shilling, until he had died slowly and painfully of cancer three years ago. After he had gone, buried in the graveyard in the village, the silence in the cottage had become deafening, booming in Henry's ears like the sea, and so thick in the empty rooms that he felt the effort of moving about, as if he were wading through deep water.

It was loneliness that had settled about his shoulders like a heavy weight and which dragged at the corners of his mouth and drew the lines on his face. 'Miserable old bugger!' the children in the road called after him. 'He can't smile, his face would crack!' It accompanied him when he went down to the pub for a pint of an evening, so that the other drinkers, enjoying a chat and a laugh, would turn away and talk amongst themselves. Sometimes Henry wondered whether his voice would come out all right when he did open his mouth to say something. He thought that one day he might only be able to croak like the coarse-voiced rooks that gathered in the trees behind Home Farm.

He didn't know about Jodie, even though he must have heard Marion yelling out in the road. Later on, when the police asked him, he said he supposed he'd heard her shouts but it didn't register, and he knew it sounded daft. The police sergeant gave him a disbelieving look. The truth was that he could be out in the allotment most of the day and yet not notice the goings-on in the road, the to-ing and fro-ing, the mothers walking down to meet the school bus with their little ones in pushchairs. 'In a world of your own, are you?' said the policeman sarcastically, but that was about it. Every now and then one of the older villagers came by and would call across to him and exchange a few words and he would remember that all right, like Jessie Harcourt who had been at school with him and Fred when they had been evacuated to Dorset from the East

31

End of London in the war, or Billy Wright whose son, Kit, brought him a parcel of fish and chips of a Friday when he came to see his dad. The rest of them, he didn't notice, the kids racing about on their bikes shouting at one another or kicking a football down the road. He knew a few of the older boys directed abuse at him but he chose to ignore it. In his day they would have had a clip round the ear if they had dared to cheek an adult, but it wasn't so today.

He didn't hear about Jodie until the following morning when he wheeled his bicycle out of the shed and down the path to the gate onto the road. As he was opening the gate, Billy came past with his three-legged terrier, Bingo.

'You heard, then, Henry?' he said as Bingo examined the gatepost.

'Heard what?'

'A kid's gone missing. That fat lass of Marion's. Been gone all night. Done a runner, so it seems.' At that moment a police car turned into the road and drove past the two old men before pulling up outside the Foots' house. A policeman and a policewoman got out and without looking right or left, opened the gate and went to the front door.

'No, I haven't heard anything,' said Henry, pushing his bike out onto the road and lifting his leg over the crossbar. Billy Wright would have said he didn't care either, the miserable old bugger, but he would have been wrong because as Henry cycled slowly away in the direction of the nearby, larger village where he could buy bread and a rasher or two of bacon, and the few things on his weekly shopping list, his mind was full of sudden vivid images that rushed into his head. He remembered how when they were nippers, he and Fred had run away more times than he could count, and once spent nearly a week living rough. They'd had a plan to walk back to London to look for their ma down the Roman Road in Bethnal Green where she'd gone to stay in her sister's flat over the greengrocer's. They'd got as far as Salisbury before they got picked up by a Home Guard patrol and brought back to the misery of the Bettses' farm where they had been billeted.

It had been Fred who got the worst of the beatings because he was slow and got under Jack Bettses' feet, and because he was a puny boy with a wheezing cough and large jug ears. They stuck out from his head like a pair of handles and with his hair cropped so close on account of the nits, old man Betts couldn't resist catching hold and pulling Fred about by them. Henry could remember those boy ears, the soft, flappy feel of them, the ping of the cartilage when you let them go, their red-rimmed look when it was cold.

He had had an easier time of it than poor Fred because he was a sturdy, tall lad and two years older. He was more useful about the farm and was a hard worker. Jack Betts left him alone but he hadn't been able to protect his brother, and the misery of those years smote him like a blow in the chest. He could hardly cycle straight and his eyes swam with unshed tears as he turned onto the lane at the top of the road.

Chapter Two

JULIET WAS STANDING at the bedroom window holding a mug of tea when she saw the police car and then the old man wobbling past on his bicycle. It was going to be another lovely day and she had opened the window as wide as it would go. The street outside seemed remarkably quiet, even for a village. There was literally nobody about, not a soul, not even a cat or dog. She had expected that the countryside would be up and running by now, it was after eight o'clock, maybe ploughmen plodding past, or shepherds or something – anyway, at least tractors or milk lorries. It was so utterly still that it seemed quite weird, as if she had woken up in a dream village, devoid of human life.

There had been a heavy dew in the night and the leaves of the rose which climbed the front of the cottage were glazed and silvery as if with frost and the air felt fresh and cool although the morning sun on her face and arms was already warm. Over the stone-tiled roofs of the old cottages opposite, the sun was a misty halo in a pearly blue sky and the far-off fields floated like mysterious islands on a sea of white. Juliet had promised herself that she would not endure another New York heatwave when the air was wet and thick and stifling, even at night, and just moving about was exhausting but she had almost forgotten how beautiful English summers could be.

The dawn chorus had woken her after a night of fitful sleep and, disbelieving, she had turned over in bed to consult her watch. Four thirty, and the birdsong was tumultuous. The one who had started it all – a thrush or blackbird? – first tentatively, and then gathering confidence in whole liquid phrases of notes, had swiftly been joined by others with less melodic songs and then a line of house martins began their rapid cheeping from the telephone wire outside her bedroom window.

She got up and closed the window and drew the curtains but it was impossible to sleep again. Bloody birds, she thought crossly, anticipating the day ahead spoiled by heavy-eyed tiredness. If it was going to be like this every morning, she would go mad, but she supposed the birds were unstoppable, programmed by some mechanism in their tiny pea-sized brains to carry on like this at dawn.

There was nothing for it but to get up and go downstairs and make a cup of tea which she would bring back to bed and maybe sort through some of her papers which weighed down her briefcase.

The kitchen tiles were cold to her bare feet and the electric kettle took ages to boil while she searched through the cupboards for mugs. She found them in what she considered a peculiar place, next to the sink, not where she would have kept them at all, and they were horrid, hand-crafted in thick, lumpy clay with a nasty shit-coloured glaze. She would have to buy herself a teacup – something light and pretty in bone china, she caught herself thinking, and then had to almost laugh. God, she really was turning into an old maid. Exactly like Aunt Dorothy whose strict rules about tea-making turned the whole thing into a performance with tea caddy and caddy spoon and warmed pot and silver strainer. Never in her life had Aunt Dorothy been seduced by a tea bag.

Somewhere amongst the plastic carriers of super-market shopping she had stopped to buy yesterday en route from London were tea bags and coffee, and she began to unpack and put things away. The fridge was small and ancient – at least by American standards. She could have kept a corpse in the fridge in her apartment and it always rather depressed her to open it up and find it empty except for milk, a bottle of gin and a lemon. The vacant shelves seemed to reproach her, like a lifestyle coach advising that she should get out there and live in a more abundant style.

This one, circa 1960, didn't seem to have any such high expectations. The shelves were narrow and cramped and the plastic bits were yellowing with age. The freezer compartment was so small it would only take a tray or two of ice. Still it was clean, and when she had switched it on, it rumbled into life.

She was looking forward to proper English tea, she thought, as she poured boiling water on the tea bag, and added cold milk. Why was it that it never tasted the same anywhere else in the world? She picked up the mug, collected her briefcase from the hall and mounted the steep stairs and got back into bed.

After quite a short time sipping the tea and sorting papers, she felt extraordinarily tired and leaned back on her pillows. She must have slept, not waking until half past seven. Now, leaning out of the cottage window, she saw the first sign of life as the police car came slowly down the street. How odd, she thought. It seemed so unlikely that the police should patrol such a sleepy village where crime was surely hardly heard of. She watched until she saw it signal a left-hand turn and then disappear round a corner.

A few minutes later an elderly man on a bicycle appeared from the same turning. He came straight out with his head down, not pausing or looking right or left. He shouldn't ride like that, thought Juliet, he'll get knocked off. If a car had been coming the other way it could not have avoided hitting him. Ridiculously, she wondered if he was evading the police. She watched as he came down the street and passed under her window. He was wearing a country-style flat cap and thick grey hair emerged like wings from either side. From where she was standing Juliet could only glimpse his face but it was set in lines of such misery and despair that it made her draw back, a hand to her mouth, as if she had unwittingly glimpsed some deep and intimate sorrow.

When the alarm rang at its usual time, Rachel had forgotten about the disappearance of Jodie Foot. She struggled to surface from a deep, dreamless sleep and forced herself to get straight out of bed. To lie there a few moments longer in the warm cocoon was a strong temptation that had to be resisted. As usual, Dave slept right through the insistent ring. She looked across at him as she slid her feet into the sandals she had kicked off the night before, and opened a drawer to take out clean knickers and a fresh T-shirt.

There had been a time when they had woken deliberately early to enjoy morning sex; they had turned to one another, still sleepy, but ravenous for the other's warm and compliant body. Where had it gone to, all that urgency? Worn away, she supposed, by the baby and toddler years, the lack of sleep and then the lack of time. Nowadays the whole of life seemed to be set against the clock. Still, she went and sat on Dave's side of the bed and reached under the duvet to take his hand.

She had always loved his hands, so square and capable looking. She loved the hard calluses on the pads of his palms, the scars on his thumbs, the places where he had nicked the skin with some tool or other. They were the hands of a proper workman, a man on whom you could rely. She remembered the soft, pappy paws of her stepfather, resting on the cut moquette arms of his chair where he sat in the front room of the London flat in which she had grown up. She remembered how they reached for the fag packet and the lighter also resting on the arm, or flicked the television controls. What an idle sod he had been, while her poor mum had worked her guts out and hardly ever sat down.

She took one of Dave's hands and kissed the fingers one by one. He stirred in his sleep but didn't open his eyes. She put the hand gently on the top of her thigh, naked under the long T-shirt she wore to bed, but there was no response. She sighed. No time anyway. She picked up her clothes and went to the bathroom to get dressed, banging on the boys' doors as she went.

It was the same old weekday routine, day in, day out. She cleaned her teeth and washed her face and slapped on skin cream and pulled her brown hair into a pony-tail, all without glancing in the glass above the basin. Jeans, the clean T-shirt and she was already down the stairs, opening the windows to sniff at the freshness of the summer morning and to get the kettle on for a cup of tea.

Going to the gate to fetch the milk bottle she saw the police car. Shit, she had forgotten all about Jodie.

Perhaps, after all, her disappearance was serious. Terrifying images flashed across her mind – police cordons, search parties, frogmen diving to probe the depths of rivers and lakes. Standing at the gate, milk bottle in hand, she looked down the road at the Foots' house and thought of the anxiety – agony, really – of not knowing where your child was and if she was safe. She couldn't begin to imagine what it must feel like to have her missing for a whole night. How long had she been gone the last time? A couple of days at least and the police, for some reason, never engaged in a real search. They must have known from the start that a crime had not taken place, that the kid's disappearance had another, less sinister, explanation.

Although she had no real faith in God, as she went back inside Rachel found herself asking Him to make it OK, to bring Jodie back safely.

'There's a police car outside the Foots',' she said to Dave as she put a mug of tea beside him on the bedside table.

'What have that bloody lot been up to now?' he said, still half asleep.

'It must be Jodie. You know, missing. I don't know what it means. Whether she's back or not.'

'She'll be OK,' he said, sitting up. 'It's not the first time, like you said last night. And, let's face it, that sort of kid will always be trouble. There's hundreds of girls like her, truants, runaways, get themselves into the cities and get in with a bad lot, get on drugs, go on the game.'

'Dave!' Rachel was shocked at how indifferent he sounded.

'It's true. Don't pretend otherwise. She's just the kind of kid you'd expect to do that sort of thing.'

'But that's what she is, Dave. A kid! She can't be more than thirteen. She's the same age as Jamie. How would we feel if it was him?'

'That's not very likely, is it?' Dave leaned out of bed and drank the tea without thanking her for it. He seemed angry, or maybe indignant, as if even the suggestion was an affront.

This was Dave all over, Rachel thought as she went downstairs, banging on the boys' doors again as she passed. He was always so confident, so sure that if you didn't go expecting trouble, if you were smart and did things right, life would be OK. There was no reason to expect the worst, to wait for disaster to strike, as she instinctively did. He had such belief in himself that she believed in him, too, and the world seemed a less terrifying place as a result. In the seventeen years they had been together he had never let her down and she had learned to be less apprehensive and less fearful that if she dared to be happy, the chances were it would all be taken from her.

She put plates and cereal bowls on the table and started to make toast. Jamie appeared, his face still puffy with sleep. She knew just by looking at him that he hadn't washed. She caught his hand as he reached for the cornflake packet. It was dry and warm and sticky with grubbiness.

'Upstairs!' she said. 'Wash properly. Go on! Now!'

'Mum! I can't! It's not my fault,' he complained in a whining voice. He was still a child in many ways. 'Pete's in the bathroom. He'll be in there for hours. He's got to be such a *girl*. He won't let me in.'

'Here, then,' she said. 'Wash here,' and she handed him a bar of soap and the kitchen towel. She watched as he dipped the ends of his fingers under the rush of water from the tap, his head bent as if in concentration, but more in doziness, as if he could go back to sleep standing there. His thick crown of golden-brown hair stood up, unbrushed. He was aiming for the shaggy, surfer look.

He was an uncomplicated boy; a good, smiling,

contented baby, he had grown up with a sunny, loving nature and was not given to moodiness or brooding. His face was open and freckled, his eyes blue and bright with humour – an easy boy who made friends without trying and whose passage through life seemed assuredly smooth.

She didn't worry about Jamie. It was Pete who got to her, with his awkward gangly frame and his inflamed teenage skin. Over the last few months he had grown uncommunicative and secretive – the classic teenager, Rachel supposed, although his behaviour was never openly rebellious and the reports from school were always good. It was more that he seemed to have moved away to occupy a different country of his own, somewhere secret and remote where he preferred to be left alone, and what upset her most was that she felt that he suffered there. She didn't know what it was, a girl perhaps, unrequited love, or much wider despair at what he saw on the news about the world that he was growing into. Famine and war and poverty and injustice and the destruction of the planet were the sort of things that they seemed to discuss now that he was in the sixth form, and it was enough to depress anyone. He wouldn't talk about what was bothering him and grew impatient and blushed hotly when she asked him what the matter was.

'Nothing!' he would cry. 'Leave me alone, Mum!'

He had become almost utterly silent around Dave who, in turn, grew impatient with Rachel when she tried to talk to him about her concern. 'Let it go, Rachel. Leave the lad alone. Stop getting after him. He's just growing up, that's all. He doesn't want his mother forever interfering.'

'I'm *not* interfering. I just want to know what's wrong. I want to know whether we can help.'

'For God's sake, Rachel! Leave him alone. It's normal, isn't it, for a teenager? Just let him be.'

This morning he came sloping downstairs, so tall and thin that his shoulders looked stooped, and moved his long hair out of his eyes with a slender, almost girlish hand as he sat down and hunched over his cereal bowl.

Passing the back of his stool, Rachel touched his head, and he brushed her away irritably as if she was an annoying fly.

'The police are here,' she said to both the boys. 'There's a patrol car at the Foots'. I don't know whether Jodie's back or not.'

'Everyone's been texting her,' said Jamie, getting up

and going outside to see if the car had gone. 'It's still there,' he announced as he came back. 'Just the one, and no one in it. They must be inside, taking statements.' His eyes grew wide. Rachel could see him forming a police drama in his mind, lifted straight from television programmes.

'Have you had an answer?' asked Rachel. 'To the texts?' It would be a relief to hear that Jodie had been in touch.

'Nothing. Her phone's been switched off,' said Jamie, sitting back down and taking a second bowl of cereal. He looked up. 'Hey, Mum! Do you think she's been murdered?' His tone was interested and matter of fact.

'Don't say that! Don't joke about things like that. It's horrible! Poor Marion!'

'Poor Jodie, more like!' He made a strangled face, eyes crossed, tongue sticking out.

'She'll be all right,' said Pete, speaking for the first time. 'Why shouldn't she be? She's always doing stuff like this.' He got up impatiently and pushed his bowl away.

Jamie sniggered. 'Look at this, Pete!' he said, passing over his mobile telephone. 'This text from Shane . . . "What's the difference between Jodie Foot and a police dog?"' Both boys guffawed, passing the telephone between them. Rachel shook her head and turned away.

Later on, after breakfast, when she went out to work, she'd see if there was anybody around who had any news. If there had been developments there would be someone on the lookout to pass on the details. That was what villages were like. Of course the woman at Jasmine Cottage where she was going this morning wouldn't know anything, because she was a stranger to the village, only moved in last night.

Jasmine Cottage was the closest of her various cleaning jobs, and Dr Ballantyne was hardly ever there, always up at Oxford where he was a professor, or away travelling in the holidays. She didn't know why he had the cottage at all really. You could hardly call it his home. All she had to do was dust round, air the place a bit, wage war against spiders and mice and forward any post. Having this American woman there for a few months would make the job a bit harder, but she couldn't complain because in the past she had been well paid for what amounted to hardly more than caretaking.

As she got mince out of the freezer for supper, she

wondered what the woman would be like. Dr Ballantyne had telephoned her to tell her about the arrangement he had made but he couldn't tell her much more.

'There's an obvious risk, Rachel,' he'd said, 'in letting your home to someone you have never met. I'd be grateful if you'd keep an eye on things. I don't know this Dr Fairweather from Adam, you see. She's an academic who's got a flat I can use in New York. A hairy old lesbian feminist spinster, I should think, so I'm not expecting her to throw wild parties or wreck the place. Just see she doesn't do anything daft, would you?'

She'd promised him she would and he asked her to email him if there were any emergencies. She'd have to get Jamie to do it for her, she wasn't that competent, but the new laptop Dave had bought the boys for Christmas did just about everything bar the housework.

Dave came thumping down the stairs, still buttoning a fresh work shirt and shoving it into the waistband of his jeans. He ruffled the heads of the boys and patted Rachel on the bottom as he went by to put two slices of bread in the toaster.

'All right?' he asked the room at large.

'Yeah. Dad, can we go to rugby club this evening?

They've got passing practise for the under fourteens.' Jamie's face lit up with enthusiasm.

'If I'm home in time. I should be early tonight.'

'You're always saying that,' grumbled Jamie mildly, 'and then you're not.'

'Well, I can't promise, but I'll do my best.'

He fished the bread out of the toaster and brought it to the table. Rachel pushed a mug of tea over to him.

'What time then tonight?' she asked.

Dave looked up at her, his eyes very blue, made bluer by the denim shirt. 'Look, I said I'd do my best. Get off my back, will you?'

'I only asked. I wasn't complaining, was I?'

Dave hooked his arm round her waist and drew her to him. 'Not half, you weren't. I know that tone of voice. That's women for you, boys, grumble when you work overtime, grumble when you don't!'

'I'm not like that!'

Jamie was watching them, his face bright. He loved it when they sparred affectionately. He jumped up and pushed his head between them.

'Break it up, you two!' he instructed and they both laughed and messed with his hair.

'Yuck! What's this muck you've got on?' said Dave,

recoiling in mock horror as if he had touched something disgusting. 'Oh, no! Not another styling gel victim.
One in the house is enough!'

Jamie squealed and tried to get away while Pete
ostentatiously ignored the dig at him. Rachel went to
the sink with the dirty bowls.

'I'm doing the new woman today,' she announced,
thinking aloud. 'The American I told you about who's
moved into Dr Ballantyne's for the summer.'

'We saw her, Mum,' said Jamie, breaking away from
his father. 'Yesterday evening. Didn't we, Pete? She was
moving stuff in yesterday.'

'What did she look like?'

Jamie shrugged. 'Boring.'

'What do you mean, boring?'

'Old, then. She was old and boring-looking.'

'Well, that's all right by me.' Rachel laughed. 'I don't
mind if she's boring. She's not going to be my new best
friend, is she?'

'Anyone over eighteen is old to you guys,' said Dave,
eating toast.

'Too right,' said Jamie, ducking out of the way as his
father swung his arm in his direction.

Pete brought his bowl and plate to the sink. Glancing

at him, Rachel thought that he looked tired. There were shadows under his eyes and he had hardly spoken.

'You all right, Pete?' she said quietly. His face had a blank, impenetrable look.

'Yeah,' he said defensively. 'Why? Oh, don't bother . . .' and he was gone, back upstairs. She heard him pause on the landing. He'd be looking out of the window. She often stopped there herself, drawn to the view of the quiet road and the line of the neighbours' houses and the hills beyond. He'd be looking at the police car parked outside the Foots' house. Of course, that was what was bothering him. He covered it up by pretending that he didn't care, but she knew better. He always had been too sensitive and imaginative and got upset about things when he was a little boy. He hadn't really changed, not on the inside, and he'd be thinking about Jodie as he stood on the landing and looked out of the window. About whether she was still missing and, if she was, what had happened to her.

Almost the moment Rachel left her own gate she bumped into Cathy, eager to tell her the latest news. Marion, it seemed, had not reported Jodie missing until after ten o'clock the night before. She hadn't wanted to get the police and the social services involved, said Cathy, seeing as the last time Jodie had turned up all right. She didn't want the social workers saying Jodie was out of control or not supervised properly and slapping a care order on her. Well, Rachel could see that. Once you got that lot involved, the whole thing went out of your control and decisions were made on behalf of your child by people who knew nothing about her.

She, of all people, could appreciate that. She remembered Mrs Roland, with her clipboard and file and car that smelled of the pine car freshener that dangled from the driver's mirror in the form of a little green fir tree. She could remember thinking that if forests smelled like that, she didn't want to go in one. She was eleven years old and her mother was in hospital for the first time and her stepfather had said he couldn't cope. She was being driven to a care home, and into the clutches of the social services from which she wasn't to be properly released for five years.

'So what do the police think?'

Cathy shrugged. 'Same as last time. They don't think she's been abducted. Not yet, at least. They're making inquiries, like. They'll put a missing persons out on Southern TV this evening if they've not found her. The

TV crew are coming this afternoon. They're going to interview Marion.'

She'll enjoy that, thought Rachel and then felt guilty. It was a terrible thing to think about the mother of a missing child, but all the same she knew that Marion would rise to the occasion, sitting on the sofa with her make-up on and a tragic face, the squinting toddler on her knee and the other kids crowded round her. Last time it hadn't got to that. Jodie had turned up again before the appeals went out. She'd only got half an inch in the *Western Gazette*, 'Girl Missing', and then two days later, 'Missing Girl Found'. Not even her name had been mentioned.

'Let me know, will you, Cathy? If you hear anything. Are you all right, by the way? You look a bit tired. It's terrible at the end, isn't it? Just hanging on and wait-ing.'

'Yeah, I'm all in.' Cathy patted her drum of a belly. 'Terrible heartburn I had last night, thanks to Fred, here. I can't make up my mind whether babies are more trouble in or out. Either way, they keep you awake all night. I'm just off to the clinic now – I'm due on Thursday.' She undid the door of her car and heaved herself into the driver's seat. 'Where are you off to?'

'Jasmine Cottage. There's someone moved in for the summer.'

'Well, I don't know what they'll think about all this. It's not what you expect, is it? Not when you come to the country for a bit of peace and quiet.'

Juliet was in the bedroom trying to work out why her laptop computer wouldn't work when she heard a knock at the back door and hurried down the stairs to answer it, running her hands through her hair in the way she did when she was distracted. She hated bloody technology and was still so ignorant that she wasn't sure how she could attach herself to the internet. Would it work on someone else's telephone connection in another country? How should she know the answer to such a question? Because she didn't, she would have to try and find someone who did. She had grown so used to being able to telephone the university's technical support people to solve any problems and she hardly bothered to listen to any vaguely technical explanation, computer jargon so mystified and bored her. So here she was, pig ignorant about the thing and yet totally reliant on it, both for her work and her private life, and it made her mad that she was stupid enough to be in this situation.

It was with a look of frustration on her face that she went to the door, which stood open to take advantage of the beautiful morning, and saw a round-faced, pleasant-looking youngish woman, whose shoulder-length curly brown hair was tied back in a ponytail, wearing a T-shirt and jeans.

'Oh, hello,' she said.

'Hello. I'm Rachel.' The young woman only half smiled. It's because I look so cross, thought Juliet. I've given her a fright.

'Hello,' she said again, still unsure what the caller wanted, until the penny dropped. 'Oh, *Rachel*!' she said again. Dr Ballantyne's 'help'. 'I'm so sorry. For a moment I couldn't think who Rachel was. I'm in the middle of a terrible battle with my computer, that's why I look a bit distraught.'

'Oh, dear!' said Rachel, still looking uneasy. She hesitated. 'Do you want me to come back?'

'No! No, of course not! I'm really glad to see you. Dr Ballantyne told me that you would call. I suppose I wasn't expecting you so soon. I only got here yesterday evening.'

'I know. My boys saw you unpacking,' said Rachel. 'Normally I'd just let myself in. I've got my own key,

56

but since . . .' her voice tailed off. She thought of Jamie's description, which to her mind was wrong on both counts. This woman wasn't old or boring, although she was fierce-looking and had a direct sort of manner.

'Oh, right. I see.' Juliet laughed. 'It's the old story about villages, isn't it? Everyone knowing everything about everyone else.'

'Well, they only said they'd seen you,' said Rachel. She wasn't a gossip and she didn't want this woman to think she was.

'Come on in,' said Juliet, stepping aside and throwing out an arm to indicate the way. 'Look, I've made an awful mess already. Stuff everywhere. I can never settle to anything domestic and see it through to the end, which is why I've only half unpacked and half put things away in the kitchen.'

'I can do that for you.'

'Oh, that would be wonderful. I've already got a load of stuff for the washing machine but I was defeated by the lack of water. It doesn't seem to fill.'

'It's switched off under the sink,' said Rachel. 'Didn't Dr Ballantyne say?'

'Oh, perhaps he did. I may have forgotten. He sent me reams of stuff about the place which I printed off the computer and which I now can't find. That's why I was trying to get my laptop to work just now. You couldn't have arrived at a better moment. You can talk me through it all, if you don't mind.'

Juliet followed Rachel through to the kitchen and watched her squat down to reach into the cupboard under the sink, disturbing a brace of little silverfish which shimmered away across the floor.

'This old place is full of creepie-crawlies,' she said. 'I hope you don't mind mice or spiders.'

'Well, I'm not that thrilled by them but I don't stand on a chair and scream,' said Juliet. 'I suppose it's what you expect in country cottages.'

'Yeah,' said Rachel. 'I'm a townie myself, born and bred, but I'm getting used to it now. After ten years.'

'You are?' said Juliet, watching as she loaded the machine and showed her the drawer where the soap powder went. 'Me too. I was born and brought up in London. Now I live in New York, via various other cities.'

'I'm a Londoner, born in lovely Tottenham. I thought you were American from what Dr B said.'

'Oh, really? No, I just live there. In fact living there makes me more conscious of *not* being American, if you know what I mean. It makes me feel more British.'

'I see,' said Rachel, although she didn't. She hoped the woman wasn't going to stand and watch her all the morning.

'Coffee? What about a coffee? We could go and sit outside for five minutes and you can tell me about everything.'

'Yeah, all right.'

'I had it here somewhere,' said Juliet, rummaging amongst the groceries still in the bags on the counter. 'I've found the tea already . . . Ah, here it is!' She held up a packet. Real coffee, thought Rachel, that would mean finding the jug thing that Dr B used. She would rather it had been instant, less formal and made in a minute. She didn't want to sit down with this woman and have a social, although she seemed pleasant enough. You couldn't call her pretty, her nose was too large and bony and her chin too determined, but there was something attractive about her. She had a lean, brown face and hazel eyes. She moved quickly in energetic bursts and talked fast and seemed half amused all the time, as if she was about to laugh. She wore her dark hair quite long for a woman of her age and completely straight. She kept tucking it behind an ear as she talked.

Rachel took two of the ugly mugs out of the cupboard

and put them on a tray. 'Sorry about these,' she said. 'Horrible, aren't they?'

'Disgusting!' laughed Juliet. 'I've got "new mugs" at the top of my shopping list.'

No ring, thought Rachel, seeing that the slender, brown hands were unadorned. Perhaps Dr B was right and she was a lesbian, although she didn't look like one of the butch, dungareed lot. She wore jeans and a white shirt with the sleeves rolled up, and flat Indian-looking leather sandals. Her feet were brown and long as well, and Rachel was surprised to see that she wore two silver toe rings. She was a bit of a surprise, altogether. Not what she had been expecting at all.

'My name is Juliet, by the way.'

'Oh, right.' She wanted to be called by her first name, then, not Dr Fairweather. Fleetingly, Rachel hoped that Juliet wasn't going to be over-friendly. It always complicated things in a working relationship. She preferred to keep it straightforward so that there weren't misunderstandings. Once she had worked for a lonely old lady who talked the hind leg off a donkey and then wanted to pay only for the time Rachel was actually working.

Juliet led the way outside, carrying the tray, and the two women sat on the chairs in the sun. Rachel perched on the edge, feeling the wooden seat cutting into her thighs. She didn't want to sit back and look too relaxed. After all, she was still at work.

'There!' said Juliet, pushing down the plunger of the cafetière and passing Rachel a mug. 'Milk? Sugar?'

They both sipped their coffee for a moment, and then Juliet asked various questions about the hot water boiler and the general running of the cottage. There wasn't much to say, it wasn't as if it was complicated, and then into a silence Rachel blurted out, 'A kid from the village has gone missing. I don't suppose you've heard. She's been gone all night.'

Juliet went very still and put her mug down slowly and looked across at Rachel with shocked eyes.

'God!' she said softly. 'How ghastly. How absolutely awful.'

They sat in silence for a moment, weighing up the potential horror of what Jodie's disappearance might mean.

'Yeah, well, it may not be as bad as it sounds. She's done it before, this girl. Last time she turned up right as rain.'

'Who is she? What's her name?'

'Jodie Foot. She comes from a big family that lives

down my end of the village. There's only the mother, like. A single parent. There's never been a dad around as far as I know. Of course she's in a terrible state.'

'She would be. I heard a woman screaming yesterday evening. I thought it was just a row, you know, what they call a domestic. I suppose it could have been her. Then I saw the police this morning,' said Juliet, slowly, remembering. 'I was surprised, actually. It was the first car I saw coming through the village and it made me wonder. In New York I'm so used to the sirens that I don't even notice them any more. They used to keep me awake all night when I first lived there, but here, in a village like this, in England, it didn't seem quite normal.'

'No, it isn't. We're the village the police forgot, as a rule,' said Rachel. She stood up and picked up the tray. 'Anyway, I'd better be getting on.'

'Would you let me know?' asked Juliet, following her into the kitchen. 'Would it be an awful nuisance to let me know if you hear anything? I mean, obviously I don't know the Foots, but all the same, now you've told me and in a small place like this, I somehow feel involved.'

'Yes. If I hear anything I'll give you a ring. Let's hope

it's good news.' What stupid things you say, thought Rachel, at a time like this; stock phrases trotted out to cover what you really feel but could not say or even think.

'There was an old man too,' said Juliet, suddenly remembering. 'He came out onto the main street on a bicycle. He cycled straight out without looking to see if anything was coming and there was something so peculiar about him. He had this terrible expression on his face. He looked haunted by something. First it was the police car and then he came careering along and I thought they were somehow connected.'

Rachel stopped washing the mugs at the sink and looked back over her shoulder.

'Oh,' she said, 'that would be Henry. He lives down near me, on his own since his brother died. He's a funny old thing, a bit peculiar, but he's completely harmless. He's retired but does a lot of gardens round the village. He comes here, in fact, about once or twice a week in the summer, to keep things tidy and cut the grass. He'll be round soon, I expect.'

'Oh, I see.' Juliet wasn't sure that she was pleased by this piece of information. She felt somehow reluctant to take on the strange old man on top of the news of the missing child. It seemed as if her life in this village was already being crowded by unsettling events and she had only just arrived. She stood in the door as Rachel dried the mugs and felt slightly uncomfortable, as if she should be doing something useful. I'd better finish unpacking, she thought, and slowly mounted the stairs.

She went into the bedroom and began to pull clothes out of her suitcase and put them in the clean drawers of the chest. What she really wanted to do was telephone Gavin and have a long gossipy chat. She wanted to tell him about the missing child. The awfulness of the event seemed to trigger in her an eagerness to share the terrible news with somebody else. She wanted to hear him saying how dreadful it was, and to be as shocked and horrified as she was. It was as if this child's disappearance coinciding with her move to the village transferred some drama to her own life and made it seem more interesting. Appalled at herself, she could even imagine telling the story to disbelieving friends when she got back to New York. It felt horridly like a sort of tragedy voyeurism.

She clattered back down the stairs to where Rachel was still putting things away in the kitchen.

'Is there anything I could do, do you think?' she asked, as if in atonement. 'Anything at all? I mean, I've got a car outside. I could drive someone, or do shopping or something.' Isn't this what villagers do? she thought. Rally round.

Rachel turned to look at her. 'I shouldn't think so. The Foots are an enormous family. There are hundreds of them round here. I think they'll take care of their own.'

'I see.' Juliet felt a tiny frisson of disapproval. She realised that subtly she had been put in her place. As a complete outsider she had overstepped the mark. 'OK. Well, I just thought I'd ask.' She went back upstairs. She longed to lie full length on the bed, which she still hadn't made, and close her eyes and sleep, but she couldn't with Rachel working downstairs. She would have to get back to sorting out her stuff and maybe get on the telephone to try and find someone to solve her computer problem. Effing bloody thing, she said to it where it sat plugged in on the floor, its screen blank and unresponsive.

But first, Juliet thought, she would ring her mother. She would be longing to know what the cottage was like and she would arrange to take her and Aunt Dot out to lunch. Now she was back in England she intended to make up a little for being an absent daughter.

In the small and over-furnished house in Highgate the telephone was only allowed to ring twice before being snatched up by Aunt Dot, who bellowed, 'Who is that?' into the mouthpiece. Really, thought Bobbie Fairweather, Juliet's mother, it was like an event in the Olympics, seeing who could get to the telephone first, and it was generally her sister who won because she allowed herself the unfair advantage of siting her armchair in such a way so that even if she was dozing she only had to wake with a start, as she had just done, and reach out to pick it up. She was often in such a hurry that she failed to adjust her hearing aid and, flustered, could not catch who it was on the other end, which led to the shouting.

It was being in control that Dot minded, Bobbie understood that, and generally allowed her sister the ascendancy with good grace but this rivalry over the telephone she found most trying. More often than not, the calls were for Bobbie, from her children or even, joy of joys, her grandchildren, and rarely for Dot, who nevertheless liked to act as a filter and glean any information before she passed over the receiver to her sister.

She then became a self-appointed authority and corrected Bobbie when she got things wrong, although more often than not, it was Dot herself who was mistaken, what with all the shouting and repeating. Sometimes Bobbie found herself so irritated that she felt quite violent and was alarmed by what she could only describe as a moment or two of hatred for her sister. Of course, the feeling passed and then she was ashamed of herself but it gave her an understanding of how an otherwise devoted person, tried beyond reason, could pick up a bread knife and commit murder.

This morning it was Juliet on the telephone and by the time Dot passed over the receiver, Bobbie, always alarmed by the size of telephone bills, was feeling anxious not to talk too long. She did not want poor Juliet to have to repeat everything; what the cottage was like, how she had slept on her first night, and what were her immediate plans.

'I'll tell you all when I see you!' said Juliet. 'I want to come to London at least once a week.'

'Well, that will be lovely, darling!' said Bobbie. 'We can hear all about everything then.'

Regretfully, she put down the receiver. She and Juliet had always been close and there was a certain bond between them that was quite different from that between Bobbie and her sons. However, distance meant that they inevitably had far less contact than when Juliet lived in England and the fact that she had not married and had no family of her own denied her mother the closeness of sharing love for a child and grandchild. As it was, Juliet's life as an independent career woman was something Bobbie found it hard to imagine, having lived her own life entirely through her family.

The fact that Juliet had been unhappy and was quite bravely making the best of it, did not escape her mother either, although it was something they had never talked about. I wouldn't want her to think that I am disappointed in any way, Bobbie thought. I just want her to know how proud I am of her. To teach in a prestigious university was a wonderful achievement, and even if Bobbie wondered whether it was *enough*, she never said so.

Of course it was Dot who felt that she and Juliet had most in common – 'We are both teachers, you see, and single career woman,' she kept pointing out, and Bobbie had to bite her tongue not to retort that there was rather a difference between a retired games mistress and an academic.

Anyway, Juliet was coming to see them very soon and that made Bobbie very happy indeed, and as she put down the receiver she turned to Dot with a bright smile. 'Won't it be lovely! Having Juliet here for the whole summer.'

Later, as Rachel walked home, the village was absolutely quiet. Most of the cottages and houses stood right alongside the lane, their front doors opening straight onto the street, but even on this lovely sunny morning, windows and doors were firmly closed. This was not a picturesque place filled with sprightly newly retired couples from the London suburbs. It was a proper working village where families were up and gone early in the morning, returning home from the afternoon onwards. It had a pub, but no shop, a church, no school, no village hall and the two dairy farms set within the village itself had both gone out of business in the last five years, their land taken over by a land management company, the farmhouses sold off at prices which had to be seen to be believed. Once there had been a small slaughterhouse and bacon factory on what was known as Top Lane but EU regulations had put it out of business. The premises now stood empty and overgrown with brambles, the chain-link gate heavily padlocked. Rumour had it that it had been bought by a developer who was waiting for a change in planning regulations to clear the site and put up some executive homes.

There was a scattering of new houses and bunga-lows, some sheltered housing, two cul-de-sacs of coun-cil houses, a Victorian manor house set behind high grey stone walls and the rest was just the usual hotch-potch of cottages of various sorts, some thatched and mostly built of golden local stone. A bus came through twice a week, running between the two nearest towns, and that was that.

It wasn't a village that tourists made a detour to visit. It was a nothing dump, Jamie and Pete complained, but nevertheless it had a sense of iden-tity and place because of the way it was sited in the cleavage of two gently rounded hills, in a valley so lovely that it was still a marvel to Rachel. Almost any way you looked there was a curve of small hedged fields and woodland and in the distance the higher hills that marked the edge of the vale. This morning the abundant green of early summer surged and frothed from every hedgerow, garden and field, and birds were darting busily in and out of the beech hedge that bordered Greenhill Cottage, past which Rachel walked. She still couldn't have told you what they were, just small brown garden birds, although she knew it was a blackbird that was singing from the top of a telegraph post, plump and black, his beak a bright yellow against the tender blue sky.

When she turned off the main street and onto the lane on which she lived, she could see at once that there was a lot going on at the Foots' end. Vehicles were pulled up on both sides of the road and there was a crowd of people outside and going to and fro through the garden gate. The police car was still there and had been joined by a large white police van with a chequered stripe along its side.

Cathy was standing at her gate, one hand on her swelling stomach. 'They're going to make door-to-door inquiries,' she said to Rachel in a solemn and excited voice. 'They're starting this afternoon.'

'How's Marion?'

'Under sedation. The doctor gave her something. She was climbing the walls this morning. You should have heard her screaming at the police.'

Rachel nodded. It was sure to be like that. You'd be deranged if you had lost a child, even if the chances were she would be found. It would be the not know-ing that was the agony. She opened her gate to go in.

'Was everything all right with the baby?' she asked.

Cathy's face changed to the dreamy inward-turned smile of pregnant women. She smoothed a hand over her belly. 'Yeah. The head's not dropped yet, the lazy little so and so. It's going to keep me waiting – a bit slow this one, like its dad. I just hope that I won't still be here next week.'

Rachel smiled sympathetically. 'I hope so too, for your sake. I was two weeks late with Jamie, too big to move, blobbing about like a barrage balloon.'

'What was the new man like? At Jasmine Cottage?'

'He's a woman,' said Rachel. 'She seems OK. Fine, really, although she was upset by all of this.' Rachel indi-cated the activity at the end of the road.

'I'm not surprised. Anyone would be,' said Cathy. 'It's like a nightmare, isn't it? A kid missing.'

Chapter Three

THAT SAME MORNING, after he had cycled home and put his shopping away, Henry Streeter worked in his allotment. This time he could not claim that he did not notice anything going on. You'd have had to be blind and deaf not to see the cars coming and going, the clanging of the Foots' gate, the police vehicles parked outside, and then Marion carrying on like that. He'd heard her screaming like a stuck pig, on and on, but he'd kept on hoeing between his rows of beans, concentrating on the tiny green shoots of weeds which had to be taken out.

It was a terrible thing to hear a woman scream. He tried to block it out but he couldn't ignore a sound like that. It went through his head and seemed to penetrate his chest to set his heart pumping. He went on hoeing, back along the row that he had already done, scratching at the fine tilth, and he didn't stand up and straighten his back until the sound had stopped.

Then he saw the doctor's car. It was Dr Chandler, who was Henry's own doctor, although he hadn't seen him for three years, not since he had written out Fred's death certificate. He'd been a frequent visitor in those final weeks of Fred's life, when he had tried to ease the pain and offered to arrange a nurse to help Henry cope, as he called it. Henry had refused, of course. He knew Fred would have hated to have a stranger looking after him, a woman at that.

When he understood that he was soon to die, so weak that he could hardly lift his head, and his voice was the merest whisper, Fred had asked to be carried out to the garden. He said he wanted to die outdoors where he could hear the birds singing. 'Something familiar, like,' he'd laboured to say. Henry could hardly make out the words and then didn't know if he had heard it right.

Please don't let him die at night, he'd prayed. At least grant him that one wish, God knows he'd had little enough in life. In the end it happened in the early morning. Henry had wrapped Fred in his old eiderdown and carried him in his arms out to the patch of garden just as it got light and together they had heard the first bird sing, and then another and another until the whole earth seemed to be ringing with song. Fred's wasted body was so light he could have been a child and Henry had looked down at the waxy face of his brother and saw that he was at peace and the terrible pain had gone.

He'd bowed his own head and wept then, his tears dropping on Fred's upturned face, and then he'd carried him inside and up to the bedroom and laid him gently on his bed and gone downstairs to sit in the chair in the kitchen. He'd waited until nine o'clock to ring the doctor.

'Fred's gone,' he said. 'Gone this morning.'

After he'd done his morning surgery, Dr Chandler called round and filled in forms and arranged for the undertakers to come and take Fred away. He was kind and gentle with Henry and as he was leaving said, 'It's normal, you know, to grieve and feel unable to face life without your brother. You did so much for him. I can arrange for counselling if you would like it. We have very good bereavement counsellors and many of my patients find it helps to talk to someone outside the family.'

Henry looked at him as if he was speaking a foreign language. Talk to someone? What was there to say? How could talking make anything different? He'd refused of course, and Dr Chandler had said that he'd like him to make an appointment to come and see him in a few weeks' time. 'I'd like to check you over,' he said, kindly, 'and see how you are getting on.' He felt the oppressive silence in the tidy cottage, and the stiffness of misery in the old man left behind and wished that there was something he could do.

Henry never made the appointment and this was the first time he had seen the doctor since then, and what with Marion's screams upsetting him, he suddenly felt light-headed and strange. He leaned his hoe against the chain-link fence and made his way out of the allotments and crossed the road to his cottage. Back in the kitchen, sitting at the table with the door closed, he felt a bit steadier. In a minute he'd put the kettle on the stove and make himself a cup of tea with a spoonful of sugar. That should set him right.

He was sitting there with the Weymouth mug in his hand when he heard feet crunching on the gravel path and then there was a knock at the back door. Stiffly he got up to answer it and found Billy Wright and Bingo standing there.

'Heard the news then, Henry?' asked Billy, coming inside while Bingo sniffed excitedly round the shed where Henry knew there was a rat.

'No,' said Henry. 'I've heard a lot of carry-on, that's all.'

'The lass is still missing,' said Billy, sitting down without being asked. He was a small round man with a belly that now sat on his lap like a football. The waistband of his trousers disappeared somewhere underneath, having long ago given up trying to reach round his middle. Today he wore a Yeovil Town T-shirt that his grandson had given him for his birthday.

'The police reckon someone must have seen something. They're going to do house-to-house inquiries. They'll be round here, Henry, asking a lot of tomfool questions about what you were doing yesterday evening.'

Henry didn't answer, but looked gloomily into his mug at the cold remains of his tea.

'So where were you, Henry?'

'I was here,' he said, looking up. 'Here, and in the allotment. Where I always am if I'm not out working somewhere else.'

'But can you prove it?' persisted Billy. 'That's it, you see. Can you prove it?'

Henry looked at the contents of his mug again. 'I was here,' he said again. 'I didn't see or hear anything.'

'And I was at home having a nap in the armchair and then I took Bingo for a walk, but how can I prove it, Henry? I didn't see you and you didn't see me. Do you get it? It's proof they'll be after, and we've got no proof between the pair of us.' He tapped the kitchen table with a forefinger.

Henry sniffed. He didn't really see. What would the police want with an old man like him? He couldn't tell them anything and neither could Billy. It would be a waste of time talking to them.

Billy sat on, looking round the kitchen with a disapproving expression. 'You want to get this place done up, Henry. Get a new kitchen put in, get up to date. Terrible this is. Hasn't been touched for thirty years, has it?'

'It suits me well enough,' said Henry.

'Did you look at that Argos catalogue?' persisted Billy, who, through his son and grandchildren, felt confidently in touch with modern life, and in a position to advise his friend. 'You want to get rid of that old telly and buy something that gives you a better picture and with remote control. You can change channels from your chair and don't have to be up and down all the time, and you should get a proper washing machine, an automatic. No one has one of them old top-loaders any more. You've got the money, haven't you? You're a mean old bugger. Never spend a penny, do you?'

Henry said nothing. The thick catalogue that Billy had dropped round was full of stuff he didn't want or need, so much of it that he couldn't wade through all the pages of cameras and video recorders and computers and gardening equipment. He'd had a look, just to be able to say that he had, and then he had put it by, on the shelf of the television table in the front room, and there it had stayed.

It was Fred who had enjoyed the television. He had it on every evening and watched it right through to bedtime, anything that came on, programme after programme. He knew the characters on the soap operas and followed their turbulent lives with unfeigned interest, particularly the escapades of the women.

'Ooh! She's a right one!' he used to say. 'She's a devil, she is,' or, 'She's ever so nice, is that one. Got a right soft heart, she has.' Once he had said, 'Ooh, I'd like to give her a kiss, I would. She's a lovely girl is that one,' and Henry had looked at him sharply, and seen only his smiling, childish face.

He often wondered whether Fred had ever realised what he had missed, never knowing a woman, never having held a girl in his arms. He was sentimental and soft-hearted and lavished affection on the series of cats and dogs that they had had over the years but he had never shown signs of being interested in sex, which was a good thing and made life easier. It meant that Henry didn't have to worry about him being friendly with the children of their neighbours, and even if their mothers were suspicious and wary at first, they soon realised that there was no harm in Fred and often asked him to keep an eye on their young ones playing on their bikes outside while they nipped to the shops, or ran an errand.

You hear of people being called childlike and that is exactly how Fred was. Mentally, he hadn't grown up much beyond his tenth birthday and Henry often wondered whether it was because of the war and being evacuated and the knocking around he'd got at the hands of old man Betts that Fred's development had got stuck in childhood.

After their mother was killed in the Bethnal Green

underground station disaster in 1943, they hadn't much hope left in either of them. There was no one who wanted them then. Their dad had done a runner before the war and they wouldn't have known where to begin to look for him, and their mother's relatives were too hard-pressed scratching a living themselves to take on two hungry boys, so they had no option but to stay put. By the time he was fifteen, Henry had left school and got himself a job with a dairy and found lodgings for himself and Fred with a Mrs Parsons, a kindly widow of a railwayman. They shared a small back bedroom in a damp cottage with an outside privy and she cooked them their breakfast and had tea waiting when they got home. To be away from the Bettses' farm was to be in paradise.

Henry often thought that these days they'd sue some-one for what happened to them as children. They'd sue the social services or whatever government department handed them over to the Bettses and forgot about them. You'd call it abuse these days. Back then it was what a lot of children suffered at the hands of even their own families, and you didn't think to complain. Mostly you thought you deserved any rough treatment you got, and school could be as bad. It was for Fred, because the teachers punished him for being lazy and careless and inattentive, when he couldn't help it. He was that slow to read and write that they kept him down until he was so big for the infant desks that he couldn't get his knees under them.

The only time Henry had ever been in trouble in his life was when Fred was beaten by the headmaster for not knowing his tables and Henry had waited for Mr Forster after school and seized him by his collar and tie and pushed him up against the wall and said, 'If you ever lay a hand on my brother again, I'll break your neck.'

Billy Wright remembered it and at Fred's funeral he had reminded Henry. 'You were good to Fred, Henry, that you were. From a kid onwards, you looked out for him. I'll never forget the day you knocked old Forster's glasses off. My word, that old bastard deserved it. He'd be put in prison these days for how he treated us boys.'

Now Billy could see he was wasting his time, trying to keep Henry up to date with his domestic arrangements. In his own bungalow he had every modern convenience going, electric this and digital that, even an electric toothbrush his daughter had given him last Christmas.

'I'll have a cup of tea, if you're making one,' he said, although he could see that Henry had just finished his. He watched as Henry filled the old kettle and put it on the stove. At home he'd got a one-cup electric kettle, energy saving and designed for a person living on their own, but he didn't bother to mention it. It would have been a waste of breath.

'So where do they reckon she's to?' Henry asked as he put a fresh tea bag into his brown pot. 'The lass of Marion's?'

'It was Bournemouth last time. They found her hanging around with a rough crowd down the arcades. She's a load of trouble, that girl, but you've got to remember she's had no discipline. Not like we had. They've not been taught any respect, these kids. They know about their rights, but not how they should treat other people. They don't think that the rules apply to them and what do they get when they go wrong? An ASBO! They collect them orders like Green Shield Stamps.'

Henry had heard this many times before and although he believed a lot of what Billy said was true, he'd never advocate a return to the old days. There was too much cruelty in those days, too much suffering. He'd rather kids got out of hand than any child had to go through what Fred did.

He filled a mug for Billy. The tea was black and strong and deep orange when he added milk. In a cupboard he had a tin of biscuits. It was one of the things he allowed himself. Nothing fancy, just a rich tea biscuit or a gingernut. A cup of tea and a biscuit was always a good pick-me-up. He got the tin out and put the mug on the table in front of Billy.

'What's this then?' said Billy, looking at the tea suspiciously. 'You're not using full fat milk are you, Henry? You shouldn't be doing that. It's bad for you. You need to get the semi-skimmed. It's the cholesterol, see.'

'It's what I've always used and what I'll go on using,' said Henry. 'Milk is milk. I don't want mine buggered about, thank you very much. Now drink it or leave it, it's all the same to me.'

Billy sipped his tea. It was his daughter had got him onto the low-fat malarkey and he couldn't say he enjoyed it. Henry's tea tasted much better, but he wasn't going to tell him so.

'Just as long as you know what you're doing. The damage, like.'

Billy always had to have the last word.

They were sitting there in companionable silence enjoying their tea when there was a knock on the front door that set Bingo jumping madly at the side gate and barking in the hysterical manner in which he greeted all callers, whether on his own turf or anybody else's.

The two old men looked at one another.

'That'll be them,' said Billy ominously. 'That'll be the police, Henry. Come to ask you questions.'

By lunchtime Juliet had finished arranging her things in Jasmine Cottage and looked round with satisfaction. With all the windows open and sunlight streaming in, the place was bright and cheerful and had an atmosphere that was welcoming and benign. She had decided that she would work in the second bedroom where there was a small table in a suitable spot, from where she could look over the garden and out to the hills. Today she noticed that the big black bales had all been shifted and the pale green grass that was left on the cut fields looked as if it had been swathed by the teeth of a giant comb. She guessed that this room was where Dr Ballantyne chose to work, because of the position of the electric socket and telephone point on the skirting board beneath the table and the fact that there were box files and folders full of papers on a long set of shelves which took up one whole wall. The rest of the shelves were laden with books, some stacked double and others in leaning piles on the floor.

Other people's books were always a fascination and Juliet found herself wasting a lot of time examining Dr B's library. Many of the titles were familiar, the sort of thing every student of history read at university in the sixties and seventies. There was also a collection of novels, including many of the classics, especially some well-thumbed Dickens, but no Jane Austen or George Eliot. This made Juliet smile, thinking that on her own shelves the opposite was the rule. Further along the shelf and it became clear that Dr B was a keen reader of Dostoevsky and Conrad, both of whom Juliet found gloomy, while on a shelf below was a collection of P.G. Wodehouse, a writer whom Juliet couldn't bear, although she knew lots of men who relished the humour that she found so dire. Finally, she hit on what was obviously Dr B's chief passion – row upon row of lurid murder mystery thrillers, the sort of thing she would never choose to read, hating the gruesome killings and bored by the subsequent investigation with all its ridiculously contrived twists and turns.

So, she thought, we've nothing in common, Dr B and I, at least regarding our taste in reading matter. She imagined him studying her own shelves and groaning when he found *Middlemarch* and *Mansfield Park* and all the clever twentieth-century women writers she enjoyed. She guessed that he would not be tempted to read any of them.

Mildly curious, she opened one of the folders and found inside a sheaf of lecture notes. They were laboriously handwritten and must have dated from years back, from before everyone used word processors. The writing was in black ink, very small and regular and extremely neat. It went straight across the paper as if resting on a ruled line, and sub-headings were underlined in coloured pen. There were no doodles or embellishments and the very tidiness impressed Juliet, whose mess and muddle of papers were always covered with her own drawings and scribbled afterthoughts. What a tidy mind this man had, and no imagination, she would guess. No flights of fancy here.

She was starting to form a picture of Dr Ballantyne – the unfashionable clothes in the wardrobe, the choice of books, the tidy files and the neat handwriting were all clues. His cottage was safely tasteful in an English way with faded linen loose covers on the comfortable old armchairs downstairs and a few antiques, but there were also some rather surprising modern pieces that made it a bit more interesting. The other thing which took her aback was that he had only modern art on his walls, of the splashy colourful variety, and also some rather surprising female nudes in a line on the landing, where she might have expected hunting prints, or something a bit less naked. They were pen and ink drawings of the same model, a dark woman with long hair and a lazy, unsmiling stare, lying on a rumpled bed with a whippet who posed very elegantly with its long nose resting on its paws. What should she make of that?

At first she had wondered if Dr B was homosexual and wished that she had asked Gavin a bit more about him, and at the same time realised that he was probably thinking exactly the same thing about her as he investigated her apartment and realised that there were no signs of male occupancy. To be in your fifties and single, as she was certain he was, invited that sort of speculation. You had to be either gay or a bit weird was what most people assumed, not allowing for the fact that to be alone could be a valid life choice rather than an unwilling state that was forced upon you by your failure to find a mate.

Recently she had noticed that a number of her married female friends expressed envy of her. In middle age they seemed weighed down by family burdens; adult children still living at home, aged parents and relatives and long marriages that had grown commonplace and stale. 'What bliss,' they would sigh, looking round her tranquil apartment with its empty fridge, bright colours and flowers on the polished table, its white rugs and bathroom full of expensive organic potions. 'You are so lucky to have this space of your own. I'd give anything to be able to escape to somewhere like this,' was the sort of thing they said. That was how they saw her life, as an escape from what they felt they had become at the hands of those they loved.

Turning from the shelves she put her laptop computer on the table and plugged it in, using an adaptor. She hadn't made any progress in getting it to work and felt another wave of frustration at not being able to send and receive emails which had become her chief method of communicating with her friends and colleagues. She was yearning to get in touch with Gavin, even if it was only to tell him that she had arrived safely at

Jasmine Cottage. Just occasionally, the dreaded Sonia went to visit her ancient father who lived with one of her sisters in Cumbria, and in the past he had telephoned Juliet when his wife was safely heading up the motorway, and they had managed a meeting, for old times' sake.

Juliet told herself that it was the prospect of spending some time in England after so long abroad that directed her thoughts towards Gavin. It couldn't have been anything else because she had got over the pain of parting years ago, which had anyway come about at her request. 'I can't stand it,' she had said tearfully as they sat together in his car in a discreet lay-by outside Oxford. 'When I'm with you I'm the happiest I can imagine ever being, and when I'm away from you, the most miserable. If we could only see one another more often, it might be worth it, but bloody Sonia has scotched that possibility. What you can offer me is not enough. It's not enough, this little tiny piece of you, just once in a while. It's not enough when being with you is the most important thing in my life!'

He had looked pained, which she knew he truly was, but there was never a suggestion that things could be different. He had three daughters, at that point at Oxford

High and the Dragon school, and his family life was rich and rewarding.

The imbalance in what they could individually bring to their relationship was what ultimately destroyed it. Although, on the one hand, just by seeing her, Gavin put his position in his family at risk. Sonia, as he often reminded Juliet, was a formidable woman. 'She would make it her business to exact revenge,' he had warned, 'of a Shakespearean magnitude,' and Juliet could see that he was exhilarated by the danger. In some perverse way he enjoyed playing Sonia up.

Juliet, for her part, felt that she brought her whole life, such as it was, and laid it humbly at his feet and more often than not he trampled over it in his anxiety not to be found out. Cancelled dates, interrupted telephone calls, long silences and inexplicable absences littered the path of their love affair, and each one left a little wound which never quite healed until, finally, it was too much to bear. She realised that when, with her heart full of love, she battered against his door, asking to be allowed in, if only to occupy a small corner of his life, how feeble her knocks must sound against the huge edifice of his family and what it represented.

She did not allow herself to regret the decision to

finish the affair because ultimately it freed her of the fairly constant disappointment which threatened to turn into bitterness. She certainly did not miss the sickening lurch of the heart as she was pitched from despair to joy and back again, and they managed to part with a fondness for each other that had survived a further decade, and which had matured into a loving friendship that she valued above all others. Now, at a safe distance from actually being in love, she could see that Gavin was a man who perhaps could never have brought her lasting happiness anyway, because before too long she would have been transformed, like Sonia, into his keeper.

It is no secret that infidelity is so seductive to the married of both sexes because it delivers an unrealistic amount of sex and excitement and the joy of being found adorable, and Juliet understood that the intensity and giddiness of illicit love that she had shared with Gavin was probably the best act on offer in his repertoire, his star turn. He had made her feel so good about herself, so beautiful, so clever, so witty, and during the stolen afternoons they had spent together she basked in the full beam of his attention. However, like all virtuoso performances, before too long it would have started to flag, and then, when things between them inevitably became more humdrum and commonplace, he would have begun to exasperate her.

Charming as he was as a lover, she wondered how irritating he might have become as a permanent and full-time fixture in her life. He required such a lot of attention for one thing, being, in those days, the sort of man who couldn't tolerate a dull moment. Had he been a child, his parents would have said he was over-active and had him on some kind of medication. He was ambitious, actively carving a place for himself in the university department, and always had to have something on the go, some project or plan, some new enthusiasm to be embraced. His restless energy took him out and about, making an impression, getting himself noticed, and all the time there was Sonia, solid in the background, making large, grey shepherd's pies for his students, and bringing up the girls.

To Juliet, inclined to be quiet and introverted, Gavin had seemed dynamic and thrilling, but as she had grown older, her life without him settled into a routine and a gentle pace at which she felt most comfortable and steady. She realised that he would have made this peaceful existence impossible and she wasn't sure that she would have been able to live with the clamour and rush that surrounded him.

There were other things, too. He was forgetful and untidy, unpunctual, and obsessively concerned about his health. He was wildly extravagant and generally bad with money and, worst of all, neurotically fearful of being on his own. He absolutely craved company and a day that went by without a meeting or a luncheon or a drinks party or dinner or a few friends round for supper was, in his view, hard to endure. This relentless sociability would have been hateful to Juliet; she enjoyed being on her own and purposely cleared whole days in her diary when she did not have to see anyone at all.

Their affair had been wonderfully erotic and still was when they managed to sneak a bit of time together. They still fancied one another, which was lovely, and just lately she had sensed that Gavin had perked up a bit in that department. Perhaps he was scared of finding that in his late fifties he was losing his attraction for women, or wanted to remind himself of the passionate sex they had enjoyed. Juliet, no longer scared of becoming pregnant and past caring too much about her ageing body – what did it matter, they were both saggier and had lost the lovely tautness and shine of youth years ago – was more relaxed about making love and giving and receiving pleasure than ever she had been before. Sex no longer seemed quite so performance-related as once it had been, and was all the better for it.

The other great bonus was that Juliet felt no longer trammelled by being in love with him. At last I am free, she would think as she made her way home after a sensational afternoon in a hotel bed. I can love him and leave him with none of the anguish and despair I used to feel. She didn't collapse in misery if he failed to contact her the day after they had met to say how wonderful it had been and to thank her, or if he made an assignation and then telephoned the night before to cancel. She didn't mind if she didn't hear from him for a couple of months, and then might very well be the first to make contact again. She could reverse all the rules that used to dominate her courtships and ruin her youthful love affairs. Theirs was an arrangement that they had arrived at as old friends, and was founded on deep affection and mutual respect. She had even grown to be grateful that he had Sonia in his life to keep him from doing anything silly. The last thing she herself would have wanted was to have to deal with a man like Gavin going through a tumultuous male menopause.

He had manifested the symptoms of this in a foolish way a couple of years ago when he had a brief affair with the wife of a colleague. She was too young and inexperienced to understand the rules of this sort of encounter, and overcome by remorse and too much sherry at a Fellows' drinks party, confessed everything to her husband. The fall-out was considerable and Juliet had found the whole episode extremely irritating. She was jealous, too, she realised, although Gavin took the trouble to tell her that he wouldn't have been interested had the girl not, quite literally, thrown herself sobbing at his feet. 'You should never have left me, darling,' he complained. 'If I still had you, I wouldn't have been tempted.' Despite the flattery, Juliet's sympathies were with Sonia, who did not deserve to be so humiliated.

Later she could only admire her when she stepped in smartly and sorted the whole thing out. A sabbatical was suddenly organised and Gavin was packed off to Belgium for three months, a country he loathed because, as he said, he didn't like beer, the food was horrible and the women were fat and ugly. It was a beautifully judged punishment and he had been so desperate to get back to Oxford that Sonia was able to extract every kind of promise of good behaviour. By this time the young wife was pregnant with her husband's baby and had been bundled off to the country to live amongst the flat wet fields of Brize Norton and the whole thing blew over.

So Sonia definitely had her good points although Juliet still heard with a pang about the long summer holidays at a villa in Italy, the Christmas skiing trips, and the weekends away. She thought what a waste that it wasn't her sharing Gavin's bed, and how much more she would have enjoyed his company than Sonia evidently did, with her bad back and migraines brought on if she drank wine.

Now that Juliet was here in this village, knowing no one, she had begun to think how very nice it would be to entice Gavin down for a few days. She imagined them drinking their morning coffee outside the back door, the bricks warm under their bare feet, and lying in each other's arms under the crooked eaves of the bedroom, talking and gossiping and slugging the expensive white wine that he would bring with him.

But staring out of the window and daydreaming about Gavin was not solving her computer crisis. Before she left, Rachel had suggested that the best way to find a technician who could sort out her problem was to go into the nearest small town and buy a local newspaper. 'There are always ads for PC troubleshooters,' she said. 'You should be able to find someone to help you.' This seemed such a thoroughly sensible thing to do that Juliet collected the hire car keys, found her bag and was just going out of the front door when she saw a policeman and woman walking purposefully towards her. With a sudden rush of remorse she realised that she had completely forgotten about the missing child.

Jodie's disappearance caused a surprisingly small ripple of concern at the school bus stop that morning. The older village children who caught the secondary school bus down at the crossroads hardly bothered to comment on her absence. Her poor attendance record and the nature of her family set-up meant that she often stayed away from home, with an aunt or a cousin or her nan in Sturminster. The fact that this time no one knew where she was and the police had been called in was accepted as heavy-handed interference on the part of the law. Jodie was a well-known truant and the general opinion was that Jodie's mum would be in trouble if she didn't turn up soon.

'If you skive off school so many times, they can send yer mum and dad to prison,' said Sam Davis, a red-haired eleven year old, and Jamie passed round his mobile telephone to share the text messages. The children sat on the wall in the sun and laughed and joked until the bus lumbered round the corner.

Pete, the oldest of the group, who had not joined in the chat, got on last, and swung down the aisle to sit at the back beside Gary, who grunted a greeting. As usual, he was half awake and it was only by chance that he happened to glance out of the window as the bus drove past the top of Pete's road and he spotted the police car.

'What's that about then?' he asked, sitting up and wiping the window with his sleeve. 'Who are the rozzers come to nick this time?' Although a patrol car was an unusual sight in the village, it was something that Gary had more experience of than most. The local police were often bumping down his farm drive to question his wayward brother about something or other.

'It's Jodie Foot,' said Pete, with no emotion in his voice.

'What's she done now?'

'Gone missing.'

'You're joking.'

'She's been out all night.'

'Little tart.'

'Yeah.' Pete slumped back into his seat and closed his eyes. He didn't want to think about what it would be like to be Jodie. He didn't want to exercise his imagination and wonder where she was or who she was with. It was easier to adopt the careless, joking attitude that did not betray how he really felt. He was grateful that Gary did not refer to what had happened on the bus the previous afternoon. It helped him to believe that it was not important, just a bit of mucking around. That's all it was, after all. There was no need to make a big thing of it. No need to mention it to anybody. No need to even think about it ever again. But he couldn't stop the image of Jodie's flushed, distressed expression from flashing into his mind. Angrily he chucked his bag to one side and kicked the back of the seat in front. Doing something violent blew the vision of her face away.

The police were patient, especially the woman constable who called Henry 'sir' and allowed him to take his time when he got muddled about when he was in the allotment yesterday and when he had crossed the road to his house. Despite what Billy had said, they weren't interested in what he had been doing as much as whether he had anything to tell them, which he hadn't. No, he said, he hadn't seen anything and neither had Billy. Yes, he knew Jodie well enough by sight but he hadn't spoken to her for a long time. She was always with her friends, just hanging around. The policeman made a few notes and then they asked if they could look in his shed. He'd been startled at that. What did they think, that he had the lass in there?

'No, no, sir,' said the woman constable, patting his arm, 'but we need to make sure that she's not hiding anywhere. You'd be surprised how often these missing children reports end like that – with the kid found somewhere close by after a family row. That's what we hope will be the case with Jodie Foot.'

He'd got the key down from where it hung behind the kitchen door and all four of them crossed over the bright square of sunshine to his garden shed. It took him a while to get the bugger in the lock straight, and all the time Bingo jumped up and scrabbled at the door with his one front paw. He'd lost his other front leg in an accident with a chain harrow when he was a pup, and Billy started telling the policewoman how it happened. Why doesn't he shut up? thought Henry. They didn't want to hear Billy Wright's stories when they had a job to do.

The door swung open and they all looked inside while Bingo ran round as though he was demented, nose to the ground, his little tail going like clockwork.

Henry kept a tidy shed. There was his bicycle leant up against the shelves where he kept the bone meal and the pesticides and the jam jars of seeds and all the other gardening paraphernalia. His spades and forks and hoes were hung in ranks from the wall. There was nowhere here a child could hide, especially not that galumphing girl of Marion's.

They stood in silence for a moment, just looking, breathing the hot wood and creosote smell of the place and then the policeman shut his notebook and put it back in his front pocket.

'That's it then, sir,' said the policewoman. 'You can get back to your cup of tea, now.'

'What about my shed?' complained Billy. 'I've a big shed behind my bungalow. An old hen house too.' He didn't want to be left out.

'We'll get to you, sir,' said the policewoman. 'We're

working our way round, see? That way we know we won't miss anything.'

Regretfully, Billy watched them go through Henry's side gate and set off up the road. At the rate they were going the lass would be back safe and sound before they even got to his place.

Gavin himself answered the telephone on almost the first ring.

'Hello, it's me,' said Juliet.

'Juliet?' There was surprise and pleasure in his voice. 'Where are you? I didn't recognise the number.'

'I suppose you wouldn't. I'm here, in Dorset, at the Ballantyne cottage. I moved in yesterday.'

'What's it like? Not a damp, medieval hovel, I hope.'

'Not at all. It's bright and sunny actually, not at all olde mouldy. I wanted to send you an email but my computer won't work.'

'That's a bore. Can you get it fixed? So, tell me, what are your plans?' There was something formal in his tone that alerted Juliet.

'Is this a good moment?' she asked guardedly.

'No, not really. *J'ai du monde.*'

'Oh, I see. OK, some other time. I just wanted to let

you know that I'm here. My mobile doesn't work either, so this is the only telephone number you can get me on and there isn't an answer machine.'

'Oh dear, that all sounds most inconvenient. Get yourself organised, please, darling. Listen, I shall have to go but let's speak very soon.'

Juliet put down the telephone without saying good-bye. Even now that sort of conversation had a lowering effect on her spirits and was a sharp reminder of all the years she had spent as an undemanding mistress at the mercy of Gavin's professional and private life. She realised it was foolish of her to have tried to telephone him at all when the chances of him being at work and able to talk were minimal. Now she felt more irritated than anything else, which was irrational and unfair because it was hardly Gavin's fault.

It was the tone of his voice that had grated. He had spoken in rather a showy-off, actorish manner as though he were entertaining an audience. She felt that he had actively wanted to invite speculation about the conversation that discretion meant he was unable to continue. She supposed that it endorsed the view he liked to project of himself as a man of enticing secrets. She imagined him putting down the telephone and turning to his companions and saying, with a small but meaningful smile playing about his lips, 'Now, where were we?'

Juliet had wanted to tell him about the missing child and the visit by the police and share with him the irony that she had come from New York and buried herself in one of the quietest corners of the country just when a drama was unfolding. Now, picking up the car keys, she went out and shut the front door for the second time. If he phoned her back he would find no one at home, and she was pleased by the thought of that small revenge.

By the end of the afternoon Cathy was able to tell Rachel that the police had nothing to go on. She'd got that piece of information from Dixie, one of Jodie's half-brothers whom she had cornered when he was unlocking his red Honda car which was parked outside her house. By the time they were adolescents, the Foot boys all looked the same to her – pasty faces, bad skin, shaved heads. They weren't what you'd call an attractive lot, and they didn't do anything to improve the hand that nature had dealt them.

'Nah,' he'd said. 'They haven't got nothing to go on. They're a right dozy bunch, they are. They keep saying Mum's got to think where she might be to, as if she knew! They don't seem to get it that if she knew where she was, she'd be round there to get her back and give her hell.'

'What are they doing now then?' Cathy had asked.

'Buggered if I know. Collecting statements, they say, and searching outhouses. Well, she's not likely to be in a fucking shed, is she? Not our Jodie. They need to shift their arses and look for her in town somewhere. Bournemouth or Poole or Weymouth. That's where she'll be. She's always talking about how she's going to work in Bournemouth when she leaves school. Fancies herself in Top Shop.'

Cathy's attention was distracted as another van drew up.

'That'll be the dog handlers,' said Dixie, looking nervous and getting into the car. 'I'm off out of this. What the fuck will that lot find, sniffing round our place? They're just looking for something to nail on me. See yer!' He slammed the door and roared off.

'They didn't have the dogs last time,' Cathy told Rachel as she sat at the kitchen table with a cup of tea. 'It never got that far, did it?'

'No, I don't think it did. What about the television?'

'They were here this afternoon filming. It's going out

on Southern tonight. Six thirty local news. Oh, Rachel, I can't bear to think of what Marion's going through. Do you still think, you know . . .'

'I think Jodie's all right,' said Rachel slowly. 'I don't know quite why, but I have the strongest feeling she'll turn up, right as ninepence.'

'What I'm scared of,' said Cathy, one hand resting on her unborn baby which was pushing up against her ribs, 'is that something dreadful will happen and that my baby will be born on the same day, and . . .' She couldn't go on. Her voice cracked and tears filled her large, gentle brown eyes.

'Don't think like that,' said Rachel, taking her hand in her own. 'Don't get upset. You've got to look after yourself now. It's you and the baby you should be bothered about. There's plenty of others to care about Jodie, and I'm sure she's all right.'

'Marion doesn't know why she's gone. Last time they had had a fight about something. That's what the police have been asking, was Jodie upset, was there anything worrying her at home or at school.'

'That makes sense. There's got to be a reason. Someone out there must know what was going through her head yesterday afternoon.'

'They're doing more house-to-house inquiries this evening, the policewoman told me. They want to speak to the kids off the bus and the people who come home from work in the evening. They'll be round here, Rachel, later on, I shouldn't wonder. I rang Phil on his mobile to tell him and he didn't like it. He didn't like the feeling they was going to be questioning him, like. You know, him being a man and that. As if they suspected him of something.' Phil was Cathy's husband, a large, bulky man who worked at the timber yard at the old railway station, a few miles away.

'They have to do that,' said Rachel, to reassure. 'They have to interview everyone. It's not that they're suspects. Sometimes people don't realise that something they've seen is important.' She tried to imagine the police questioning Dave and him telling them that yesterday evening he was miles away, working late. She suddenly wondered, with a start, whether he'd had someone with him, someone from work, to provide him with an alibi, to testify for him. It's horrible, she thought, but Cathy's right. It'll be the men the police will be interested in. It was always some woman's husband or boyfriend or brother who was taken away with a blanket over his head.

She glanced at the clock. The bus would be arriving in the next five minutes and maybe the boys would bring some news from school. She remembered that Dave had half promised to be home in good time to take Jamie to rugby practice. She hoped he wouldn't forget. She wanted him home, especially this evening.

Chapter Four

NOTHING WAS SAID at school about the disappearance of Jodie Foot. Pete spent all the morning waiting for something to happen, for police cars to come zooming into the car park with lights flashing, or officers to appear in the corridors, or the bell ringing for a suspension of lessons in order to break the news. Instead there was nothing – not a mention, and he could hardly bear the tension, which made his head ache dully from somewhere behind his eyes.

The hours dragged by and he sat by the window, numb with unhappiness. The sun was too bright through the plate glass. It hit the side of his head and fell across one shoulder and made him feel hot and sick. Perhaps he was really ill, and this whole panicky feeling was because of that. Maybe he would come to and find himself at home in bed with a fever, or in hospital, with meningitis or something that made your brain blow to pieces, and the whole Jodie thing would have just been in his head. He knew that how he was feeling wasn't right; he couldn't take in a word of his lessons, and he didn't trust himself to speak. He avoided his friends because he didn't think he could appear normal and then one or other would ask him what the matter was, and then what would he say?

The only person he wanted to talk to was a girl in his year, Honor Ritchie. She was a posh girl, a doctor's daughter, the sort of girl he never would have believed would notice a lad like him, but all last term they had been friends. More than that. He had loved her with a yearning ache, and still did, although in the end he had blown their friendship by acting like an arse. Now she would hardly speak to him or look in his direction.

They had got to know one another because they did drama together and played opposite one another last year in *The Merchant of Venice*. He had only had a relatively small part but she had played Portia and he had had to give her a fatherly embrace from time to time and he'd loved it, *loved* it, taking her in his arms. She'd felt so frail and, well, like a girl which was something entirely new to him, not having sisters, and she had rested her head on his chest and he could smell her hair. They had grown really close during the rehearsals and with all the emotion and everything that you put into drama productions. She had cried sometimes, saying that she was hopeless and couldn't remember her lines, and they'd taken to going into town afterwards and having a coffee, and she had told him a lot, how she always felt under pressure and how her parents wanted her to do medicine at university while all she wanted was to be an actress and to get into drama school.

They had never been an item, never properly gone out together because right at the beginning she had told him how stupid she thought that was. She said that because they were still at school she would rather they were just friends and so he had had to opt for that while all the time he yearned for more. He thought it must be because she didn't fancy him, not as boyfriend material, but then she confused him by wanting to hold hands and to spend a lot of time alone with him. Her parents were pretty relaxed about things and they spent hours together in her bedroom and she would change her clothes in front of him, stripping off a T-shirt so that he couldn't help but stare at her small round breasts cupped in a little bra, or stepping out of her jeans and walking round in tiny pants while she looked for something else to wear.

She was so beautiful with her long reddish-gold hair and body the colour of skimmed milk. At school she tied her hair back and wore glasses and baggy old clothes, and all the time, underneath, there was this wonderful, magical being which only he knew about. Sometimes they would lie on her bed together and she would put her bare arms round his neck and he would study the texture of her skin, so smooth and unmarked and brushed over with fine golden hairs and smelling of the expensive organic lavender soap her mother bought in France. They would lie so close, facing each other, that he could breathe in her just-exhaled breath, slightly sweet and warm, and he felt utterly lost in his longing for her.

One evening, after he'd drunk a lot of vodka at a party and his friends were finding places to have a shag with their girlfriends, they had sat together on the stairs and on a wave of frustration he had asked her what exactly it was she wanted from him. 'You just use me,' he said bitterly. 'You're just making a fool of me. I'm like your bloody eunuch.' He was pleased with that word. He had only just come across it in an English lesson and had to look it up to find out what it meant. It was the first time he had said it out loud. They had argued for a bit and his voice was loud and angry. Somewhere inside him there remained the person he really was who listened in dismay to this drink-fuelled self but could not subdue his horrible hectoring tone. Honor had cried and said that he was so wrong, that she loved him but now he had ruined everything between them. She had got up from the stairs and stood in the hall, telephoning for a cab from her mobile. He'd lumbered after her, trying to say he was sorry, that he hadn't wanted it to be like that, but she had shaken off his arm and told him to piss off. After that he didn't know what to think and they avoided one another for ages and he had felt alone and wallowing in misery. It seemed they couldn't even be friends any more.

That didn't stop him thinking about her all the time, or seeing her, for that matter. She was on the school council and was always up there on the stage and having her say in year group meetings, and she hung out with a gang of what he thought of as posh kids – mostly girls, who would go on to good universities, who carried books around all the time and sat by themselves talking about literature or planning their gap year travels. They were always going on about saving something or other, elephants or tigers or blind kids in India, or getting worked up about recycling. None of them seemed to notice the smelly old people knocking around neglected and lonely in this country, or the kids in care, or the home-grown nutters. They weren't glamorous enough and helping them didn't involve wearing sarongs on some palm-fringed beach for six months. He thought these girls were shallow and spoilt and silly, and he hated Honor when she was with them.

But now she was the only person he wanted to talk to. All that they had felt for each other was still there, he was sure of it. You couldn't just wipe out all the stuff they had shared, but he didn't know how to reach her again. Their old friendship was like a lifebelt thrown to a drowning man, bobbing about just beyond his reach. If only he could stretch out and take it, he would be saved. He needed Honor's attention and her judgement of what had happened. He needed to have her listen to him with her head bent a little and then look up at him with her clear grey eyes, full of understanding. He had to talk to her.

Ever since the break-up he knew his mum wanted him to tell her what the matter was with him. She was always looking at him with pain in her face but he couldn't dig all the stuff out of his heart and put it into words. Of course it wasn't that he didn't love her or care what she thought, but there were things that you couldn't tell your mum, things that didn't belong in the space there was between them. All the stuff that had happened to him since he stopped being just a kid like Jamie was private. It couldn't be spoken of in the kitchen at home, or while they were sitting watching television, or in the car, or anywhere. It was stuff he had to deal with behind the locked bathroom door or in his bedroom when he was alone in the house. When she asked questions, although he could tell she was trying to tread carefully round him, she just sent him further into his own self. He had to shrug her off to shut her up and he hated himself when he was like that, surly and sullen, when she was trying to be kind.

Now, in the early part of the afternoon he skulked about the main school corridor, longing to see Honor's bright head bobbing along in front of him, coming out of a classroom or going up the stairs. Any minute now the bell would ring and there would be a surge of students let out of lessons and she would be amongst them and that would be his chance. His heart thumped as he watched the clock at the top of the staircase, and waited for the electric bell to shrill. It was hot in the corridor, the glass windows all along the front of the school let in great squares of sunshine, which slanted on the dusty, scuffed linoleum. The dull headache was thumping behind his eyes and his stomach felt strangely light and fluttery.

At ten past the hour the bell began to ring and was the signal for an eruption of movement. Doors banged open and talking and laughing surged like a tidal wave down the corridor. He knew which classroom she would come out of and leaned up against the opposite wall. It was a small class. Honor and five other weirdos were taking Latin GCSE. Now it seemed they were never going to come out. The door remained firmly shut as all the other rooms emptied and the mass of movement down the corridor thinned out. Perhaps she wasn't in there at all. Perhaps he had read the timetable wrong.

Just as he was thinking this, the door opened and the few students trooped out, talking amongst themselves, but she was not with them. And then, there she was, the last out, discussing something with Miss Price, the batty old teacher. She looked up and saw him but did not respond. She seemed to deliberately turn her attention back to Miss Price, who was so small that she only reached Honor's shoulder. They moved along the corridor together and he was left there, standing against the wall, unable to intercept her, and then suddenly she halted with her back to him. Miss Price nodded briskly at something she said and then set off down the corridor towards the staffroom, her trade-mark wicker basket of books over her arm. Slowly Honor turned to him.

He felt relief and gratitude flood his face.

'I was waiting for you. I want to talk to you,' he said. 'Please.'

'Talk away,' she said.

'It's not about us.' He saw her face stiffen and her mouth set. 'Please,' he said again, desperate. 'I need to tell someone. I think I've done something really, really bad. I think something terrible might have happened.'

Her face changed into a look of incomprehension and concern.

'What? What have you done?'

'It's about Jodie Foot.'

'Who? What about her? Who is she anyway?'

'I can't tell you here,' he repeated. 'Can we go for a walk?'

'Yeah, I suppose so. I've got a double free.'

'I know. I do remember.' It was the one time in the school week when both of them were free of classes and they had made a habit of spending it together.

'Come on then,' and she slipped her arm through his. Instantly, for the first time in weeks, he felt happy, despite everything else.

Later, sitting opposite one another on high stools in a coffee shop in town, he began to spell out what had happened, talking quietly and glancing every now and then at the chatting middle-aged and elderly women who were the other customers.

'It's about Jodie. Jodie Foot. She's a kid in Year Eight. She lives in our village, in our road, in fact. It started on the bus, see, yesterday afternoon. Gary and I were sitting in the usual place at the back and Jodie was about two down from us.'

'What's she like, this Jodie?'

'Not so little. You'll remember her older brother, Darryl. He was two years above us . . . always getting into fights. Painted his nut red, white and blue before the World Cup and got himself suspended.'

'Yes, I remember now. I supervised her class for library periods last year. She was a pain in the butt, actually. She wouldn't ever do her work properly and just messed around.'

'Yeah, that sounds like her.'

'So what's happened?'

Pete looked at Honor and the happiness of being here with her, of talking to her again, of having her attention, of watching her bony cream-coloured fingers, like little skinny sticks, folding and creasing a paper napkin, filled his heart so full that he could hardly breathe.

'Well, it's difficult to explain, but Gary Russell and me, on the way home, we sort of get at the girls a bit, at Jodie and Karen Mills. It's not much, we just tease them.'

Honor made a face. She knew teasing was a euphemism for what she had suffered lower down the school. For two years her life had been made a misery because she was 'different'. She still couldn't think about that time without remembering how her whole world was filled with dread and the feeling of there being no escape.

'I don't know why you hang around with Gary. He's such a moron, a bag of shit, a waste of space.'

'I don't "hang around" with him. Come on, I just go home on the same bus, that's all.'

'So what are you saying? I still don't know what this is about.'

'Yesterday,' said Pete, carefully tracing a finger through a little pile of spilt sugar on the table, 'Karen was off school so Jodie was on her own. Anyway, on the way home, she was sitting in front of us, like she always does, and she was wearing this tight shirt and Gary started off about her tits, you know . . .'

Honor glared at him. 'God!' she said, grimacing.

'Yeah, I know, but she's the sort of kid who asks for it. She kind of flaunts herself. She, like, invites that sort of thing.'

'That's no excuse. That's the sort of thing men on rape charges say.'

'I know. I'm not saying it's an excuse. I'm trying to tell you what happened. Listen, please, Honor.'

'You joined in, did you?'

'No! Not with that sort of stuff anyway.'

'What then?'

'I might have said she'd got a fat arse, that's all.'

Honor frowned. 'All personal stuff, was it, this abuse? The finest example of your wit and intelligence?'

'Please, Honor, I'm not proud of what happened, but I need to tell you the truth.'

'What happened then?'

'Well, after a while she got up and moved down the bus and sat with some of the others. She looked a bit upset.'

'Huh!' Honor rolled her eyes. 'Does that surprise you?'

'Honor! It wasn't that bad. After that we left her alone, and she just sat there looking out of the window. When we got off she was just in front of me and then she stopped and I walked past her. She was texting someone on her mobile. She didn't look upset or anything. I just walked past her and went on home. The thing is, she hasn't been seen since.'

Honor frowned. 'What do you mean, not seen? Not at all? She's disappeared?'

'Yeah. She never went home. It seems she's done a runner. The police have been called in. They were outside her house this morning. They've started a search for her.'

'Oh, my God!' said Honor, shocked. Pete watched as

understanding crossed her face. 'So you think . . . that what you did, or said, or whatever, made her do it? Made her run away?'

'I don't know. How can I know? It wasn't much, what we did. Gary said a bit of stuff – you know, crude, but nothing really bad, and I said what I've already told you. But maybe, you know, she was upset about something else and it was like the last straw.'

Honor sat silent and thoughtful and then picked up her spoon and began to stir her coffee.

'You can't know,' she said finally. 'Maybe it's partly your fault, maybe it's not, but you can't get away from the fact that you and Gary were bullying the kid. You were picking on a girl four years younger than you. There were two of you, great boys both of you, like men, really, and one of her. She's just a young girl. It was horrible and cowardly, the sort of thing I really, really hate.'

Pete bowed his head in misery. 'I know, I know. The thing is, should I tell someone? Should I tell the police? Does it make a difference?'

'Well, I suppose it provides a possible reason for her running away. They might be less worried if they knew that. Maybe what you say makes it more likely that she's gone off on her own accord and less likely that she's been abducted by some pervert.'

'She's done it before, you know. The last time she was away two or three days before they found her. She was hanging out with some smackheads in a squat in Bournemouth.'

'I can't see what harm it can do if you tell. It doesn't make you look good, but apart from that . . .'

'It's Gary. He's on his last warning. I can't tell anyone, can I, without involving him. Even if I say it was only me, it will involve him as soon as they know he was there on the bus with me.'

'He's not worth bothering about.'

'Honor, come on. I can't shop him for no reason, and there's another thing.'

'What's that?'

'My parents would have to know, wouldn't they? The police would get them involved. You don't know what it's like in a village, the chat and all. I really, really don't want to put them through it. My mum, anyway. My dad wouldn't give a shit, but Mum would.'

'It's a bit late to think of that.'

'Honor! Come on! You KNOW me! You know I'm not a horrible person, but if I tell the police, it looks as if I am. It makes what I did seem much worse than it was. You should hear some of the stuff that Jodie and Karen come out with, things she says to me and Gary. She's bloody wised-up about stuff. She's not like an innocent kid.'

'That doesn't make any difference to the fact that you were bullying her. I can't believe it of you, Pete.' Honor's eyes brimmed with tears.

'Please,' Pete implored, trying to take one of her hands. 'I don't know why I did . . . it just didn't seem bad at the time.'

'Yeah, but it's Gary, too. I know what he's like. He's really cruel, the remarks he makes, and you could have *stopped* him, couldn't you? You could have told him to shut up, but instead you joined in and now you seem to want me to be sorry for you.'

Pete sat in misery, acknowledging that what she said was true. Of course he could have tried to shut Gary up, but it wouldn't have worked. What Honor didn't seem to understand was that boys were different from the do-goodie girls she went around with, who were always loudly comforting each other and parading how sensitive and caring they were. He didn't know why it was that yester-day afternoon he had felt like hurting Jodie; he just had, that's all, and at the time it hadn't seemed such a bad thing to do, but now he was truly sorry for it. It was as simple as that. He wanted Honor to help him decide what he should do next, not to give him a Sunday School lecture. He wished now that he hadn't told her. Suddenly the enormity of someone else knowing what had happened became clear to him. It would be typical of her to insist on telling the headmaster.

'So,' he said, 'forget it, OK? I don't know why I told you.' His voice sounded cold and Honor looked across at him.

'No,' she said, 'you can't do that. You can't tell me and then say I'm to forget it.'

'What then?'

'I'll have to think.'

'Maybe she's been found already. Maybe I'm worrying for nothing.'

'If she's still missing then the police will start making inquiries, won't they? They'll start interviewing people. I think you should tell them before that happens otherwise this thing is going to get worse. It will seem as if you were withholding information. You'll have to tell someone, Pete. Tell your parents, if you don't want to go to the police. Or someone at school. You can't protect

Gary. Any trouble he might get into isn't as important as finding Jodie.'

'Why should me telling anyone help find her? I mean, I don't know where she's gone.'

'I don't know! I'm not the police! But they always ask for *any* information, don't they? What you have to say might count. It might be important.'

Pete sighed. 'OK,' he said. 'OK. I will. Sometime.'

'That's not good enough. You must tell someone today.'

'All right. I will when I get home. If she hasn't turned up, I will.'

Briefly Honor touched his hand and he looked up, surprised.

'I'm glad you told me,' she said. 'I won't tell anyone else.'

He searched her face, looking for a sign of softness or affection, but there was none, just a sort of calm, detached expression. All the same, he felt a sense of relief.

Later, walking up the road in the glaring sun, she slipped her arm through his. 'What scares me is that it feels as if there's a side of you I don't know,' she said in a thoughtful voice. She withdrew her arm and gave a little shake.

'I feel as if I don't know myself that well,' Pete said.

At the back of his mind lurked powerful images of a gang of youths kicking another to the ground, the sort of violence you saw on television. Dreadful, mindless stuff that afterwards, chastened, each would blame on the other. Just lads like him who hadn't stopped when they knew they should.

It was a perfect evening, warm and golden and still, and at six o'clock Juliet had a glass of wine in one hand and her novel in the other and was sitting in the garden enjoying the peace. The next morning she intended to drive back up to London to return the hire car and after a series of missions would go and visit her mother and her aunt before coming back to Dorset on the train – at least that was what she would do if she couldn't rouse Gavin to suggest something more exciting. So far there had been no word from him and she was not going to try and contact him again by telephone.

Upstairs her computer was whirring quietly as it recharged its battery. She had successfully found someone to come and sort out her problem, which turned out to be absurdly small, just a piece of re-programming completed in a matter of minutes. It had taken one telephone call and then a visit by a young man in a van from a local computer firm – same day service, which was better than she could have hoped for.

The wooden chair she sat on outside the back door was still warm from the sun that had now moved round to shine on the front of the cottage, flooding the upstairs rooms with mellow evening light. Juliet settled herself more comfortably and sipped her wine. She could smell the stocks that had been planted in an old trough outside the door and remembered that she must water all the pots and containers that were set about on the flagstones and on the side of the stone steps up to the next level of the garden. In them, as well as flowers, she had found two types of parsley, mint and thyme, oregano and sage, chives and rosemary and had picked a large bunch and put it in a big glass jam jar on the kitchen window sill. She planned a supper of a green herb salad and grilled lamb chops marinated in garlic and olive oil and rosemary. She realised that she had drunk her wine so fast that she was going to have to go inside for a refill when the telephone rang. Gavin! Hastily she got up, scraping back her chair and bolted to the telephone in the kitchen.

'Hello?'

'Is that Juliet?' It was a woman's voice that she did not recognise and her heart lurched in disappointment.

'Yes?'

'It's me, Rachel.'

'Oh, hello, Rachel.' The missing child came rushing back into her consciousness. 'Is there any news?'

'Not really, but I thought you might like to know that it will be on the television news in a minute. *South Today*. Jodie's mother has given an interview.'

'Thank you so much. I'll go and put the television on right away. I had the police here this afternoon. They wanted to look round outside. I couldn't find the key to the garden shed at the top of the garden, which was what they seemed most interested in. They said that they thought Jodie might not have gone far, that she might be hiding out somewhere in the village. They said that they'll come back. Do you think that old man has the key? You know, the one on the bicycle?'

'Henry? Yes, I expect he does. I'll tell him to drop it round, if you like. He only lives a few doors away.'

'Would you? Thanks a lot. I don't want them forcing the door.'

'Yes, I'll send one of the boys over later. Anyway, best be going if we don't want to miss it on the news.'

Juliet thanked her again and put down the telephone. She went into the sitting room and switched on the television and found the right channel. There was an item about the invasion of hospitals by a new strain of super-bug and then the smiling presenter introduced the regional news and weather and there was some music and whirling graphics and then a couple appeared on the screen, perching opposite one another on high stools at what looked like a very state-of-the-art kitchen counter. As the music faded away they stopped talking and turned to smile a greeting at the camera as if the viewer was a visitor who had interrupted them at a prearranged moment.

Jodie's disappearance was the second item. It was introduced with a grave face by the pretty young woman.

'Police today are stepping up their search for twelve-year-old Jodie Foot who has been missing from her home in the Dorset village of Kings Ashton for twenty-four hours. Her mother, Mrs Marion Foot, has appealed for help in finding her daughter.' The scene changed to the Foots' front room where a fat woman in a tight T-shirt with a lot of auburn hair sat on a sofa between two glum-faced youths who looked down at their hands splayed on their knees. Both were chewing gum. The woman had a large, squinting infant on her knee, a shaven-headed child with a gold earring, who stared at the camera. Juliet made an instant judgement of what sort of family this was. She wondered that Rachel hadn't hinted as much.

Then Marion Foot began to speak, appealing for help in tracing her daughter, and Juliet heard a cigarette-roughened voice and a Dorset accent. The camera zoomed in and the woman's make-up was more obvious, the outlined fuchsia mouth, the bright eye shadow and – Juliet couldn't believe this – what looked like false eyelashes. But what she said, the usual pleading and imploring with a catch in the throat, was strongly expressed and moving. There was real anguish in the brimming, made-up eyes. 'She's a good kid, is Jodie,' she said, 'and I just want her back safe. That's what we all want,' she glanced either side at the slack-jawed, chewing boys who made no response, 'and little Ewan wants his sister.' The child on her knee began to pick its nose and then swivelled its head to look up at its mother as if it was suddenly conscious of her distress. With an artless and touching gesture it raised a hand and patted her cheek and suddenly Juliet felt so deeply touched by this desperate family that her own eyes filled. 'Oh God,' she found herself saying out loud. 'Please bring the wretched child back safe and sound.'

There followed a statement from the inspector who was heading the search, delivered in the police-speak that was routinely used when making appeals to the public, as if the inquiry had to be dignified by grandiose phrases. What it boiled down to was that they hadn't a clue and there must be someone out there who had seen a twelve-year-old girl answering Jodie's description. Then the camera swept around the village, and the voice-over spoke of the sleepy atmosphere and the absence of crime. It passed along the quiet main street, the church, the pub, two women on horses clopping past some cottages and then back to the Foots' road where it all began. Two old men and a three-legged terrier were coming out of a nearby cottage gate. 'How do you feel about the missing child?' they were asked. Juliet clutched her head at the inanity of the question but the small round man wearing a cloth cap edged forward eagerly and expressed alarm and concern as if he was the spokesman for the taller man, who stared into the distance, his craggy face expressionless. Juliet looked at him hard and was sure that he was the same old man she had seen on the bicycle, the man who had the key to the shed and who at some point would be coming round to Jasmine Cottage to look after the garden.

'Terrible, it is,' said the small man. 'It's not what you expect in a quiet little place like this. Our kids could run anywhere when they were growing up, all day long they could be out playing and just come in for their dinner. These days they can't do that any more. It's not safe. Not even in a little place like this. Used to know everyone in the village back then. Now it's full of strangers.'

The taller man said nothing, looking over the head of the interviewer as if he wasn't there, seeming to detach himself from the scene, which anyway lasted only a second or two and was followed by a school photograph of Jodie as a smiling moon-faced child, wearing a uniform shirt and tie, gap-toothed, her hair in bunches, and then a telephone number to ring with any information.

That was it. The news moved on to the next item which was about water shortages in the district. The young presenter sat up straighter on her stool, like a performing seal waiting to be thrown a fish and Juliet switched off the television and went to refill her glass, thinking about what she had just seen.

She had been in the village a little over twenty-four hours and already she was being inextricably drawn into the drama. Now she thought about it, she was disturbed by the immediate assumptions she had made concerning Marion Foot and her family when she knew nothing about them. She had instantly judged her to be a poor sort of mother because she was blousy-looking and sounded ill-educated and Jodie, she had guessed, was not a child who benefited from a caring or conscientious home. Children like her, from dysfunctional, sprawling, bottom-of-the-heap families were the ones who were abducted whilst playing unsupervised, or knocked over on roads or killed trespassing on railway lines, or burnt in ghastly home fires while their parents were out at the pub. Juliet wished that she hadn't had these thoughts but she could not deny them. Tragedies like that which threatened the Foot family were rare in safe, well-ordered middle-class families with stay-at-home mothers and children who were supervised from the cradle onwards.

She was shocked to realise that she had felt a little distance, a bit like the compassion gap that existed when she saw images of terrible famines in Africa. Those people were poor and black and the shock was less profound than it would have been had they been middle-class and white. It was an uncomfortable thought that class and cultural divides should be so intrinsic and so strong and so undeniable.

She was getting the wine bottle out of the fridge when the telephone rang again. Who now?

'Hello?'

'Juliet, darling!'

'Gavin!' She couldn't say his name without a smile. Holding the telephone under her chin, she finished filling her glass.

Henry, fascinated, watched himself on television, sitting close to the screen, leaning forward, his hands on his knees. Billy had wanted him to go round to his bungalow and watch on his large screen TV with the bloomin' remote control he was never allowed to hear the end of, but he'd said no. He didn't take to the idea of being in and out of other people's houses, even if he did count Billy as a friend.

In fact, 'friend' was not a word that Henry used. There were people he knew and people he didn't. He happened to have known Billy for years. When he thought of it, Billy and Jessie were the folk whom he had known longest, and with that long acquaintance came an easiness and familiarity which could pass as friendship. He dropped off home-grown vegetables on their doorsteps and helped Jessie with outdoor jobs, and shared a pint with Billy every now and then, but he didn't want to go interfering, poking his nose into their lives, which was what he reckoned passed as friendship these days.

If he had ever thought about it he would have realised that there had been little room in his life for friends in the accepted sense because of Fred. He didn't have the freedom to spend time with other people when Fred was alive. They did things together, took coach trips with the old folks club, which Fred loved, but their social life was always dictated by what Fred enjoyed, and he required a lot of Henry's attention. He was as good as gold, Henry used to tell people, but it was easy to see that he had to keep an eye on him when they went out together. Skittles or darts, for instance, which Henry enjoyed, and which were the mainstay of village social life, were possible with Fred around although he didn't have the co-ordination to play himself. Henry could sit him in the corner with a half-pint of shandy while he played himself, but afterwards when the drinking and socialising began, it was time to take him home.

After he died, Henry didn't have the heart to start playing again.

It was a strange experience, seeing himself like that on the television screen. He wasn't a man who bothered much with how he looked. He only had the little shaving mirror propped on the bathroom window sill, and now there he was, a great gaunt, scarecrow of a man, looming behind Billy and staring into the distance as if he wasn't the full shilling himself. If that was what he looked like, no wonder folk seemed to keep out of his way.

It was Billy who was doing all the talking, full of himself as usual, and then it was all over and the next item was being introduced by the young woman with her blond bob and big glossy smile. Henry leaned forward and turned off the television and sat for a moment, absorbing what he had just seen. He thought about Marion, just a few doors down from where he lived. She was loud-mouthed and looked a cheap kind of woman but she was a proper mother, he reckoned, one that would do anything for her kids. She might be heard to shout and swear at them at times but they were a family all the same and he could bet she would lay down her life for any one of them. They might not be disciplined and respectful, he had to agree with Billy there, but they knew what it meant to have a home and to belong to a family.

He didn't like to think of that lass of hers gone missing. Something must have happened to make her run off like that. Children suffered more than adults realised because often grown-ups didn't have the eyes to see what things were really like, or the sense to ask the questions which might reveal the truth. He could remember the times he and Fred had been told how lucky they were to stay with the Bettses because that was how it seemed from the outside and it was what it suited people to think. It caused less bother all round.

He'd known what it was to be a happy child, because he could remember things from the London days, like attending the Board School in Whitechapel, playing football in the streets, going to St Simon's, Bethnal Green, on a Sunday, where the young curate took an interest in poor boys like him and Fred, and got them to join the choir. It was worth the tedium of attending services and weekly choir practice for the choir

Christmas dinner and the summer outing when they went by train to Margate for a day at the seaside.

He could remember his mother as clear as anything although he had only got the one photograph that he'd managed to hide from the Bettses and had kept all these years. It showed a frail young woman with soft fair hair, wearing an ill-fitting coat, her skirt trailing below the coat hem, and holding the hands of two small boys. Him and Fred. He supposed that she had sent them away because she was terrified of the bombing raids. Everyone was then, and parents were told that it was the right thing to do, to send your kids off to the country where they would be well looked after and benefit from fresh air and better food. His whole school were evacuated, as far as he could remember, all packed off, like a load of parcels, with labels tied on their coats, their gas masks round their necks. They went by train, and spirits were high, with singing and excitement. It had seemed like an adventure. They'd each been given a brown paper bag containing a smaller, blue bag of custard cream biscuits and a tin of corned beef. They ate the biscuits on the journey, a rare treat they were; the corned beef they never saw again, not after the Bettses had got their hands on it. When they arrived at the other end they got taken by bus to a village hall and then they just waited to be chosen. Nobody seemed to want two boys – probably thought they'd eat too much – until Mrs Betts came along. She reckoned they were strong enough to be useful on the farm.

Their mother cried when she said goodbye at Waterloo, or at least that's what Henry liked to think. All the mothers were boo-hooing and waving their hankies as they left. She couldn't have known that she would never see them again. It was the curate who wrote and told them that she had been killed. He wrote from hospital where he was recovering from a leg injury caused by metal from a flying bomb. Later on he came down to visit them and Henry could remember how Mrs Betts cut him bread and butter and a slice of fruit cake. 'You're a lucky pair,' he'd told them, 'being looked after like this.' He thought they had landed on their feet because Mr Betts was a church warden, and he remarked on how they'd both grown and how brown they had become.

Henry remembered that the curate told him that he should leave school at fourteen and get a job. It was better that he and Fred stay in the country, he said. 'There's nothing for you in London, not now your mother has gone. The Bettses have agreed that you can lodge with them.' Now, sitting in his own front room seventy years on, he could remember his feeling of rising panic, as if the walls were closing in on him, shutting out all hope of escape.

'We're not staying here,' he had blurted out. 'Not a day longer than we have to.' He could remember the courage it had taken to speak out like that. Mrs Betts froze, her back to them, as she was putting the cake back in its tin on the big mahogany sideboard.

Somehow he must have convinced the curate that he was telling the truth when he said that they had been mistreated and after that they moved to live with the railwayman's widow and their fortunes had looked up, but what they had missed out on, him and Fred, was having a mother all those years.

The other thing that troubled him was that he couldn't remember crying or grieving for her. He supposed that they must have done because he knew that they had loved her, but their unhappiness went unexpressed and unremarked upon. There was a war on and tragedy was touching a lot of people's lives every day. Nobody took any extra notice of them because they had lost their mother, even if it had changed their lives forever.

But it didn't do any good to dwell on things, Henry thought, as he got out of the chair. It didn't alter anything and it had all been so long ago and there were many far worse off than he and Fred had been. They had made out all right in the end. Meanwhile, there was Marion to think of and that missing girl of hers.

He went out of the back door and collected the old watering can from where it hung on the wall. Its metalled sides were still warm to touch from the heat of the sun. His tomato plants would be thirsty. He had them in growbags along the side of the shed and their dense branches were already beaded with little green tomatoes. Later on in the summer he would harvest them, sweet and round and red. There was nothing to beat a home-grown tomato with a piece of cheddar cheese. Every few days there would be more to pick and when he went off early to work he would leave a bag of them hanging on the handle of Jessie's back door. 'You're a miracle with them plants,' she told him, and although he scoffed and said anyone could grow tomatoes if there was enough sun and you gave them plenty of water, he was pleased. Jessie agreed there was nothing to touch them, and once when he'd called round to mend a bit of broken fencing he'd found her little grand-niece, the one they would have called a mongol when he was a boy, sitting up at Jessie's kitchen table eating a bowl of them with bread and butter. 'She loves them, Henry,' Jessie had said, 'and she won't touch the shop variety. Say thank you to Henry, Taylor,' and the little girl had turned round in her chair and given him a real beaming smile.

Now it was a bit cooler he could smell the honeysuckle that grew over the back door. The fragrance always seemed that much stronger in the evening. He broke a bit off as he waited for the can to fill from the outside tap. The scent was so sweet, it made his head swim. Above, the sky was softening from hard enamel blue to a dove grey and house martins swooped backwards and forwards to their mud nests under the eaves. He could hear the shouts of children from the road outside. They were back out there on their bikes and skateboards as if nothing had happened.

Chapter Five

HALF AN HOUR after the news programme came to an end, the same two constables who had visited Juliet knocked on the Turners' front door and Rachel got up to let them in. She and Dave had been kept informed by Jamie of the police progress up the road and knew it wouldn't be long before it was their turn and she felt on edge and nervous, even though she had nothing to hide. The normal length of stay in each house was ten minutes at the most, followed by a look round the premises and a brief search of sheds and outhouses.

There was no need for explanations, but the policewoman was formal, explaining the situation as if Rachel did not know about Jodie's disappearance, and asking if she and Dave would be willing to answer a few questions. 'Yes, of course. Come in,' she said. As she shut the door behind them, Jamie appeared at the garden gate, evidently hoping to be included in the interview, but Rachel motioned to him to make himself scarce. She didn't want him there, all ears, while his parents answered police questions. It didn't seem suitable, somehow.

There followed a moment when the three of them stood awkwardly in the narrow hall, the dark uniforms somehow absorbing the light and filling the space, until Dave put his head round the door of the sitting room and said, 'Come on through. You don't have to stay out there. We were just watching it on the news. There's no news, in fact, is there? Come on in. Where are you going to sit?'

His manner was relaxed and easy because he was a confident man who was not subdued or overawed by the police. It was Rachel who was uncomfortable. Uniforms and any figures of authority filled her with misgivings and this visit, not social and yet taking place in her sitting room, felt awkward. She'd tidied up specially, straightening the sofa cushions and taking a duster to the mantelpiece. She was proud of the front room, so clean and bright with the polished wood floor that Dave had put down and the new shelving full of books and the pieces of china that she'd collected over the years.

The house was not a traditional country cottage but a solidly built, semi-detached villa constructed in the thirties. It, and the two identical houses on either side, had never been council properties, unlike those at the end of the road, but put up by a local builder for the white-collar workers moving into the area between the wars. Rachel was glad of that. It gave her and Dave a bit of standing, she thought, especially with people like the police, who could see they were owner-occupiers and treat them accordingly. It wasn't so much snobbishness or that she looked down on the council-house dwellers, it was more that she felt they needed all the clout they could muster. The childhood years of being helpless in local authority care had seen to that.

She did not consider offering any refreshments and was surprised when Dave did, and the policewoman said they could do with a cup of tea. She went off into the kitchen to get out mugs and a tin of biscuits. Through the open door she could hear Dave answering questions. He was working on a rushed job the evening in question, he said, on a new trading estate near Dorchester, and the police noted down the name of the firm that he worked for and a rough estimate of the time he got home. No, he hadn't seen anything out of the usual on his way through the village, certainly not Jodie, but he couldn't say that he was surprised at her going awol. She was out of control, in his view, as were the rest of the Foot kids. In the kitchen, staring at the kettle as she waited for it to boil, Rachel wished that he would stop. He should keep his views to himself. It didn't do to volunteer that sort of stuff to the police.

She made the tea and put the mugs on a tray with the biscuits arranged on a plate and took it through. Dave's face was animated and he was sitting forward on his armchair, his legs apart, his hands on his knees, facing the two constables who were sitting side by side on the couch. Their faces were impassive and by contrast Dave seemed over-excited, his voice too loud, as if he was putting on a performance for their benefit. Rachel moved between them, passing the tea and handing out the biscuits and the sugar. The interruption caused Dave's monologue to subside and the policewoman turned to look at Rachel and say, 'And you, Mrs Turner? You were here all yesterday afternoon and evening?'

'Yes,' said Rachel. 'I was here all the time, but I didn't know anything about Jodie until my neighbour told me in the evening.'

'And your two sons travel home on the school bus

with Jodie. That's right, isn't it?' She was a heavy young woman with a large bosom that was not flattered by the cut of her uniform jacket. She was wearing trousers and businesslike lace-up shoes. If called upon, she looked as if she could pursue and bring down quite a large criminal. By contrast the policeman was rather slight and puny. He had very pale hair and wishy-washy blue eyes and his hands were long and thin.

'Yes, that's right. They didn't have anything to say, though. Nothing out of the ordinary happened, according to them.'

'We may have to a chat with them later on,' said the WPC. 'But hopefully we'll have Jodie back before that becomes necessary.'

'Let's hope,' said Rachel. She longed for them to drink their tea and leave but they seemed in no hurry. Dave began to talk about Neighbourhood Watch and how he thought it was a waste of time and then, thank goodness, they got up and said that they would have a look at the shed, if that was all right, and they all went out. Jamie appeared from nowhere and hung about, watching and listening. There was no sign of Pete.

The police poked about amongst the lawnmower and gardening tools and outgrown plastic toys and then re-emerged looking slightly ridiculous, coming out of the door, one behind the other. Dave locked up behind them and they started down the path to the gate. On the way they passed Jamie and stopped to have a word with him, checking his name and age.

'Oh, yes,' said the policewoman, as if in sudden recognition, 'we've already spoken to your brother, haven't we?' She consulted her notes. 'Peter, isn't it?'

'Yeah, that's right,' said Jamie. Rachel frowned. What did that mean? Already spoken? Hadn't she just said that they might have to interview the boys later? Now it seemed that they had already done so. Wasn't it necessary to have parental permission before they did?

The minute the police constables had crossed the road and were out of hearing, she got hold of Jamie and said, 'What was that they said? They've already spoken to Pete? What was all that about?'

Jamie shrugged out of her grasp. 'I don't know. He said he wanted to speak to them. He said he had something to tell them.'

'When was this?'

'Mum! Chill! A while back. Just in the street. They were coming out of the Kings' house and we were hanging around and he just went over and told them that he wanted to tell them something and they went and sat in the patrol car with him.'

'What? What did he want to tell them?'

'Mum!' wailed Jamie again. 'I don't know. He hasn't said anything to me.'

Rachel turned to Dave, who was dribbling a football about, unconcerned. 'Dave, did you hear that? Pete has been speaking to the police about Jodie.'

Dave stopped what he was doing and said, 'So what? So what if he has?'

Rachel felt a flush of irritation that he failed to respond to her concern. She understood that he was making the point that she was over-reacting.

'Well! What has he got to tell the police? He hasn't said anything to us, has he?'

Dave went back to playing with the ball, knocking it from side to side between his feet, jigging up and down in a way Rachel found intensely annoying when she was trying to have a serious conversation.

'Heh!' he said, concentrating on the ball. 'What's the matter with you? You make it sound like he's *involved*. Is that what you're saying?'

'Of course not! Of course I'm not. I just don't think the police should talk to our son without us knowing.'

'He's over sixteen. He's not a juvenile. Anyway, it sounds as if he wanted to speak to them. Perhaps he's remembered something that Jodie said or did that he thinks might be important.' Dave finished by kicking the ball up into the air and catching it neatly. 'I don't get why you're so worked up about it.'

'I'm just concerned, that's what. That's not unusual, is it, for a mother to be concerned?' She heard her voice rising.

'Oh, for God's sake,' Dave said under his breath but not so quietly that she couldn't hear.

She stared at him, now thoroughly affronted, but he ignored her by tossing the ball to Jamie. She wasn't ready to give up and caught his arm.

'Why are you like this?'

'Like what?' His blue eyes were cold and she was frightened by what she had started.

'Like I'm making a fuss or something. Like I'm making a big deal.'

'Ask yourself.'

'So is that what you're saying? That I'm out of order being concerned?'

'Maybe. Yeah, maybe. All right, if you want to know, yes, you make a big deal out of everything.'

154

'Like what?'

'Oh, come on, Rachel. Everything. You're always on about something. At me or the boys. You're like a bloody dripping tap.'

She let his arm go, the bitter taste of acrimony in her mouth. 'How can you say that? How dare you say it?'

'Because it's true, that's how.' Dave mimicked her voice. '"Pete, what's the matter? Why won't you tell Mummy? You used to tell Mummy everything. Dave, what time will you be home today? You won't be late, will you? Why do you have to be late? Why do you have to work at weekends?" It gets on my bloody wick, that's what.'

Rachel stood dumbfounded. The criticism seemed profoundly unjust. 'That's so unfair. I'm not like that. Any wife wants to know when her husband will be home from work. It's normal and it's normal for a mother to care about her son.'

'Not like you are, it's not normal,' said Dave coming over and standing very close. 'On and bloody on. You'll drive the lad away always trying to snoop into his life.'

'Snoop? You can't call being concerned snooping! There's serious stuff happening out there.' Rachel gestured with a sweep of her arm. 'There's drugs every-where, you know that, and one of the things to watch is when they get secretive, when their behaviour changes. That's what they told us at that drugs talk they had at school. It's being a proper parent, that's what it is.'

'Yeah, well, maybe, but you're a pain in the arse about it. He's a good lad, just leave him alone, and get off my back while you're about it.'

Rachel stared at him. She couldn't believe what he was saying. How had he turned all this into an attack on her? Was this really what he thought of her? Confused doubts filled her mind. Was he right? Was she unreasonable? Did she try to hang on too tight? She had often struggled with this fear, even when in the early days of knowing Dave he had told her that it was one of the things that he loved about her. A man wants to feel needed, he'd said. He didn't believe in what he called feminist bollocks; men and women were made differently and that was that, and the woman in a partnership should be looked after by the man. She had loved the idea of that, the security and sense of belonging.

In her agitation her breath was fast and shallow as she turned away to go inside. She didn't want to continue like this, slanging back and forth in front of Jamie. She felt the sting of Dave's criticism – you're a pain in the arse, you're not normal – and the cruelty of his mimicry. How could someone who loved you say things like that? Because she deserved it, that was how. But she knew it wasn't true, and even if it was, why hadn't he told her gently sometime before? Why hadn't they talked about it, instead of resentment building up and then bursting out like this? She imagined the kind of conversation they might have had, as advocated in advice columns in magazines, and realised that it couldn't have taken place in real life. She and Dave just didn't talk like that.

Back in the refuge of the kitchen she picked up the dishcloth and began to wipe the surfaces of the units like an automaton, her bruised feelings still churning inside her. That was the trouble, they never talked about anything these days, she thought. It was always the same: too busy, too tired or the boys were around. There were no longer late evenings when she and Dave sat up together like they once had, her with a glass of wine and Dave with a couple of cans of beer. These days she went upstairs, exhausted, before the boys moved off the sofa in the sitting room, and was asleep as soon as she got into bed. What had happened to the time that she and Dave had once had for each other? What had happened to the closeness that they had once shared? She had never really considered it before, not as a problem, anyway, because a marriage was sure to change as children got older. It was to be expected that there would be new pressures, but all along she had believed that things were fine between them. She was evidently wrong.

She sat at the table and stared at the lunch boxes, waiting to be made up for tomorrow. She opened the nearest, which happened to be Jamie's. She was forever telling the boys and Dave to chuck out the cling film and wrappers and apple cores and sandwich crusts but they never did. She hated having to deal with the mess every evening and it was such a simple thing to do for her. Nobody thinks of me, she heard a voice telling her in her head. They all take me for granted. It was what married women were always saying to explain why they felt discontented or miserable.

She got up again and tipped the rubbish from each box into the bin. Her heart was still thumping with the words she had exchanged with Dave. She wondered what he was doing, still outside in the garden, and hoped that he might come in and put his arms round her and say that he was sorry that he had hurt her and been unfair. But that wasn't his way. He was always so confident that he was right. It was always her who said she was sorry because she couldn't bear the atmosphere.

When she got to Pete's box she saw that his lunch remained uneaten, the sandwiches still wrapped in cling film. She put the box back on the table and sat down again. He was sixteen, always starving, and he hadn't eaten a mouthful. A renewed anxiety flooded her mind, pushing the quarrel she had had with Dave to one side. Seeing the cream cheese and salami sandwiches there – his favourites – convinced her that there was something wrong, something seriously wrong with Pete. His behaviour wasn't normal, whatever Dave might say.

What she needed to do right away was find him. She needed to ask him straight out what was going on and convince him that she could help. If he could talk to the police, he could talk to her. Where would he be? Somewhere in the village hanging out with the other teenagers, she supposed, in their usual spots.

Thinking quickly, she glanced through the kitchen window to where Jamie and Dave were kicking the ball about between them. She would go out of the

159

front. She didn't want questions from either of them.

As she pulled the door closed behind her, she saw Jamie's bike leaning against the front gate and on an impulse she took hold of the handlebars and wheeled it into the road. It would be quicker like this. She wobbled a bit but as soon as she got speed up it was easier and she set off without looking round. Jamie must have seen her because from behind her she heard him shout, 'Mum! Where are you going? Mum!' She didn't waver, just pedalled on.

It was downhill to the pub where the kids sometimes sat outside on summer evenings and she whizzed along, freewheeling, with the wind blowing her hair out behind her, but when she got there, there were only a few cars drawn up. The hanging baskets and the old barrels filled with geraniums and begonias were very bright in the evening sun and two middle-aged couples she did not recognise were sitting in the beer garden under an umbrella. She braked and skidded to a halt and they looked over at her with surprised expressions. It wasn't what they expected, to see a grown woman burning rubber on a kid's bike. A man's face looked out of the pub window and then turned away but there was no other sign of life.

She started off again more slowly as the road climbed a little. She had never noticed before that it was uphill and it was hard work, making her legs ache almost at once and she wobbled as she struggled to change gear and then to her relief the road dipped again and she pedalled easily past Jasmine Cottage.

As she went by she had a glimpse of Juliet Fairweather sitting in the back garden with a glass of wine in her hand. She looked very solitary sitting there with no husband, no children and nobody to care about. Nobody to quarrel with, nobody to be sick with worry over, was nearer to the truth, she thought as she cycled on.

She would go on round the village, hoping she might find Pete somewhere else, but really she had no idea where he would be. It was stupid of her to think that she could find him. Doubts began to creep into her mind. Dave was right, she was over-reacting, hysterical even. The only place she could think of now was an overgrown and dusty lay-by a bit further on where some of the older ones, the Foots and their friends, parked their clapped-out old cars, doors open, stereos blaring, and shared smokes and cans of lager.

He'll kill me, she thought, if he's there – his mother coming looking for him on a bicycle, showing him up in front of the older boys. She should have stopped to ask Jamie where to look for him. She didn't care any longer about the row with Dave. It didn't matter any more. It was only her feelings that had been hurt and she could get over that, and perhaps Dave was right anyway. Perhaps she was a pain in the arse without knowing it.

She pedalled past the last cottage and the old barn that had been turned into a house and occupied at weekends by Londoners. It was empty now, the curtains all drawn and two black bags of rubbish left by the gate had been torn apart by foxes and the contents scattered on the verge. Soon the lay-by came into view but she could see that there was a cattle truck parked there, up close to the hedge. Some calves jostled at a field gate as she went by and then skidded away on straight legs, their tails high in the air. The grass was thick with buttercups and the calves' round white knees were stained with yellow patches.

What now? How stupid she was to think that she could find him like this, when he could be anywhere. The hedgerow on either side was thick and high, trailing with little pink and white dog roses and tangled ropes of honeysuckle. It was like cycling along a narrow green tunnel. Rachel pressed on towards her last hope, an old bench set to look over the valley, but when at last she saw it up ahead, it was deserted, save for a single can of Diet Coke left sitting on its wooden seat. She came to a halt, her heart thudding.

It was pointless, stupid. She would never find Pete like this. She would have to go back home and wait for him to come in, which was what she should have done in the first place. It was true what Dave said, she did over-react and panic herself into believing the worst. She considered her options. Now she had come this far it would be quickest to go on, past the old slaughter-house, and then take a right-hand lane which led down into the far end of the village. From now on she would think of the bicycle ride as recreational. It was good to get some exercise on such a lovely summer evening.

It was very quiet and she could hear the blood thumping in her ears and felt her face glowing hot and red with exertion. It was further than she thought, distances were so different on a bicycle, but then she saw the high chain-link fence of the old bacon factory ahead, all grown through with bindweed and sagging and rusty. As she got closer she could see the ugly breeze blocks and the old corrugated roof, which had blown half off and was slanting up into the sky.

It was a horrid place, she thought, even on a summer evening. Hogweed and elder saplings had pushed up through the cracked concrete of the yard and black swarms of flies buzzed over the rank vegetation that pressed against the broken windows and the sliding metal door. Someone had hung a hand-painted Keep Out sign onto the padlocked gate, but beside it there was a wide hole in the wire, beyond which a beaten-down track ran through the high summer grass and nettles.

Then, as she was labouring past this unlovely place, two things happened simultaneously. She heard a regular striking noise, like one metal implement hitting against another, and out of the corner of her eye she glimpsed an unexpected flash of shining red towards the rear of the ruined buildings. She skidded to a halt, her feet scraping on the stones of the lane, and wheeled the bike round. She pushed it back to the gate and peered in. The noise continued and appeared to be coming from inside the main shed and she realised that what she had seen was the partly concealed frame of a mountain bike which she recognised as belonging to Pete.

Quickly, looking to right and left, she shoved Jamie's

bike into a gap in the hedge. She bent down and lumbered head first through the hole in the fence. She felt unaccountably frightened. Sweat trickled down between her breasts and a persistent fly buzzed about her forehead. Swatting it away, she crossed the yard in front of the building and reached the sliding door. She saw that it was padlocked and bolted, but the noise was coming from inside, so there must be some way in. The metal windows were set too high for her to see through but she was sure that Pete was in there somewhere. Maybe there was another door to the side or at the back. She made her way to the right where the bike was propped behind a broken brick wall and saw that there was another, smaller door which stood open.

Moving stealthily, so as not to alarm him, she went on until she reached the door and could peer into the old slaughterhouse. The interior was half open to the sky and the floor was littered with broken bricks and debris. At one end there was a heap of oil drums and split and sagging cardboard boxes. There was nobody there but the noise was very close now. Rachel paused and cocked her head to listen and then picked her way across the floor until she could see beyond the wall of drums.

Pete was sitting on the ground, his back against what looked like an old boiler. His head was sunk on his chest in an attitude of thoughtfulness and in one hand he held a stout metal bar which he was aimlessly banging against an upright girder supporting the roof.

Rachel felt a spasm of love and concern and relief, and stumbling over the broken floor went towards him. He looked up, startled. His face drained of colour and he looked wild-eyed and fearful and for a moment Rachel saw him as a stranger would, as an unhappy and troubled youth, who might pick up a stone, chuck it and run.

'Pete!' she said in a pleading, emotional voice, holding out one hand towards him.

'Mum! What are you doing here?' The fright she had given him had knocked him off balance. He hadn't the time to decide how to behave. Relief flooded through him at the sight of her, in her funny, too-short jeans and her old trainers, her face hot and red with her hair all over the place.

'What are you doing? How did you know I was here?' he said again. He made no move to get up and she eased herself down to sit beside him.

'Come to find you.'

'Why? For God's sake, Mum. It's all right to be here. Nobody gives a toss.'

She reached for his nearer hand. 'Look, Pete, you've got to tell me what the matter is. I know there's something wrong and I want to help. Jamie told us that you've been talking to the police.'

Pete fell silent and with his free hand started banging the metal rod again before he looked at her and said, 'I suppose you'll have to know sooner or later.'

Juliet was up early the next morning, woken again by the light and the birdsong. This time she didn't mind because she planned to be in London by ten o'clock. She had already decided what to wear and her black linen skirt lay over the chair in the bedroom. It would crease, of course, but it was well-cut, slim-fitting and exactly the right length, making the most of what she considered her best feature, her long brown legs. A simple white T-shirt and some African-looking beads, a chunky brown belt and a gaucho-inspired leather bag completed the look. She spent longer choosing her underwear because after she had had lunch with her mother and aunt she was going to meet Gavin at the flat of a friend of his in Victoria, and they would have a few snatched hours together.

These days she realised that her boyish figure was really more attractive clothed than naked. It was one of life's ironies that as one got older it was the fatter women who looked better without clothes. She had noticed at her weekly visits to the swimming pool that plump flesh sat more comfortably on shoulders and hips, whereas she feared that she looked bony and shrunken across the chest and her bum seemed to have almost disappeared. She needed the help of a pretty padded half-cup bra and boyish briefs to provide the allure she felt she needed for the semi-dressed stage of the love-making proceedings. Once she was lying down and naked, and things had got underway, she could stop worrying.

As a mistress, the planning of these encounters was another of the advantages one had over the poor old wife, who would long ago have given up caring a scrap what underwear her husband saw her in day after day. Juliet thought of one of her married friends who said that she hadn't bought a new bra for five years because she hadn't had time, and Sonia certainly looked as if she were the same. She appeared never to care how she dressed which was one of the things that Juliet found slightly intimidating about her. You had to be hugely confident to go around in droopy denim skirts and blouses and sensible sandals and a pudding haircut when you had a husband as attractive as Gavin, but Sonia did.

She looked even worse when she had made an effort because her taste was so appalling. Gavin had some framed photographs in his college rooms of the pair of them at various important functions. Juliet had often looked at them and found them very cheering because Sonia looked ghastly in them all, as if Gavin had taken his mother along rather than his wife. What was mildly disconcerting was that such disregard for one's appearance often went hand in hand with a first-class brain, and then it was only a short step to considering an interest in clothes a sign of being an academic lightweight – in Oxford, anyway. It was irritating that without any effort on her part, Sonia could make most other women feel intellectually inferior.

Gavin, in a different way, was also without insecurities about his appearance, she thought, as she went round closing windows and checking that she had locked the garden door. Men like him were so utterly confident of their desirability that they didn't have a moment's anxiety over their slack bellies or thinning hair. That was why he could be such a buoyant flirt with students thirty years his junior and actually believe that they found him attractive. Of course, quite a lot of them did, and that was the great unfairness of ageing. Men so often became more attractive as they got older.

Juliet imagined Gavin getting ready for his day in London where he had a morning meeting at the Institute of Architects. He would choose what he wore quite carefully because there was no doubt that he verged on being a bit of a dandy in a particular Oxford arty way. It would be a linen suit day today, she guessed, and a bright open-necked shirt and a colourful handkerchief and his beautiful, lightweight Italian shoes. She had a sudden vision of his face crinkling as he smiled at her, his head slightly on one side, his well-manicured hands, the heavy crested gold signet ring on the little finger of the left, reaching for hers across so many lunch and dinner tables.

She put the kettle to boil for a cup of coffee and then suddenly realised that the old man hadn't been round with the key to the garden shed and maybe the police would come back today, although she had told them that she would be out. She had peered through the shed window yesterday and of course there was nothing in there except gardening paraphernalia, so it wouldn't help their search. Perhaps, and she fervently hoped it might be so, the wretched child had been found by now.

Damn, she thought as she filled the cafetière, she should have watered the tubs and pots before she left, because it looked as if it was going to be another hot day. She unlocked the back door again and went across the lawn to pull out the hose. The dew was thick on the grass and in a moment her feet were sopping wet and the hose left a dirty mark where it brushed against her T-shirt. Fuck, she swore again, she would have to go and change. What a palaver it was having to deal with stuff like this. How simple and streamlined her life was in a city flat with only a cactus to look after.

Lunch with the elderly was, as usual, something of a marathon. Sailing up the M3 in the hire car and returning it to Heathrow and then catching the tube out to Highgate was easy by comparison. Her mother, Roberta, always called Bobbie, and her Aunt Dorothy, known as Dot, both in their eighties, upright and beady-eyed, were on watch for her arrival from the bow window of their Edwardian house in a leafy side road. Juliet guessed that they had probably taken up position there soon after breakfast and had consulted their watches at regular intervals ever since, Dot determined that she would be late and her mother defending her supposed tardiness as best she could.

Her mother, always much the prettier of the two, had had her hair done the day before and it was spun into snowy white peaks about her pink scalp, and her face was glowing with rosy powder and sketchily applied lipstick and blue eyeshadow. This morning her cushiony figure was fresh in a white blouse and floral skirt and pink cardigan while Dot was severe with her cropped hair, and dressed like a wardress, in a no-nonsense shirtwaister. They both wore polished court shoes, Dot's brown with a stacked heel which hardly flattered her stout ankles, and her mother's black patent, from which her fat little feet puffed up, like well-risen soufflés.

Juliet embraced them both, her mother first. She was soft and sweet smelling to hug, whereas Aunt Dot in her arms felt resistant and unyielding, like an old-fashioned bolster. There followed the usual exclamations – how thin she was, how tanned, was she still jet-lagged, she looked a little tired, was she still working so hard. Her mother's manner was lively and girlish, while Aunt Dot, the older sister, tut-tutted and corrected her as if she was a child.

By now, even Bobbie had given up any hope that Juliet was bringing news of an impending marriage and the subject was no longer touched upon, thank God, but Juliet was as conscious as ever of what a disappointment this was. She knew it was not for selfish reasons that Bobbie wanted her safely wed, but rather that she believed that by remaining single, Juliet missed out on the most important foundation stone for a happy adult life despite the fact that both her brothers were married, divorced and remarried with seven children between them, which you could hardly call marital plain sailing.

Bobbie's own marriage had been entirely harmonious and full of sustaining love and mutual respect, cut short when Juliet's father dropped dead the day before his sixty-fifth birthday, a week before he was due to retire as a City solicitor. His death was the only unreliable thing he had ever done.

He left his widow comfortably off but desperately lonely and ultimately at the mercy of being taken over by Dorothy, who was a spinster and long retired as head of PE at a London girls' school. This was a far trickier relationship than marriage had been and involved a complicated power struggle, in which Dorothy exerted iron control in the guise of taking care of and being concerned about her sister's well-being.

The struggle for dominance started almost the moment Juliet arrived.

'Now, if we are walking down to the restaurant you will need a hat, Bobbie. The sun is strong this morning.'

'I don't need a hat, thank you, Dot.' Juliet knew that her mother did not want to squash her freshly arranged hair.

'That's just being silly. The sun on your head and glaring in your eyes will give you a headache. You know how it was when we had that little walk in Kenwood the other day.'

'But I had a headache before we even started. I told you I did.'

'Juliet, I am going to ask you to get your mother's panama hat from her room.'

'Well, I shan't wear it if she does.'

So it went on. Hearing aids, sticks, bags, spectacles, house keys, and they were off at a snail's pace down the sunlit street to the Italian restaurant where Juliet had taken them for many years. Walking along between them, an elderly lady on each arm, she wondered how she would be when she was over eighty. Dead, she hoped. She really did. She couldn't see the point of living that long.

It was a frightening prospect, the idea of a lonely or infirm old age, and being unmarried and single intensified the anxiety. Who would look after her? Certainly not her brothers who were far too involved with their own complicated families. Where would she live and who or what would be the mainstay of her life? Newspaper scandals of solitary old ladies who lay dead in their flats for weeks, unmissed and unlamented, flashed through her mind.

You reap what you sow, she thought; it was a sense of belonging to a community that sustained her mother and aunt in their old age. They were very firmly connected to this part of London; although the great capital city had changed dramatically in their lifetime, their own particular corner of it was relatively unaltered. They had attended the same parish church for nearly sixty years, stood on the same corner to shake their tins for the Lifeboat collection, attended the

Wednesday afternoon meeting of the Mothers' Union and bought their meat from the old-fashioned butchers on the high street. Her mother still had her hair done within walking distance although the salon had changed hands ten or more times since she first went there as a young bride. It was now called Hairsoteric and was staffed by teenaged girls with navel rings and spiked hair.

Further afield they still belonged to the Highgate Historical Society, and went every year to the Royal Academy Summer Exhibition and had tea afterwards at Fortnum and Masons, and Dot had only recently retired from being secretary of the Old Girls Union of her school. The routine of their lives was what kept them going, and although they now tottered to a new supermarket to do their shopping and no longer ventured out after dark, the deep rhythms and certainties remained the same.

Juliet, who lived so exclusively for herself, knew that unless she 'settled' somewhere fairly soon, she would be denied this sense of belonging. In fact, this was the very thing she had vigorously worked against all her adult life. She loved being independent, unfettered, unconnected. She relished the anonymity of living in a flat in a huge city, with only a small circle of chosen friends. The thought of having to actively and deliberately attach herself to a community filled her with dread. She didn't consider herself especially selfish in wanting to live as she did. She did her bit for the world by giving generously to various chosen charities; in fact her choice of Christmas presents had become a source of gentle teasing, as her friends received yet another goat, or a standpipe for an African village, but she didn't see the need to get involved on a more personal level.

Her long affair with Gavin had been isolating too. They could never go anywhere as a couple and she was therefore excluded from many of the things that a woman might expect to share with her lover. She was well aware that there was a price to be paid for being the mistress of a married man and she had seen the effect of this on one or two of her friends who had chosen the same path. If they didn't play their cards right, they could see it would be easy to end up lonely and friendless in small, bleak flats because they had invested too much of themselves in what was ultimately a fruitless affair. This was one of the reasons she had pulled the plug on Gavin. However, that didn't mean she wanted to force herself into being part of a jolly community. God forbid.

They tottered along, the three of them, taking up the width of the pavement, with tree roots and loose paving stones, bicycles and prams to be negotiated, pausing to greet a Turkish window cleaner, who came down off his ladder to kiss their hands and promise that he would be round tomorrow. The next person who loomed into their path was an enormous blonde Russian girl with cropped hair and a ring through her nose and a pair of shoulders in a tank top that made her look straight off pulling a plough on a collective farm. 'This is Olga, our carer,' explained Juliet's mother, as pleased to bump into her as if she were a wonderful and un-expected visitor. 'Olga, this is my daughter, Juliet, whom I was telling you about.' The girl mountain beamed and seized Juliet with both hands, kissing her on each cheek several times.

When they reached the restaurant, Dot was put out that their customary place was already occupied by three businessmen. The waiter showed them to an alter-native table and she made the point by asking doubt-fully, 'Will this do?' in the same ringing tones that had carried across several hockey pitches. 'I think it's a little too close to the door. Bobbie should not be in a draught, because of her neuralgia and that seat is too much in the sun. Could we sit a little away from the window?' All the time glaring at the businessmen, who did not even look up.

Then when they were finally settled there was the business of choosing what to eat, and nothing on the menu was quite right for her mother.

'Could I have the sole but without the butter sauce, and just some mashed potato not the croquettes? Oh, but perhaps,' after the waiter had laboriously written all this down on a small pad, 'I'll change my mind and have the duck, but without the red wine sauce.'

Dot would not allow this to go unchallenged. 'Duck will give you indigestion, Bobbie. It's much too fatty for you. You should have the veal if you don't want the fish.'

'But I don't *want* veal, Dot, thank you very much! I'd rather like to choose my own lunch, if you don't mind.'

Juliet smiled apologetically up at the waiter who stood patiently beside the table. He looked only about eighteen but was a natural with the customers, know-ing exactly the right, slightly flirtatious tone to use as he leaned forward and said to Bobbie, 'For you, signora, today I would suggest the Pollo Spago. Free-range chicken with parsley and garlic. It is very good; light and perfect, I think.'

Juliet's mother beamed up at him and said, 'What a very good suggestion! Thank you so much. That's exactly what I would like! How very clever of you to know!'

People love my mother, thought Juliet, because she is so generous and gracious and simple-hearted, but I'm afraid I'm much more like Aunt Dot.

It required a special sort of patience to listen to the same loop of anecdotes and stories, revisiting the long feud that Dot had enjoyed with the headmistress of her school and how, ultimately, she had delivered the winning blow, how the local dry cleaners, now run by offhand Polish girls, had lost a Burberry raincoat and tried to compensate for the loss with a ten-pound voucher, how Bobbie could not replace her summer sandals because the English footwear company had gone out of business and their shoes were now imported from China, and what did Juliet think of *that*. Juliet had to respond kindly and appropriately as if she was hearing it all for the first time. At the back of her mind she hoped that through her dutifulness she earned her time to come with Gavin.

'I'll visit once a week, Ma,' she promised later as she settled the two old ladies back into their own armchairs for a nap. They had so enjoyed their outing, her mother told her as she raised her downy cheek to be kissed, and Juliet felt a stab of remorse that by the end of lunch she had been looking surreptitiously at her watch and working out how long it would take her to get across London to Victoria.

The nearby primary school had just closed for the afternoon and as she waited to hail a taxi, the pavement was crowded with mothers and children going noisily home. Juliet suddenly thought of Jodie Foot. With a sudden rush of concern she wondered if there was any news.

At about the same time, Rachel was sitting in her front room with the two police constables. To her surprise she had opened the door to answer the bell and found them standing on the doorstep for the second time.

'When would we be able to come and have a little chat with your husband, Mrs Turner?' asked the policewoman, her meaty thighs spread on the seat of the sofa, her sturdy black shoes planted well apart on the floor.

'Why?' asked Rachel, her face feeling suddenly hot and red. 'Why do you need to speak to him?'

The policewoman coughed and looked sideways at her colleague. There was something in the shared glance that made Rachel feel sick. This would be about Pete, she thought, about what had happened on the bus. They were going to get him into trouble, report him to the school, get him suspended even.

'It seems there is a discrepancy in his statement,' the policewoman went on. 'We ran a routine check, you see, where he works, and there was no overtime on the evening in question. We're quite sure of that. He left the site on the dot of five. We need to have a chat with him and clear up the matter of his whereabouts between then and, when was it?' She consulted her notebook. 'About seven forty, when he said he arrived home for his tea. Don't worry, Mrs Turner,' she went on, seeing Rachel's dumbfounded face. 'These things can usually be sorted very easily. It's often a case of something having slipped the memory. I'm sure your husband will be able to give us an explanation.'

Chapter Six

PETE WENT TO find Honor at breaktime. He felt considerably better and more cheerful than he had done the day before and he had to thank her for that. Today the television news item had set the school buzzing with talk of Jodie's disappearance and the headmaster had acted by summoning a special assembly to address the upper school. He spoke in careful phrases, designed to encourage any pupil with information to come forward but at the same time quelling hysteria and wild rumours.

He was wearing a dark suit, as if the occasion called for a certain formality, and he came forward from behind the lectern so that he could better engage with his pupils. That was his style; a modern headmaster, who liked to think that he related well to young people and talked a language that they could understand.

'Now look,' he said, after explaining her disappearance, 'let's get this clear. There's nothing to suggest that anything *bad* has happened to Jodie, but the longer she is missing the more concerned we all are. Any of you out there who has any information at all must come and share it with me, it doesn't matter how unimportant it might seem. I don't have to tell you that anything you bring to me will be treated with the utmost confidence. You know me well enough to trust me on that one. You never know, what you have to say, however trivial, could be the very clue that we are searching for that will lead us to getting Jodie Foot back home safe and sound.'

His gaze fell on a lad in Year Ten who had unwisely chosen that moment to exchange a smirk and a whispered word with his neighbour.

'Yes?' he said, raising his voice and pointing to identify the culprit. 'Stephen Draper, what's that you've got to share with us? It must be something important.'

Every head turned to stare and the boy, realising that he had been targeted, blushed hotly and hung his head and mumbled, 'Nothing, sir.'

Pete looked down the rows of faces in the Sixth Form to find Honor. He knew where she should be sitting but she wasn't there and then he remembered that she had an early flute lesson that kept her out of assembly. He wanted to catch her eye and give her some sort of indication that he had done what she said was right.

It was a relief to have spoken to the police, and a bit of a let-down too. When he'd gone up to them in the street and told them that there was something he thought they should know, they had asked him to go and sit in the patrol car and he had slid across the back seat and the fat woman constable had got in beside him. The policeman got in the front, in the driver's seat, and the radio crackled the whole time, like it always did in police dramas on television. The policewoman asked if he would like a sweet and he refused, but she unwrapped a toffee and put it in her mouth and began to chew. She folded the paper into a small neat square and put it in the ashtray. 'Well, son,' she said, shifting round to look at him. 'What have you got for us?'

It was hot in the car and his hands were sweaty and he wiped the palms on the legs of his jeans. He had rehearsed what he was going to say so many times but now he couldn't find the words. It was as if they had slid off the surface of his brain and had gone for ever.

He traced a finger round the edge of the window. He had to say something. He could see the policeman's pale eyes looking at him in the driver's mirror.

'Yeah, well,' he started. 'It's about Jodie, see . . .' he trailed off.

'Yes?' encouraged the policewoman. 'Know where she is, do you?'

'No, no,' he said. 'Nothing like that. It's just that I think I might know why she's gone. Why she's done a runner.'

'Why's that then?' Now he had said that he didn't know where Jodie was, the policeman stopped watching him, as if he was no longer interesting. Instead he picked up a clipboard and began to rifle through some typed pages secured by a bulldog clip.

'Go on, then,' said the policewoman. 'We haven't got all day.'

'It was on the bus,' said Pete. 'Me and another lad, we were like, teasing her a bit, and she got upset, like . . . and it could be because of that she's gone.'

The policewoman didn't react. 'Who's the other lad? A friend of yours?'

'Yeah. He's in my year. He doesn't live here, though, not in the village.'

'So what were you two saying to Jodie, then? What were you saying to upset her?'

'Nothing much. It was just a bit of teasing, mucking about like, but she was on her own because her friend Karen's off sick, and she seemed to get stressed out. That's all. I just thought I should tell you.'

'Did you touch her at all? While all this was going on?'

'Touch her?' Pete could feel himself blushing. 'No, of course not. We never *touched* her. It wasn't like that.'

There was a pause and then the policewoman said, 'This Jodie is one tough kid. I wouldn't lose any sleep over what you've just told us, but it was right to tell us all the same. She was a bit of a bully herself, so we've heard, but still, it gives us a possible reason for her running away. Right little bastards you can be to one another, can't you, you kids? Here, are you sure you don't want a toffee?'

'No thanks,' he said again.

The policeman spoke for the first time, his pale, fishy eyes again seeking Pete's in the mirror. There was menace in the quiet way he said, 'We may have to take this further, lad. We may have to inform the school and Jodie's mum. Have you told your parents?'

'No,' he mumbled.

'Well, I should get on and tell them. It will be better for them to hear it from you.'

Although this was said as a suggestion, he somehow made it seem like a threat.

'Yeah, OK.'

And that was it. All over in about three minutes flat. He hopped out of the car and went back to where he'd left his bike, leaning up against a garden fence. The other kids were still there, all wanting to know what it was about. He told them to eff off and just got on his bike and rode away. He needed to go somewhere on his own.

Sitting in the old bacon factory he'd tried to sort out in his mind what difference it had made, telling the police. They hadn't seemed that bothered, as if what he had said wasn't a big deal and yet the policeman had talked about telling his parents, which was what he most dreaded. That, and the policewoman asking about touching Jodie. He knew at that moment that they thought it was about sex, that he and Gary had been coming on to her, and the idea made him feel desperate. Of course it wasn't anything to do with sex. She was just a kid. She wasn't even pretty or potentially sexy like some girls of that age were. It was sick to think like that. He felt dirty, soiled by the suggestion, and horrified that this was what his parents might think as well. The papers were always full of paedophile stuff and how perverts groomed kids for sex. Was that what they would suspect of him?

Then his mum had turned up. She'd scared the shit out of him, creeping in like that, and he couldn't believe it, that she'd actually found him, and she came and sat beside him and took his hand. Hot gusts of feeling came sweeping over him and tears clogged his nose and throat as he began to tell her what had happened. She had been great and listened quietly. She didn't put her spoke in at all, or start fussing or getting worked up. It seemed that it was the fact that he had opened up to her that mattered. She told him that when she was a teenager she hadn't had anybody she could trust, and how she had promised herself that when she had kids of her own she would make sure they understood that they could always turn to her. Always. Whatever. After a bit he had felt more under control and swallowed hard and wiped his eyes with the back of his hand. He was comforted just by her being there as he had been when he was a little kid and came crying to find her with a grazed knee.

She had said that she would tell his dad for him if he didn't feel that he could, and that he shouldn't worry any more because they would stand by him if it came to anything, although she couldn't believe that it would. She said that she wished he hadn't had any part in whatever it was that had happened on the bus but that she was sure that it would have been Gary rather than him, and he felt pathetically relieved and grateful that she should see it like that.

He still felt rotten about himself and ashamed and confused that the person he thought he was had not prevented him, protected him, from becoming part of this horrible chain of events. He'd have liked to rewrite the whole scene and make himself some sort of fucking hero, telling Gary to lay off and preventing the slagging Jodie had been given. It wasn't that he didn't have the balls, it was more that at the time it hadn't even occurred to him. He kept thinking of some poem that they'd studied at school about not speaking out to defend people like Jews and communists and how in the end, when it was your turn to get arrested, there would be no one left to speak for you. Nearly everyone in the class claimed that they'd stick up for what they thought was right and he'd agreed, really believing that he would.

Now, the first time in his whole sodding life something like that had happened to him he'd done fuck all to stop it.

He wanted to find Honor to thank her for listening to him yesterday and sorting out his head, because he knew that even if there was more trouble coming his way, he had made it less serious by coming clean.

The assembly came to an end and the headmaster half ran down the platform steps to remind everyone that he was young and vigorous, accompanied at a slower pace by the deputy head, Mrs Browne. She usually smiled from side to side, like royalty on a walkabout, but her face this morning was sombre. An immediate buzz broke out and Pete shoved his way through the crowd to get to the swing doors. He felt a sharp bang on his shoulder and turned round to see Gary and one of his mates, Nick Deacon, behind him.

'How about that then, Pete?' said Gary, laughing. 'Where's the stupid bitch gone to then? She got off the bus right in front of you, mate! Did you roll her into a ditch on the way home? She'd have been up for it. Gagging for it, she was.' Nick sniggered. 'Has she been abducted, like? Raped and that? Is she in a plastic bag in your dustbin?' Gary cracked up at his own wit.

Pete caught hold of his hand and thrust it violently upwards.

'Just shut it!' he said vehemently. 'Just . . .' he couldn't find the words to express his revulsion. 'You could be in deep shit,' he said to Gary. 'You know that. Deep, deep shit, so don't fuck with me.'

'Ooooer!' said Gary in mock dismay. 'Why? What have I done?'

'You *know*!'

'I don't, mate. You'll have to tell me. You're not a little telltale tittie, are you, Petey boy? I don't think so!' He spaced the last words out with a sort of joking menace, ''Cos if I'm in it, so are you, mate!'

Pete sent him a withering look and walked away. Honor was right, he wasn't worth protecting.

He saw her then in the corridor in front of him. Mrs Browne must have stopped her and they were talking seriously, heads down. There was something about the tension between the two figures which suggested to him that they were talking about Jodie and maybe even him. A sudden thought came to him that Honor was shopping him to the old Browne cow and just thinking that made him go red and hot. He stopped by the glass-covered noticeboards on the wall to his right and pretended to study the timetable, all the while keeping an eye on Honor. She was wearing baggy denim dungarees, peculiar things that came from a weird catalogue of clothes that were made from organic cotton somewhere up a Welsh mountain. They wrapped over at the back and were secured by a large metal buckle. Underneath she wore a small shrunk white T-shirt and her arms were bare. Just thinking about her arms made Pete feel weak. He could remember them so well, the scattering of pale freckles, the fine golden hairs and the soft cream undersides.

She and Mrs Browne finished their conversation and their heads suddenly came up and their voices rose as they changed the subject and broke apart, and then Honor turned, saw him and half smiled and he started forward towards her. Mrs Browne was walking away in the opposite direction.

'Hi!'

He drew her to one side. 'I've done it. I told the police last night. And my mum.'

'Cool! I'm really, really glad.'

'I wouldn't have if it hadn't been for you and although it's still all shite, it's better than before. I just wanted to thank you.'

'Yes, you would have done,' Honor said. 'You'd have worked it out for yourself that it was the only thing to do. Eventually. What were they like about it?'

'The police were OK. They didn't think it was that important. They still seem to think Jodie's just bummed off somewhere. My mum kind of found out, so I told her. She was great about it. She said that she would tell my dad, but she didn't. Not last night. They'd had a row about something and weren't talking and this morning he was off to work early.'

Honor sighed. 'God, parents! They're worse than kids sometimes. Mine aren't speaking either. They're quarrelling about where to go on holiday. It was all door-slamming and stuff last night and my mother's being all martyred because Dad wants to go somewhere where he can play golf and she says that's all he does at home. Anyway,' she heaved a sigh, 'there's still nothing come up about Jodie, is there? It kind of puts everything else into perspective, thinking of her and what might have happened – worst-case scenario sort of thing.'

'Yeah. The police said that they may have to report the bus thing to school, like as if it was a real incident of bullying or something.'

Honor nodded sympathetically. 'I guessed they might.

I'm really sorry, Pete. It seems unfair somehow, because even if you were kind of involved, it's just so not you. You're the last person.'

'Except like you just said, I was kind of involved.'

'Don't be daft. If you can't see the difference between you and that arse Gary, well, I despair.'

'Don't despair. Not of me, anyway. Please.'

'I won't. I did try to think the worst of you after all that stuff between us, but just talking to you again reminds me of, well, how we used to be. Anyway, I've got to go. I'm late already and old Filbert will murder me.' Mr Filbert taught history in a Portakabin in the car park.

'I'll walk with you.'

'Don't you have a class?'

'Yeah, I expect so, but I can't face it. Not today. Not with all this stuff in my head.'

'It's really cool, you know,' said Honor as they pushed open the heavy swing doors and went out into the blinding sun of the concrete pathway. 'It's so cool that you were brave enough to do what you did. Face it and everything. I'm really proud of you. Now all we can do is hope that the loathsome little tart turns up, unmurdered.' She gasped and held a hand to her mouth. 'I never said that. I don't mean it like that.'

'I know what you mean, and so do I.'

Later, as Pete walked back across to the main school building, his heart was singing.

Juliet would have preferred it if she and Gavin had met in a hotel rather than a friend's flat. There was something so neutral and removed from the every day about a hotel room with its window shrouded with thick drapes and dense net curtains through which only the dimmest light filtered from outside. It could be any time of day or night, any season, any weather, any city street in any country, and inside there was a secret, sealed world waiting for them. The anonymity of the room and the heavy, thick-carpeted, well-padded comfort was like a stage set designed especially for illicit lovers.

The crisp bedlinen and thick towels could be rumpled, stained and left twisted on the floor for someone else to deal with, and the miniature shampoos and bath oils were just enough for this one occasion – no more, no less, to be used and discarded. At the end of their tenure the room would be cleared and cleaned and all traces of their time sprayed, wiped and vacuumed away while they would emerge, secretly transformed by glorious sex, and no harm done to anyone else.

Unfortunately Gavin's friend's flat in Victoria was not at all like this. It was on the fifth floor of a turreted mansion block of glowering red sandstone, reached by a creaking old lift. Its owner, an academic writer now living in Italy most of the year, had offered it to Gavin should he ever need a bed in London during the summer, when he came backwards and forwards from Oxford for dinners and meetings. It was very convenient, Gavin said, to have a London pad and Juliet had laughed and said that she hadn't heard anyone use that word since the sixties.

However, when he unlocked the door and let her in, Juliet looked round in dismay. It was very definitely already fully occupied, to the last corner, the last inch of shelf, by the presence of its owner, whose clothes, books, papers and personal possessions overflowed onto every surface.

'But it's completely free, darling,' said Gavin, noticing her glum face, and propelling her forward with a hand in the small of her back. 'And no questions asked. It's much less risky than a hotel where one could bump into anyone.'

There was no point in complaining and she felt better after Gavin had opened the bottle of champagne which he'd brought in a chill bag and they had exchanged their first kiss. He was looking older, thought Juliet, his hair greyer but still luxuriant and worn long at the back, tucked behind his ears to curl in a raffish, boyish way. She was right about his clothes, the crumpled linen suit and sea-island cotton shirt with buttoned-down collar, open at the neck, and he looked exactly what he was, cultured and arty and interesting. His face was lightly tanned with healthy-looking full pink lips and a large, slightly Roman nose and amused smile lines round his very blue eyes. He had put on a little weight and his face looked heavier and there was more flesh around the cleft that divided his chin.

He was not a tall man, slightly shorter than Juliet, and as they kissed so expertly and their bodies leaned one into the other, she felt the tremors of sexual awakening and a sense that this was where she belonged, that this was the man with whom she would always feel most at home and be most herself. However, as things progressed and she found herself lying in a narrow double bed between maroon and brown sheets of the sort she loathed, she found it harder than usual to switch off other thoughts and get into the mood that the occasion called for.

The room itself was all wrong. The shafts of sun, streaming through the dirty high window, danced with motes of dust and were too bright and too harsh and fell thickly to illuminate grey balls of fluff beneath a bedroom chair. Under the tallboy opposite the bed she noticed that there lurked a dark, round object and she couldn't stop herself wondering what it was. A lost pair of socks, perhaps? A tennis ball? An orange, rolled away and forgotten, turning green and mouldy?

If she turned her head only slightly she was then distracted by the overloaded bedside table, a stack of books and a pair of spectacles, a bottle of pills and a dirty glass with a skin of something yellow and sticky-looking clinging to the bottom. It was sordid, that's what it was, and she felt irritated that Gavin didn't appear to realise that she might feel that she deserved something better. Of course, he would be pleased with the fact that it was free. Paying for hotels was always a problem when Sonia went through credit card accounts with a toothcomb.

But he was such an accomplished lover and they knew one another so intimately and yet had been apart for so long, that eventually she forgot about the depressing room and gave herself up entirely to the enjoyment of being with him again and being made love to so expertly. Oh, yes, it was wonderful. After all these years she knew all his moves so well and how to respond to them. First this, then that, it was like a well-rehearsed dance. Then a horrid little nagging thought crept into her head. Did he make love like this, whisper these endearments, sigh so lustily, move his hands from here to here when he was pleasuring his other lovers, and maybe Sonia, too? She tried to banish the idea but it was stubborn and refused to be erased entirely.

Afterwards, when they lay in one another's arms and chatted like the old friends that they were, Juliet wondered if this form of intimacy wasn't really what she enjoyed most about being with Gavin. In the days when she had dreamed of marriage she had imagined that it would be like this and more so, when the fondness and closeness they felt for one another was intensified by the tenderness of regular love-making. So what demon was it that made her spoil things again by asking, 'How is Sonia?' as she lazily stroked his shoulder. She felt herself tensing just a little as she waited for his answer, knowing that whatever he said would create a tiny snag on the smooth surface of the peaceful moment.

'She's very well, actually. Busy with this and that committee, and of course the girls are home for the summer.' Gavin paused and took another sip of champagne, which was difficult to do lying down. He raised his head and rested his chin on the wiry, grey hairs of his chest. 'She's been asked to chair a government working party on reoffending juveniles. It will require a hell of a lot of ghastly meetings and mean that she has to be in London at least two days a week starting in September, but they're very keen to have her, which is flattering, of course.' Juliet thought she detected a hint of peevishness in his tone.

'Will she accept it?' she asked.

'Of course. It's not the sort of thing you turn down. It's quite a feather in her cap.'

Juliet went on with her stroking and considered this piece of information. She wondered whether Gavin thought it disloyal of Sonia to want anything more than him in her life. She imagined her in a businesslike suit, preoccupied with young offenders and carrying a heavy briefcase backwards and forwards to London, and guessed that he would find such a situation irriating. Gavin surely preferred his women to be planets orbiting his sun.

'Is she happy, do you think? I mean, with things in general?'

Gavin thought about this for a moment, staring up at

the ceiling. 'Well, one of her great strengths is her organising ability and now the girls are older she probably considers that she doesn't have enough to do. Actually,' he added after a pause for thought, 'I don't believe that clever women like her consider happiness as one of life's goals. There are more important things to achieve. They are not, as a rule, very good at placid contentment. They would rather have their teeth into something gristly.'

'Too bloody bright to be fobbed off, possibly,' said Juliet, wondering if he included her in the clever category, 'and not sufficiently bovine.'

Gavin laughed and tickled her, which set her wriggling and squealing like a schoolgirl.

'You're so easy to wind up,' he said fondly, and then, when they were calm again, 'How is the cottage working out? You've only been there two minutes and are already in London, so I guess you're stultified with boredom. I always thought you would be, darling. I did warn you.'

'I'm not at all, as a matter of fact. There is the terrible drama of the missing child, for one thing, with police everywhere and the mother on the telly last night, appealing for information.'

'What a dreadful thing to happen.' Gavin's large eyes suddenly filled with welling tears. He was a tremendously sentimental man and easily moved. It was one of the things she loved about him. He's thinking of his own daughters, thought Juliet, and what it would be like if anything happened to one of them. She supposed she should comfort him but didn't know what to say and felt suddenly excluded. Childless women were generally supposed to be a bit deficient in the feelings department. She had often noticed that mothers, in particular, liked to think they had attained a higher level of compassion just through the process of having given birth.

The champagne had started to give her a headache and it was damnably hot in the room with its dirty window stuck tight with paint and impossible to open.

'Honestly,' she said, changing the subject, 'much as I've loved seeing you, I don't want to come here again if you don't mind. It's such a horrible flat. Let's do something better next time,' and she got out of bed. Conscious of not being sixteen, she walked across the room to the bathroom, which was equally grim with a stained basin and a dripping tap, and a shaggy brown bath mat flattened with wear, and looked at herself in the glass. She saw a shadow of disappointment in her face and it made her look old and tired.

Gavin's voice came from the bedroom. 'Come back

to bed, darling. Don't go off in a huff like that. Why do you ask about Sonia if it makes you cross? Anyway, it's *you* I want to talk about. I do worry about you. I often think if it hadn't been for me . . .'

When Dave came whistling up the path that evening, Rachel was waiting for him. She had made sure that the boys had already eaten and were out of the house.

'Hi, love!' he said, putting his sandwich box on the table and kissing her cheek as he passed to wash his hands at the sink.

She stood behind him, just a foot or two away, looking at his back, at his denim workshirt tucked into his waistband under the leather belt of his jeans, at the pale stubbly hair on his brown scalp. He made a lot of splashing noises with the tap turned on full and from either side of his body small sprays of silvery droplets showered sideways.

'All right?' he said, turning back, the towel in his hands, and looking at her as if he already suspected that all was not well. Her just standing there might have told him as much.

'No, not really,' said Rachel in a voice as neutral as she could make it.

'Why? What's up?'

'The police have been round again.'

'Yeah? What did they want this time?' His tone was casual and unconcerned and he met her eyes with a steady blue gaze.

'They wanted to speak to you, Dave. About your statement.'

'What about it?'

'That it wasn't true. That you weren't on overtime.'

He paused, head on one side. 'They what?' His tone made it sound as if she was talking nonsense.

'You weren't doing overtime. I rang the office this afternoon and they told me there hasn't been any overtime for months – the opposite in fact. Work has been a bit on the short side.'

'You rang the office?' he said slowly, his face grown hard around the mouth and eyes.

Rachel almost faltered, but pressed on. 'Yes, I did, Dave. I had to know, and that's what they said. So, if you haven't been doing overtime, where have you been?'

'Well, this is very nice. Very nice, indeed. My wife checking up on me. Doubting my word.' Dave turned away from her as if in disgust.

'I want to know, Dave. The police will be here soon and you'll have to tell them.' She couldn't keep the anguish out of her voice.

'Tell them what exactly?'

'Well, don't ask me! I don't know, do I? Where you were the night before last, and all the other nights, come to that, and the Saturdays, too.'

'I was working, like I said. Look, what is this?'

'But you weren't. Her in the office, Shirley whatever her name is, said you weren't.'

'So what do you think I was doing then?'

'Don't keep asking me the questions. I don't know. I don't know what to think.'

'I'd like to hear you say you trust me.'

'I do! You know I do. I don't think . . .' Her voice trailed off. 'I just need to know what you were doing if you weren't at work like you said you were.'

'I was at work. I was bloody moonlighting, wasn't I? Christ, you've really landed me in it now.'

'What do you mean?' Rachel found her hands were shaking and she leant them both on the kitchen table to steady herself.

'I do a bit of freelancing, don't I? Out of hours. Undercutting the quoted price.'

'You've never told me. You've never told me that before.'

'Because it could get me into trouble, that's why. It's not the sort of thing you talk about, is it? The less said the better.'

'Well, the police will have to know now. They're coming round to ask you questions. You'll have to tell them the truth.' Rachel felt as if all the solid surfaces of the kitchen had begun to give way. Fixed objects on the extremities of her vision seemed to move and dissolve. She realised that the banging in her ears was the thumping of her heart.

Dave looked at her, cold and angry. 'I'd have thought there would be a bit more in the way of support from you. A bit more loyalty. Jesus, it's you I bloody do it for, remember, you and the boys.' Suddenly he was making it seem as if she had done something wrong when surely it was the other way round.

'You didn't have to lie to us. Not to us, or to the police. That's one thing you didn't have to do.'

'Oh, please!' said Dave impatiently and then added in a tone that invited her to try to see it his way, 'What's the point of telling you something that would upset you? You know what you're like. You worry about everything.'

Rachel fell silent. She realised, without quite knowing why or how, that she was being lied to. It was the same feeling that she had had all those years ago when her stepfather had explained to her in a kind and patient voice that he was doing what he could to get her back home and out of foster care when all the time he was telling the authorities he couldn't cope with her.

She went over to the sink and took a glass from the draining board and filled it with water. Her hands were shaking.

'I want to be with you,' she said after she had finished gulping it down. It tasted bitter with chemicals. 'I want to be there when you speak to the police.'

'That's up to them,' said Dave evenly. He came to stand behind her and put both hands on her shoulders. 'Now, look,' he said, his voice full of reasonableness. 'What's this all about? All this upset. Getting all worked up over a spot of overtime. Haven't you ever heard of the black economy? Jesus, Rachel, everybody's at it.'

She turned to look at him. His face was the same as always, sensible and reassuring. 'It's about being told by the police that your husband is a liar, that's what it's about. It's about wondering where you've been and what you've been doing. It's about Pete thinking it's because of him Jodie's run away. That's what it's about.' Rachel put her hands to her face.

'Pete? What's Pete got to do with it?' Dave's tone changed and became instantly sharp and alert.

'I was going to tell you last night, but after we'd quarrelled about all that other stuff, I didn't. I didn't want to, not with you being so sure that I was wrong about him and saying those things about me.'

Dave gave an irritated gesture. 'Leave that out of it. I want to know about Pete. He's my son too, remember.'

'It all came out when I went off on Jamie's bike to look for him. I found him in the old slaughterhouse, just sitting about on his own, really miserable. It seems he and that boy, Gary, had been teasing Jodie on the bus, on the way home from school.'

'What do you mean, teasing?'

'It didn't sound like much, but schools all have these bullying policies these days and it would probably pass for sexual harassment or something. He's got himself in a proper state about it.'

'He couldn't sexually harass a kid like Jodie. She'd harass him more like.'

'She's only twelve. It would look like bullying to

anyone that didn't know her. Or him. And that lad, Gary, he's got a reputation as a bully. I've heard that from Jamie.'

As she spoke she heard the garden gate bang and then, the front doorbell rang.

'That'll be them,' she whispered, watching Dave's face which showed not a flicker of anxiety. I never asked, she thought, whether there'll be trouble about this moonlighting. She suddenly had visions of him losing his job, of unemployment, of a downward spiral into debt. Oh, God! How could everything suddenly go so wrong?

Dave went to answer the door and she heard his voice from the hall, confident and perky, as if he was welcoming guests to a party.

'Come in. That's right. My wife's just been telling me that you've caught me out. Economical with the truth, is what a politician would call it.' He gave a short laugh, like a snort, which was met by silence.

The two constables came through to the front room while Rachel stood in the doorway, and the police-woman began at once. This time her voice was quite different. There was no attempt to be friendly and even her jutting bosom, instead of looking motherly and comforting, was imposing in a threatening way. The tall policeman's pale face wore a pained expression.

'Just a few further questions, then, Mr Turner. You told us you were doing overtime on the evening Jodie Foot went missing, and after a routine check we found out that was not true. We need to know where you were and we also need to know why you were lying. At the moment this is an informal interview but it may become necessary for us to issue you with a caution and take you into the station for further questioning.'

The policewoman looked across at Rachel but did not smile, and nobody made a move to sit down.

Dave spread his hands, 'Yeah, well, I can see it looks bad,' he said, 'but I can easily explain. I agree I wasn't being strictly honest with you when I said that I was doing overtime. It wasn't overtime in that sense, it was more like working late.'

'Working late?'

'Yeah, doing a bit of freelancing here and there. Working on my own, see. That's what I was doing yesterday evening. Helping out a friend with a wiring job.'

Rachel felt a curious sensation in her stomach as if a weighty stone had been thrown into a pool, sinking down into the depths and sending out little ripples of fear.

The policewoman stared hard at Dave while the policeman was writing notes.

'All right, Mr Turner. What is the name and address of this friend?'

Rachel could see that Dave was ready for this. He swallowed hard but did not falter.

'Mike Dryden,' he said, naming someone Rachel had heard of from the Rugby Club but did not know. 'I can't exactly remember the house number, but it's in Meadowside Avenue, Shillington. House halfway down on the left with a camper van in the drive.'

'And that was where you were after work yesterday evening, Mr Turner?'

Dave nodded.

'Between what time would you say that was?'

'Half five until a bit before seven.'

'And what was the nature of the work you were doing for Mr Dryden?'

'Loft conversion. I was doing the wiring for a loft conversion.'

'I see. We'll have to speak to Mr Dryden, get him to confirm your story, and you'll be hearing from us again no doubt. You're lucky we're not having you in for wasting police time, sir.'

'Yeah, well, I didn't mean to cause all this.' Dave spread his hands. 'Overtime, working late – come on, there's not much difference, is there?'

The two constables eyed him coldly.

'It's a question of misleading information,' said the policewoman while the policeman put his notebook back into his top pocket. 'It doesn't help, sir, not in an inquiry like this.'

'No, no, I understand and I'm sorry. It was stupid of me, a slip of the tongue, you know.'

As he was showing them out of the front door and Rachel was wondering if she would ever breathe normally again, there was a bang on the back door and she heard Cathy call out her name. Oh no, she thought, please, not now. 'Yeah, I'm through here. What is it?'

As soon as she saw her neighbour's face she knew. Cathy was flushed and hectic looking, her eyes bright and her hair dishevelled. She was wearing an apron over her kaftan top and jeans, as if she had just run out of the kitchen.

'My contractions have started. Half an hour ago. Olly

was born in forty-five minutes so I don't think I should hang around.'

'Where's Phil?'

'Gone to get a spare tyre for the car. He had a puncture on the way home and didn't want to take the risk of not having a spare. Not with me like this, but it looks as though I've beaten him to it. I've been trying to get him on his mobile but he's not answering. I've left him a message.'

'Do you want me to take you in? Yeovil, isn't it?'

'Would you mind, love? They're coming on really hard now.'

'What about Olly and Ben?' Cathy had two small square boys of four and six.

'Mum's on her way, and Carol from the other side has got them in with hers. I thought, seeing Dave's van was back, you might be able to take me.'

'Of course, I will,' Rachel said without any hesitation. 'I'll just get my bag. Sit here a sec.' She pulled out a kitchen chair and Cathy lowered herself heavily and then gasped, hand on her enormous belly. Rachel found her other hand and held it tight until the pain had passed, and then bolted from the room. As she shot through the hall she heard Dave's voice from somewhere upstairs. He was talking quietly into his mobile, leaving a message for someone.

'So, be a mate, Mike, and do us a favour. I don't suppose they'll ask many questions. Just say that I was over with you, will you? Thanks, chum, and give us a ring when you get this message.'

Rachel stood in the hall below, her heart lurching. Unnamed terrors bobbed around the surface of her brain, things she could not bear to contemplate and which, as long as she did not allow herself to think about, she could bat away. She grabbed her woven straw bag and scrabbled for mobile and purse and car keys.

She shouted up the stairs, not sure how her voice would work. 'Dave! I'm going out. I'm taking Cathy to hospital. She's in labour.' She heard a movement from above but didn't wait to see his face over the banisters or hear his feet treading the stairs down to her.

'Come on,' she said to Cathy in the kitchen. 'Wagons roll!' and with a hand under her elbow she manoeuvred her up and out through the back door.

Cathy walked slowly, stiff-legged. 'God Almighty!' she sighed. 'Here we go again. Why do we do it, Rach? Us women? I've got me bag packed and some towels and things in case you have to be a midwife on the way! They're just inside my gate.'

'You keep your legs crossed!' ordered Rachel. They reached the car and she unlocked the door. 'You don't want to have to call this baby Yeovil or after somewhere else on the way, do you? You know like people do – Brooklyn and Chelsea, stuff like that.' She was amazed at how a normal person still seemed to be occupying her head, one that could joke and reassure and act as if nothing else was happening in her own life. 'Here, let's put the seat back. It'll be more comfortable like that. Just hang on there while I run and pick up your things.'

Inside Cathy's gate was a striped beach bag with two folded towels on the top as if she had prepared for a holiday. Rachel picked them up and threw them into the back seat of the car.

'Thanks, love. I can't do the seat belt up, not by a mile.'

'You'll just have to hold on tight, then. Right, we're off!'

As she accelerated away from the kerb she saw from the driver's mirror that Dave had come out of the gate and was standing looking after them in the road, and there was Carol in her front garden, trying to make Cathy's boys wave, but they were too busy turning their bicycles in very small, slow circles to look up.

'That was the police round at your place again, wasn't it?' said Cathy, heaving her bulk about in her seat, trying to settle more comfortably.

'Yeah. They had something to check with Dave. Something about where he was working the evening Jodie went missing.' Her voice sounded casual and normal. She met her own gaze in the driver's mirror and it was like watching someone else talking. Her words seemed to have nothing to do with the real tangled confusion of her thoughts. This is how liars are, she thought; criminals, murderers, who cover up the truth.

'Oh, bloody hell, here we go again,' and Cathy closed her eyes and began to breathe through parted lips in little pants, like a distressed animal.

'Perhaps we should have called an ambulance.'

'You must be joking. By the time they get an ambulance out here, I'd have had this baby twice over.'

All this time there was another conversation going on in Rachel's head. She was trying to discipline herself, saying over and over, I must think, I must think. She needed to explore the worst possible explanation for what she had just heard. Was he having an affair? It seemed the most likely explanation. He had lied to her, twice, and to the police. Surely it could not have anything to do with Jodie's disappearance? But to lie to the police! It made her feel physically sick and her hands trembled on the wheel and all the time she was talking inanities to Cathy, trying to keep her calm.

She drove as fast as she dared out of the village down the narrow lanes which in the early weeks of summer had cow parsley frothing in great swathes from the hedgerows and brushing against the sides of the car. The low sun smote in bright flashes from behind the lacy canopy of trees.

Cathy alternatively groaned or chatted beside her. The contractions seemed to be coming every few minutes and getting stronger. She was remarkably calm and Rachel marvelled at her stoicism and the fact that she seemed devoid of any sense of the drama in which she could rightfully have played a starring role. Cathy was the sort of modest, self-deprecating woman who was more impressed by other people's lives, as if she didn't consider herself interesting enough in her own right. It wouldn't have occurred to her to make a fuss.

In between the contractions she tried to get Phil on his mobile, but reception was patchy and she couldn't get a proper signal. 'Typical!' she said cheerfully. 'Where the hell has he got to? Never there when you need them, are they? And under your feet when they're not.'

I must just concentrate on this one thing, thought Rachel. I must get Cathy to hospital and later on I can think about Dave. Then she remembered what Cathy had said to her, about her baby coming on the day of terrible news and she was struck by a fear that it might be true, like a premonition of disaster.

They had reached the main road now, and Rachel drove faster through the golden evening, slowing down in the villages where there were a few people about doing everyday, normal, unhurried things, unaware of the drama within the passing car. She saw a man standing on a stepladder, cutting his hedge, and a blond-haired young woman steadying a toddler on a tricycle along the pavement. The fields on either side were busy with tractors or full of black and white cows, lying down in the evening sunshine in companionable-looking groups.

'They're cutting the silage,' said Cathy, nodding out of the window during one of her moments of respite. 'They'll be wanting to get it done before this weather breaks.' She was a country girl, daughter of a dairyman and born in a farm cottage only a mile or two from the village. It seemed amazing to Rachel that she should be interested in silage-making when she was just about to give birth, but that was country people for you.

At last they reached the town and crawled through traffic lights and roundabouts, halted at crossings where the red lights showed but there was no one waiting to cross, until finally they turned onto the road to the hospital. Rachel's heart sank to see that it was congested with the cars of evening visitors. People were traipsing across the road from the car park with bunches of flowers and carrier bags and disappearing into the entrance. In the bright sunlight it looked almost as if a festival event or a performance was taking place in the hideous modern complex with its swinging doors and sinister chimney stack. The car park appeared to be jammed full and cars dithered about in the road, passengers pointing one way while the driver looked in the other.

'Bloody hell!' groaned Cathy. 'Just take me to A&E. Pull up outside where the ambulances go. I can't hang on much longer. I'm wanting to push. I don't want this baby here in the bloody road.'

Desperately Rachel wove through the traffic, hooting her horn as politely as she could and then stopped, jumped out and ran round to open Cathy's door. Cathy was clutching the sides of the car seat, her face tense with concentration.

'Oh God!' cried Rachel. 'Hang on, Cath!' She called out to a young woman walking past. 'Can you run in there and get some help! She's having a baby!' and a man appeared and helped her to manoeuvre Cathy out, and then another said, 'Leave the car! Don't worry. I'll watch it. There's room enough for the ambulances to get through.'

Between them they got Cathy to move, bent over, stiff-legged, like a very ancient creature, into the foyer and the two women behind the desk saw at once what was happening and started to press buttons and call for help. The people sitting round the walls on spindly plastic chairs stared, suddenly silenced by the drama. Rachel noticed that the back of Cathy's trousers were stained darkly and guessed that her waters must have broken, and then the next set of doors crashed open and a team of green-suited medics rushed out with a trolley and took over the situation and Cathy was heaved up and rolled away.

'I don't want to leave her,' Rachel said in panic to the receptionist. 'It's only me she's got with her, but my car's just outside.'

'You'll have to move it, love. It can't stay there. She'll be all right now. She's got all the help she needs.'

Damn. Rachel had no option but to run back out and thank the man who was standing guard.

'That's all right. Looked as if you only just made it.'

'Yeah, but they won't let me leave the car here. I've got to find somewhere to park it.'

'Bloody ridiculous, this place is,' the man said. He was about sixty and even though the evening was still very warm he was wearing a thick acrylic jumper patterned in a snowflake design.

Rachel noticed that his breath smelled strongly of alcohol and that his chin was sprouting bristly silver stubble and then that his shoes were broken down and he wore no socks. Immediately she looked inside the car and saw that her bag was still there, safely on the back seat, and felt guilty that she should have been suspicious of him just because he looked a bit derelict.

'Thanks ever so much,' she said and got in, wondering if she should offer him any money but worrying that it might cause offence if she did.

'That's all right, my lover,' he said cheerily. 'Let us know what the baby is!'

'Yeah, I will!' As if she would ever see him again, and as if he should care, but there was something re-assuringly kind about the conversation that made her feel better for a moment, as if she was part of something warm and human that connected her safely to the mainstream of life.

She trailed round the narrow residential streets searching for a parking space but it was hopeless, hopeless, and she thought of Cathy having no one of her own to be there with her and felt panicky and desperate. At last, after what seemed like at least twenty minutes, she found a car about to leave and waited while the woman driver took her time to adjust her mirror, fiddle with something in her bag and fold her jacket on the back seat before she moved off.

Rachel quickly parked her car, wrenching at the wheel and shunting to and fro into the small space, and then ran, hurtling along the pavements past the garden gates and the smell of lilac and hot dinners and barbeques and the shouts of children playing and music and the far-away applause of television game shows.

When she reached the entrance to the hospital and

ran to the door through which they had taken Cathy, the man in the jumper was still there, sitting on a low wall, and she realised that this place provided his evening entertainment. She waved at him as she ran past and he gave her the thumbs up. At the desk the reception-ist looked up and smiled and said, 'Go right in. Her husband's got here. They're in theatre three.'

Thank goodness Phil's made it, Rachel thought as she half ran down the corridor, conscious of her old trainers squeaking on the polished lino, past a knot of green medics who hovered round another who held up a large, shadowy X-ray plate to the light, the illu-minated bones glowing a spooky white. A fat nurse pushed a trolley of clinking equipment in the oppo-site direction, her legs bottle-shaped in black tights. No one took any notice of Rachel. They were used to urgency.

She found the theatre and peered through the round window in the swing door and there was Cathy still wearing the clothes she had arrived in, lying on a high bed, covered by a white cellular blanket. Phil was by her side, half sitting on the bed with his arm round her shoulders, and cradled in Cathy's arms was the tiny, blood-smeared head of a dark-haired baby. Rachel pushed the door open gently and they both looked up, their faces changed with wonder.

'Oh, Rach!' said Cathy. 'Come and look! I only just made it. They wheeled me straight in here and it took me as long to have the baby as it did for you to park the car! We won't have to call it Yeovil after all. It's a girl, Rach! Come and say hello to Hope.'

They don't need me there, thought Rachel a little while later as she walked back down the corridor. She was only accidental to the story. Now they should be alone, the three of them, to share the first minutes of their baby's life. Memories rushed back of how it had been for her and Dave in those precious moments of meeting each of their sons and the fierce tenderness they felt as they saw the reality of the little human scrap that they had created. She remembered examining with pure wonder the perfect miniature hands and feet, the delicate pink whorls of the ears, stroking the silky, mottled skin of the funny little bowed legs which kicked feebly, and gazing into the strange, inscrutable face with its puckered anemone mouth and gummy unfocused eyes. However much you're prepared for it, however much you think you know what to expect, a new baby still bowls you over.

In her state of distress and agitation, Rachel suddenly felt comforted because those births had meant something, hadn't they, something huge which changed her and Dave forever? Before, they were just two people who loved each other. Afterwards, as parents of a tiny red-faced baby, with perfect curled fingers and little pink, yawning mouth, they were bound in a way that could never be undone. Whatever Dave had done could not shake any of that and Rachel told herself off for being so easily frightened and for having such little faith in him.

A man was moaning from a cubicle, low notes of misery and pain, and an ancient woman with thin white hair called out feebly from where she lay on a trolley, raising one old, yellow arm to attract attention. It was a shock to see this side of life, unravelling at the edges, and normally hidden from public view, and Rachel felt as if the same thing was happening to her, but inside, where no one could see.

Outside, her new friend was still sitting on the wall. He had found someone else to talk to, a small, tidy couple, both with neat silver hair, who looked as though they were dressed for church until you saw that the woman carried a stiff cellophane cone of yellow freesias.

Rachel caught his eye and gave him a little wave as she passed and said, 'A girl!' and he saluted her back, with his derelict's smile of wrecked teeth.

It was still congested outside the hospital and as she waited to cross the road, a police car went past and drew up outside the main entrance. A policeman got out of the front and went to open the back door from which a fat woman with bright coppery hair struggled to get out, her heavy thighs straining against her denim skirt as she stood up. She turned to wait for a girl to duck out after her and with a shock that made her gasp out loud, Rachel saw that the woman was Marion and it was Jodie who was with her in the back of the patrol car.

Chapter Seven

FROM WHERE SHE sat at her open sitting-room window, Jessie Harcourt had a good view of the road and had been watching the police activity as if it was a show put on for her entertainment. She wondered at the second visit to the Turners and guessed that it was the husband, Dave, whom they had come to see. It did make you wonder, she thought to herself, because it was so often men who were behind these disappearances of young girls. She couldn't believe that Dave could be involved. She didn't know him well, but he was a good sort of man, she would guess – a hard worker and devoted to those two lads of his. He'd helped her once when she had a mains water leak and even found out where it was under the ground. Just watching the dial of her water meter spinning round had been enough to give her a funny turn, but he'd told her not to worry and found the helpline number she had to ring. She'd always be grateful for that.

The wife was a strange one, though. They'd been in the village nearly ten years but she still hardly spoke. Stand-offish, was the general opinion. Thought she was better than anyone else was what Marion said. Right up her own arse, were the exact words she'd used. That was Marion for you.

It wasn't long after the police left that Jessie saw Cathy turn into Rachel's gate – what a size she was – and then a minute or two later they drove off together. Jessie guessed that Cathy's time had come and that her big simpleton of a husband had somehow managed not to be there when he was needed.

In a minute she'd get up and go and put the kettle on for a cup of tea, although Smokey wouldn't like her stirring. She'd got the cat asleep on her lap, purring loudly. It was too hot to have a great lump like him sitting on her, but she hadn't the heart to push him off. There was nothing for it, though. 'Come on, Smokey boy. Off you get. Mummy wants a cuppa.' He opened his yellow eyes and glared and unsheathed his claws to dig very lightly through the cotton of her skirt. She pushed him off sharpish then and he landed with a heavy thud on the floor and stalked off in a temper, his tail upright as a poker.

Jessie got to her feet and had another look through the window. There was a strange sort of hush about the evening air. It felt heavy and still, as if there was a storm on the way. Let's hope so, she thought. She couldn't abide the heat. It made her ankles swell and she couldn't sleep at night. She could still hear tractors going backwards and forwards through the village. They'd be in a hurry to shift the bales off the fields before the weather broke. They were so enormous, these modern machines, that they made the ground shake.

She could remember when she was a child riding back through the village on a hay cart, pulled by a pair of horses. Mr Betts, that was the farmer's name, a miserable old bugger if ever there was one. What a time of it poor Henry and Fred had had, living on that farm. Common knowledge it was in the village, but no one thought anything of it in those days. Children's rights hadn't been invented. No wonder Henry was like he was. Marked him for life, it had.

She was just thinking about him when she saw him cross the road to his allotment.

★   ★   ★

After he had eaten his tea, two rashers of bacon and the first runner beans from the garden, Henry had washed up and dried the dishes and hung the cloth over the tap. The long empty evening stretched out in front of him and he had gone over to his allotment to see about earthing up a row of potatoes. He had always found it better to be occupied. His large bony hands and feet were restless when they had no work to do and he could not sit at peace in his armchair while the summer sky was still bright and the birds were singing.

Although the evening sun glared down with a white intensity, there was a sultry heaviness, a weightiness, in the atmosphere, which suggested to him that a thunderstorm was on the way. As he crossed the road carrying his spade, he noticed that things seemed a good deal quieter than in the last day or two. Some of the older boys were kicking a ball listlessly back and forth across the street, but they seemed subdued by the oppressive evening air. There wasn't the usual shouting and whooping and energetic bursts of scuffling activity.

There was only one police car parked outside the Foots' house, with a couple of plain-clothes officers sitting inside, both talking into telephones, and the house itself had a closed look, with all the curtains tightly drawn. The dog must have been taken away somewhere because a silence hung over the place. Someone had cut the grass in the front garden and the newly exposed stalks were a sickly pale green.

Henry had been thinking a lot about Jodie. She had been on his mind most of the day and although he couldn't quite visualise her face, or hear her voice, he didn't know her well enough for that, it was the thought of her, unhappy, confused and troubled, that bothered him. He couldn't abide cruelty to children, and day after day the television news brought him stories of suffering and pain at the hands of adults. The sight of weeping toddlers caught in the arms of desperate, fleeing mothers, droughts and famines where starving, hollow-eyed children languished listlessly in refugee camps, and stories from closer to home of children abused and abandoned upset him so much that he had to get out of his chair and switch off the set. What kind of world was it that allowed these things to happen?

Now something bad had taken place right on his doorstep and there was no way to press a button and switch it off. What bothered him about Jodie was not the thought that she might have been abducted, raped, murdered, he hardly considered these possibilities, but more that her running away triggered a sympathetic response somewhere inside him. It felt as if a floodgate had burst and a whole lot of dammed-up memories had come rolling out like a tide. He couldn't control the great surge that swept him along and it was not a comfortable experience or one that he would have chosen.

Last night he had found it difficult to sleep. His room was stuffy, even with the window wide open, and he had lain, staring open-eyed into the darkness while wild thoughts galloped through his mind. Why now, in his old age, with so many intervening years, did he remember the past so vividly? All that was done with, he told himself sternly. No good came from dwelling on his childhood. He had made a point, all his life, of not harking back because, above all, he despised self-pity. He'd got no reason to feel hard done by. There were many more worse off and, in the end, he and Fred had set themselves up all right. It was true that after they had been evacuated they had missed out on being part of a proper family, but at least they could remember clearly what it felt like to have a mother who loved them. It wasn't as if they had grown up never knowing.

In the dim light of his bedroom as he tossed and

turned under the hot sheet, his mother's girlish voice and her smile came back to him as vividly as if she was there beside him. He could remember some of the things she said, how she once had called him her hero. He had just put his wages into her hand from his Saturday job at the brewery stables where they kept the dray horses. 'Henry's a hero to me,' she said to her sister Edie as they sat at the kitchen table with the brown pot under its crocheted tea cosy on the oilcloth between them. 'There's nothing he wouldn't do for me, is there, love?' and she had pulled him into her arms, even though he was already a big, clumsy boy, wearing his dad's cut-down trousers and boots, with two pairs of stockings to keep them on.

She always had a cotton handkerchief in her coat pocket, or in her apron, or up her sleeve, and she would pull it out and spit on a corner to rub at a dirty mark on his face. He could remember the slightly sweet smell of her saliva, and her soft breath as she bent close to his face. He could remember her coat too. Brown it was, a colour they called 'nigger' then, with a half belt at the back. It had a single row of brown buttons as big as old-fashioned copper pennies down the front and in it she looked as smart as paint, except that the pile of the wool around the buttons and at the very edge of the cuffs was worn away and sad, bare cloth remained. He remembered thinking that when he was older, with a proper job, he'd buy her a new coat and take her to the pictures, and afterwards for a bun and a cup of tea at Lyons, but then, of course, he never got the chance.

For years and years after they heard that she had been killed, he and Fred knew nothing of the circumstances of her death. No one saw fit to tell them and they never thought to ask. They hadn't even been allowed to go to her funeral. Henry supposed there had been no one to arrange it for them. He couldn't remember how, years later, he found out that the people who had died in the disaster had been crushed to death in a panic to get down the tube station steps to safety, but when he did, it distressed him very much. It made him think of the terror of knowing that she was going to die, because it wouldn't have been instant, like a hit by a bomb. He couldn't stop himself wondering how long it had been before she lost consciousness and he knew that during these long minutes she would have thought of her two boys, and all the time they didn't know and hadn't known for years and years. What had they been doing when she was trapped down there? Were they lying asleep in their beds? Henry hoped that perhaps he had been thinking of her, because he often did at night. He used to make Fred say his prayers every evening and they were always the same, 'God bless Mum and keep her safe.' God must have had other plans and Henry had not had much time for Him since.

In fact, Henry had never told Fred of his discovery of how their mother had died. He could at least spare him that, and his brother had gone to his grave thinking that she had been killed outright in their bombed house. Sometimes Henry wished they had died with her. It would have been neater that way, if the three of them had gone together, because you couldn't say that their lives had gone on to amount to much. All he could claim was that he had done his best for Fred and had worked hard and didn't owe a penny.

Usually he was strict with himself about allowing this vein of thought. He set himself a limit and generally stuck to it during the day, when he kept busy, but nights like this when he couldn't sleep, it was harder not to dwell on things. Thinking about his mother led swiftly to thinking about the Bettses, and from there it was only a step into the darkness of that part of his life.

Jodie Foot's disappearance had created a short cut

into his childhood and lying in the dark he could remember how it was to feel that he had nothing to lose, that anything that happened to him as a result of running away could not be as bad as how things were. He could remember misery like a clamp around his heart. He remembered it as a physical pain and wondered whether because of this constriction something inside him had withered and died away, and if it was the capacity to love. His feelings for Fred were complicated by duty and loyalty and mixed up with the irritation and exasperation of looking after him. He never considered whether he had loved him or not. It was more like a deep, organic attachment. They only had each other. When they were growing up it was Fred and Henry v. the Rest of the World.

Looking back he wasn't sure that at the time he had even realised the extent of their abuse. Children accepted what was handed out to them in those days and he remembered plenty of carefree times, mucking about with Billy and the other lads at school, playing football, summer swimming in the pool where the cattle drank and the mud was soft and silky between their toes. Maybe he thought then that he deserved the punishments handed out and he probably did. Some of them, at least.

So why had running away been such an imperative? Partly it was prompted by homesickness and a longing for their old life with their mother, but all evacuated children must have felt the same way. He could remember a girl who had been evacuated from their London school, Barbara Laws, she was called, crying every day at school. Every single break time she sobbed in the playground, she was that homesick. The boys took it in turns to climb up on the wall that separated boys from girls and hang on the railings and have a laugh at her. Once he'd knocked a lad over for singing, 'What's the matter with Barbara Laws? Her face is red 'cos she don't wear drawers.' Evacuee kids stuck up for one another.

With him and Fred it was more like a fierce survival instinct. To be free of the Bettses was to give Fred a chance, even if they were cold and hungry and wet and hiding in a ditch. There was no one else to help them, no one to hear their voices, and it was this helplessness that he remembered so clearly which now made him worry about Jodie. Running away and staying away as she had done, or so they seemed to think, was the action of a troubled girl who had nowhere to turn. Running was an escape from something. What had she got herself into that made her life so bad?

239

He knew that Jodie wouldn't have been beaten and half-starved as he and Fred had been. That Marion Foot might be a loose sort of woman with all her carryings-on, but she had a warm heart and she loved her children. It was the other things kids had to face today that could make their lives unhappy. He'd read about it in the paper – the dreadful, cruel bullying that went on and couldn't be escaped. It was what they did to one another with their mobile phones, the messages they sent each other on their computers, the threats, the cruel photographs, and there was no getting away from that.

Even when they got home from school, they weren't safe. Henry didn't understand the half of it, texting and emailing and the chat rooms, it was a foreign language to him, but it seemed to have made name-calling and the like worse, more vicious and deadly. Last week he'd read about some big, fat lass who had come home from school and gone up into the bathroom and taken an overdose of her mother's pills and killed herself. Where had the country got to, a rich country with everyone driving cars and having holidays abroad, even if they were out of work and on the social, and sending soldiers to fight in other people's countries and having bloody great knees-ups for Africa, while all the time, at home, that sort of thing could happen?

He'd studied the girl's photo, taken on a beach with her arm round her sister, another big girl. They were both laughing into the camera, and she'd got a lovely smile, a wide grin and dimples in her round cheeks, but she hadn't been allowed to be happy. Like Fred, she was picked on for being a bit different until eventually she couldn't take it any more.

Yesterday he'd heard three of the young women who lived on his road stopping to have a chat where he was working in the allotment. One of them, who had a child in a pushchair, was saying that Jodie must have been in trouble with some of the older kids. She was too full of herself, she said. Another said that she'd heard she'd been selling drugs in school for one of her step-brothers. They all agreed that she was a bully herself. None of them had a high opinion of her, that was obvious. He had wanted to throw down his hoe and stand up straight and shout over the fence at them, 'That's a *child* you're talking about!'

Now he finished what he was doing and looked around him. The bindweed needed pulling out where it clambered along the chain-link fence but he had grown to like its white trumpets of flowers and to admire its determination. He would leave it be. He glanced up at the sky which was darkening with ominous purple clouds. It felt as if all the air had been sucked out of the atmosphere. It was so still that he heard the rustle of a yellow leaf fall from the wigwam of runner beans.

He crossed the road back to his house as the first large warm drops of rain began to hit the ground. There was going to be a storm all right. That would be the last of the hot settled weather. A car pulled up outside the house opposite. It was a familiar car, driven by the young woman with the two lads and the husband who drove the white van. She was a nice enough lass. Reserved, he'd say, and minded her own business. Her boys were all right, too. Decent lads, not the lippy sort.

He gave her a nod as he went by. She was still sitting in the car and hardly seemed to notice and her face looked set and remote. Henry wasn't bothered. Folks could exchange a greeting or not. It was no skin off his nose.

He'd hardly got in and got his boots off when he heard the gate bang and Billy and Bingo were at the door. What did he want now? Well, he wouldn't have to wait long to find out.

'You heard the news?' Billy wiped his forehead with his handkerchief. He looked hot and red in the face.

'What news?'

'Marion's lass is back. Little tart was found in Weymouth with a man old enough to be her dad. Met him in a chat room or whatever they call it. He's in custody and she's back with her mam. What do you think on that, then? I always said she was trouble, that one.'

Henry grunted. He didn't know what to think. All that stuff he'd had going round his head, the girl running off because she was unhappy, had been way off the mark. It just showed what an old fool he was.

Billy, watching his friend's face for a response, was disappointed. He'd expected a bit more of a reaction to his news. Miserable old sod, he thought. He doesn't give a bugger one way or the other. If you weren't careful, that's what happened when you got old. You got that selfish you couldn't think of no one but yourself. It wouldn't happen to him, not likely, not with all his outside interests and his get up and go. Gas-fired barbeque was the next thing on his list, to accompany the patio chairs he'd ordered, although to be truthful he hadn't been too impressed by the quality when they were delivered. Made in China it had said on the box, and he could quite believe it. Made of bloody matchwood. He'd had to get his son round to help him put the bloomin' things together and he'd have to be a bit choosy who he let sit on them. His lump of a daughter-in-law was one he'd have to warn off for starters. Good lass she was, but by God she'd got an arse on her.

'That'll be an end to it, then,' said Henry. 'To all the commotion. We can get back to normal now.'

'Us on the telly and all,' said Billy regretfully. 'You'd be surprised at the people that saw us, Henry. Ever so many have rung up to say they'd just switched on to catch the headlines and there we were.' He spared Henry's feelings by not pointing out that it was his own appearance and not Henry's that had prompted the calls.

By now Billy had worked his way in to sit at the kitchen table. He wiped his forehead again. 'Hot enough for you?' he asked. 'There was a few drops of rain when I was coming along here. There's a storm on the way.' Bingo, ever nosy, had hopped upstairs, uninvited, and from above came the rattle of his claws on the lino as he carried out investigations in the two bedrooms.

'Lass yonder's had her baby,' said Billy. 'I've just seen Carol. That daft lummock of a husband nearly missed the calving. He was out getting a spare tyre fixed, so she said. That Rachel opposite took her in to Yeovil. Anyways, she's had a little lass, which is what they wanted, so Carol said.' Carol was some relation of Billy's, Henry thought. A niece, perhaps.

'That's all right, then,' he mumbled, not knowing what else to say.

'How about a drop of something?' said Billy, looking up at the darkening kitchen window. 'Reckon we need a bit of a stiffener, Henry. What have you got that would hit the spot? Wet the baby's head while we're about it.'

'Whisky,' said Henry, heaving himself to his feet. 'That's all I've got. Half bottle somewhere in the larder.'

'Come on, then,' said Billy. 'What are you waiting for? Get it out, you mean old bugger. Left from Christmas, I'll be bound.' He paused while Henry got to his feet and started to knock about in the larder.

'Will you listen to that?' he said, as a sudden roll of thunder cracked overhead.

'Weather's broken, Henry. That'll be an end to this heat.'

Rachel sat for a moment in the car before getting out. Now she no longer had to worry about Jodie, she had thought of nothing but Dave all the way home, rehearsing what she was going to say to him, but now it came to it, her mind was a blank. Within the next few minutes she had to go into her house and face him and she didn't know how to do it. She didn't know how her voice was going to come out and she didn't know what expression to put on her face. She felt as if she had been asked to play a part without guidance as to what was expected of her, as if she had been handed out a role for which she was unprepared. She even tried to think of stuff she'd seen on the television, how women behaved when they found out their husbands had lied to them. She wasn't the screaming and shouting type. When she was upset she went quiet, turned inward. She never wanted to talk about what was on her mind. Her strongest impulse was to leave a dangerous subject alone, just ignore it, take the view that whatever it was would sort itself out.

The childhood years of trying to appease her stepfather came back to her, of trying to be invisible, so that he wouldn't turn round in his armchair in front of the television set and see her, in her ugly brown school uniform, trying to cut herself bread and butter in the kitchen without him hearing. If he didn't notice her then he couldn't say that she was too much for him. He couldn't tell the social workers that he couldn't cope. For months, when her mother went into hospital, she would creep in from school and drop her bag in the hall and go silently upstairs to her bedroom and only come down when she was so hungry she thought she would faint. Big fry-ups he made for himself, fat pink and grey sausages glistening in the pan, thick wavy strips of streaky bacon, chunks of fried bread, a tin of beans. The smell drifted up the stairs, tormenting her where she sat on the edge of her bed with her nose pressed against her bare arm sniffing her own skin smell instead. If he offered her anything, which he sometimes did, she said she'd already had her tea with her friend Susan, in the belief that the less trouble she caused, the better.

She felt exactly the same now. Don't go looking for trouble, advised a voice in her head. If you go in asking questions, treating him like he's done something wrong, you'll put him on the defensive and he'll get angry.

He'll flare up and you know how you hate that, and he'll accuse you of not trusting him and he'll say what has he ever done to let you or the boys down, and he's right.

But he's been lying, said another voice. He's been lying about what he's been doing after work and I need to know the truth.

He's told you. He's been working, moonlighting, that's what he said.

Then why should he lie? Why couldn't he have told the truth?

What does it *matter* where he said he was? What difference does it make?

It does make a difference. You know it does. It means he's hiding something.

And so on.

There was nothing for it. It had to be done. There was no hiding here. She got out of the car and walked up the path as the first fat drops of rain spread dark stains on the concrete. The kitchen door was open and she could see the room was empty but the door to the sitting room was flung back to let in some air. She could hear the television and see Dave's feet sticking out from where he was sitting on the sofa. He was lying back, relaxed, his legs stretched out in front of him, his ankles crossed. His feet, in their old trainers, looked so normal and familiar that Rachel couldn't believe that anything out of the ordinary could have happened in their lives.

He must have heard her put her bag and the car keys on the table because, without moving, he shouted through to her, 'What's the news? You went off in a hurry. I didn't know what the hell was going on.' His voice was perfectly normal too, cheerful even.

'I told you,' she said, standing in the door but not looking at him. Instead her eyes fixed on the television screen. It was that programme about the woman police surgeon, the one who never smiled and was always rolling corpses in and out of mortuary drawers as if she was in the kitchen preparing dinner. This evening she was talking to a male colleague in a white coat and lifting her chin up to him in a perky, challenging way and he was twinkling a smile down at her, all across the body of the poor old stiff. Rachel found herself wanting to concentrate on the programme, absorb herself in it, and had to wrench her mind back to why she was standing in her sitting room avoiding eye contact with Dave.

'I had to rush Cathy in to Yeovil. She's had her baby.

A girl.' Now her voice had come out, it sounded strange, as if she was talking over the thumping of her heart.

'She has? Did Phil get there in time?' She knew he was scanning her face, already half sensing there was something wrong.

'Yes. I had to go miles to find anywhere to park. He was there when I got back.'

'I reckoned she wouldn't go much longer. She was the size of a house. Hey, is something the matter?'

Rachel shook her head, still avoiding his eye. 'No, no. The baby's fine.'

'Come on then, love. Come and sit down.' He patted the space beside him on the sofa. 'Do you want a cup of tea? You look a bit shook up or something.'

She suddenly remembered. 'Jodie's back. I saw her at the hospital with Marion. They were getting out of a police car.'

He looked up, his face broken into a smile. 'Well, thank God for that. Apart from being glad she's all right, that gets the police right off my back, doesn't it? They won't be poking about in my business any more, the bastards.'

Rachel didn't move. She stood with her hand to her mouth. If she was going to say anything it had to be now. Her voice came out in a sudden rush, high-pitched and strained, not as she wanted to sound. 'I can't believe you lying, Dave. Lying to me and the police. Why did you have to lie?'

Dave slumped back on the sofa and closed his eyes. 'Come on, love. We've been through all of this.'

'But why the lying?' she persisted, her voice trembling. 'I don't understand what it's all about.'

Dave sat up and stretched out an arm towards her.

'Come on, Rach,' he said, in a cajoling tone. 'What's up with you? Are you paranoid or something? I've told you, haven't I? I was working late. For myself. For us,' he corrected. 'For cash. I suppose I thought you didn't need to know.'

'Where? Where were you working?'

'Like I said. Hey! What is this? You'll be getting the bloody thumbscrews out next. I was doing a bit of work for Mike. OK? Ring him if you want. Bloody hell! I'm sick of this!' He stood up, hands on hips, and stared out of the window, looking away from her as if exasperated by her attitude, as if she was being unreasonable. 'What are you getting at? What are you saying?' His tone was offended.

Rachel paused, thinking, he's still lying. Please don't

let this be happening. He doesn't know that I heard him on his mobile. She took a deep breath.

'OK,' she said. 'OK.' She went to sit on the sofa, very quiet. Jodie's back, she thought, and Cathy's had a lovely baby, and here we are, doing something awful to ourselves. She felt as if everything, all their future happiness, depended on her and how she behaved in the next few minutes. 'I'm sorry,' she said, finally, because it was a way out. 'I'm sorry. It got me upset, that's all. The police coming round and everything. It was horrible.' This will make it right, she told herself. This was what he wanted from her.

Dave came to sit beside her and took her nearer hand in his. She looked down at it lying there. It was rough and unkempt from the housework. The summery pink nail varnish she had painted on weeks ago was mostly chipped off. I don't take care of myself, she thought. His own hand had short, clean nails and felt warm and dry.

'I know, I know,' he said. 'I'm sorry, love.' His voice was kind and gentle now. Rachel felt huge relief sweep through her. It was really so simple. That was all it took to put things right. 'Come here,' he said and pulled her towards him. 'The bloody police sticking their noses in, causing trouble. You've got nothing to worry about now, Rach. Not now the kid's back. Pete can stop worrying, too.'

'Yes,' she said. 'Thank God for that, and Jodie looked all right, too. Same as usual, really. After all the fuss she's caused! I suppose it's all's well that ends well, isn't it?' They sat in silence for a moment.

'I'll make us a cup of tea,' she said starting to get up, and then added, 'And the baby! A lovely, perfect little girl which was what they wanted. I couldn't really be happy for Cathy and Phil because I was so sick with worry.'

'My poor love,' said Dave, catching hold of her again and putting his arms round her waist. 'Forget the tea,' he said softly in an altered, cajoling voice. 'The boys are out. Why don't we go upstairs?'

On her way through the mainline station, Juliet scanned the headlines on the newspaper stands, dreading 'Girl's Body Found' or something similar and was relieved to read 'Congestion Charge Shocker' instead. She bought an evening paper and searched its pages as she waited for her train but there was no mention of the events in the village. Probably teenage girls disappeared every day off the streets of London and most other cities, and the case of Jodie Foot was no big deal. Still, Juliet thought, maybe when she got back to the cottage there would be some news. Surely there must have been some developments by now. A child couldn't just vanish from such a small community and leave no clues at all for the police to uncover. On the other hand, when she thought of the shed-searching operation by the two rather dim-witted police constables, she supposed it could. She wondered whether she could telephone Rachel for any news when she got back, but guessed that by then it would be too late by country standards. She would have to leave it until the morning.

The train journey was long and slow. The air conditioning wasn't working and to begin with it was intolerably hot in the carriage. Really, she had been hotter and more uncomfortable since she arrived in England than ever she was in New York where they managed things so much more efficiently. It proved impossible to open the train windows until the guard passed through and released them with a special tool and then the wind rushed wildly down the carriage, fluttering the pages of Juliet's paper and blowing her hair across her face and she huddled into her jacket and felt chilly and tired.

The commuter rush was over by now and her immediate fellow passengers were a pair of teenage boys sitting opposite, their heads nodding to the faint tinny vibrations from their headsets. Their limbs sprawled restlessly as if rampaging testosterone made it impossible to sit tidily. They had got on the train looking self-conscious in dark suits but lost no time in taking off their ties, pulling out their shirts and rolling their jackets into balls and tossing them onto the rack above their heads. They had the fresh, pink complexions and clean, floppy hair of public schoolboys and she guessed that they had been to London on some work experience scheme in a stockbroking firm, or a bank, organised by one of their fathers. They were both beautiful in a lean, long-limbed, well-bred way, with all the insouciance and assurance of youth and privilege. God, she thought, imagine being responsible for boys like that, who were probably highly sexually active and working their way through the sixth-form girls.

She watched, amused, as they stocked up with as many miniature bottles of vodka as they could afford from the refreshment trolley, counting their change to the last pence into the hand of the waiting attendant. He was not much older than they were; a tall eastern

European-looking youth, with broken English, and his name, Stefan, on a badge on his jaunty uniform waist-coat. His face was grey with fatigue, his eyes sunk in dark sockets. He had long, sensitive-looking hands, like a pianist. Juliet wondered at the circumstances that had led him to pushing a refreshment trolley down an English train with such an air of gravity and forbearance.

The older woman sitting next to her, who showed early signs of wanting a proper conversation, had informed her that she was on her way from her home in Kent to stay with her son in Shaftesbury. Photographs of the grandchildren were produced and in order to secure a bit of peace in which to think about Gavin, Juliet, after expressing polite interest, closed her eyes and pretended to sleep.

It had been lovely to see him, of course, but she wondered why, the horrible flat apart, their meeting had made her feel less rather than more happy than before. To start with, their time together had been too short. Ideally, they should have spent the evening together, maybe gone to a film or walked along the river and then had a meal somewhere before going back to bed. The most luxurious love-making came later in her experience and there was all the wonderful tenderness of lying in each other's arms and drifting off to sleep, rather than keeping an eye on the clock before snatching up one's clothes, dressing hastily and saying goodbye. Re-entering the hot dirty London evening and walking alone through the seedy streets to the tube had depressed her.

The other thing, she admitted, as the train pulled out of Basingstoke, was that she was still jealous of Sonia. She might not want Gavin full time herself, but the fact that Sonia had him, had always had him and would have him in the future was a thorn in her side. It annoyed her that he had loved Sonia enough to want to marry her in the first place, that they had produced three daughters who were talented, well-balanced and good-looking, and that if and when it ever came to it, God forbid, it would be Sonia that Gavin would choose above all others.

He might tell Juliet how much he desired her and call her his love, but the absolute bottom line of the whole thing was that he didn't want her more than he wanted to hang on to Sonia and all that came with her. Juliet was, and always would be, second best, and this was a lowering sort of thought, however much she told herself it shouldn't matter and that what they had suited them both.

Juliet also knew that she had to take responsibility for causing damage to the marriage and inevitable pain to Sonia, who was far too intelligent and perceptive not to notice that Gavin was playing away from home. Subtly, the signals would go out. A heightened excitability, a new indifference towards her, a sense of his interest ebbing away in another direction – all these signs would get picked up by her well-tuned, wifely antenna. Gavin would not be very good at furtiveness, he was much too careless and expansive for that, and no doubt clues were scattered fairly thickly on the ground at 124 Caldicott Road, North Oxford.

Juliet supposed that in the early days, in the full flood of their affair, he might well have been perkier, more cheerful and pleased with himself as he rode on a wave of thrilling extra-marital sex, and maybe overdid the compensatory, guilt-induced niceness to his wife. Juliet guessed it would cause quite a bit of suspicion if a husband broke the habit of a lifetime and started to come home late and flushed, bearing bunches of un-expected roses and wearing a satisfied expression.

There was some consolation in thinking that she was certainly not the first of Gavin's lovers and would not be the last, and therefore Sonia, by putting up with it and staying with him, was compliant. The truth, however, that Juliet had knowingly and deliberately set out to sleep with another woman's husband and was not sorry that she had done so and intended to continue, given the chance, did not sit easily on her conscience. She would not like her mother to know, for instance, or her aunt, and there were certain of her married friends who would consider her behaviour treacherous, selfish and destructive.

Early on in their relationship she had realised that one way to feel better about herself was to nurture a dislike for Sonia, to run her down and mock her and pity her. Once her rival had been reduced like this, Juliet felt less guilty. It was easier to sin against a woman one disliked, and the many kindnesses that she had received at Sonia's hands only intensified her antipathy. If only you knew, she would think, when Sonia left a message asking her to join a supper party, that a few hours ago I was in bed with your husband, it would wipe the smug smile off your complacent face.

As the train flashed through meadows lit by evening sun, Juliet wondered at the reprehensible person she feared she was. In other areas of her life she reckoned that she was kind and reasonably unselfish, a woman who had lots of friends who valued her, and she had to hope that if her moral character were to be held up for inspection, this could be used to counter-balance the truth that she had behaved badly towards Sonia.

And poor old Sonia hardly deserved her antipathy. After all, it was the wife who was supposed to be jealous, not the mistress, and jealousy, everyone knew, was the most corrosive and damaging emotion. It didn't do her any good at all to wish Sonia ill but she saw now, as she thought about it, that it was when Gavin told her about Sonia's young offenders' appointment that she had felt her spirits sag. She must still be jealous of Sonia's cleverness, just as she found it hard to think about the Edwardian house in Oxford, brimming with books, with its oak floorboards and lovely rugs, and filled everywhere with the presence of bloody Sonia. She was there in the stone-flagged conservatory with its charming old cane furniture and miraculous vine which yielded clusters of perfect green grapes, and in the garden, rampant with lovingly tended roses. 'Oh, this is all Sonia's department,' Gavin said airily at summer parties where his guests drank Pimms amongst the enchanting arbours and trellises, and exclaimed at the beauty of the cascading, scented boughs. There would be Sonia in an unflattering, bunchy skirt and flat sandals, having made no effort whatsoever with her appearance, walking round with the keener gardeners amongst their guests, modestly pointing out her spectacular success with Lady Hillingdon and triumphant absence of green-fly and black spot.

And there would be Gavin, Juliet could see him so clearly, in his beautifully cut pale linen suit, perfectly creased and crumpled, his handsome patriarch's face alive with animation as he talked to the prettiest girl at the party, maybe one of his students, who would be gazing adoringly back at him. Gavin was as he was *because* of Sonia; she allowed him to be like this, and set the stage for his bravura performances. They were a double act, a duo, and even now, years after Juliet felt that she had recovered, she still minded that the man she felt closest to, with whom she felt at her best in every way, belonged so completely to someone else.

Aunt Dot would say that you make your bed and then you lie in it, she thought. It was freedom of choice that had led her to take this particular path. She did not regret it for one moment, but she wished it could have been different. The melancholy she felt now – she was sure the French would have a word for it – was the price she paid. The loneliness of the future, as she and Gavin both got older and the desire and the opportunity to meet for illicit love went into decline, was inevitable.

But, hell, thought Juliet, it's been worth it. Every moment has been worth it and when I am nodding in my armchair in some dreary old people's home, because there will be sod all family to look after me, at least I will be dreaming about bloody good sex and companionship with a man I loved.

As the train slid through the tranquil green water meadows outside Salisbury, the sky darkened to a murky purple. There was a tremendous crash of thunder and then sheets of slanting rain hit the windows and came showering through in huge exploding droplets. The wild wind tore down the carriage, flapping and whipping as it went.

The two boys sitting opposite jumped up and slammed the windows shut, laughing as they leaned across the tables. Juliet and the woman smiled and thanked them.

'Thank goodness. That's the end of the heatwave,' the woman said, nodding towards the window. 'I knew a storm was on the way. I've had a headache all day. I think everyone feels out of sorts in that sultry heat.'

Perhaps that's it, thought Juliet. Perhaps it's just the weather that makes me feel so at odds with everything.

Chapter Eight

O VER THE VILLAGE, the sky piled up with dark plum-coloured clouds streaked underneath with lurid yellow and darkened so dramatically that the kids hanging around outside looked up in sudden fear. Then there was a crash of thunder so loud that the ground shook and the rain came as if a giant hand had torn a dark curtain from the sky and flung it to the earth with such force that the droplets bounced off the road. A wind whipped past, picking up the dust and dirt and straw, the dried-up litter of the heatwave, and tossed it in stinging gusts into the air, bringing with it the smell of hot, wet earth.

Pete was up in his bedroom when he heard his mother's car draw up outside. He'd been up there all the evening, since after supper and all the time that the police had been there, talking in the front room. He'd sat on the bed, his hands wet with sweat and fear, and then he had heard them leave and the front door shut. He'd sat on, too apprehensive to go downstairs, waiting for someone to start looking for him, but nothing happened except he'd heard Cathy calling and then gone to the window to see his mother helping Cathy into the car and then driving off with her. He'd guessed it was some mercy mission because Cathy was so enormous she could hardly walk.

Now his mother took a long time getting out of the car and then he heard his parents talking downstairs and although he couldn't catch the words he knew from the tone of their voices that they were arguing. Later there was the sound of his dad's voice, wheedling and silly, on the stairs and his mother answering softly. He had stood still as a stone, not wanting them to realise that he was there and yet not wanting to hear them go into their room and shut the door. Then there was silence before he heard the rhythmic grunts and low female gasps that so sickened him.

It was disgusting that they did it like that, urgently, as if they couldn't wait. He couldn't bear to think of his mother wanting it, naked and willing, and his dad doing it to her. It had been weeks, he thought, since they last had, and he had hoped that it was over, that they had reached an age where they didn't want to fuck any more.

Fuck, fuck, fuck, they went . . . his parents, for fuck's sake. He was glad that the storm was right overhead and drowned the noise. He dragged himself off the bed and went to watch from the window and wished that he didn't feel so disturbed. What sort of pervert was he? It was disgusting to get a hard-on from listening to your parents, for fuck's sake.

The familiar view of the road and neighbouring houses and the hills beyond was transformed in the malevolent light and by the sudden violent assault of the wind and rain. He saw a jagged fork of lightning flash across the sky followed by another crash of thunder so loud that he ducked back from the window in shock. Then he heard the gate bang and looked down at the top of Jamie's head, his mop of golden hair greenish and wet as seaweed, as he raced for the back door. The next moment he was shouting from downstairs, wondering where everyone was, and then his feet came crashing up the stairs. It took a moment or two for Pete to take in what he was shouting.

'Jodie's back!' he was yelling. 'Jodie's back!'

Pete went to the door as his father came out of the bedroom opposite, still tucking his shirt into his jeans. He caught hold of Jamie and swung him round. Jamie's hair spun wet drops across the landing, like a dog shaking, and his white T-shirt was soaked and clinging to his body.

'We know!' Dave said. 'Mum saw them at the hospital. She took Cathy in to have her baby and when she was leaving she saw them in a police car. Jodie and Marion. Right as rain!' His voice was loud and excited. Jamie ducked away from his arm and made to go into their bedroom but Dave stood in his way and pulled the door to behind him. 'Mum's having a lie-down,' he said. 'She's worn out with it all.'

Fucking liar, Pete wanted to shout. He went back into his room to sit on his bed. It was so dark now that he had to turn on the electric light. So Jodie was back. The news knocked the other stuff out of his head and he knew suddenly what it was to feel a wave of relief wash over him. He lay down flat and closed his eyes but Jamie banged open the door and rushed to the bed and punched at his belly, forcing him to jerk into a curl to protect himself.

'Did you hear?' Jamie was shouting, too, against the roar of the wind and the rain clattering against the window. 'Jodie's been found. She's been texting everyone. The police found her in Weymouth. She's been shagging some really old man.'

'Yeah, I heard,' said Pete, kicking out at his brother with both feet, although he hadn't, not that last bit anyway. The relief was such that he was scared that he was going to cry.

'She met this bloke in a chat room. He's been grooming her for sex. The police have got him and now he'll get banged up. Life, probably.'

'Who did you hear all this from?'

'We just heard. Just now, from Dixie.'

His dad was at the door then. Christ, why couldn't people leave him alone? thought Pete. He hated it when his family thought they could just barge into his room.

'What did I tell you?' Dave demanded, as if someone had contradicted him. 'Didn't I say she'd be back? Instead of poking their noses into other people's business – decent people, at that – the police should have listened to me. I'd have told them!' He seemed more than just relieved. He was elated and exuberant. He came over and seized Pete's arm and pulled him off the bed in a playful show of force. 'Those police bastards look pretty stupid, now, eh? Calling you a bully! Snooping round asking questions about me at work! Round here tonight upsetting your mum! We could have them for damages, you and me. Defamation of character!'

Pete, lying in a heap on the floor, looked up at his father, unable to match his mood. It didn't seem to be anything much to do with relief that Jodie was safe and it didn't feel much to do with her when later on his mum went out in the car to get fish and chips as a treat for them all, and they sat laughing and chatting and drinking lager round the kitchen table. The storm had passed on but now it was raining steadily. The road outside ran with water and the garden dripped, the heads of his mum's flowers bowed nearly to the ground and the grass littered with twigs and leaves blown off the tree.

The atmosphere at the table was almost festive. It was partly to do with the baby arriving safely. Cathy's belly had looked so gross and Pete tried not to think about it all emptying out of her furry, dark hole. In his view, the whole thing was a fucking miracle. Fucking, literally.

Although she was a nice person and all that, the idea that Cathy, with her plain face and frizzy hair and great big tree trunk legs, and Phil, who had a heaving beer belly and was covered in a pelt of black body hair that sprouted out through the neck of his shirts, fucked each other was more disgusting than thinking about his parents doing the same thing.

Several times as they sat eating Dave got up to get something and stopped to massage his mum's shoulders as he went by her chair. Once he leaned across the table to take her hand and she smiled back at him. Pete realised that something or other from the bedroom still clung to them and it made him want to slam back his chair and get out of there. His father was in one of those moods when he wanted to dole out treats. He said that they should plan a summer holiday, that they could afford it with all the overtime he'd been doing, and Jamie started to jump around and shout about going to Florida.

Pete sat there, eating his fish and chips but feeling as if he was at the wrong party. He felt that something more had happened, somewhere underneath the surface, that nobody was talking about. It was as if there was a truth that was being deliberately by-passed, but he didn't know what it was and he didn't know how to begin looking for it or even if he wanted to.

It had been such a strange day. He wanted to think about Honor because he still felt muddled about her feelings for him. He wanted to think about sex, especially with her. He wanted to think about Jodie and work out, now that she was back, whether he was dumb to have felt so ashamed about what had happened on the bus. His dad seemed happy to think that he was off the hook and had got one over the police, but he couldn't see that it altered any of what had actually happened, or gave him an excuse to feel it was now OK.

The effort that had gone into his distress of the last few days left him feeling empty now it was over. He certainly didn't want to make a party of it. He looked round the table at his family and felt the gulf between them so wide that he wanted to get out of the kitchen and be on his own. As soon as he could he would go and lie on his bed again. He'd already tried to get hold of Honor to tell her the news but her mobile was switched off. There was no one else he could think of who he wanted to talk to.

★　★　★

Over the next few days the village came to terms with what had happened. Someone tied a string of balloons to the Foots' gate and a hand-painted sheet hung on the front of another house, with WELCOME HOME JODIE in wobbly red letters that dripped and ran in the rain until it looked like the spooky writing of a horror comic. Rachel noticed that the sheet came down when the stories started to spread that Jodie had been found with a man in Weymouth and that she'd hood-winked him into thinking she was seventeen. The balloons stayed where they were, dangling from the gate and looking less and less celebratory as they drooped and shrivelled.

Jamie came home from school with the news that Jodie had bullied a girl in their year to hand over her mobile telephone and when her parents found out – she was too scared to tell them at first and pretended she had lost it – the police were able to trace the calls Jodie had made. She had been too smart to use her own mobile and the absence of calls had been one of the worrying mysteries about her disappearance. The mistake she had made was to rely on the power she had over Gemma Threep, who was uncool and friend-less, in the belief that she wouldn't dare tell on her.

It turned out that she had been planning the escapade for a few days and that Marion hadn't been truthful when she said there had been no trouble at home. She and Jodie had had a row over the hours she spent on internet chat rooms, and Marion had threatened to confiscate the computer. That was what sparked the whole thing off and as Rachel said to Cathy, none of it came as a surprise when you thought about it.

The social workers moved in on the case. There was often a strange car parked outside the Foots and twice Rachel saw a young woman with a briefcase knocking at the door. The latest rumour was that Jodie wasn't returning to school. She had been put under a supervision order and was being sent away somewhere, to a boarding school, and only coming home at weekends.

The sympathy for the Foots ebbed away. Someone reported them for cruelty to the barking dog which had reappeared after a few days and was then taken away in a RSPCA van, and Dixie was had up for an out-of-date tax disc. The curtains in the downstairs windows remained closed and the house had a defeated, disappointed look.

'So that's that,' said Rachel to Cathy, sitting in her neighbour's kitchen watching her feeding Hope. 'You can't help feeling sorry for Marion. They won't be in such a hurry to put her on the television the next time. I don't know how she had the nerve to go through with it when she knew she hadn't told the police the whole truth.'

'It was because she was scared they'd take Jodie away,' said Cathy, kissing the dark downy head that lay in her arms. 'That's what she'd got at the back of her mind. She'd do anything to stop that happening.' She didn't think Rachel sounded sorry at all and wondered at how hard she could sometimes be on people. She knew she didn't like Marion, but all the same. Of course, Rachel didn't know her like Cathy did. They'd been at school together, primary and secondary. She'd known her all her life. She wasn't everybody's cup of tea, but she was all right, Marion was, and you wouldn't wish the anxiety of a missing child on anybody.

'All she's done is cause a lot of trouble to everybody,' said Rachel.

Cathy didn't answer. She moved Hope from one breast to the other and guided her daughter's perfect little pink mouth, with its pearly sucking blister, towards her nipple. What trouble had it been to anyone to answer a few questions? she thought. What was that compared with the agony of not knowing what had happened to your daughter?

'Anyway,' said Rachel getting up and taking the coffee cups over to the sink. 'Thank God it's over, for all concerned.' The sink was filled with breakfast dishes and last night's saucepans by the look of it. She turned on the tap and started to run the hot water.

'There's no need for you to do any of that,' said Cathy, glancing over. 'I'll catch up with it all. One day!'

'It's something I can do,' said Rachel, squirting washing-up liquid into the water. 'I'd like to do something to give you a hand,' and Cathy felt hot, unexpected tears in her eyes. Her hormones were all over the place and the smallest act of kindness set her off.

Two days after her trip to London, Juliet woke late and listened to the sound of steady rain falling. God, she'd forgotten what an English summer was really like. At least the grey light seeping through the curtains had allowed her to sleep longer and it seemed to have shut the birds up, too. She could still hear them, but the volume was definitely turned down.

As she lay there, half awake, she gradually became aware of another noise, a rhythmic scratching that sounded quite close, as if it was coming from the garden. She listened a few moments longer and then, puzzled, got out of bed and went to the window. She saw it was the strange old man, the one she had first seen on the bicycle, raking up the debris of the storm that littered the patch of grass. Behind him the shed door stood open.

She glanced at her watch. Half past seven. What an hour to turn up and disturb people! She watched him as he raked, regardless of the rain, his thick white hair bushing out from under his old tweed cap. She couldn't see his face from up here, but she remembered his stony, craggy profile and rather dreaded having to get dressed and go downstairs and introduce herself. She wondered what was expected of her. Should she offer him coffee or tea? Should she invite him into the kitchen, out of the rain? Rachel had told her that he was a bit strange. Odd, but harmless was what she had said.

Twenty minutes later she stood at the kitchen door with a freshly brewed pot of coffee on the counter behind her.

'Hello!' she called into the wet garden. 'Good morning!' There was no response. The rain had slackened and was now no more than a grey mist which crept over her bare feet and clung damply to her face and arms.

'Hello?' she tried again, and started up the brick steps to the square of lawn and the flower beds. She could see him then, Henry, she remembered his name was, at the far end, turning over the compost heap with a fork, his back to her. Damn. He hadn't heard her. She picked her way over the wet grass.

'Hello! Good morning!'

He turned to look at her. Really, he had the most unusual face. It was hollow-eyed and looked as if it was carved out of granite, with deep lines running down his cheeks and a downward turn to his mouth.

'Hi!' she said, approaching with a bright, social smile and extended hand. 'I'm Dr Fairweather. Juliet. I expect you will have heard that I'm here for the summer!'

He ignored her hand and did not return her smile and then she realised that he had looked down at his own hand and decided that it was too dirty to offer to her.

'I wondered if you'd like some coffee? I've just made some. Or tea? You were here very early. I expect you'd like a break. It's such a dismal morning.' How long would she have to witter on before he responded? He really was as odd as Rachel had warned.

Henry stared. He didn't know what to say. It wasn't usual to be asked if he wanted anything. He came and went to his various jobs and apart from the occasional conversation about what needed doing in the garden, he had hardly any contact with the people for whom he worked. He'd only seen Dr Ballantyne maybe a dozen times in the ten years he'd worked for him. The woman who had come out of the house was tall and slim with brown hair and she had a pleasant, friendly voice. She talked to him in a confident manner, like a nurse or a teacher, and he felt that he was obliged to accept her offer, although it wasn't something he liked the idea of.

'So!' said Juliet. 'Tea or coffee? I'll bring it out here for you if you prefer, but it's still rather wet, isn't it?'

Henry found his voice at last. 'It's not what I'd usually do, like, but a cup of tea would be welcome.'

'Come on, then!' she said and turned for him to follow her over the grass and down the steps to the back door. She'd got bare feet, he noticed then, which struck him as very peculiar. Who went wandering about outside in the wet without shoes? Her feet were long and brown and left a dark imprint on the grass. To his surprise he noticed that on two of her toes she wore silver rings that glinted as she walked. A hippie, then, he thought. It would be all free love and smoking roll-ups, he wouldn't be surprised. He regretted that he had accepted her offer, but he couldn't get out of it now.

He followed her to the door and then hesitated outside. His boots were cleanish but wet and, hippie or not, she wouldn't want him treading over her kitchen floor.

'Come in, please!' she said, turning back. 'Oh! Don't worry about your boots. Look, put your coat here. It can drip on the floor, it doesn't matter. Now. Tea. I've only got Earl Grey, is that all right?' and she was getting a bloomin' teapot out of the cupboard and a proper old-fashioned tea caddy. Years ago he'd given up loose tea. He thought everybody had.

'Milk? Sugar? I've got biscuits here. Rather good ones. You know, made by Prince Charles. Although probably not by his own royal hand. Or Camilla's, come to that.' She gave a little laugh.

Henry didn't know what she was talking about so he kept his mouth shut.

'Please sit down!' said Juliet, thinking, God, this is

heavy going. He looks as if he thinks I'm going to have him for breakfast. 'There!' she said, filling the pot with boiling water and putting it on the table together with milk, sugar, teaspoon and the biscuit tin. She was terribly tempted to pour her coffee and take it back to bed with her, leaving the strange old man to it, but that didn't seem an option, although he looked so uneasy, she was sure he would prefer it.

Henry stared at the pale grey liquid in his mug. Gnat's piss, it was. It scarcely passed for tea.

Juliet sat down opposite him and then seizing on what she felt would be a safe topic said, 'Isn't it a huge relief that the child has been found? Rachel told me that they've arrested a man, but it seems he hasn't harmed her, thank goodness. It could have all ended so differently.'

'Aye.' Henry stirred his tea.

'Is it OK, to call you Henry?' Then hoping that a bit of well-earned praise might help, Juliet went on, 'You certainly do a good job on Dr Ballantyne's garden. It looks immaculate. Not that I am a gardener. I'm a Londoner, born and bred. I live right in the middle of New York now and hardly ever step off the concrete, but I can see how well kept everything is.'

Henry took a sip of tea. It tasted as bad as it looked. Like scented bath water.

'Ah,' he said, and then added, 'I was born in London. In Bethnal Green.' He didn't know why he told her. It just came into his head from nowhere.

'You were? Really? I imagined you were a Dorset native. When did you come to the village? What brought you here?' Juliet took the lid off the biscuit tin and passed it to him.

'It was the war. Me and me brother were evacuees. We came here when we were kids.'

'Really? Evacuated to this village? But you didn't go back to London? Not when the bombing was over?'

'Nothing to go back to,' he said shortly.

'What do you mean?'

Bugger this, he thought. All these questions. Like a bloody terrier, she was, like the woman who came round doing the census, ticking boxes on a fact sheet.

Despite himself he said, 'Our house wasn't bombed, not that I know of, but like I said, we never went back. We lost our mother, see, and there wasn't no one else as would take us on. So we stayed put. After, there wasn't nothing to go back for, was there?' It wasn't really a question.

'No other family? What about your father? Was he killed too?' Juliet didn't hesitate to ask the question. It didn't seem insensitive when what they were talking about had happened so long ago.

'No, not my dad. Or, like I said, not that I know of. He'd done a runner years before. Left my mother with us two kids to bring up. All we ever had from him was his name. On my mother's side we came from a big family. It was like that then in the East End. Everyone knew everyone else or was related. A lot of uncles and aunts and cousins we had, I forget them all now, but there was none as could take us in. Life was harder then. Proper slums they were, down the East End. Hackney, Poplar, Stepney, Bow, Bethnal Green.' The old names rolled off his tongue and he felt a flash of contempt for this woman with her posh lady's voice, who wouldn't know anything about hardship but who found it all so interesting. She'd never had to wear a worn-out coat, but, when he glanced up, she was nodding sympathetically.

'I know,' she said gently. 'You realise, of course, that I'm not a medical doctor. I'm actually a social historian and years ago, when I was a student, I wrote a paper on kinship in the pre-war East End of London. I read a lot about what it was like. Did you lose touch with the rest of them? The aunts and uncles?'

'They never came looking for us and we never looked for them. I sometimes wonder about Mam's sister, Edie, the one closest to her. I sometimes wonder why she never came for us boys. She was fond of my mother and lived just round the corner from us, but she had a drinker for a husband, a rough sort of man, and I daresay he wouldn't let her. Jealous he was of her, our mam used to say. Jealous even when she came round for a cup of tea with her sister. Used to knock her about. So we didn't go looking for any of them and it was just me and Fred after the war.'

'Fred was your brother?'

'Yes,' said Henry. He'd had enough now. He didn't know what he was doing, blathering to this stranger. He'd never talked to anybody like this before. Everything pouring out, stuff no one wanted to hear. He must be going soft in the head.

'What year was it?' asked Juliet. 'The year your mother died?'

'March third, nineteen forty-three. In the Bethnal Green tube disaster.'

'But the blitz was over by then, wasn't it? There

would have been a lot of London children who had returned from being evacuated.'

'There were some from this village that had gone back by then, but not Fred and me. We had to stay put. Our mam couldn't come for us. She'd got nowhere to live by then. She worked in a factory that got bombed out and she couldn't keep up with the rent on the house. She couldn't have us back even if she wanted. She wrote and told us we were to stay put until she found somewhere.'

Juliet was silent. It was hard to picture this old man as a child, as a knobbly-kneed boy, but she could imagine the feeling of alienation and bewilderment at being cut off from everything you knew. It must have felt like abandonment. Although, of course, there were evacuee children who had loved being in the country, who looked back on their time away from the cities as an escape into a new and different world of animals and fresh air and wholesome food.

'What were they like, the people who took you in?'

She didn't think she had asked anything to offend, but the atmosphere between them changed abruptly and Henry stood up as if he hadn't heard the question.

'I'll be getting on, thank you very much. I'm not

one for talking. Not when there's work to be done.'
He clamped his mouth shut in a tight line and took
his mug towards the sink.

Juliet had to jump up and bustle after him, saying.
'Leave the cup, I'll do it.' She watched him from the
door going back up the garden. Something had upset
him, that was obvious.

Later, when she was sitting upstairs at her laptop, she
typed in Bethnal Green, 3 March 1943, and waited to
see what would come up.

Henry cycled home still feeling upset. There was no cause
for the woman to ask him questions and no need for
him to have answered. He didn't know what was happening to him, all this stirring up the past, delving into what
had been laid to rest long ago. He gripped the handlebars tightly and lowered his head into the rain which
had begun again. At this rate he wouldn't be able to go
and work at his afternoon job and he dreaded the long,
empty hours ahead. He sometimes thought he should
get another dog, a stray, perhaps. The last one had
belonged to Fred and had been a pretty little cross-bred
bitch that had been dumped out of a car on the A30.
Pip, Fred had called her and they'd had her for years.

A dog would be company and give him something to do when he wasn't working. He could take a dog for a walk on an afternoon like this and it would get him out of the empty, sighing house with its grey shadowy corners. But then the dog itself would have to be left while he was out, shut in the kitchen or the shed, waiting for him to come home, lifting its head to listen for his footstep, and he didn't want to do that to a dog.

He was grateful that he was able to cycle to his gate without meeting any of his neighbours. His was the sort of loneliness that was made worse by seeing other people. He swung his leg over the bicycle and pushed it through the gate and up the path to the back of the house. It wasn't until he went into the hall to go upstairs to change his wet trousers that he saw a blue envelope lying face down on the mat. He stooped to pick it up and turned it over. The address was handwritten and the writer had got his name correct but had left out the house number, and even the road name. Someone at the sorting office had circled the space where it should have been in blue pencil and added, 'Try No. 8, Green Lane.'

He took the envelope into the kitchen and sat down

287

at the table. It was unusual for him to get a hand-written letter and he was baffled by this one. He peered at the postmark for a clue but the stamp was too indistinct to read. Putting the envelope on the table he went to the sink and washed his hands, soaping them over and over before drying them on the roller towel behind the door. Then he took up his kitchen knife and slit open the envelope. Inside were two sheets of tightly written paper. The writing was small and tidy, straight across the page, line after line, in blue Biro. He glanced at the address at the top, 129 Vale Road, West Drayton, Middlesex.

This isn't for me, he thought. The silly buggers have sent it to the wrong house and now I've been and opened someone else's letter. Then his eye fell on the first line.

'Dear Cousin Henry,' he read. 'I'm sure this will come as a surprise to you.'

Henry sat down and began to read.

Rachel found herself excessively busy the first few days after Jodie's return. Life seemed to have picked up speed and she told herself that she hardly had time to think, at least not about Dave. Together they went to a Year Eight Parents' Evening to discuss Jamie's progress and they heard what every parent wishes for, that their son was helpful, well-balanced, a good influence on others, maybe a little lazy academically in subjects he wasn't interested in, but in nearly every way a model student.

They drove home feeling pleased with themselves and pleased with Jamie. There was nothing like having your child praised to make you feel good about yourself, thought Rachel. It was a reinforcement of everything you'd tried to make of your life, a public pat on the back for good parenting. Of course there had been a lot of talk amongst the parents about Jodie and by now the relief was heavily diluted with criticism. Rachel made a point of not joining in. She was one of the few mothers who actually knew Marion and there was no need for her to say anything because other people said it for her. Dave, of course, put in his twopennyworth, saying, you only have to look at the family, and practically calling Marion a prostitute. Rachel felt uncomfortable with that. She couldn't see that it did anyone any good, not now that it was all over and Jodie wasn't coming back to the school, to go criticising and pointing fingers. It was enough to hear the nice things said about their own son without wanting to run down other people.

What's more, the recent crisis that she and Dave had been through was a storm they had weathered and in a way she had Jodie to thank for that. Sometimes it took a crisis, she thought, as they drove home from the school through the grey light of another dismal evening, to give you a jolt, to make you realise how important marriage was and how it was at the heart of everything and how you should pay attention to it. Somehow she had managed to bury her fears and she congratulated herself that she'd been able to do so without ever letting on to Dave that she knew he'd lied to her, and she had managed to convince herself that it didn't matter.

She looked across at him as he drove, still talking about how well Jamie was doing. He had been in this expansive mood for days, ever since the night Jodie got back. Now he was promising Jamie that he would buy him a surfboard as a reward for his good assessments, and he had been as good as his word about having a holiday later on in the summer. He and Jamie had spent hours on the internet looking for deals on holidays in northern Spain where they could find surf and sun and Rachel had got their passports out of the drawer by her bed to check they were in order. The idea was that they should drive, taking a ferry from Plymouth and finding somewhere to camp along the coast. Rachel wasn't sure that she was keen on the idea of camping. What sort of holiday was that for her? But Dave promised that they would hire a proper tent with all the equipment, and that they would eat out a lot at restaurants in the evenings.

'Sunshine, wine,' he said, putting his arm round her. 'You, in a bikini!'

'Not a chance!' She laughed. 'Look at this!' and she pinched at the roll of flab round the top of her jeans. 'I'll be stuffed into one of those Look Ten Pounds Slimmer swimming costumes!'

'Just so long as it's tight and sexy.'

That was how they had been. On a sort of high. Rachel couldn't help but appreciate the atmosphere created by Dave's good humour, especially after the anxiety of the last week. His conviction that things were good and that they had a lot to celebrate was infectious but there were times when she was on her own when she couldn't help thinking about what exactly had happened. Somewhere buried inside her there was a certainty that all was not well. It made her think of her mother carrying the cancerous cell which would eventually kill her, and how no amount of denial or hope made a scrap of difference in the end.

I've discovered that my husband has lied to me, she thought one morning as she made their bed, and he doesn't know that I know, and we're both relieved to have got away with something. We both feel we've had a narrow escape. She sat on the edge of the bed with her head in her hands feeling physically sick. That's the truth of it, she thought, and all this happiness is just make-believe. With terrible clarity she knew that Dave must be having an affair. There was no other explanation. She didn't want to believe it, but the knowledge was there, like a trap, waiting for her.

So she and Dave, the whole family, were clinging to what she saw was a leaking raft and things only appeared to be well because they were keeping secrets from each other, paddling frantically to disguise the truth, that the craft was doomed. But she had no alternative. She had to try and bury her suspicions and behave as normal and keep the family ship afloat because of the boys. It was they who mattered most.

She was reassured that Jamie was all right and although Pete had gone back to being moody and silent at home,

Rachel saw that there was a new lightness about him. Last night he had come into the kitchen when she was getting supper ready. He had been up in his room working, he'd got an exam the next day, and he was wearing his glasses and his hair was stuck on end. He picked up the wooden spoon and stirred the pasta sauce that she was making, round and round the pan, when it didn't need stirring at all. His big knobbly feet, young feet with no disfiguring corns or bunions, were bare, and he stood there stirring, and the silence had felt easy between them and for once she didn't need to spoil it with anxious questions.

She was draining the pasta of its boiling water into the sink when he had left the spoon and came and put his arms round her waist and laid his head between her shoulders.

'Careful!' she warned, and then the moment was over and he moved away and Dave came in the back door and looked at them both with the questioning face of someone who thinks that they have just missed something. She had to turn her head so that neither of them would see the tears that had sprung into her eyes.

'What's all this?' he said, coming over and kissing the nape of her neck.

'Watch out, this is hot!' She elbowed him out of the way but he took the pan from her hand and put it on the draining board.

'Come here!' he said. 'I want to give my wife a kiss when I get home from work.'

It can't be true, she thought as he put his arms round her. This is real, and the other can't be true. I mustn't even think it.

Chapter Nine

WHEN SHE WOKE the next morning Rachel lay waiting for the alarm to go off. Last night she and Dave had made love and the sex had been better than for a long time, more exciting – more urgent. It was as if her body was intent on giving her a stronger message than her head. He wouldn't make love to me like that, she thought, if he was seeing someone else. I'm mad to even think it. She glanced at the bedside clock and found that she had woken half an hour too early. I'll get up, she decided. There's bacon in the fridge and I'll do a cooked breakfast for us all. Things are going to be fine, I know they are. Dave loves me and I love him, and that is all that matters.

She crept out of bed and got dressed. Down in the kitchen she sang softly to herself as she set the table.

With the bacon rashers sizzling in the pan, she fetched her make-up bag and put on some lipstick and mascara. Things would be fine from now on and one of the changes she was going to make was to take more time for herself. If you feel good about yourself, she told her reflection in her mirror, then you feel empowered to deal with other things in your life. This was a fact established by every women's magazine she had ever read.

Today she was going to Jasmine Cottage and she was looking forward to seeing Juliet again and hoped that she would be at home. A lot had happened since the last time she had seen her and although she had no intention of gossiping, she knew that Juliet had been genuinely concerned about Jodie. She had telephoned the morning after Jodie was back and Rachel told her about taking Cathy to hospital and seeing Jodie and Marion getting out of the police car and, as far as everyone knew, she was unharmed. Now she could tell her the latest news that Jamie had brought from school.

She decided this morning, affected by her new optimistic mood, that she also wanted to have a proper look at exactly how Juliet dressed. Although she had only met her once she had been impressed by her style. Most of the other people Rachel worked for were elderly and did not provide much interest in that way. Juliet had been wearing jeans and a T-shirt, all casual stuff, but she had looked elegant and sophisticated and Rachel wanted to work out how she did it. Perhaps it was the battered leather belt with the heavy-looking buckle, or the simple sandals, or the cut of her jeans or her loose hair, or the silver jewellery – there was just something about her. She was a lot older, of course, but Rachel recognised a clothes sense that she envied.

It was Dave's rekindled interest in her and the thought of going away on holiday that made her consider her own appearance for once, and as soon as you started down that route, she thought, you were surely in for a nasty shock. She would be a good candidate for one of those television makeover programmes where neglected women were taken in hand by a team of experts and as a first step were shown exactly how they had let themselves go. They'd be photographed walking down the street in their ordinary everyday clothes, hair untidy, no make-up, mouth turned down and a preoccupied expression as they went through a shopping list in their heads or thought about the day ahead, with nothing much special to look forward to. This is what you look like, they were told. This is what you have become. This is the person your husband and children see.

The women often wept at the sight of themselves and Rachel could hardly bear it, it seemed so unfair. Then they were displayed at the end of the programme, with new, hairdresser-teased hair and full make-up, posing in specially chosen and flattering clothes and looking quite transformed and tearfully grateful that they had been saved in the nick of time from what was really only themselves.

Although Rachel wanted to cheer that these women had been pulled back from the brink in the nick of time, the programmes were also dispiriting. The husbands or boyfriends were always so pleased with the improvement in their women, and she wondered how they dared, when they themselves stayed exactly the same, with their beer bellies and bad teeth and thinning hair. Couldn't people who loved one another let the years pass without noticing or minding, maybe even loving, the inevitable physical changes in each other? Wasn't that the whole point of love and marriage? Anyway, these women didn't have this confidence and it seemed to Rachel sad and hopeless, like trying to hold back the tide, because in the long run they would all grow old, come what may. Unless they were unlucky, like her mother, who had died when she was thirty-six.

Rachel remembered that as her mother had shrunk, eaten away by cancer, she had looked younger and younger, with her flat chest and transparent skin and wispy, infant's hair, until just before she died Rachel felt that they had swapped roles and it was her mother who had become the helpless child. She had sat by her bed feeling large and clumsy with her long, teenage legs wound round the metal tubular chair and her size-six feet in her new stacked heel shoes making marks on the shining lino floor of the hospice. She remembered staring at her own skin which was pink and glowing, her veins full of bright red blood. If only she could have lent some of that pulsing good health to her mother and given her the opportunity to live long enough to worry about the signs of ageing.

Nevertheless, all this didn't mean that Rachel couldn't try and make a bit more effort with herself, especially with things being as they were, and a hard look at Juliet Fairweather seemed a good place to start.

When she arrived at Jasmine Cottage and let herself in, she found Juliet on the telephone in the kitchen, deep in conversation and looking rumpled and distressed, running a hand through her hair, and standing with one bare foot resting at an angle on the arch of the other.

She looked across at Rachel and mouthed a welcome and then turned away to continue her conversation. As Rachel went to get the Hoover from the cupboard under the stairs, she heard enough to guess that there had been some sort of family crisis involving Juliet's mother. Not wanting to be a distraction, she lugged the Hoover up the stairs to keep out of the way and to start work cleaning the bedrooms. A few minutes later, Juliet came running up to find her.

'Oh dear,' she said, and Rachel turned off the Hoover and turned to listen. She could see that Juliet wanted to talk, and far from looking chic, this morning she looked quite old and tired with no make-up and her skin almost yellow in the gloomy sunless light. 'That was my brother on the telephone. My elderly aunt, who lives with my slightly less elderly mother, has had a fall and broken a hip. She was taken to hospital yesterday morning, poor old thing. It actually happened in the night and she wouldn't allow my mother to call for help. Apparently she kept saying that she would be all right, and then passing out. Eventually my mother attracted a neighbour's attention in the morning by knocking at the window as they were going out early for a newspaper and, thank goodness, they called for an ambulance.'

Rachel made sympathetic noises.

'Anyway,' went on Juliet, talking fast and using her hands for emphasis, 'now my mother can't be left on her own. She relies on her sister in all sorts of ways and really can't cope. One of my brothers is away in France for a month, and that was the other one on the telephone. He wants to put her in a residential home for a few weeks, but she's terribly upset at the idea. She makes it sound like being locked up in a maximum security prison. She says that if she gets put in one, she will never come out. She telephoned me this morning in a terrible state. She thinks in no time at all she'll be stuck on a commode with mindless daytime television in the background. "It's the slippery slope, Juliet," she kept saying.'

'What does your brother say to that?'

'Well, he thinks she's just being difficult. He's a great organiser, you see, and wants to tidy the whole thing up and get on with his life with a clear conscience, knowing that she's being looked after somewhere. The fact that she doesn't want to be organised is just an irrelevant annoyance that must be firmly overridden.'

'I see.' Rachel realised that Juliet had told her all this because she was uncertain of how she felt about it herself. 'Well, it's always difficult with old people. They always want to hang on to their independence, don't they?'

'I just don't know what's best. They are both appealing to me for support and I can see it from both sides. My brother is obviously right from a practical point of view, but I do empathise with my mother, who has always loved her home above all else.' She paused and then asked, 'Are your parents alive, Rachel? Although of course they wouldn't be ancient like my mother.'

'I don't know about my father,' said Rachel. 'I've never had anything to do with him. He wasn't married to my mother and I don't think he even knew she was pregnant with me. Then she died when I was fourteen. She was ill off and on for a long time and my stepdad put me into care when she was in hospital. He died about five years ago. Smoked and ate himself to death apparently. I didn't see him after Mum died.' She could say it now. That was one good thing that had happened as she got older. She no longer felt that her childhood was her fault.

Juliet looked genuinely moved and reached out and touched her arm. 'Oh Rachel,' she said. 'Oh, I'm so sorry. What a very sad story.'

Rachel shrugged. 'It was a long time ago,' she said. She wasn't asking for sympathy.

'Look,' said Juliet impulsively. 'Leave the bloody Hoover. It's too early, I suppose, for a drink? But let's have a cup of coffee. Something to perk us up. I can't believe this grey weather when it's supposed to be summer. Honestly, it's enough to get anyone down. I'll go and put the kettle on and give you a shout when it's ready.'

Later, as they sat opposite one another at the little polished table in the kitchen with the ugly coffee mugs in front of them, Juliet said thoughtfully, 'It's strange, because only the other day I had Henry in here, you know, the gardener, and he told me the most awful story of how his mother died at about the same age as you lost your mother. He told me she was killed in a civilian disaster in London, during the war. After he'd gone I looked it up on the internet. It was a dreadful thing – nearly two hundred people, mostly women and children and the elderly, of course, were crushed to death one night in a panic at Bethnal Green tube station, where they were taking shelter during an air raid.'

Rachel stared. This piece of information was news to her and she suddenly realised how little she knew Henry, even though they lived nearly opposite. 'I've never heard about that. All I know is that he was an evacuee who never went back to London. I suppose I thought that he'd chosen to stay because he'd liked living in the country.'

'Well, he might have done, but it seems he had no one to go back to. I'm sure you know that the East End of London bore the brunt of the air raids and apparently people were expecting retaliation from the Luftwaffe after the heavy bombing of Berlin a few days before. A siren had gone off and then there was a salvo from some new anti-aircraft guns nearby, which made a hell of a noise, like bombshells in fact, and people panicked. I suppose they thought that the bombing had started before they had got safely underground. You can just imagine it. It was pitch dark outside and had been raining and the tunnel was very dimly lit. A mother carrying a baby in her arms slipped on the steps, and those behind all piled down on top of her and were crushed by the people crowding in from the streets above.'

'Oh, my God!' cried Rachel, holding her hand to her mouth. 'What a horrible thing to happen. It must have been a terrible way to die and a terrible thing for Henry and his brother to live through, losing their mum like that. It's dreadful what you don't know about people you practically live next door to.'

'I got the impression that he's never talked about it much. He's one of those people who bury things, isn't he? One of those men who don't, or can't, articulate their feelings. He suddenly started to tell me out of the blue and then clammed up completely when I asked him more about it. As I said, he and his brother were only boys, and they never went back to London and never saw their remaining family again. They were on their own from then on. I don't know how old Henry would have been – thirteen or fourteen, I should think.'

'I never knew any of that,' said Rachel, shaking her head. 'I've never heard anyone even mention it. People always think that in villages people know everything about everyone else, but it's not true. Poor old man. No wonder he's a bit peculiar. You don't ever get over it, having your mother taken from you like that. Eventually you get used to it, like people do when they lose a leg or something, and you have to learn to live a different life, but you never get over it. I was just thinking of my mum this morning, on the way here. I think of her most days, actually. Not sadly really, more just wondering about her. I was thinking of how old she'd be now – nearly sixty – and how young sixty-year-old women seem these days, and how much life they still seem to have to live.'

As she spoke, Rachel realised that Juliet couldn't be far off this age herself and wondered if she might be causing offence, but it was too late now. 'I was thinking how much I'd like to have known her as she got older and wondered what she'd be like. So I envy you, still having your mother. Although I can see the problems now she's elderly, especially with your sort of life.' Oh shit, she thought, I've made a right mess of this conversation. I've blundered right into it now.

'What do you mean?' asked Juliet as Rachel guessed she would. 'What sort of life?' Her tone was more interested than anything else.

'Well,' said Rachel, realising that she had got to go on now and wondering how she should put it. 'You seem so free and independent. No ties. You can do what you like when you like. Live where you want. Don't have to answer to anyone. All that sort of thing. So your mother might seem like a bit of a hindrance, I can see that.'

Juliet sat for a moment considering. She could tell that Rachel was uncomfortable with what she had said in case it sounded like criticism.

'Well, you're absolutely right, of course,' she said. 'People always think that single women are selfish – and very often with good reason, because living on your own means that you do only have yourself to consider, but on the other hand there isn't anyone else to look after you. Think of it like that. As you get older you can't rely on a husband's salary or pension, or companionship in your old age, or the comfort of grown-up children, or the pleasure of grandchildren. So, in a sense, if you are single, I think you have every right to take bloody good care of yourself!'

'I didn't mean that I thought you were selfish.'

'No,' said Juliet, smiling. 'Look, don't worry. I'm used to it. It's how married people often react. Anyway, it's more or less what my brother was saying to me just then on the telephone. If I won't support him in putting our mother into a home, he suggested that I look after her, that she comes here for the summer.'

Rachel didn't comment. She felt that she had said

too much already and it was nothing to do with her anyway. She thought instead of what she had just heard about Henry. She couldn't believe that ten years she had lived opposite him and she had never known anything of what Juliet had told her. The truth was that although they said hello when they met, she had never had a proper conversation with the old man. He wasn't the sort to stop and want a chat, not like his friend Billy Wright who you had to avoid if you were in a hurry to get anywhere on time.

She used to talk more to his brother Fred, who was a bit simple, and was often at the gate looking for a chat. All smiles, he was. Everyone in the village liked him, and when he had died Rachel had meant to call with a pot of jam, or bake Henry a cake or something, but she had never got round to it. She hadn't wanted to go upsetting him, and his manner was off-putting for one thing, but it had made her cry buckets when she had heard that Fred had gone. She and Cathy had sat at her kitchen table and blubbed into a box of tissues. There was just something about Fred — innocent, he was, like a child, and always happy, even though he seemed to have so little in his life.

'And maybe that's what I'll do,' said Juliet, thinking

aloud. 'Or I'll ask her, anyway, and see what she says.' The truth that the years were slipping by and lately she hadn't had the time to be close to her mother was undeniable, and that they both might enjoy time together suddenly seemed a possibility. She looked across at Rachel and smiled. 'You've made up for it, though, haven't you?' she said, wanting to end on a comforting note. 'It seems as if you've made a real family yourself and given those boys of yours a proper home and a great start in life.'

'It's not making up, though, is it?' said Rachel and Juliet mentally kicked herself for her clumsiness. 'You can't "make up" for your mother dying at thirty-six. You never lose the feeling that you've had something stolen from you, that a big piece of your life is missing. Even having your own children is a reminder of what you've lost, because you'd love her to have known them and vice versa.'

'No. I can see that. I just mean that maybe you realise the importance of family more than other people might do.'

'Yeah,' said Rachel, giving Juliet a little smile. 'Maybe I do,' and she stood up to take her mug to the sink. 'Thanks for that. I'd better be getting on.'

Juliet drained her coffee and poured herself some more and thought about her own situation. Of course she shouldn't get carried away. There were practical difficulties to consider regarding her mother. She mustn't be too impulsive. What would she do if she had to go away for a few days, for work or, more importantly, for Gavin? She couldn't leave her alone in the cottage any more than she could be alone in London. She would have to find someone to keep an eye on her. Perhaps she should make some inquiries about home help and that sort of thing before she committed herself.

Rachel, on her way upstairs, was wondering much the same thing. Would Juliet be prepared to give up her freedom, if only for a few weeks? She somehow doubted it. Like she said, she wouldn't be used to putting anyone else first. As she bent down to switch on the Hoover, she heard the bleep of her mobile from the pocket of her jeans. She fished it out. She had a new message. From Dave. 'Working late,' she read. 'Job to finish. C U. xx.'

She put her mobile back in her pocket and stood a moment at the window. Outside, the garden still dripped with rain and the fields beyond had darkened to a dirty yellow where the hay had been taken off.

She realised how much she had been dreading this moment because, with a terrible certainty, she knew that Dave was lying.

Henry slid the letter back in its envelope and took it into the sitting room. He stood for a moment wondering where to put it for safe keeping and propped it on the mantelpiece over the fire, next to the clock that old Mrs Parsons had given Fred. The blue of the envelope was a bright rectangle of colour against the drab wallpaper and caught his eye as he went to go back to the kitchen. You couldn't miss it, sitting there, and it gave Henry an uneasy feeling, like an unexploded bomb. What if Billy came round? He'd be on to it like a flash. 'What's that then, Henry? You had a letter?' Henry didn't want questions, not yet, not until he'd got used to the idea.

He'd read it all the way through several times, unable to take in the contents at one go, and then he'd put it into his pocket and gone over to the allotment and worked there in the rain, and all the time he could think of nothing else. He'd come back for his dinner at twelve o'clock and put the envelope on the table, where he could see it, and after he'd warmed a tin of tomato soup and cut himself some bread and butter, he read it again, every word, from the address and the date at the top – four days it had taken to get to him from the day it was written – to the signature at the bottom.

Now he picked it up again and took the pages out of the envelope and sat down in his armchair. It was dark in the front room. The sky looked like a fuzzy grey blanket pressed against the window, and he had to get up and put on the electric light before he could see well enough to read. The paper was quite thin and the blue had already become smudged along the creases from the number of times he had unfolded the pages.

Dear Cousin Henry,

I expect this letter will come as a surprise to you, if it finds you at all. It's what you would call a shot in the dark, me writing to you out of the blue. I call you Cousin Henry because I have reason to believe that you are Henry Streeter, son of my Auntie Connie, who was killed in 1943.

You probably don't remember me, but my mother was Edie, your mother's sister, and we lived round the corner from you in Globe Road, Bethnal Green. I was only three years old when your mum was killed, so if you do remember me at all, it would be as a baby.

My mother and I were down the tube station along with your mother when the disaster happened. Of course, I don't remember it, but my mother was pulled out alive, with me in her arms, but your mother was not so lucky. Mum took it ever so hard, losing her sister, and I do remember that she talked a lot about you and your brother and she always meant to get in touch with you after the war. She used to show me photographs of the two of you, but of course it didn't mean much because I couldn't remember you.

My mother had a hard life and I have many regrets, but you only learn as you get older and now it is too late. She passed away aged 84 ten years ago. She divorced my father after the war and brought me up on her own and I never saw him since, which just goes to show, blood is not always thicker than water.

I am getting to the reason I am hoping to be in touch after all these years. I was recently on a coach holiday in the Isle of Wight with an old friend (a lady friend) and I happened to see a news item on the TV in the hotel about a child missing from a village in Dorset. The name of the village rang a bell with me and I remembered it was the same one that you were evacuated to during the war. It's strange how you remember these things, but it came back to me like a flash, and also because my mother kept your address for many years, always meaning to get in touch with you again. I said to my friend, Nora, that this was the village that my cousins had been sent to and then the interviewer talked to two men, and I caught the name of the one, Henry Streeter. You can imagine my surprise. I never thought that you would still be there after all these years and considering the many changes and moves in my life.

I am now a widow of ten years having lost my husband a few weeks after my mother died. The loneliness has been terrible, not having been blessed with children, but I keep myself busy and lead an active life since I retired last year, so please don't think I am sorry for myself.

I am writing to you in the hope that I heard right and it wasn't just wishful thinking or my ears playing tricks on me. As you can see I don't know your proper address, or if this will find you, but fingers crossed. I would like to get in touch because my mother missed her sister all her life and I think she felt guilty that she never made more of an effort to find you, but she had enough on her plate as it was. I have many family photographs and also your mother's wedding ring and a few other things that might be of interest.

I expect you know that two of our uncles were killed in the war and that our mothers' eldest sister, Ida, went to Canada with her family, and Auntie Rose to New Zealand. Our grandad died in 1948 of lung cancer. He was a shocking smoker. Our nan lived for many years after and was always a comfort to my mum. She stayed in the old house on the Roman Road until it was demolished and she was put in a council flat with all mod cons, but she missed the old place and was never the same again. She passed away not long after and that broke the family up for good.

I am hoping that this letter finds you and that you have it in your heart to reply. I don't know any of the details of your life, whether married or single etc. or how life has treated you and Fred. I haven't told you much about my life either but that can come later.

With affectionate greetings from your long lost cousin,

Betty (Milward)

PS I hope there is good news of the missing girl. I have looked in the papers, TV etc. but haven't seen any mention.

Henry folded up the letter and put it back in the envelope and sat with it in his hand in the fading afternoon. He didn't know what he felt but it was more like panic than anything else. He didn't know what his unknown cousin wanted, writing to him like this, after all these years. He couldn't remember her at all, not as a baby or anything else, but he couldn't doubt her word. You couldn't make up the things she had written.

Why can't I be left alone, he thought miserably, left in peace? He didn't want a stranger, even if she was a relation, poking around in his life disturbing everything. Next thing he knew, this Betty Milward would be on his doorstep, knocking on his door, and what a shock she'd get then, when she met him face to face. Who's this great scarecrow, she'd think, this peculiar old man, and he'd have to ask her in and then there'd be all her questions, and what was the point of it all? What was the point, at this stage of their lives? It was better to let things be.

But what he couldn't get out of his head was that this woman had been with his mother when she died. That's what he couldn't believe. She'd been down the shelter with her own mother and they would have been together, the two sisters, and her mother had survived, been pulled out alive with her baby in her arms, and his hadn't.

He unfolded the letter again. She'd got his mother's wedding ring, and photographs and 'a few other things that might be of interest'. He couldn't believe it. No wonder his heart was pounding and his throat was dry. It felt to Henry as if there was a mysterious and in-explicable plot afoot to bring his childhood back, what with him being drawn to the past so much over the last few days and then the woman at Jasmine Cottage with her questions, and then this letter arriving on his mat, out of nowhere.

Well, he thought, I shall have to reply. He sat for a long time with the letter in his hand and knew that if he did, he wouldn't know what to say. He had never written a personal letter in his whole life and he didn't know where to start. He was going to need some help, a second opinion on what he should write to this woman who said she was his cousin. One thing he did know was that he wasn't going to consult Billy Wright. Oh no. He could remember how he'd been at school. He couldn't put two words together on paper. Talk the hind leg off a donkey, but writing was a different matter.

The more he thought about it, he could see that it was a good letter that his cousin Betty (Milward) had written. It said just enough and no more, and not too much about how sorry she was that things had turned out as they did. He liked that, and he liked it that she said she wasn't asking for pity, her being on her own and the loneliness of it when you were used to living with someone all your life. They had that in common, the pair of them.

He thought all this but it didn't help. Not a single sentence came into his head beyond, 'Dear Cousin Betty, your letter came as a great shock to me.' He said these words over and over in his head but each time came to a full stop when nothing else suggested itself. He folded the pages again and put them back into the envelope and the envelope into his trouser pocket. He'd had an idea. This afternoon he'd planned to cut Jessie Harcourt's hedge. He'd told her he'd come round when he had time and the wet weather meant that he couldn't get on with mowing grass. Jessie would help him out. Just as he could remember Billy at school, he could remember Jessie, too. She'd had lovely, light brown hair and she had a desk over on the far side of the classroom and the sun bathed her head in gold when it shone through the high window, as if it marked her out as someone special. She was a clever girl and it was no surprise that when she left school she went to work for the Milk Board as a clerk, and ended up doing the accounts.

Yet it turned out that it was only in her career that Jessie fulfilled the promise she had shown as a girl. Her home life had been shaped by her mother in the same way that Henry's had been shaped by Fred. Mrs Harcourt made sure that Jessie, her youngest daughter, had remained unmarried in order to look after her. She saw off any young men who showed any interest, and at one time that had even included Henry, when he had made a half-hearted attempt to walk out with Jessie. She'd grown plain by the time she was twenty, thick round

319

the middle and bespectacled, but she was the same nice girl, kind and humorous and uncomplaining.

Old Mrs Harcourt was a devil, thought Henry. She'd ruled Jessie with a rod of iron, playing on her good nature and the fact that she'd got a dicky heart, and then the old girl lived until she was nearly ninety. When she was alive, she'd well and truly scotched any chance that Jessie ever had to lead her own life, but now she was gone, Jessie was making up for lost time. She'd inherited the bungalow and her mother's nest egg and, unlike Henry, she seemed to have a great appetite for life. She was always out and about: once a week on the bus into Shaftesbury to the supermarket and lunch out, a regular taxi for bingo on a Saturday night, even taking a coach trip to the Italian alps last year and bringing him back a bottle of a yellow liqueur which she said was made by monks who lived up a mountain. It was a thank you for feeding her old cat, Smokey, who sat like a warm pudding in the sun on her doorstep every day she was away, and glared at Henry through slitted yellow eyes. He and Billy had had a try of the stuff in the funny-shaped bottle but it had tasted like bitter cough medicine and it still lurked at the back of his larder. 'Centuries old, secret recipe,' Billy read off the label, holding the small print to the light. 'You could say the same for creosote, Henry. You could paint the fence with this stuff.'

Out in his shed, Henry lifted down his stepladder from where it hung on the wall and collected his hedge clippers and then set off down the road. There was a car pulled up outside Jessie's gate and when he went round to the back door she was sitting in the kitchen with a blonde girl in tight jeans standing over her, painting sections of her hair with a thick mauve paste and then winding them round tight little blue curlers. Henry had never seen anything like it. He felt as uncomfortable as if he had walked in on a secret ritual. Was it mauve hair she was going in for now?

Jessie twisted her head round as far as she could and looked under the girl's raised arm. 'Oh, it's you, Henry. Come in, love. Don't stand out there. You know Belinda, don't you? She's Stan Forrest's granddaughter.' The girl nodded to him and went on with what she was doing. 'She's come to do my perm. I'm off on Thursday for a week. Eden Project and a tour of Cornwall. Cream teas and sea views and four-star hotels, so I've got to look my best!'

Henry realised at once that this was not the moment.

He couldn't get his letter out, not in front of the silent, unsmiling girl. He had thought that he would just put the envelope on the table and say, 'Take a look at that, Jessie, and tell me what you think.' He had imagined himself waiting while she read, watching her face as she absorbed the news, but today the table was cluttered with bottles and hairdressing paraphernalia and Jessie's mind wouldn't be on it, not with all this palaver going on.

'Heard any more about Jodie Foot?' asked Jessie, although if anyone had heard anything it was much more likely to be her than Henry. 'Billy says she's going to get sent to a boarding school. Posh uniform and everything. He says it costs the taxpayer more than sending a girl to Roedean. I don't know where he gets his information from, do you? Makes up the half of it! I was coming round later,' she added 'to ask if you'd feed Smokey and keep an eye on him while I'm away. Same as usual.'

Henry nodded. She could take it for granted that *he* wouldn't be going anywhere.

'And water my hanging baskets if we get another dry spell. Thanks ever so much, Henry. I hope you don't mind me asking.'

'That's all right,' said Henry, stiffly. 'I've come round to do your hedge, seeing as it's too wet for anything else.'

'You're a good friend, Henry. What would I do without you? We'll have a cup of tea, dear, later. When Belinda's finished she'll put the kettle on, won't you, love? It's ever such a long business, a perm is. What price beauty, eh?'

'Lovely hair you used to have,' said Henry suddenly and then wondered what he was doing, blurting that out. You couldn't say it was lovely any more. Hard, dry, iron-grey curls she had these days, like little metal springs all over her head, but Jessie only laughed. 'My crowning glory, wasn't it, Henry? I didn't have much else to recommend me! It was the one thing people could say, "You've got lovely hair, Jessie!" Thick and light brown it was, Belinda, with a bit of a wave to it.'

'It's still thick, mind,' said the girl, dabbing away with the mauve brush. 'Your perm takes me twice as long as most of my other ladies.' She looked at her watch. 'I've got to keep my eye on the time. I'll be needing to get down to the school bus to collect Kia Marie at quarter past.'

Henry suddenly remembered who the girl was, that

her father worked for an agricultural contractor and that her grandad had been at school with him and Jessie. So she had a child, he thought, and he would have said that she was only a child herself. She looked like a teenager. He imagined the whole web of this interconnected local family, reaching out ever wider to each new generation, while his own family had one short branch, chopped off like a dead bough until this Betty Milward had come springing out of nowhere.

He couldn't stand here any longer like a spare part. He put his hand in his pocket and felt the edge of the envelope. It was still there. He hadn't imagined it.

'I'll be getting on then,' he said. 'Shouldn't take me long. I'll put the clippings on the compost.'

'Thanks, love, and thanks for keeping an eye on things when I'm away. Cat food is in the shed as usual. Do you hear that, Smokey? Your Uncle Henry's going to look after you.' The fat grey cat sitting in a solid lump on the kitchen counter glared back.

'He don't look too pleased!' said the girl, and she and Jessie laughed.

Chapter Ten

RACHEL KEPT OUT of Juliet's way for the rest of the morning, which was easily enough done because she was on the telephone most of the time, arguing with her brother and speaking to the ward sister about her Aunt Dot. Work was the best thing, thought Rachel. While she was working, she could keep the panicky, sick feeling at bay and the most important thing was to appear normal. She even stayed a bit later than she needed, giving the spare bedroom a good clean in case Juliet's mother was indeed coming to stay, which she guessed was most likely from the snatches of telephone conversation she overheard.

Finally, she put on her coat, gave Juliet a brief wave through the open door to where she stood, telephone clamped to her ear, and went out of the back door.

It was raining again and she turned up her collar and walked briskly. The village street was still littered with the small debris of the storm, straw and stones and twigs and leaves that had been carried in the eddies of rain-water. You could hardly believe that it was June, she thought, and that only a while ago she had cycled up this road sweating in the heat. That evening felt like the beginning of the unravelling of her life, and with disturbing clarity the row she had had with Dave came back into her mind. She remembered his criticism of her, and although at the time she had been taken aback, now his words fell into place. He was sick of her, that was obvious. His compliments and loving words since then seemed worthless in the light of her new conviction that he was having an affair. He was only like that, said those things, to keep her quiet, so that she wouldn't suspect the truth.

It was the middle of the day and the village was quiet. She passed a woman she did not know out walking a large golden retriever. They nodded at one another as they passed. All Rachel wanted was to get on home without seeing anyone with whom she had to talk, and she was grateful that as she passed the pub there was nobody about. A few cars and a very dirty Land Rover were parked outside with a black and white collie in the back. The day was so dark that they'd got all the lights on in the bar.

She hurried on. A car went past and the woman driver waved. It was the lady who was church warden or something, the one who had got her enlisted on a rota to clean the church brass. Rachel remembered how Dave had said it was a good thing to do. We're part of a community living here, he'd said, and he had offered to help when the heating in the church had gone wrong. He used to take the boys to family services when they were younger. Oh yes, he was good at being the family man. She used to stay at home and get the Sunday roast in the oven. She loved those peaceful Sunday mornings, peeling the veg and listening to the radio, with the house to herself.

She was nearly home now and as she turned into her own road she saw Henry Streeter coming towards her and then, to her relief, turning into Jessie Harcourt's gate. I ought to speak to him, she thought. One day I will, but not now, not with all this on my mind. I'm no use to anyone in this state.

She almost ran up her own garden path to the back door. The kitchen looked calm and tidy, just as she had left it, everything straight and the dishcloths put to dry over the stove. She took off her wet coat and hung it in the porch and then sat at the kitchen table. It was very, very quiet. She heard the motor of the fridge start and stop and the ticking of the wall clock. She did not know how long she sat there or what exactly she was thinking. She was waiting for something to come into her mind to tell her what to do next. Then she picked up the telephone and dialled Dave's mobile number.

'Hi, Rach!' he answered cheerily, almost at once. 'Get my message?'

'Yes. That's why I'm calling.' Although her hand shook and her breath fluttered in her chest, her voice sounded normal and unconcerned. 'What time will you be home do you think? Jamie's got football tonight, remember.'

'Oh, right. Well, can you get Ricky's dad to take him, love? I don't know what time I'll be clear of this job I'm on.'

'Where are you working?' How easily the loaded question slipped out and the trap was laid.

'I'm finishing off that loft conversion. I promised I'd have it done before Mike and his partner and kids go on holiday next week. Shouldn't take me more than a night or two. Don't worry about my tea. I'll pick up

something on my way home. Sorry, love. I've got to
go. Bye.'

Rachel sat on. Loft conversion. That's what he'd told
the police and he'd been lying then. He was using the
same lie to her now. Of course, she could get in the
car and drive to wherever it was Mike lived and check
the whole thing out, but Dave was not stupid. Mike
would be prepared to cover for him. After all, if Jodie
hadn't turned up it might have been the police who
were doing the checking. Rachel couldn't very well
demand to see what work it was that he was supposed
to be doing, not without revealing who she was and
what she suspected.

Her mind spun with loose ends of information that
began to come together and make sense. If he was doing
all this extra work for cash, then where was it? Where
did the money go? Not into their joint account where
his wages were paid once a month by direct debit. He
told her that he had opened an online savings account
but she had no evidence of it and no way she could
check his word. She had never doubted him before and
had never asked for proof, just as he never asked what
she did with the money that she earned in cash because
he knew it went straight into the housekeeping.

How did married people manage their extramarital affairs? It was supposed to be so easy with email and mobile telephones. You could make arrangements and whisper your words of love and longing, and leave no trace to be uncovered by suspicious husbands and wives. Rachel thought of all the times she had seen men drawn into lay-bys, talking on their mobiles. Businessmen, reps, and adulterers. You just had to be careful, and that was what Dave was, she realised. He was so careful. His mobile telephone was always on his belt and only switched on when he used it. When she had asked to borrow it one day when she had left hers in a shop, he had made an excuse. It had surprised her at the time but now his reluctance was a piece of evidence. He couldn't allow her to use it. It was too risky. What might she have discovered if she'd scrolled through the history of his calls and text messages?

How many times had she seen him checking his telephone and then saying he had to go out – to the pub, to the garden centre, to pick up some beer – anything, she saw now, to get him out of the house and allow him to answer a call or send a message?

Then there were all the evenings and weekends he had worked overtime. How easy it had been for him, and she had never asked questions, always accepted his word because she believed him. She got up to fetch the big diary in which she mapped their various lives. Looking over the first six months of this year she remembered all the times he had ducked out of activities with Jamie, all the evenings he had told her not to wait up for him. It had been going on for months, she could see that now. Years, maybe.

Sometimes he came home and she noticed that his hair was damp, as if he had just showered. Once she had remarked on it and he'd laughed and said that he'd put his head under the tap when he had finished work, he was that hot and dirty after crawling about amongst the rafters of a dry cleaners all day. She'd believed him then but now it made a different sort of sense.

She had to admit that she had been suspicious before. She knew it was a tendency she had struggled to check in herself ever since she and Dave first met when they were working for the same large retail group with headquarters in Woodford. She had been new in Sales and Dave was on the store shopfitting team. He'd given her a lift home one evening when there was a tube strike and it had gone on from there. She discovered that he had learnt his trade in the army and he'd been married briefly before. It took him months to persuade her that he was serious about her. She couldn't really believe it, because he had seemed so perfect.

In the early years of their marriage she had been so uncertain of his love for her that she could hardly bear it when he talked to any other female and there had been scenes and rows when he had shouted his denials and she had grown silent and withdrawn. 'You've got to get over this,' he'd told her. 'You've got to get over being suspicious and jealous all the time, or it will kill what we've got. Do you hear me, Rachel? You've got to get over it because you're doing my head in with all this crap and there's only so much a bloke can take.' God, he'd terrified her by saying that. He'd made her see that it was her fault, that it was she who had got to change.

So this was not the first time she suspected he was having an affair. Once, during a party, she had walked into the kitchen and interrupted him laughing with one of her friends. There was something about the way they were looking at each other that filled her with terrible, sick panic and she had turned and left the room. He'd come after her and pulled her back. 'Oh, come on!' he'd said. 'What's the matter, Rach? Loosen up! We were only having a laugh!'

What had she done on that occasion? She'd grown quiet and remote, drawing herself away in the hope that if she made herself invisible then the situation which she did not know how to handle would go away, and it had done exactly that. Gradually, the old easiness returned between her and Dave, and the anxiety faded away and she told herself that she had been wrong to overreact.

There had been other girls. Linda was one, their pretty blonde neighbour when they were first married and lived in Essex, who was always bumping into Dave in the road, thrusting her cleavage at him, tossing her hair and laughing. He brought her home in his van one evening, saying her car wouldn't start and she had had to abandon it in the supermarket car park. He said she'd called everyone she knew on her mobile and he was the only one who answered. He said he was driving past anyway and had picked her up and the back of the van was full of her shopping to prove it, but they had the flushed, hectic look of lovers, and Rachel could smell it on them, the smell of sex.

Dave was older than her, he'd been posted all over

the place with the army, he'd been married before, and he was confident and assured around women. It was part of what attracted her, that he was so experienced and yet it was her he wanted. He told her that she was different from all the others because she was shy and uncertain and he loved that in her. You're so innocent, he said. You're so untouched.

She wasn't fool enough, even in those early days, not to recognise that he was a man who liked women and couldn't help seeking their attention. It was part of him, part of his nature, and he wore his masculine charm like a banner, but he had taken her so gently and kindly, promising never to hurt her and she had believed in the goodness of him.

I'm sick of it all, he told her. I'm tired of one-night stands and nightclubs and easy girls. Now I want something different. I want a home and a family. I want a good woman waiting for me. I want you, Rachel. I want you to be the mother of my children. I want to look after you for the rest of our lives. I want to grow old with you. What a pair we'll be, hand in hand at eighty, and she had believed him.

So that was it. All lies. Her mother had married a man Rachel hated and had told her that she could love him too if she would only try. Her mother told her that she was difficult and possessive and spoiling her chance of happiness. Then she had died and left her, and Rachel felt her heart shrivelling like an apple neglected in the bottom of a fruit bowl. Every drop of love was squeezed out of her until she met Dave, and his handsome face and stocky body and buoyancy and confidence and assurance, his hold on life, and the amazing fact that he loved her and wanted her, had eventually persuaded her that she was not a hopeless case.

And all the time, Rachel thought, without knowing it she had kept this splinter of ice in her heart, just in case, just in case it was all lies, and now she could feel the cold spreading inside her. All she had to do was find Dave out, track him down and prove what she had really known deep down all along, that nothing and no one could be relied on and love was just something people made up because they wanted it so badly, and that their marriage had been a shallow, shaky affair from the very start.

As she roamed restlessly about the house in the grey hours of the dismal afternoon, she found she couldn't remember what it was to feel in love, or to be in love with Dave. She felt a tigerish passion for the boys. She'd die for them, no question, but towards Dave she could only touch a gaping hole where there had once been something else. It seemed as if love had never really belonged to her. It had been stitched on like a patch that had now been ripped away.

Suddenly, looking out of the landing window, she thought of Marion with her sly, knowing smile, her fat complacency, and knew that she had always guessed at the truth of Rachel's marriage, and that was why she sneered at her nice home and well-behaved boys. Marion, despite her hopeless, doomed relationships and good-for-nothing lovers, would never have been fooled as she had been. Marion kicked out any man who did her wrong, screaming abuse and throwing his clothes out of the bedroom window. She'd actually done that, Rachel remembered. There had been an unappetising pair of greying jockey shorts caught in the bare branches of the tree in her garden for months one winter, when the tanker driver she'd shacked up with got the order of the boot.

Marion and Dave were two of a kind, cut from the same cloth. They must recognise it in each other, the confidence in themselves, the unshakeable belief in who they were and what was owed to them. Even after the

Jodie affair, Marion refused to be put down by the police or the social workers or the village gossips. Cathy said that she'd heard that she was back on her stool in the pub, holding forth to anyone who would listen how the bloke should be castrated and she'd do it herself given half a chance. She was getting up a petition, she said, about victims' rights.

People like them were born with a survivor's grip on life which would always be out of her reach. She had thought she was safe when Dave had taken her on and that she could share in the strength of his convictions, but now she saw that all he had done was to make her more vulnerable. False security it had been all along and it was almost a relief to find that out. It was the relief of knowing the worst.

Now she had to work it out, her strategy. It felt as if two great forces were battling inside her head. One was the need to hang on to everything for the sake of the boys because they were all that mattered. She would suffer anything for their sake. The other feeling was so angry and destructive that it terrified her. It was the compulsion to smash and break and stamp on what held her to Dave, to expose the lies and deceit and prove once and for all that nothing lasted, and there was nothing and no one to trust. Somehow, it felt as if that would be a sort of triumph.

As she stood there, a cold little voice of reason came to her. I have got to stop myself doing anything mad and destructive. I must carry this knowledge about with me and be so quiet and secretive that no one will suspect. It's like having a terrorist bomb strapped to my middle, which could blow my whole family wide open. I must do what is best for the boys. Dave's a good father. They both love him. I must remember that. I must find a way out of all of this, even if I can't see how at the moment.

Somehow she got through the rest of the afternoon and evening. She arranged for Jamie to go to football with Ricky and cooked the boys their supper and waited for Dave to come in. When he did he made it easy for her by appearing so completely normal and unaffected by his lies.

'Hi!' he said, throwing down his bag and kissing her in passing where she stood at the sink. 'Everything all right, love? Sorry I couldn't get back to take Jamie. Go all right, did it?' He glanced at the clock. 'Christ, look at the time. I'm knackered. Got the job done though, which is the main thing.'

'Finished it, did you?' asked Rachel with her back still to him.

'Yeah. Mike's well pleased. They're off to Australia on Friday. He got a bonus, he said, from that steel stock-holders he works for and he's blowing it on a trip to see his brother who lives out there. You don't fancy Australia, do you, love? I reckon I could get a good wage out there.' He picked the morning's post off the counter as he talked and looked through the envelopes. Then he went to the fridge for a beer while Rachel watched him with a sense of detachment.

Here was a lying, cheating husband, she thought, and you would never know the difference. He could lie to her and to the boys, and let Jamie down, without a trace of guilt showing on his face. If she wished, they could go on like this for years and years, until she was old and tired and then maybe he'd tell her it was over between them. Lots of men did that. Dumped their dull old wives after long marriages and when there always seemed to be a younger woman ready to take them on.

And here she was, with the means to destroy them as a family, and he was quite unaware of it because he was so secure in his role as a great husband and father.

It seemed that he could keep the other part of his life completely separate. How can he do it, she thought, as he started to talk about the holiday, comparing prices and ferry times, telling her that they should book as soon as possible, that August was the busiest month.

Listening to him, watching his brown hands leafing through the sheets he had printed off the internet, Rachel had a sudden fear that she was mad. The gap between the truth which she had arrived at that afternoon and the fiction which posed as reality seemed too great to encompass. The kitchen was tidy, the supper things put away, the lunch boxes ready on the counter for the morning, the floor swept; everything in order and prepared for the next day of their lives. The very normality was like an anchor, holding their lives steady, but the truth could knock the whole thing sky high.

But she had to know for sure. She had given birth to this monstrous suspicion, dragged it up to the surface, and it wasn't to be buried again now; it was growing teeth and claws and becoming bigger and stronger by the minute. It occurred to her that the easiest thing would be to kill herself. She could go out now and get in the car and go somewhere to swallow pills, or gas herself, or walk into the sea until the water closed over her head, and the terrible thing would die with her and that would be the end of it.

But she couldn't do that because of the boys. Like a legacy, what she and Dave had created between them would live on after she was gone. You only had to think of Princess Diana to see how it could happen, even in an ordinary little family like theirs. It would be the boys who suffered, just like those poor princes, and she couldn't do that to them. She had to deal with this in the right way and for the moment she didn't know what she would do or how it would turn out. Watch and wait, she told herself. The calm of the kitchen re-assured her and Dave's plans for the holiday gave them something to talk about and then he watched football on television and that was the evening taken care of, manoeuvred through as if she was a secret agent on a mission or, as she had felt before, like an actress play-ing a part which bore no relation to her real life.

Lying beside him in bed, listening to his steady, untroubled breathing, Rachel wondered how the woman, whoever she was, felt about Dave going away on a family holiday. Had he told her? Would she be jealous? Would it be a reminder that he belonged else-where, to his wife and his sons? Did she even know

341

that he was married? Perhaps when he was with his lover, she and the boys no longer existed for him. She had read in the newspapers about men who were able to do that, to live fantasy lives, even to go as far as marrying bigamously and raising a second, secret family.

Across the landing her two boys slept peacefully and through the open bedroom window she could hear the church clock strike the quarter hour. The night was very dark and still. She got out of bed and went to the window. There was no moon to be seen and no stars, just murky black over the houses and gardens, farms and hills. Then she saw a light go on next door. It shone onto the square of garden at the front and she knew it would be Cathy stumbling out of her warm bed to feed little Hope.

Across the way Henry's cottage was in darkness and Rachel thought of him lying there, alone and lonely, with Fred gone, and deprived forever, she supposed, of the loving touch of another human being. We all need it, she thought, that connection to other people, or we wither and die inside, but at least then there isn't the pain of losing what you once had. She thought of what Juliet had told her about Henry. She could understand him better now, see him in a new light. No wonder he was as dry as an old stick, backwards and forwards to his allotment, hardly speaking, living on his own, not needing anyone else. He was wise, that was what. He knew that love was not intended for the likes of him and he had saved himself a lot of heartache by not pretending that it was.

A hundred miles or so away, the same murky night lay like a blanket over London, but here it was underlit by the ugly orange glow of a million street lamps. Bobbie Fairweather, who could not sleep, had very slowly come downstairs to make herself a cup of tea. She glanced out of the kitchen window as she waited for the kettle to boil; it was impossible to guess the time when the first streaks of dawn were blotted out by the artificial half-light. It was comforting that it was never dark, especially to someone who had lived in the city all of her life, and who had grown afraid of gloomy passageways and unlit streets. It had been different in the war when the blackout shrouded the whole city in complete darkness and only the beams of the anti-aircraft lights lit up the sky. Until London was burning, that is, and then the fiery glow billowing into the dark was something to dread and fear.

It was never quiet either. Although Bobbie was deaf

343

and needed her hearing aid to catch conversations, she could hear the rumble of traffic from the main road, which went on all night, the shouts of the drunks being turned out from the pubs and, much later, the clubs, the slam of car doors, the underground rumble of the tube trains when they started to run again at dawn and the sound of the police sirens that pierced the dark hours as the city lurched towards another day.

Bobbie lifted the kettle carefully. Her hands were weak and arthritic and this was one of the things that Dot did not allow her to do. Poor Dot. Bobbie thought of her lying in her hospital bed and hoped that she had been knocked out by painkillers and a sleeping pill. She would never sleep otherwise. She would be restless and fretful, worrying about everything.

It was dreadful to admit, even to herself, that she was enjoying being on her own. It made a change from being dominated all the time by her energetic older sister, and she could manage perfectly well, whatever her family said. But they would not let her be, and one of the reasons that she was wide awake now was because tomorrow morning her son, Anthony, would be arriving at ten thirty to drive her down to Dorset to stay with Juliet.

She had done her best to argue that she would rather remain in her own home but when one was old, one was easily overruled, and upstairs her case was packed and ready. Poor Juliet, she thought. What a nuisance for her to have me landing on her, the last thing she would want when she was used to living a completely independent life. In the middle of the country, too, where there would be no diversions, no nearby cafés or restaurants, no shops to browse, no libraries, nothing to help pass the day. She would have to try to be useful. She could still cook but she was slow and sometimes made mistakes, and of course Juliet didn't eat the sort of food that she was good at preparing, baked fruits and egg custards, tarts and pies, braised meats and stews. It was all too old-fashioned.

There was a time when she would have had to leave a note for the milkman to stop the milk and to cancel the newspaper, but no one delivered any more and when she tried to think of who she should tell that she was going to be away, apart from the agency who sent in the carers there was no one who would miss her. So many of her friends had died or were incarcerated in homes. At my age, she thought, I've become one of life's extras. Nothing depends upon me any more. Instead

I rely on the kindness of others and so I must be grateful that my children look after me, and after all, she was glad, really glad to be spending time with Juliet. Juliet, dear Juliet, whose life she so little understood, and who she so wished could find the happiness that Bobbie felt sure every woman yearned for. A good man, that's what Juliet needed.

Over the next few days, with the care of a detective, Rachel went through every one of Dave's pockets, collected every scrap of paper, searched every drawer and, when she had the opportunity, cleaned the inside of the van, reaching under the seats and turning out the compartments and pockets. From under the passenger seat she drew out the top of a lipstick, dusty and furred with dirt, and then her fingers found the little gold keeper of an earring. It glinted in the palm of her hand; a small, hard piece of evidence.

Don't think it, one half of her seemed to argue. You know the van was second-hand and was never cleaned out properly before Dave bought it. You know that other people have borrowed it from time to time. This isn't evidence. It's just supposition. At the same time, the warring partner in her head demanded, who is this woman? Is there more than one? Is she a friend, a neighbour, someone at work? Does she wake in the morning with a smile on her face because she has a lover like Dave, who makes her feel beautiful and sexy with his hard body and his urgent desires? Oh, I'll find out, Rachel promised the demon. I'll find out.

She carried her secret about with her but longed to share her unhappiness. She was aware that when you kept unspoken stuff in your head, you only saw things one particular way, and talking to someone was what she needed more than anything else. If only she had a sister or a really close friend to whom she could pour out what had happened, but adults who had been in care as children missed out on friends from way back, who knew them from when they were growing up.

Once or twice she was on the edge of going round to Cathy to unburden herself, but it wasn't fair to do that, not with the new baby, and there was a tiny doubt in her mind that she could really trust her, being such a talker, and belonging so firmly to the village. Rachel felt the disparity of their situations. Cathy had all the friends she needed. She might have asked Rachel to take her to the hospital but that was only because she was a neighbour. If she had a crisis in her own marriage, it would not be Rachel to whom she turned.

She thought of all the women of every age, shape and class, all over the world, who were going through the same thing. Women in mud huts and shacks in African villages, Chinese women in teeming cities, unhappy American women lying on their analysts' couches, women all over Britain, in every town and every village, who suspected that their husbands were unfaithful. She thought of them all, bitter, deceived, revengeful, discarded. Please God, she prayed, prove me wrong. Don't let me be one of them.

The first day that the weather was dry, Henry cycled to Jasmine Cottage to mow the lawn. He was concerned that it had not been cut for nearly two weeks and after all the rain it looked as if the grass had grown by inches. It would be hard work using the old mower that Dr Ballantyne kept in his shed, even though he had had the blades sharpened in the spring.

Today he would make sure that he did not get trapped by the woman staying in the cottage, whatever she said her name was. He'd make sure he kept well out of her way. It was the middle of the morning and with any luck she wouldn't be in, but when he let himself in the side gate, he could see that the kitchen door was open, and then glancing up he saw her at an upstairs window, her head bent as if she was sitting there reading.

It was an old motor mower that was a bugger to start, and after all the damp it was more stubborn than usual, but eventually he got it to spark into life and began to cut the lawn in neat straight lines, back and forth, with the upward stretch away from the cottage towards the top of the garden. He had to push hard to get up the slope with the grass as long as this, and stopped often to empty the box of clippings onto the compost heap behind the shed.

It took him longer than usual, and although it wasn't a warm morning for June, he felt hot and tired and could see his heart working overtime, his chest lifting and falling under his checked shirt. He was getting too old for this malarkey, he thought, but then what? With any luck he'd have a stroke or a heart attack and that would carry him off. Decrepit old age didn't bear thinking of.

Going back with the grass box, he looked again at the back of the cottage and saw that it wasn't the same woman sitting at the window. He could see now that

it was an elderly lady with white hair who was looking out at him and smiling and who raised a hand when
she saw that he had seen her. He gave her a nod and
went back to his work but it wasn't many minutes
before he saw Juliet coming across the grass towards
him. Bugger, he thought. This morning she was wearing sandals and a long, colourful skirt that clung to her
legs as she walked. A gypsy she looked like today, or a
fairground fortune teller.

'Good morning, Henry!' she shouted above the clattering motor. 'The kettle's on. Come and have a cup
of tea and meet my mother.'

Henry shook his head. 'Not this morning. I'd best
be getting on,' he said, not looking up.

'Oh, come on. Only for a few minutes. That looks
such hard work.'

Just at that moment the motor let him down, splut-
tering to a stop. It was overheating with the extra effort
required by the long grass.

'That's better!' said Juliet in a normal voice. 'We won't
keep you long, I promise. She has come to stay with
me for a few weeks, you see, and I know she'd like to
meet you. She went through the Blitz as a young woman.
She was in the WVS. I was telling her about your story,

and she said that she could remember the terrible acci-dent that killed your mother. Anyway, come and meet her.'

Against his will for the second time, Henry found himself following Juliet towards the kitchen, where the white-haired lady was standing at the stove wearing an apron. She turned to greet him, holding out her hand and smiling.

'Oh, my goodness,' she said, 'I've been watching you. How hard you have to work pushing that enormous lawnmower. I'm Juliet's mother, Bobbie. A cup of tea? I've made a pot. I asked Juliet to buy some proper Indian tea, which I'm sure you prefer to that horrid, weak, scented stuff she drinks. Does that look right for you?' She held out a mug of dark brown tea that was exactly as Henry liked it.

'Come and sit down. Juliet has told me what happened to you as a child. Such a sad story, but as I said to her, they were hard times, which her generation don't really understand. My father was a London vicar, you see, and he stayed there right through the Blitz and so did I. He tried to join up but they wouldn't have him – he was far too old and had very poor sight as a result of being wounded in the Great War. He had a piece of metal lodged in his head, so he claimed. He ran a soup kitchen in the crypt during the war and kept the vicarage open to anyone who needed help. Some terribly sad cases there were.'

My, she was a talker all right, thought Henry, taking the seat she indicated and watching as she moved with the aid of a stick to sit opposite him. She looked across at him with bright blue eyes, not piercing or cold, but rather soft and vague, in a face that he could only describe as sweet and open, like a pansy. She wasn't like that daughter of hers, who had gone out of the room to take a telephone call. She was like an excitable horse, all brown and bony with long arms and legs, clattering about. He'd never have guessed they were related.

'Juliet told me that you were evacuated as a child and, do you know, after I joined the WVS, we were given the job of organising the evacuation quite early on in the war. My goodness, I shall never forget it, the scenes at Victoria station. You just had to remind your-self that it was for the children's own good, but it was heartbreaking when you had to prise little fingers from a mother's sleeve, and of course the women were ter-ribly upset as well because we all knew that each farewell could be for the last time.' She touched Henry's arm. 'As it was for you and your brother, I believe.'

'Aye,' said Henry. She was easy to listen to. It was no effort because she didn't expect him to say anything in return.

'But you know,' she went on, 'the strange thing is that I can remember the Bethnal Green disaster really well. I can remember it happening. Of course, the tube station was used as an air-raid shelter all through the bombing raids and by nineteen forty-three the worst of the raids were over, but the East End of London, because of the docks, I suppose, went on being hit. It was a really deep shelter, you know. They had a canteen down there, bunk beds, even a library. One of my friends helped with the canteen and I can remember her telling me that it was terribly crowded, thousands and thousands of people took shelter there every night during the worst of it.'

Henry sat listening, his tea cooling in the mug.

'On that particular night I had been at the cinema with rather a dear friend, who was on leave. I remember it, Henry, because it was the last time I saw him. He was in the RAF and he was killed shortly afterwards. The film had just finished and we were coming out of the cinema and deciding where to go afterwards. He was in very high spirits, we both were. You had to be, because life was so uncertain, and he wanted to go on somewhere rather grand, like the Ritz, and then to a nightclub, but I was a vicar's daughter, Henry, poor as a church mouse, and the Ritz was full of debutantes, dressed to the nines, drinking champagne, so I didn't want to. I was a homely sort of girl. Instead we went to Lyons Corner House for toasted cheese and a pot of tea. Isn't it strange, dear, that I can remember all this as if it was yesterday, and yet I can't remember what day it is or where I've put my glasses?

'Anyway, as we were coming out of the cinema, the sirens went off and we ran down the road together, and took shelter under a railway arch. We didn't want to spoil our evening down in a shelter, and so we sat it out, watching the sky light up over the East End. The noise was tremendous, the loudest I think I ever heard, and then the next morning we heard that there had been a direct hit on the station and all those people, mostly women and children, had been killed.'

'But that wasn't what happened!' Henry almost shouted. 'That's what we were told, and that's what I thought for years but the station wasn't hit at all. It was panic that killed them. They were crushed in a panic to get down the steps.'

'Juliet told me that yesterday. She looked it up on the interweb, or whatever it's called. But, at the time they said it had been hit by a bomb. I don't know why it was hushed up. Perhaps the government thought the truth was too dreadful.'

They sat for a moment in silence.

'So you see,' said Bobbie. 'I've never forgotten that night and never will.' Her eyes had filled and grown glassy bright and she took a handkerchief from the pocket of her skirt and dabbed at them gently. 'I'm so sorry, Henry. Old age makes one terribly sentimental, and I live so much in the past these days. Being old is boring more than anything else. With all the time I have to sit and think, I suppose it's no wonder that I'd rather remember when I was young and had everything to live for and there was so much happening and so much excitement.'

Henry sniffed and rubbed his nose. On a rare impulse he had made up his mind what he was going to do. He took the blue envelope from his pocket and put it on the table in front of Bobbie.

'Take a look at that,' he said, and sat back to watch while her old fingers fumbled to pull out the pages.

'Glasses?' she said. 'Where are my glasses? Oh, here they are, round my neck, all the time! Now, Henry, what is this about?' and she began to read.

When Juliet came back into the kitchen she was surprised to see Henry still sitting opposite her mother at the kitchen table, and what was more they appeared to be in deep conversation. He must have been there for nearly half an hour, all the time she had been on the telephone to Gavin.

'I'm sorry,' she said, waving at the door to the hall. 'That was rather a complicated call.'

'Oh, darling,' said her mother, looking up. 'Henry and I have had a wonderful talk, and he's shown me a remarkable letter that he's just received. We've been thinking about what he is going to write in reply. I say, are you all right, Juliet? You look rather upset.'

Juliet hardly heard. She couldn't think about Henry and his wonderful letter or whatever it was, and wished very much that she was alone to collect her thoughts. She needed time and quiet to take in what Gavin had just told her, that Sonia had informed him she was leaving him. Or rather, that she had asked him to remove himself from the house, apparently for good.

It had been a bolt from the blue. 'I'm totally shell-shocked,' he said. 'We had had a perfectly pleasant week-end, people to dinner on Saturday, a concert on Sunday, and then this morning she looked across the breakfast table and said, "Gavin, you need to know that I intend to divorce you." Just like that. I thought she was joking at first, but as you know, Sonia doesn't go in much for humour.'

'But why?' said Juliet, incredulous. 'Why on earth does she want to divorce you?' Of course, there were plenty of reasons, she realised that, but which one in particular? 'Why now? What about the girls, for one thing?'

'Exactly.' Gavin's voice sounded completely despondent.

'Well? What did she say?'

'She said the girls were old enough to deal with it. She said she had discussed it with them.'

'*Discussed* it? Without telling you?'

'Yes. She made it sound as if it was an item on one of her bloody agendas.'

'She must have given you a reason! You don't just bring a marriage like yours to an end in that way. You always said it was rock solid!'

'I thought it was.'

'So what did she say? Come on, Gavin, tell me!'

'She said . . .' Juliet could hear evasion in his voice, 'that she would no longer put up with . . . various things . . . aspects of our relationship.'

'You mean your adultery?'

'In a word, yes.'

'So who has she found out about?'

'I've no idea. She didn't say.'

'Why didn't you deny it?'

'Juliet!' His tone was pleading. 'You know perfectly well. Over the years . . .'

'Yes. You've shagged for the university, haven't you, Gavin? If there was a Blue for extramarital activities, you would have earned it years ago.'

'Juliet! Please! I didn't telephone to get it in the ear from you as well.'

'Did she mention me, by any chance?'

'Mmmm. She might have done. In the past historic tense.'

'Oh, bloody hell!'

'Why? Why does it matter to you?'

'Look, Gavin, I don't want my name bandied around as a reason for you and Sonia divorcing. It simply wouldn't be fair.'

'She knows I was with a woman in the flat in London.'

'What? How could she possibly know that? Oh, shit!'

'I don't know how. She's much too clever to reveal her sources.'

'You denied it, I hope.'

'No, not exactly. I have a horrid feeling that we were set up, or I was. It seems that bloody Rupert isn't the friend I took him for.'

'Gavin! What are you saying? Who is Rupert, for God's sake?'

'Rupert Mallory. The old todger who owns the flat. Who offered it to me. Who must have bloody well known what I would use it for.'

Juliet took a deep breath. 'You mean that we were photographed or something? That there was a private detective hiding in the wardrobe? This is *ridiculous*. We're far too old for this sort of thing.'

'I don't know, Juliet. I keep telling you. She won't say. She just says she *knows*, she has *evidence*, and that she has had enough of it.'

'Oh, shit!' said Juliet again. 'Do you think she means it?'

'Juliet! You know Sonia.'

'So when does she want you to move out?'

'I have already.'

'What? You only had this conversation at breakfast this morning!'

'She said that she would give me an hour to pack a case and that she had booked a cab to take me to the station. She said that she didn't care where I went from there, and that she would contact me through the department office and at a mutually convenient time I could arrange to come back and collect my things. The whole thing was stage-managed to the last detail.'

'Bloody hell.'

'Yes.'

'So where are you?'

'At first I was going to the department but then I thought better of it. I couldn't very well arrive with a suitcase, having been turned out of my own house, could I? What sort of fool would I have looked?'

No, thought Juliet, that wouldn't suit your image at all. She wondered why she felt annoyed with him. Far more annoyed than sympathetic.

'So I caught the London train. I'm sitting in the café at the National Library having a cup of coffee. I suppose I will have to go and find a hotel. Everyone I know is away and my club is closed for a month for refurbishment.'

Almost before he said it, Juliet knew what was coming next.

'So I wondered if I could come down to you? You did invite me, if you remember.'

And now, as her mother looked at her in concern, the phone rang again. Juliet went back through to the hall and picked up the receiver.

'You have one new message,' said the electronic female voice. And then Juliet heard Sonia's unmistakable, businesslike tone. 'Ah, Juliet. You appear to be having a very long telephone call. From Gavin, I suspect. No doubt pleading his case. You've always wanted him, haven't you, so I am just ringing to tell you that he's all yours as far as I'm concerned. He has an amount of stuff here that I would rather like him to remove, and I have hired a man and van for Thursday of next week to bring it down to you in Dorset. I know it's only a rented cottage, but you should have room and if you don't, Gavin will have to arrange to put it into storage somewhere. I hope Thursday will be convenient. If not, please get in touch and we can agree on another day. Sooner rather than later, if you don't mind.'

Chapter Eleven

'DEAR COUSIN BETTY', wrote Henry, sitting at the kitchen table, the writing pad laid on a clean sheet of newspaper. He'd had to cycle into the nearest town to buy the pad and matching envelopes at the post office. He'd never had any call for that sort of thing before, but he knew the spiral notepad he'd had for years in the drawer of the sideboard was not fit for the purpose, its cheap, lined pages now furry and yellow with age. However it was good enough to use for the first rough drafts, which he now had in front of him.

Bobbie, as she'd told him to call her – although he felt uncomfortable doing so – had given him a good steer on what he ought to say. They had mapped it out together, and she had seen at once that he had to take it slowly at first, be a bit cautious, because although

Betty was a cousin, he knew nothing about her and he didn't want to say too much first off.

She was a grand old lady, Bobbie was. Henry was not one to be impressed by la-di-dah manners. He'd been a socialist all his life and if it hadn't been for the Reds behaving worse than the Nazis, he would have been a communist. He didn't hold with tugging his forelock to the gentry, and so he wasn't what he would call well-disposed to get along with her, a lady who came from what he thought of as the upper class.

But he saw at once that she was a lady in every sense of the word, with the charm and manners that went with it. She had put him at ease at once with her chatter and her sympathy and understanding that went just far enough not to make him feel awkward. Instead, it seemed that she welcomed the opportunity to share her memories with him and what she told him had led him to get the letter out of his pocket. After all, she had been part of what the letter was about. She'd heard the guns and seen the sky light up over the East End on the very night his mother had been killed.

Henry couldn't believe that Bobbie remembered that night in particular and that it had stayed with her all these years because it had been special for her too, what with losing her young man immediately afterwards. He was glad now that Jessie had been having her hair done, because if she hadn't been sitting there with mauve paste all over her head, his letter would have ended up on her kitchen table. As it turned out, it was Bobbie who was the right person to help him. He couldn't believe the luck of it; and there he had been, he chided himself, miserable old bugger that he was, doing his damnedest to avoid meeting her.

With many long pauses for thought, he wrote.

Your letter was a great surprise to me. After all these years, I have got accustomed to thinking of myself as having no family after Fred passed away on May 23rd two years ago. He had cancer and had not been well for a long time. The end was quick and he died at home which is what he wanted.

I am sorry that I can't remember you as a baby, but remember Fred and me were evacuated before you were born and our Mother wasn't one for writing letters to give us the news. I remember your mother well. She was our Mother's favourite sister and was around our house a lot in those days. She was a laughing, happy person – not a care in the world.

I am glad she was with her on that night. It is a comfort to know that Mother had family by her, Fred and me being so far away. We were not told the Truth of her death, not until years later, and to this day I do not know where she is buried. This is something that you might know and I should be grateful for the information. I sometimes feel that Fred and I were like forgotten boys to the rest of the family, but then, everyone had their troubles and new lives to make after the war.

As to my own life, it has not amounted to much. Fred and I stayed put here after the war. We were advised we had nothing to go back to, so better to stay. We had to make our own way. Fred had small jobs, being 'simple' but a good worker. I am now retired and keep busy with gardening and maintenance work here and around. I never married, what with Fred, and there being no opportunity. I own my own house and have all I want, but not what you would call well off.

As to Mother's bits and pieces, wedding ring

etc. I would like to have something of hers and to see the photographs. Perhaps we could meet and have a chance to get to know each other? I have only been to London on the one occasion – to travel with a Guernsey cow to the Dairy Show in 1978 – but I daresay I could go again. There is a train goes to Waterloo, or coach from Wincanton to Hammersmith. The coach is cheaper but there's only the one in the morning. Just let me know what you think is best. I haven't, as yet, thanked you for writing to me. I am very grateful that you took the trouble.

Yours ever,

Cousin Henry

It had been Bobbie who had helped him with how to sign off. He didn't like 'yours faithfully' or 'yours sincerely' that was for business letters, and 'with love' wasn't right at all – not for a lady he had never clapped eyes on, even if she was family, and what she had put, 'affectionate greetings' and all that, didn't sound right coming from a man.

He had decided not to put anything about the war years and the Bettses. That didn't need to come out, not now or ever. He hadn't commented on the family news because none of it meant anything to him after all these years. They had all turned their backs on him and Fred and he couldn't forgive them for that, and he didn't care what happened to any of them. It had been Bobbie's idea that he and Betty might meet in London. 'I think it would be best, Henry. You could get up on the train or the coach. Juliet says it only takes a little over two hours and you could have lunch somewhere and a chance to chat and get to know one another. I think it's wise to leave visiting each other's homes until later. After all, you might find that you don't want to take this contact any further, in which case it is better not to raise false hopes in Betty. She talks about being lonely, and you know, after one loses one's husband, one can be desperate for other relationships and maybe that's what has prompted her to write to you. I suppose it's about trying to replace a little of what you've lost. After my husband died, my sister Dot insisted that I move in with her and, you know, it was a mistake. I was vulnerable at that time and hated being on my own.' She had paused and looked at Henry knowingly, head a little on one side. 'But, my dear, you'll understand exactly what I mean because you lost your life's companion, didn't you? Your brother. And not very long ago, Juliet told me. I'm so sorry.'

With most people who tried that tack, Henry would have clammed shut and bolted at the first opportunity, but Bobbie was so gentle and kind and her chatter just went on, and she poured him another mug of tea and Henry, for the very first time since Fred died, felt something shift and loosen in his heart.

He reread his letter. There were several things that worried him about it. He didn't much like the way he had stated his position; that he owned his own house but wasn't well off, but had all he wanted. It struck him as out of place to write like that, but Bobbie had pointed out that he should make it clear that he did not want anything material from Betty. There are people who cultivate friendships with long-lost relatives because they hope to benefit financially, she had said, and it would be reassuring for Betty to know that he was not going to take advantage of her in any way. He would never have thought of that. That was a woman's point of view for you.

He was more worried about the phrase 'get to know one another'. He didn't know what was meant by it. Surely Betty had told him all he needed to know about herself, and he'd done the same in his reply. For a man who could sit in a crowded pub week after week, year after year, and down a pint in silence, this idea of getting to know people was a mystery, but Bobbie said that was what Betty would want to hear. 'She'll feel nervous about meeting you, Henry, of course she will. It's very brave of her, I think, to write to a man who is really a stranger, and offer friendship. You must reassure her that you want to get to know her as well.'

He wasn't at all confident about going to London. The very idea made him feel panicked. He imagined the crowds and the streets and the traffic and wasn't sure that he could go through with it. The furthest he had been for years was Yeovil in one direction and Weymouth in the other, and even then he'd been on a coach trip and herded about like a sheep. How would he ever manage on his own? He'd end up getting a train in the wrong direction, like Billy's brother, Stan, who went to Exeter instead of Waterloo, and only discovered his mistake when he noticed after an hour or so that the landscape outside the train window was getting greener and less populated, the hills were higher and there were more sheep, when he'd expected the opposite. The London Eye, he was supposed to be going on, with his daughter meeting him off the train at Waterloo and half frantic with anxiety. But Bobbie seemed quite confident that he could manage the journey without mishap, even offering to accompany him. 'Look, dear,' she said. 'I am well over eighty but if you help me in and out of the carriage and give me your arm when I need it, I'll go with you. I've lived in London all my life and Dot and I use public transport every day. In fact, I've never owned a car. There's nothing to be worried about. It's what you're used to, you see. If you put me in a field of cows, I'd run a mile!' They'd had to laugh at that. Run a mile, when she could only shuffle about the kitchen with the aid of a stick and holding on to something all the time!

He read his finished letter through again. It had taken a long time to write and his hand felt cramped from gripping the Biro. He was quite pleased with his handwriting which was neat and legible, nothing to be ashamed of there, but he still had a sense of unease about the correspondence and a feeling of dread about where it all might end and what it would require of him. His very nature rebelled against it and if it hadn't been for Bobbie and her optimistic outlook, he would have given up and not replied at all. As it was, he had promised that he would get on down and show her the finished copy before he put it in the postbox. Four o' clock in the afternoon the post was collected, although from his observation of the post van, it could be any time at all.

Taking up his pen, he added a postscript: 'The missing lass turned up safe and sound.'

'I'm not going with them,' said Pete, lying in Honor's arms in her narrow bed. 'I don't know how they can think I want to. I mean, it's not real, is it? I'm not that sad, to want to go on holiday with my family.'

Honor said nothing. This was a particular battle she had never had to fight. Her parents were already golfing and arguing their way round Spain and she was supposed to be staying with her friend Mel for two weeks. 'I don't know,' she said. 'Mine were a bit too keen to want to go without me, to be honest. It was cheaper to book out of school holidays.' She sounded a bit wistful. 'My mum gave me that talk, you know, about knowing she could trust me, and for the first time in my life, I thought, well, fuck it, maybe I *will* throw a party while they're away and invite everyone I know to come round and bring their smackhead friends. I mean, why should she trust me? I'm seventeen, for God's sake. If she can trust me now, how sad is that?' Pete smiled and stroked her arm. It was an ongoing theme that Honor was sick of being thought of as responsible.

'What would they say if they knew that we were doing this?' he asked.

'All they'd want to know is if we were practising safe sex,' sighed Honor, 'and after that, I don't think they would mind. In fact, my mother has been longing to give me sex advice since I was about nine. She thinks I'm retarded or something. I've really disappointed her by keeping her waiting this long to show how liberal and unshockable she is. You know, she would really much rather be my sister than my mother.'

'I'm glad you waited,' whispered Pete into her hair, which he wound round his arm in a thick hank and held against his face.

'Anyway, how is it at home now? Has everything settled down after the Jodie thing? What's the talk in the village? Has anyone seen her since it happened?'

'She was back for a few days but she kept indoors. Karen was the only one who saw her and she said she was all right. She's started at this special school now. They send a taxi for her on a Monday morning and bring her back on a Friday. Nobody even talks about her any more. She's, like, yesterday's news.'

'I suppose that's good, then.' She paused. 'Pete?'

'Yeah?'

'That stuff about the bus on the journey home. The stuff that got you so upset.'

'Yeah? What about it?'

'Was there more to it than what you said?'

'What do you mean?' Pete felt his whole body tense.

'It's just something that Gary's been saying. That Jodie and Karen had been whispering stuff about your mum and dad. Winding you up.'

'Honor, please.' He closed his eyes. 'That was all such bollocks. Please.'

'OK. Sorry. I thought maybe you wanted to talk about it.'

'I don't, because it's bollocks. It was stuff that Jodie's mother was saying. She's a right cow, an old slapper. She's jealous of my mum, that's all. I didn't want Jamie to hear because he might have believed it and got upset.'

'What sort of thing?'

'That Jodie's mum fancied my dad and stuff like that. That she thought he was up for it because he didn't get it at home.'

Honor pulled a face. 'Pathetic. As if she would know! Some people just can't bear it, can they, when other people seem to be happy.'

'I don't know whether they are. How can you tell with your parents, what's going on between them? Mum is the same as usual and Dad's out a lot. He does a lot of overtime. They're like married couples are, I suppose, just doing their thing.'

'At least they don't row all the time, like mine do. God, can you imagine this holiday they're on? Mum didn't want to go golfing anyway, so she was arsey before they even left the house. I don't know why they don't just call it a day, really. It isn't as if they're staying together because of me. I wouldn't mind if they split up. In fact, divorce is one of my fondest dreams. It couldn't be worse than them fighting all the time, could it? I sometimes imagine each of them in a nice little house with a room for me, one in London, preferably, and one down here in the country, and both anxious to make it up to me – you know, coming from a broken home and being damaged for life. It would be good, wouldn't it? I'd exploit them without mercy.'

They both laughed.

'Anyway, I'm not going,' said Pete again. How could

he want to go on holiday with his *family*, for fuck's sake? Not when he and Honor had started sleeping together and all he wanted to do was spend all day, every day, in bed with her.

'Shall we go somewhere?' he said. 'Shall we go like camping or something? Why don't we go to Cornwall? Get your mum to lend you her car and we could go away, just the two of us.'

'Yes,' said Honor. 'I'd thought of that too.' The pale grey walls of her bedroom suddenly glowed with a yellow light which fell in a warm slant across their naked bodies. Honor dipped her fingers into its golden shaft and felt the heat on her skin. 'Lovely sun! At last! I was beginning to think we'd had the summer.'

'It hasn't even started,' said Pete, kissing her neck. He felt as if his whole world, everything he cared about, was here in this narrow bed.

Juliet waited for a long time after Henry had gone back out to the garden before she went back into the kitchen to face her mother. She felt physically shaken by the message from Sonia, and very angry, too. How dare she treat her in such a high-handed manner? For goodness' sake, she had gone through agonies of conscience before breaking up with Gavin because he was married; it was a bit much for Sonia to start treating her as the guilty party now, when she'd had only such very temporary possession of him. I've seen him about five times in two years, she thought. Sonia can't suddenly make me responsible for what has happened between them.

'What's the matter, darling?' asked Bobbie. 'You seem awfully upset. Who was that on the telephone? It's not bad news about Dot, is it?'

'No, no. Nothing like that,' Juliet said irritably. Did her mother imagine that everything that went on in her life revolved around her and her ancient aunt? Old people could sometimes seem so self-centred. Her mind was working furiously. Of course she wanted to see Gavin, to give him the support he needed, and now she had time to get used to the idea, she was terribly glad that it was to her that he had turned. After the extraordinary message from Sonia she knew that they must stand together and she had started to like the idea very much, that for the first time he really needed her. She would be his ally and best friend as well as everything else and she began to feel elated at the thought. It was the presence of her mother that made things difficult.

How could she and Gavin sort this thing out, or even enjoy being together, if they were shut up in a small cottage in the middle of nowhere, with her mother as an elderly chaperone? On the other hand, she loved her mother dearly and it made her feel quite awful to want her out of the way, or treat her as a nuisance, when she had only just arrived. She felt completely torn between desire and duty, and the demands of love of two different kinds.

'I'm so sorry I snapped at you, Mother,' she said. 'That was a friend on the telephone, an old friend, who has run into a crisis in his personal life. He was asking to come here for a few days. I haven't said yes, but I very much want to help him, and see him, in fact.' Bobbie sat listening, her head cocked in an alert fashion. What on earth does she make of all of this? thought Juliet. She ploughed on. 'What I think would be a much better idea, given that he needs time to think and sort things out, is that he and I go away for a few days. I don't know where. Not abroad – Cornwall or somewhere.'

Isn't this cottage 'away' enough for anybody? thought Bobbie. It seemed very much away to her. Then she suddenly realised that 'away' meant *away from her*. This man was a lover, of course. She could see it now, the awkwardness of having to share a small space, and her just being there, an unwanted third party at every meal and every moment of the day.

'Oh dear. I was determined not to be a problem to you, Juliet. I knew I should have stayed in London. I was perfectly all right on my own, if only you all hadn't fussed so about me.'

'Don't be silly,' said Juliet, quite crossly again. 'I love having you here. You know that. Only, you can see that in this case . . . and it will only be for a few days. I'll have to see if I can find an agency to help – you know, to provide an emergency carer. Some nice lady who could come and live-in.'

'Juliet, please!' Bobbie's voice was exasperated. 'Don't treat me as if I need a keeper. I'm not completely in-capable. I can look after myself perfectly well for a few days.'

'Well, maybe not live-in care, but someone to come in morning and evening and do your shopping, help you up and down the stairs, be here while you have a bath. That sort of thing. I can't just go off and aban-don you, you can see that.' Juliet's tone was kind now. She felt awful that she had been irritable.

Bobbie was silent. She wasn't stupid and knew that she needed help, especially in this inconvenient cottage with its steep stairs and uneven floors and lack of hand-holds and all the things which made living in the London house so much easier for an elderly person. And plonked in a village in the middle of nowhere, where she knew no one! Why had Juliet insisted she come here, only to make her feel a nuisance? All her life, Bobbie had fallen in with other people's plans for her, and more fool her, often knowing in her heart that things would be better done differently.

Seeing her stricken face, Juliet threw her arms round her mother. This was all Sonia's fault. 'Look, Ma, I'll do a bit of ringing round and see what I come up with. Just don't worry and please, please, don't let me make you feel a nuisance, because you're not, I promise. It's just that . . . well, I'm sure we can arrange something, and if I can't, I shall have to tell Gavin that I can't go away with him. It's not the end of the world. Now why don't you go and sit in the sitting room and I'll bring you a glass of sherry. I think we could both do with one, don't you?'

Bobbie allowed herself to be led to an armchair where she sat obediently, her ankles crossed and her hands in her lap, like a good child. She stopped speculating about Juliet and her mysterious man in a crisis. Talking to Henry had brought back a defining moment when she might have altered the course of her own life. That one night she had shared with Roddy had remained with her, and would to her dying day, which, when she thought about it, was probably not that far off. She had been a young, married woman then and utterly and totally in love with a man other than her husband. That night, after they had made love in a London hotel, she had promised him that after the war she would divorce Stephen and marry him, and put right what she could see had been a terrible decision, taken because she was sorry for Stephen, heroically enlisting and going off to fight, and thinking he was so in love with her. She would have gone through with it too, despite her mother's conviction that a divorced daughter was worse than if she had fallen under a bus.

Then fate intervened and Roddy had been killed days afterwards, shot out of the sky in his aeroplane somewhere over the Channel and his body never found, and that had been that. A door slammed shut and the different life that she had only glimpsed was gone forever.

Stephen came back after the war was over and they picked up the pieces and went on. Nobody, not a living soul, knew about that decision she had made, and Henry was the first person to whom she had ever even mentioned Roddy.

'So who is this friend of yours?' she asked Juliet when she came back with two glasses of sherry on a tray and a dish of salted almonds.

'He's a man I've known for years. A married man,' said Juliet, almost defiantly.

'Really? You know, darling, you don't have to sound defensive. I'm hardly likely to be shocked.'

'Oh, Mother!' Juliet, sighed. How could Bobbie, with her own tremendously conventional married life, possibly understand the awful complexities of her situation?

'Are you in love with him?'

'I used to be. Very, but it wasn't possible. He was married, as I said, with children and so on, and I don't know whether I love him any more. I've spent an awful lot of time training myself not to.'

'Oh, I see.'

'What do you see? I thought you'd ask me what's changed. Let me tell you. His wife has just told him she wants a divorce. Completely out of the blue. It's a situation that he never expected and was quite unprepared for, and so he is in a state of shock. He's turned to me more as a friend than a lover and that's how I want to help him – as a friend.'

Wanting to go away together so desperately seemed to suggest that Juliet had in mind something a bit more than friendship, Bobbie thought, but she didn't say anything.

As if she'd read her mind, Juliet took a gulp of sherry and said, 'But it doesn't sound like that, does it?' She gave a short laugh. 'As you can see, I'm in a fearful muddle about him.'

'And what about his feelings for you?'

'Good question. I don't know that either. He did love me, I'm sure, but wanting someone who is out of bounds is different, isn't it? If he suddenly finds himself free, and me served up on a plate . . . oh, I don't know.'

'You said you've known him for a long time.'

'Yes, I have. Since I was twenty-four. Nearly thirty years. From when I was first at Oxford. He was a young don then, and is still there, as a rather older one.'

Here was the answer, then, thought Bobbie. This man was the reason Juliet was still single and living in New York. She suddenly felt terribly sad that so much that her daughter had to offer had been lost by loving the wrong man.

'And you never – oh, what is the expression you all use – managed to "move on", as it were?'

'Of course I did,' said Juliet, needled. Her mother was talking as if her life had been wasted. 'I haven't sat around moping, for goodness' sake. I've met a lot of other men, some of whom I've also loved, but never quite like Gavin. He became a sort of benchmark, and I've never been prepared to settle for anything less.'

Anything less, thought Bobbie. That's exactly what she had settled for, and it hadn't been so bad, although guilt had played a part in her resolve to be a good wife to Stephen.

'Does his wife know about you?'

'Yes. Apparently. I don't know that she knows I cleared off because I was sick of the deceit and lies. As much for myself as for her and the children. It was made clear from the beginning that Gavin would never leave her and I told myself that it was enough to be his mistress, but it turned out not to be, and I was consumed with guilt. It was a no winner, really.'

'But you remained lovers?'

'Very part-time. I went halfway round the world to

avoid it being anything more. Also, Gavin's a serial adulterer, Mother. If it hadn't been me, it would have been someone else.'

'Oh dear.'

'Yes.'

'He's obviously a very good lover.'

Juliet could hardly believe she was having this conversation with her mother of all people.

'Honestly!' she protested. 'What a thing to say!'

'Don't be prudish, Juliet! What I am trying to say, dear, is that truly wonderful sex is an immensely powerful thing, and once experienced, not to be underestimated. It can alter everything.'

Juliet stared at her mother. What on earth was she getting at? How could she know?

'Yes, well, he is,' she said rather brusquely.

There was a silence while the extraordinary nature of their conversation seemed to charge the atmosphere in the room.

'Go away with him, then. Have what time you can together and wait and see how you feel afterwards. It can't do any harm and might do you some good.'

'I have to admit that that was my first reaction.'

'And your wretched old mother is standing in your

way! Oh dear, Juliet. This is too awful. I insist that you take me back to London where I can manage perfectly well on my own, as I said from the beginning. You could have him here with you, couldn't you, if it wasn't for me?'

'Well, yes, I could, but it isn't only you. I don't know whether I can bear to start it all over again.' Juliet stood up and moved restlessly to the window where she stood looking out. 'I have put an awful lot of effort into building a life independent of Gavin and half of me tells me that I don't want him back. You could describe him as an ageing philanderer, whose wife has very sensibly seen the light. I'm afraid that he's boyfriend material only, and actually, "boyfriend" seems a ridiculous term to use for someone rather stout, in his fifties. It suggests arrested development, doesn't it, which is probably pretty apt, come to think of it. For both of us.'

'I see. Well, you are both older now and perhaps wiser and maybe, Juliet, this is your time. Perhaps if he had had you he would not have needed anyone else.'

'I think you're being very charitable, Mother, and characteristically kind.'

'Well, do be a bit understanding. Poor chap. He needs his friends now.'

'Yes, I know.' Juliet sighed. 'He can be terrific fun and extremely charming, but at the moment he can think only of his own situation. He simply can't believe that he's out on his ear.'

'Oh, Juliet, invite the poor man to stay even if you don't love him, and I'll look after him. I can take out my hearing aid and let him talk. That's what men in his position need to do.'

What can Mother possibly know about 'men in his position', thought Juliet, amused. She got up and refilled their sherry glasses and realised that she felt much better and calmer. She would never have imagined that talking to her mother about Gavin could be either useful or helpful. But then Bobbie had a way with people. Look at how she had been with Henry, for example.

'You certainly had an astonishing effect on Henry, Mum. Rachel, the sweet girl who comes to clean, told me that he's really rather a strange old man, almost a recluse. He's terribly wary of me. I practically had to herd him into the kitchen with a stick the other morning and I was only trying to get him out of the wet and offer him a cup of tea.'

'Strange? No, he's not. He's lonely, that's all. He's

coming round later to show me his reply to the letter he's received from a long-lost cousin.'

'Oh, yes, that business about his letter,' said Juliet. 'You'll have to tell me . . .' but Bobbie could see that she wasn't really interested in Henry. She had too much else on her mind.

'Do you know, I'm just wondering about Rachel,' said Juliet. 'Whether *she* would be able to come in and out while I'm away. I might give her a ring.'

'I thought I could make a crumble with those wrinkled apples you have in the fruit bowl,' said Bobbie, changing tack. 'Do you have some plain flour?'

'Oh, goodness,' said Juliet. 'I don't usually bother too much about lunch. A bit of bread and cheese does me . . . and I know for sure that I didn't buy any flour,' but Bobbie had already got out of her chair and was heading through to the kitchen, her stick tapping like Blind Pugh. She began to search in the larder.

'Wonderful!' she said, emerging with a packet in her hand. 'Plain and self-raising! I am rather warming to this Dr Finlay.'

'Ballantyne.'

'What?'

'It doesn't matter.'

'Juliet, dear, you go and get on with whatever you have to do. I'm very happy pottering about here. Now all I need is a pie dish. Where do you think I would find one?'

When Juliet at last escaped, she went to her bedroom and closed the door and lay on the bed, feeling guilty. She wished she was nicer, and more patient; she should also be getting on with her research, which so far had amounted to nothing at all. She hadn't even telephoned to make an appointment to go over to the great house and view the library, and assess the quantity and quality of the source material to be found there. Now, in no time at all she would be going to the station to meet Gavin off the London train, which in itself was fine – what she had wanted, in fact, when she first saw the cottage – but not under the present circumstances, which seemed dangerously out of control.

Ever since she had arrived in the village things had gone wrong, starting with the missing child, although she supposed that particular drama had ended as well as it could possibly have done. She regretted that she had been so eager to make contact with Gavin, and their afternoon in London now seemed like a disaster.

How could Sonia possibly have known that it was her he had taken to the horrible flat that afternoon? Sonia's claim that she had *known all along* came back to her. Juliet thought about the various occasions over the years when she had been invited to the Oxford house and had been met with kindness and graciousness. Had Sonia known then that she was Gavin's mistress? If so, had Sonia decided that she was not a sufficient threat, merely a passing fancy on her husband's part, which was best allowed to run its course? How humiliating that was, to be so demeaned, as if she was just one of the many university women, often needy and un-stable, who became a nuisance because they were in love with him. Sonia's saintliness, her kindness to these females, often taking them up as if they were one of her good causes, was one of the most powerful weapons in her arsenal, coming directly below a) the girls and b) her private income. How she reduced their appeal by her patronage! Juliet had heard her doing it. 'What a dear little thing that Ginnie Trevis, is. So pretty and bright. Weren't you at Trinity with her father, Gavin? I've asked her to lunch on Sunday.' Thus she delivered the fatal blow to a blossoming affair.

Why, Juliet wondered, had she been chosen by Sonia

to inherit Gavin when she was fed up with him? It felt like a children's party game and as if she was the one holding the parcel when the music stopped. And how had Sonia discovered where she was staying? Was Juliet, as the most recent recipient of her husband's favours, the one to get him gift-wrapped and delivered to her doorstep? Or had Sonia always known that Gavin genuinely loved her and yet had stuck to his wife and family out of a sense of duty, and that now she no longer wanted him herself she had decided it was Juliet's turn?

She also had to think about what to do about the threatened van load of Gavin's belongings. If he could not deflect its arrival, then the whole lot would have to go in the back of Hector's garage. There was room, she had already checked. After all, Hector was supposed to be a friend, and wouldn't begrudge Gavin a bit of storage space in a crisis, and at the end of her stay she could just go back to New York and leave the pair of them to sort it out. Under no circumstances would she speak to Sonia direct. She would ignore the telephone call and maintain a dignified silence. She would refuse to be drawn into the marital wrangling and would neither confirm nor deny Sonia's accusations.

Oh, hell, she thought, closing her eyes. This is all so bloody ridiculous. We are *old*, all of us! At our age, a century ago, we might have expected to be dead, and here we are behaving like . . . she couldn't think of a suitable word. *Teenagers*, maybe, but it was *fools* that came to mind. More than anything else, the whole thing seemed such an exhausting waste of time.

She got off the bed and went out onto the landing to the head of the stairs.

'Mother!' she shouted down, but the radio in the kitchen was turned up. She ran down and opened the kitchen door.

'Apple crumble is a lovely idea,' she said to her mother who was busy rubbing butter into the crumble mixture. 'But let's have it for supper tonight. It's a dish to cheer up the old adulterer, don't you think? A comforting nursery pud?' Perhaps she hadn't heard properly, but Bobbie turned and smiled.

Bobbie would have liked to have gone upstairs and had a rest after lunch, as she was used to doing at home, but by the time she and Juliet had cleared the table and done the washing up, Henry appeared at the back door with his letter in his hand.

'Come in, dear!' she said. 'We are just about to have some coffee. Would you rather have tea?'

But Henry wanted neither. He loomed awkwardly over her as she sat at the kitchen table and slid the folded sheets of paper out of the envelope and read what he had written.

'That is perfect, Henry,' she said when she had finished. 'You couldn't have done better, and you have put your address and postcode very clearly for Betty's reply. It's better, I think, don't you, not to put a telephone number? I always think a telephone call can catch one terribly off guard, and you want time to think before you make the arrangements to meet her.'

Juliet overheard 'the arrangements to meet her' as she passed by the open door. What were they hatching, the pair of them? It sounded as if her mother was running a dating agency with Henry as her first, and most unlikely, client.

'So you think it will do?' Henry asked anxiously.

'It's perfect! Exactly right. I'm sure she will reply very quickly and, I hope, agree to meet you in London. I don't know exactly where it is that she lives, but somewhere in Greater London, so it can't be hard for her to get herself into the centre. She might say that she will meet you off the train. That would be good, wouldn't it?'

Henry nodded. He had already planned that he would take Betty some vegetables from the garden. The best, mind. A few polished onions, a handful of beans, a lettuce, half a dozen new-laid eggs. The sort of things you couldn't get in town. He'd taken his tweed jacket into the dry cleaner's and he'd got a good shirt, ironed and ready in his wardrobe.

'When she does reply,' said Bobbie, 'we'll plan the next stage, and one thing, Henry dear, if I might make a suggestion? Is there a barber in the little town you shop in? I think you should get a haircut. A good trim. You've got such a fine head of hair, but it's a little unruly, isn't it?'

Henry supposed that it was. He cut his hair himself with the kitchen scissors, the wiry silver clumps falling onto a folded newspaper placed over the bathroom basin and then emptied onto the compost heap.

'We'll get you properly spruced up. You're a very good-looking man, you know. I'm allowed to say that at my great age! You remind me very much of Sir Anthony Eden, but stronger. He was rather weak about the chin.'

Henry didn't know what to think. Good-looking! No one had ever said that to him. A great scarecrow, more like. He picked up the envelope and sealed it. 'I'll be off to the postbox, then,' he said, flustered.

'Yes, off you go! Henry, I think I am as excited as you are!' and Bobbie clapped her hands. 'You must promise to come and tell me the minute you get a reply!'

My goodness, she thought as she went slowly up the stairs to her room, this was all turning out to be quite a to-do. First Henry, and then Juliet and her crisis with her married man. For excitement, it certainly beat the life she and Dot had led for the past years. Although their carer Olga had a young man with a drug habit, an illegal immigrant from the Balkans, who had turned violent and come round and beaten at their front door with an iron bar. Dot had shouted at him from an upstairs window and called the police, but he had long gone by the time they arrived.

Bobbie reached her room and closed the door. She took off her shoes, which was an effort in itself, and lay full length on the bed. She felt extremely tired and also guilty that she had hardly thought about her sister, languishing in hospital. Later she would ask Juliet if they could telephone the ward to see how she was. Poor

Dot. How she would fret about what she was getting up to without her. I can never let you out of my sight, Bobbie, she was always complaining, without you starting to talk to someone and getting involved in something.

Poor Dot. So in love with that horrid headmistress, all those years. All that quarrelling and taking umbrage, and all for love. How foolish it was. And then Juliet and her Oxford don. It seemed that however clever you were, it was no guarantee that you would run your life wisely. Cleverness and good sense rarely went hand in hand.

After Roddy, Stephen had been so very dull, but he was a good husband and a kind man and she hoped that she had been a good wife. But she was so terribly, terribly glad that she had known what passion felt like. Apart from the love for children and grandchildren, which sprang from a different compartment of her heart, Bobbie knew it was the most precious and wonderful thing she had ever experienced. Of course, it might not have lasted. If things had turned out differently and Roddy had survived, she would have gone through with her decision to divorce, and she would have married him, and what then? Would the rapture have lasted? Would marriage and a mortgage and children and a dull career in the City have killed it off? She would never know.

The few days that they had stolen together when he was home on leave and the one glorious night was all that she had. Even now, sixty years on, she could relive every moment. She could remember his smooth young body in her arms and how they had both wept after making love. If only she could arrange it, she thought, closing her eyes, she would make sure that she was thinking of Roddy as she breathed her last. With great certainty she knew that he would have been thinking of her as his burning plane pitched towards the cold grey sea. For sixty years she had thought of him as her lover, and she loved him as much today as she ever had.

She must have dropped off to sleep because when she woke she saw that the light through the bedroom window had dimmed and that it was now evening. She wondered whether Juliet had collected her Oxford man from the station. She lay and listened but could hear nothing. What a nuisance it was to be so deaf. She supposed that she would have to powder her face and tidy herself up and go downstairs to meet him. She had no intention of keeping them company and being an unwanted third. She didn't feel in the least hungry and would come early to bed with a little something on a tray.

Despite her rest, she felt very tired and weary as she reached for her stick and attempted to get up from the bed. What an effort everything was, and how horrid her ankles looked, swollen out of recognition, whereas once they had been so slender and shapely. Poor Dot had always had thick legs, even as a girl. That was why she took to wearing trousers all the time, and perhaps that, in turn, was what encouraged her to become a lesbian. Or maybe it all happened the other way round.

Shuffling across the landing to the bathroom, she thought of her sister again, alone and fretful in hospital, and felt a wave of affection. Oh, yes, she loved Dot, too, despite her bossiness. A tremendous lot. It was wonderful, really, how much love of differing sorts could be contained in a human heart.

Chapter Twelve

THE NEXT MORNING a pale sun bathed the back of Jasmine Cottage in a gentle warmth and it was pleasant enough to sit outside for breakfast. Juliet, making toast in the kitchen, remembered how she had pictured this very scene: Gavin and herself, a night of wonderful sex behind them, enjoying the peace and tranquillity of the pretty garden, their bare feet touching under the table. She certainly hadn't imagined her mother there as well.

She could see the two of them now through the open window, lover and mother, chatting to one another quite comfortably. They appeared to be getting on so well, she thought, that at any moment Gavin would be suggesting that they take Bobbie to Cornwall with them. She had already tackled her mother on that subject and told her that she had managed to arrange for Rachel to come in two or three times a day for the short time she planned to be away. 'She'll see that everything is all right and do any housework or shopping. We'll only be gone four days or so. Now are you sure that you don't mind me leaving you?'

'Of course not.' Bobbie said. 'It's very good of Rachel, but what a nuisance I am.'

'Mother! Don't say that! I feel bad enough about it as it is, but you can see that this is a bit of a crisis. I really can't have Gavin staying here – not in the current circumstances. Anyway, Rachel was quite happy about it. Her boys are at school all day. She can see them off in the morning and be there when they get back as usual. She said she would be quite glad of the extra money. They are going away on holiday next month and it must cost a fortune, feeding teenagers and keeping them in their designer clothes and those vast trainers that cost a hundred quid a shot.'

Now as Juliet made the coffee she realised that she felt extremely tired, with the thick-headed, prickly-eyed exhaustion of hardly having slept all night. They had drunk far too much the evening before and the moment they had got into bed, Gavin had fallen asleep, humped over onto her side of the mattress and leaving her only a narrow space in which to try and get comfortable. His penis lay limp against his thigh. All the trouble it had caused, she thought, looking at it, nestling there so innocently. All the angst and muddle and suffering, as well as all the pleasure.

The alcohol made her heart race and her blood pound in her ears against the pillow, and she knew she would not sleep for hours. Before too long, Gavin began to snore and then to twitch, like a dog dreaming of rabbits, and she gave him a sharp dig with her elbow. He turned over then and she studied his plump naked back, covered with freckles across the shoulders, and his grey hair curling into a duck's arse at the nape of his neck. Poor Gavin, he had done his best during the evening, but he had been totally wrong-footed by Sonia's *coup de force* and was unable to think or talk of anything else. He kept trying to telephone her. The signal on his mobile was intermittent so he disappeared out of the back door to the top of the garden and walked about up there with the damned thing pressed to his ear.

Juliet called to him to use the land line, but there was no reply from Sonia and the answer machine had been switched off. Sonia had deftly severed all lines of communication. This performance went on all through supper, with short breaks for attempted conversation, and then Bobbie, who had to be persuaded to eat with them at all, announced that she was going to bed.

When they were eventually alone it had hardly been romantic, but then how could it be, with Gavin in such a state? Instead he was grateful for having been taken in, for someone to listen to his tale of woe and for the comfort of food and a great deal of wine. Even the apple crumble had been a mixed blessing. He almost wept as Bobbie dished it up, the scent of hot apples spiced with cloves wafting from beneath the golden topping, and Juliet remembered that it was one of Sonia's signature dishes at the parties she and Gavin used to give. With what Juliet thought was a deliberate display of inverted snobbery, Sonia eschewed fancy, contemporary food – nothing Italian or Pacific Rim came out of her kitchen – and guests were presented with school dinner vats of cottage pie, and Irish stew, fruit crumbles and Queen of Puddings. People who knew Gavin well were apt to make cheap remarks about Spotted Dick. It was that sort of cooking.

Long after her mother had gone to bed they had sat up talking, or rather Juliet had listened to how Gavin's world would collapse if Sonia kept her word and went through with the divorce.

'She owns the house, you realise. She inherited it from her father. She has a considerable private income as well, but I happen to know that she has put everything in trust for the girls. I understand now why she was so busy over the last few months with her family solicitors. She was planning this, Juliet. She was making sure that I end up without a penny. And where am I going to live, if she turns me out? You know how terribly expensive Oxford is, and, of course, I have no property to sell. The villa in Italy belongs jointly to her and her brother. I am quite literally a pauper.'

'You could always live in college.'

Gavin shot her a glance. 'That's hardly a solution.'

'What about your salary?'

'A pittance, darling, as well you know.'

'Twice as much as I earn, and have to live on.'

'Oh, darling, please. That's not a helpful remark.'

And so it had gone on until Juliet asked, 'Apart from the practicalities and the financial implications, what else are you going to lose?'

Gavin was silent for a moment. 'Well, she can't prevent me seeing the girls. She wouldn't do that.'

'On the contrary, she might suggest that you look after them. Especially with this London thing she's about to start.'

Gavin looked seriously alarmed. 'No, she wouldn't do that. She knows that I couldn't possibly . . . I mean, I've got my work.'

'So has she.'

'I have to say, Juliet, that you aren't being much of a comfort to me. Why do you insist on making things appear worse than they are?'

'I don't mean to. I just think you have to consider every possibility. How do you feel about losing Sonia herself?'

'It's too soon to know. I'm still in a state of shock. At the moment I'm so angry with her, I can't feel anything else. She's my *wife*. I'm *used* to living with her. I thought we got along really rather well.'

'Were you sleeping together?'

'On occasions. Although I would say that if either one of us had lost interest, it was Sonia. She used to have a remarkable appetite for sex.'

Juliet stared. Sonia? With that haircut and those sandals?

'Oh, yes. She was always rather, um, adventurous.' Gavin sounded a little wistful.

Juliet shook her head as if to banish the thought. 'I'd rather not know, thank you. Has she been faithful to you, do you think?'

It was Gavin's turn to look surprised. 'Well, of course she has. She's never been remotely interested in anyone else.' He refilled their glasses. 'I'm well aware of how I've been a shit at times, caused her unhappiness, but the thing is she has always understood that, at heart, I'm devoted – a devoted family man.'

When Juliet gave a snort, he looked rather hurt.

Juliet loaded a tray with the coffee and toast and glanced again at the scene outside the kitchen window. Gavin looked remarkably well, considering his life was hanging in tatters about him. He had certainly slept soundly enough and now, bathed and freshly shaved, he seemed to have recovered some of his brio. He was still talking animatedly with Bobbie as Juliet went out through the back door to join them.

As soon as she was close enough, she realised the subject was Henry and his letter, which had so occupied her mother the day before. Gavin was working hard at being fascinated and tremendously sympathetic, and had even offered to accompany Henry on his projected trip to London. A more unlikely and absurd pairing Juliet could not imagine. Waspishly, she guessed that in his current position he wanted even her mother to think well of him. I might be an adulterer, he seemed to be saying, but you can see that I am also a very nice man and my wife is making a serious mistake in throwing me out. The obvious charm offensive irritated Juliet and this, in turn, made her feel generally out of sorts.

'And so you see,' said Bobbie, 'Henry and his brother arrived here as boys and never went back. After their mother was killed they had no more contact with their family. Henry doesn't even know where his mother is buried. He hopes to find out from this cousin who has suddenly appeared in his life. That is a remarkable story in itself. Would you believe it, she saw him on the television! She happened to catch the television news while she was on holiday on the Isle of Wight. There was an item about that child that was missing from the village and Henry and a neighbour were interviewed, and she recognised his name, Henry Streeter, and remembered the name of the village. She had no idea he still lived here. She wasn't at all confident that her letter would find him.'

'Oh, yes,' said Gavin. 'The missing child. Juliet was

very upset about all of that, weren't you, darling? But I gather she turned up safely.'

'Yes, she did. Thank goodness,' said Juliet, pouring the coffee. 'It was a bit of a non-event in the end. It appears that she was in all sorts of trouble at school and had done a bunk several times before. She's now been sent to some sort of remedial boarding school.'

'Not Cheltenham Ladies College, I presume?' said Gavin. 'Although I expect it costs the taxpayer just as much. After all, our great boarding schools offer exactly the same sort of custodial service to middle-class parents, who frankly can't be bothered to deal with their own delinquent offspring through their teenage years.' He spoke rather smugly, his own girls all having been at day schools in Oxford. If anyone had done the bothering about his children, thought Juliet, it would have been Sonia.

Bobbie, watching him buttering his toast and wiping his fingers on a napkin, could see that Gavin was an attractive man. He had a lovely, educated voice and beautiful manners and a handsome, genial sort of face, grown a little fleshy in middle age. He was rather on the short side, shorter than Juliet, and a bit portly, but dressed flamboyantly this morning in a bright green linen shirt and cream trousers, creating the impression of someone artistic and a bit bohemian. His hair was long and swept back. He looked like a man who might present a television programme about Tuscany, Bobbie thought, wearing a Panama hat and waving his hands about. He was a very good talker, and a listener, too, and had been so interested in her story about Henry.

While Juliet had been making the coffee, Bobbie had taken care to give any reference to his own situation a very wide berth. If he wanted to raise the subject, that was one thing, but she was certainly not going to ask any questions. Apart from checking his watch frequently, and going in and out of the house to use the telephone, he seemed relaxed for a man who had just been banished from the family home. Of course she realised that the effortless flow of conversation, the polite inquiries about her own situation and that of poor Dot was a demonstration of good manners and a social ease which must have been acquired and polished over the years, as an actor learns his stagecraft. It was a skill that must have stood him in good stead for life at Oxford, which Bobbie imagined as a series of sherry parties in historic college settings.

The other thing that Bobbie noticed at once was that he seemed to be extremely fond of Juliet, often turning to look at her, or address a complimentary remark in her direction. I do believe he loves her, she thought, or at any rate loves being with her, and is touchingly grateful to her. Juliet, on the other hand, seemed unnecessarily sharp with him, plonking his coffee down so it slopped into the saucer and ignoring his request for brown sugar, so he had to get up and go and look for it himself while she sat restlessly tapping her foot and running her hands through her hair. She looked tired and strained and it seemed to Bobbie that for some contrary reason she was deliberately making no effort to please.

They seemed unbalanced in other ways: Juliet dressed so simply, and with an understated sort of style, while Gavin was outgoing and flamboyant. They reminded Bobbie of a breed of bird where the cock is small and brilliant and full of himself, and the hen is larger and brown and much less eye-catching.

However, it seemed that it was Juliet who was making all the arrangements and Gavin was asking her advice and quite meekly falling in with her plans. She appeared to have made it clear that there was no question of him moving in with her and that the few days they were to have together in Cornwall were simply a chance for him to think, and plan the immediate future. Bobbie wondered whether Juliet wasn't overdoing all the 'you must do such and such'. She was beginning to remind her ever so slightly of Dot. Gavin was told he must insist on a meeting with his wife and come to a workable arrangement for their separation. A sensible footing, Juliet called it, using words like 'dialogue' and 'conciliation', and 'the way forward'. Gavin sat there with a long face, looking defeated and acquiescent and not saying very much.

Bobbie had wondered why Juliet was so anxious to go away, but when she thought about it, she could see that if a man had been thrown out by his wife, to move straight in with his ex-mistress was possibly not the wisest thing to do, especially if he was nursing any hope of reconciliation. Such a move also put Juliet in rather a bad light, and would make it appear to anyone from the outside that she was the cause of the marriage breaking down. So perhaps she was right to be so uncompromising, and then it occurred to Bobbie that her own presence could be useful. She could be described as a chaperone of sorts, giving Gavin's flight to Dorset a sort of respectability. Sharing a love nest with your mistress's 84-year-old mother seemed most unlikely.

With breakfast finally over, Gavin carried the loaded tray inside and Bobbie followed, taking care over the uneven paving stones. She insisted on washing up, and he stood beside her, took up a cloth and began to dry, while Juliet went in and out of the front door, packing the car.

'I don't know quite how to say this,' he said suddenly, studying the plate in his hands, 'but I would like you to know that I've always loved Juliet. I had no business to, because I was married with children when I met her, but, you know, there are some things which can't be avoided. I couldn't, anyway. She always makes light of my feelings for her. She seems to find the situation easier to live with if she paints me as a serial adulterer, but for some reason I want you to think better of me than that. It's not true, you see. There have been other women, I don't deny it, but only after Juliet left me and went to New York.'

Bobbie turned to look at him in surprise. She had not expected such a declaration and she didn't know whether to feel pleased or sad for Juliet.

'Oh, I see,' she said, thoughtfully. 'Well, thank you for telling me,' and she turned back to the washing up.

'Everything is such a mess,' he said despairingly, throwing down the dishcloth on the table. He had only dried one plate.

'Well, it's sure to be, isn't it?' she said mildly. 'I imagine that long marriages don't come apart without a great deal of anguish.'

'I think that's everything,' said Juliet, coming in with the car keys in her hand. 'Now, Mother, are you sure you will be all right? I really don't like leaving you, you know.'

No, Bobbie thought. Had I been a dog I would have been put into kennels.

'You've got my mobile number and I will ring tonight and tell you where we are staying. This,' said Juliet, waving a piece of paper, 'is the number on which you can reach Dot. You can telephone the ward and they will take the telephone on a trolley to her bed. Look, I'll put it here on the hall table.'

While Juliet talked she returned to the sink two plates that Bobbie had washed and put to drain. Bobbie saw that they were still smeared with jam that she had failed to notice. Even her washing of dishes was no longer up to scratch.

She dried her hands and followed them to the hall

where the front door stood open and the car was pulled up outside. 'Get in, Gavin,' Juliet said, which he did obediently, turning to trill his fingers at Bobbie, who thought that in more ways than one Juliet seemed to be doing the driving.

After Bobbie had waved them off she went and sat down. She felt tired and the sitting room of the cottage was pleasantly quiet. After a few minutes the whirl of the departure and the taut emotional atmosphere that had been left behind by Juliet and her lover seemed to be absorbed into the peace of the tranquil room with its thick, old walls and low beamed ceiling. Bobbie thought of all the human dilemmas, the sum of centuries of tragedy and happiness that had been stored beneath the thatched roof of the cottage. The sunshine fell in a bright pool on the rug at her feet and before long her head nodded onto her breast and she began to doze.

A few minutes later she woke with a start. It had suddenly come to her, the explanation for Juliet's behaviour. She was frightened of love. She was doing her best to deflect Gavin's feelings for her by behaving in such an unbecoming way. Oh, Juliet, she thought sadly. Oh, Juliet.

★   ★   ★

'I don't mind,' said Rachel to Cathy, watching her bath Hope in a bowl on her kitchen table. 'When Juliet asked me if I could go and keep an eye on her mother for a few days while she was away, I thought, great, a chance to keep out of the house and enjoy a bit of peace and quiet.'

'Not peaceful at home, then?' asked Cathy, soaping the pink, mottled legs of her baby who, transfixed, gazed up at her with gummy blue eyes.

'What do you think? Pete's just announced that he's not going on holiday with us this year. He says as soon as school breaks up he's going to Cornwall with his girlfriend. You can imagine how well that's gone down.'

'They all do that, though, don't they? At his age. None of them want to go on holiday with their parents. You could have expected that. It's normal.'

'He's only just seventeen.'

'What were you doing at seventeen?'

'Working. Living in a hostel.'

'There you are then. You were treated like an adult. I was working too, although I couldn't afford not to live at home. Rows all the time, there were, about what time I should be in, where I was and who I was with.

My dad was a right old tyrant and, I tell you, it made me worse. I just thought, sod him, and stayed out all night.'

'Here, let me do that,' said Rachel, reaching for Hope who was now wrapped in a towel, her black hair sticking up vertically. Rachel loved the routine of cream and powder and the sweet smell of a fresh baby in clean clothes.

Cathy went to fill the kettle for coffee as Rachel dried each tiny, jerking limb. 'She's doing really well, isn't she? Look at her lovely little fat tummy!'

'She's made up her birth weight and put on nearly three pounds,' said Cathy proudly. 'She's ever so good. A real greedy little feeder.'

Rachel stroked the baby's cheek and watched as she instinctively turned her head, her perfect little pink mouth searching for milk.

'She's hungry now,' she said. 'She's looking for you.'

Cathy put the coffee mugs on the table and unbuttoned her blouse before reaching for her baby. Rachel marvelled at the love affair between the two of them, how as Hope suckled they gazed at each other with total absorption, while Hope's tiny starfish hands caressed Cathy's swollen breast.

'Are you all right, love?' asked Cathy suddenly, looking up.

'Me? Yeah. Why?' Rachel felt a moment of rising panic.

'I don't know.' Cathy shrugged. 'You seem a bit stressed and you look tired.'

'Thanks.'

'Rach! Come on! You just don't seem yourself.'

'Yeah, well. I suppose things aren't that great between me and Dave.'

Cathy sighed and looked back down at her baby. That old story, she seemed to say. 'Do you want to tell me?'

'No, it's OK. He's always working late, stuff like that. If I look tired it's because I'm not sleeping too well.'

'At least he's a worker, unlike some, and he's a good father, and he's not a drinker. You ought to count your blessings.' Then Cathy looked up, concerned. 'He doesn't lay into you, does he, Rach?'

'Of course not! Look, forget it! I'm fine.'

'The holiday will do you good. You work hard, you know. No wonder you feel tired.'

'I don't think I'm going, actually.'

'What?'

'Not if Pete's staying. We can't both go to Spain and leave him here. It's not responsible. It looks as if we don't care. If he stays, then I will, too. Dave and Jamie can go off and do their surfing thing together. They don't need me there.'

Cathy looked up again. Although she was brain dead with tiredness, she could still detect the sadness and defeat in Rachel's voice.

'Don't say that,' she said. 'Don't talk like that.'

'Why not? It's true.'

Cathy didn't know what to say. She felt that Rachel was on the edge of something. She could feel her unhappiness seeping into the atmosphere of her untidy kitchen.

'There's something I've been wanting to ask you,' she said on an impulse, 'although I don't know whether this is the right moment, and you might want to think about it, so I'm not expecting an answer right out.'

Rachel looked at her in guarded surprise.

'We wondered if you'd be little Hope's godmum. We're getting her christened, see. We're old-fashioned like that, and I wanted to ask someone who was a good mother themselves. That's what you are, Rachel. The best I know, and if anything happened to me, I'd like

417

to think that you would take care of her.' Cathy's eyes brimmed at the thought and she wiped them with the edge of the baby blanket.

Rachel sat for a moment, stunned by what Cathy had just said. She felt a great hot surge in her throat and had to swallow hard before she could dare to speak.

'You don't have to tell me now,' said Cathy, mistaking the reason for the pause, and then, looking across at her friend, she saw that Rachel's face was congested with emotion and then tears began to gather in her eyes and spill down her cheeks.

'Oh, Rachel! Come here, love! What's wrong? Don't cry!'

'I'm just so surprised. Shocked, really. I'd never have thought . . . but I don't know. I don't know whether I can. It's not that I'm not religious or anything.'

'Then why ever not?'

'I just don't know whether I'm the right person, Cathy. Whether I'm fit, a fit enough person.'

'Don't be so daft. Of course you are. Do you think I'd have asked you if you weren't? I've known you long enough, haven't I?'

'I'm just not sure. It's such a wonderful thing to be

asked. I'd love to say yes, I really would. I'm really touched.'

'Here you are then,' said Cathy, beaming, as if that settled it. She held out the baby to Rachel. 'Hope, this is your godmum!'

Rachel took the warm blanket-wrapped bundle in her arms. Hope was already sleeping again, her little eyelids tight closed and one tiny fist curled against her cheek.

'Look at us,' said Cathy, wiping her own eyes again. 'We're a right pair, aren't we? Well, a good cry never did anyone any harm. Come on, let's have another coffee.'

'It's the nicest thing anyone's ever done,' said Rachel, still struggling to speak. 'You asking me, Cathy. I just can't believe it.'

Juliet's spirits lifted on the drive through Dorset, Somerset and then Devon. Sitting beside Gavin in the little car was companionable and as they chatted it felt as if the present anxieties were less overwhelming than they had seemed the night before. As they drove westwards, the bright sunshine, the beauty of the countryside and the fact that they had no plans to be anywhere at any particular time gave the trip a holiday feeling.

Hadn't she always longed to go away somewhere with Gavin and have him to herself for more than a snatched few hours at a time?

After all, she told herself, as they bowled along the A303, they had nothing at all to lose from enjoying a few happy days away. The long-term future of their own relationship, a subject which had leapt to the front of her mind and threatened to occupy it altogether, could be allowed to take its course for the time being. With Sonia cutting herself off so abruptly, Gavin was swaying about like an unsupported climbing plant and seemed to need and want her in a way which altered the basis of their relationship.

They diverted into Taunton to buy a guide to the best houses and churches of the West Country and Gavin stopped talking about himself and even managed to take an interest in where they might go, and began plotting their route. Juliet remembered a hotel on the border of Devon and Cornwall, with a reputation for comfort and good cooking, and rang ahead to book a room. It was mind-blowingly expensive, but bugger the cost, she thought. They might as well make the best of being together because she had really no idea what lay ahead.

For Juliet, the burning question was would Gavin want to put his relationship with her on a different, even a permanent, footing if Sonia was as good as her word and insisted on a divorce? And was this, if she was absolutely truthful, what she herself wanted?

These thoughts raced round her mind, she couldn't stop them, and neither could she share them with Gavin. She felt it was unfair to push him too far, too fast when he was finding it difficult enough to come to terms with the fact that Sonia had chucked him out.

With Sonia miraculously, astonishingly, removed from the equation, where did it leave them? Juliet remembered the terrible, tearful parting all those years ago, when she had told Gavin that she couldn't go on with things as they were, and he had said how much he loved her and would always love her, but would never leave his wife. He had said that he could not ask her to stay when he had so little to offer her and that it was right that she should try and make another life for herself. What else had he said? She had relived the moment so very often in her mind that she knew the dialogue like the words of a play. He had said, 'I'm too selfish not to hope that one day, darling, something might happen to allow us to be together.' Those were his very words, she was sure. What had he meant? She had thought about it often enough and decided they expressed a sentiment which slipped out easily in those sort of circumstances and could be dismissed as meaningless. Was he really suggesting that if anything happened to Sonia he would be *glad*, because it would open the way for herself and him to be together? Of course he didn't. He couldn't possibly nurse a hope that something might happen to his wife. It made him sound like Dr Crippen with an acid bath in mind.

What she had decided at the time, and what she had stuck to over the years of separation, was that Gavin, being ultimately a kindly man, didn't want her to believe that he gave her up too lightly. He wanted to leave her with assurances that he loved her. Not enough, of course, to break his marriage and ditch Sonia and the girls, but enough to feel her loss and wish it could be different. His words did not alter the situation but were designed to make it less painful for her.

Juliet wished that she didn't have to revisit this time of her life when she was so very unhappy. She had left Gavin that day feeling that her heart was broken, but she had plodded on with making a new life although during the weeks and then months that followed her decision to go, she was filled with anger and hurt as well as pain. It seemed to her that she had lost everything while Gavin sailed on, his life hardly altered. She was angry with herself for permitting this to happen and with Gavin for never hesitating in his choice between her and Sonia, and with Sonia for being his wife.

Only very gradually had she reached the point where she could claim that she was reconciled to the loss of him and at peace with herself. It was then that she had been strong enough to meet him again on the very irregular basis that now prevailed and it was for this equilibrium that she feared. She wasn't sure that she could bear to go through another period of emotional turmoil and upheaval and uncertainty. She had vowed that she was never going to allow herself to become a victim to all that misery ever again. If she and Gavin had any sort of future together, she would have to make sure that it was on her terms, and in the gamesmanship of human relationships, how could she ever be sure of that?

An enormous cream tea was waiting for them when they arrived at the hotel. Gavin ate greedily, spreading on the jam and cream, licking his lips with the pink tip of his tongue, while Juliet couldn't manage more than a few mouthfuls. It struck her as ironic that it was Gavin whose life was in tatters but who nevertheless managed a good night's sleep and no loss of appetite, while she, who had worked hard to distance herself, felt most affected.

The huge calorific intake had a beneficial effect, and after they had admired their sumptuous room with its wide views of an endless green valley, they made love very successfully, and later lay in each other's arms, fulfilled and at peace. The sense of physical closeness allowed Juliet for the first time to feel re-assured that everything would be all right, that the uncertainties would be resolved and that she was strong enough to deal with whatever was the eventual outcome.

'Oh, God, Juliet,' said Gavin, stroking her hair, as she lay with her head on his shoulder. 'I can't believe my luck that you were over here when all this happened. I'm so incredibly grateful to have you beside me.'

What a sucker I am to feel pleased by that, thought Juliet.

'I'm glad I am.'

'Do you mean it? I'm not a very good proposition at the moment, am I?'

'Yes, of course I mean it.'

There was a peaceful pause before Gavin said, 'It may seem a bit soon, you know, after Sonia, but would you ever consider coming back to England?'

Juliet's heart missed a beat. 'Come back? What for?'

'Oh, darling, don't be dense. What do you think for? To be with me, of course. To be together. Isn't it what we always wanted?'

'*I* did. I don't think you ever considered it for one moment!'

'Only because I was *married*, Juliet. Which I don't seem to be any more. Or won't be, shortly.'

They fell silent. Juliet did not allow herself to answer. It was far too soon to make decisions, and she was suddenly struck by a thought that Gavin was motivated by a great fear of being alone. His own company terrified him. He was one of those men who needed a woman and a domestic framework around him and now that Sonia's departure had created a vacancy, he was already seeking to fill it.

'Let's wait and see.'

'Darling, I do mean it. You've always been the one.

You know that. If it hadn't been that I was married . . .'

'But that was years ago, Gavin. The situation is not the same any longer. We've both changed since then. Well, at least, I have. I *had* to, if you remember.' She couldn't avoid a little sting of bitterness in her tone.

'Nothing has changed for me,' he said earnestly, leaning on one elbow so that he could look at her face. 'At least, as far as you are concerned. I still love you and fancy you.'

'Gavin, I've learned to live without you. It's taken me a long, long time. It's not as simple as you make out to revert to how we were.'

'Oh dear,' he said, collapsing down onto his back and staring at the ceiling. 'You do kick a man when he's down, darling. It was the first thing I thought of when Sonia said she was booting me out. When I had got over the initial shock, I thought, now Juliet and I can be together.'

'That was a bit presumptuous.'

'But didn't you think that too? Wasn't it the first thing that sprang into your mind?'

Juliet was silent again. She wasn't going to admit that he was right.

'I don't know,' she said eventually. 'Don't go so fast,

Gavin. Let's just see, shall we? You need to get through the next few weeks, find somewhere to live, even if only temporarily, and speak to Sonia first and foremost.'

'But we've got the summer, haven't we? You and I? Surely, darling, you can give me that?'

'Let's just see.'

'When do you have to be back in New York? Why do you have to go back at all?'

'Gavin! I live and work there. Of course I must go back. I've got a teaching contract and there's my research.'

'Oh bugger that, sweetheart. They only give you a year's contract, don't they, the bastards, and pay you peanuts. They can't expect loyalty as well. Hand in your notice. Don't go back. We'll find a place to rent in Oxford.' He was sitting up now, waving his arms about excitedly, reorganising their lives.

'And my research?'

'Don't be cross, sweetie, if I say it's not ground-breaking. I mean, we can all hang on, can't we, without knowing what Admiral Spyglass said about the Royal Navy when he was sitting on the lavatory one morning?'

He was so rude that she knew he was joking but

427

suddenly Juliet wondered if her whole life in New York had indeed been a displacement activity, something she did because she had to do something after Gavin. Just as quickly she checked herself. Don't think like that, she told herself sternly.

'I love you,' he shouted, catching hold of her in his arms. 'I love and admire your research. I love everything you do, but I would rather you did it somewhere we could be together.'

Later, as they sat in the drawing room waiting for dinner, Gavin strayed about among the armchairs with his customary restlessness and spotted a copy of that day's London *Evening Standard*, left by another guest on a coffee table.

He seized it eagerly and Juliet realised how he hated being removed from the hub of things. Throwing himself down beside her, he scanned the first pages and then idly flicked through the rest until he suddenly sat up and almost shouted, 'I don't believe it!'

'What? Gavin, what is it?' Juliet cried, alarmed.

'Read that!' Gavin shoved the paper into her hand, stabbing at a page with his finger.

Tory peer, Lord Coleman (65) today denied rumours that his recent separation from his wife of forty years, Helena (62) had anything to do with his blossoming friendship with colleague Sonia Trevelyan, the well-respected think-tank academic married to Oxford professor Gavin Trevelyan. Lord Coleman is Chairman of the Government's Social Policy Unit and has recently appointed Dr Trevelyan to head the inquiry into young re-offenders.

Today Lady Coleman declined to comment on the rumours. 'I haven't seen my husband since Monday when he left for a holiday in Morocco. On his own.' Dr Trevelyan was not available to comment.

Bobbie stared at the keys to Jasmine Cottage which she held in her hand. She had written a letter to Dot and had made up her mind to go along the village street and find the postbox, but now she was anxious about securing the cottage while she was out and whether she would ever be able to work out how to get back in again. There seemed to be an ordinary-looking key and Yale key for each door and if she bolted the back door and went out of the front she was concerned that somehow she might activate a latch that would prevent her re-entering. She was so used to the massive security now needed in London, where she and Dot had a steel front door and a burglar alarm, that not for one moment would she have considered slipping out and leaving the cottage unlocked for a few minutes.

Eventually she felt satisfied that she had the correct key to open and close the front door, and with the letter in one hand and her stick in the other, she set out. It was strange that there was no pavement and that the cottage opened straight onto the street, but there seemed to be no traffic to speak of and so she felt quite safe walking in the road, but her next decision was in which direction to go. To the left the street climbed a little and then disappeared into trees; to the right the higgledy-piggledy cottages seemed more numerous. It was most likely that the postbox would lie in that direction.

It was a lovely day, quite warm with only the smallest breeze, and Bobbie enjoyed her slow progress. She studied the gardens as she went and observed the names of the cottages on either side. The Old Bakery, the Old Post Office, the Old School, the Old Hall, the Old

Forge, the Old Dairy. Once, this had been a busy street, she thought, with people shopping and the sound of children shouting in the playground. Now it was utterly quiet and deserted and despite the warm sunshine, all the cottages looked closed and empty, with not a single window open.

She thought of her own London street and how it teemed with life all day long. There was never a dull moment when she sat in the bay window of the sitting room looking out at the passers-by. How did elderly people manage in a place like this, shut off from any sort of life? How lonely and isolated it would be.

What had it been like for Henry, evacuated here all those years ago, when he was used to the street life of the gregarious East End of London? Thank goodness, Bobbie thought, that he'd had his brother with him. She wondered where he lived now. There was something about these pretty cottages on either side of the road that smelled of money – the newly thatched roofs, the tasteful curtains, the discreetly painted front doors. They didn't look like the homes of what she thought of as ordinary people.

A small white car went by and pulled up at a cottage ahead and she saw a blue-uniformed district nurse get out and go up the garden path. Well, thank goodness, she thought, at least there's a sign of life, and then a young woman appeared, walking towards her with a dog on a lead and pushing a baby in a buggy.

At last, there was the postbox set into a wall, but when she reached it she found that there was only one collection and that she had missed it. Oh dear, but there was nothing she could do. Poor Dot would have to wait another day before she heard from her.

As she walked slowly back the way she had come, she checked her watch. Nearly twelve o'clock. Almost lunchtime. Time for the sherry that Dot used to pour as the clock struck midday. Dear Dot. Bobbie thought anxiously of her sister and then remembered the telephone number that Juliet had left in the hall by the telephone. As soon as she got back, she would ring the hospital. She had begun to feel, quite strongly, that Dot needed her.

She should not have worried about opening the front door. The key turned with no difficulty and she made her way to the telephone table in the hall and sat down heavily on the wooden chair beside it. She needed her spectacles to read the number. They weren't round her neck where they ought to be. Damn. Where had she left them? Surely not in her bedroom. She didn't think she could face the steep stairs. Her legs felt as stiff and heavy as wood and at the same time as if they might give way. She laid her hands on her lap and then felt the shape of her glasses in her skirt pocket. Thank goodness. She fished them out, put them on and picked up the piece of paper. The telephone was an unfamiliar shape and the buttons difficult to see and she had several attempts before she got the number right.

A woman with a foreign accent answered almost at once. 'Darwin Ward. Can I help you?'

'I'd like to speak to my sister, please. To Dorothy Medway. She was admitted several days ago with a broken hip. She—'

'Hold on, please,' the woman cut in briskly, and then the telephone went dead.

Bobbie waited and waited. 'Hello? Are you there? Hello?'

Nobody answered. Eventually she lost hope and replaced the receiver. It took courage to start all over again. The same woman answered.

'Please!' said Bobbie. 'I was cut off! I need to speak to my sister. My daughter gave me this number, and I—'

'Who do you want?' demanded the woman.

'My sister. Dorothy Medway. She—'

'Hold the line,' the woman almost barked at her.

'Please,' said Bobbie, but before she could explain the line was dead again.

She sat pressing the headset to her ear for a long time but it was no use. There was nobody there. Perhaps something had happened to Dot. You heard such awful tales of what went on in hospitals. Perhaps she had become confused and wandered off, although that seemed unlikely with her broken hip, or left in a bathroom and forgotten. Perhaps she had become seriously ill and been moved into intensive care. There were so many worrying possibilities. What should she do? She couldn't remember where she had written Juliet's mobile telephone number. She could telephone her son, Christopher, but both he and her daughter-in-law would be at work, and anyway she would need her diary from her handbag and she didn't know where she had left it. Perhaps on the kitchen table. Oh dear. She felt a rising panic. Juliet was right, she could not be left alone. Certainly not in a strange place where she felt disorientated and uncertain.

She sat on where she was for a moment to gather

her thoughts and then she heard a man's voice calling from the back door. Oh, thank goodness, it sounded like Henry.

'Henry?' she called. 'Is that you? Come in, please. I'm through here in the hall.' Then she remembered that the door was bolted. She would have to go and open it. It felt as if she was very slow, negotiating her way round the rugs and down the two steps to the kitchen, and she was frightened that he would give up and go away, but at last she was there and pulling back the bolt.

Henry was standing on the other side. 'I was coming by,' he said gruffly. 'I heard you was on your own. I thought I'd just see if there was anything that needed doing, like.'

'Oh, Henry! I was just feeling so anxious. I can't remember where I've left anything, and I've been trying to telephone my sister in hospital and I couldn't get through, and it worried me so, that something might have happened to her.'

Henry was nonplussed. The telephone was something he avoided. These days you were lucky if you got a human being on the other end.

'What is it you've lost?' he asked. Maybe that was something he could help with.

'My bag. I'm sure I had it this morning. I thought it might be on the kitchen table but I can see it's not there. Maybe I left it outside where we had breakfast.'

'I'll go and look,' said Henry. 'You sit yourself down.'

Somehow Rachel got away from Cathy's kitchen and back to her own. She would have to pull herself together because in a minute she must go down to Jasmine Cottage and see if Juliet's mother was all right. Cathy's asking her to be Hope's godmother had upset her so much that she felt quite shaky. Partly it was because she was so touched to be asked. She couldn't expect Cathy to understand how much it meant to her. All the time she had lived in this village she had never felt that she really belonged. She had assumed that she would always be an outsider and she had never honestly made much effort to have it otherwise. It was on the edge of things she felt most comfortable.

Now Cathy had changed all that and Rachel found it hard to believe that she had chosen her from all her possible friends and relations. But she couldn't accept. She would have to somehow tell Cathy that she couldn't. Not with Dave and everything. Not with his affair going on under their noses. It would make a laughing stock of her when people found out, as she was sure they would. It would be the talk of the village and Cathy would come to regret that she had asked her.

She went upstairs to the bathroom and washed her face and combed her hair. She would have to go out again. She had no option. She would have the chance to calm down on the way, although she would have to drive so that she could go to the shops if Mrs Fairweather needed anything.

She went back downstairs and collected her bag and keys and went out to the car. She drove to the top of the road and came to a stop at the T junction and then without being conscious of any decision to do so, she found herself turning away from Jasmine Cottage and driving out of the village in the opposite direction. She suddenly knew what she had to do. She would go to Shillington and check out the loft conversion. She had looked up the house number days ago in the telephone directory: 8 Meadowside. Mike Dryden had gone away on holiday, according to Dave, but there would be signs, wouldn't there, of recent work done to the house? She could ask the neighbours. Someone would know.

It took her twenty minutes to reach Shillington, a nondescript trailing village on either side of a main road, and a further five minutes to find Meadowside, on a small housing estate, and then the right number. She pulled up outside and stared. It was an ordinary red-brick, semi-detached house with an integral garage and a short drive. From the front Rachel could see nothing different about it from its neighbour, so she got out and walked to the gate. Then she saw that there was a Velux window in the roof and a new-looking patch of tiles, and that just inside the gate there was a small pile of builder's sand and some wooden planking.

For the second time that afternoon Rachel felt tears filling her eyes and she got back in the car, put her head in her hands and wept.

An hour later than she intended, Rachel drew up outside Jasmine Cottage. She saw a bicycle round by the back door and guessed that it was Henry's and then saw him up at the top of the garden, bending over the lawn-mower. She tapped on the door and went in.

'Everything all right, Mrs Fairweather?' she called. The kitchen was empty. Then she heard a voice from the hall.

'Is that Rachel?'

'Yes, it's me. I'm sorry I'm a bit late popping by. I got held up, but I'm here now.'

'It's the telephone. Could you just help me with the telephone?'

Rachel went through to the hall and found Juliet's mother sitting by the table, looking agitated. She hadn't realised how old she would be, and so frail-looking; and she wondered at Juliet going off and leaving her.

'I've been trying to get through to my sister who is in hospital,' Bobbie explained.

'Have you got the number there? Well, let me try. They're devils, sometimes, for not answering. If they're busy on the wards, they just let it ring.'

It took Rachel only a minute or two to make the call for her and this time she was given the chance to explain that two previous calls had been cut off.

'Here,' she said, handing over the handset, 'they're taking the telephone to your sister now,' and then Bobbie heard Dot's voice, very faint and faraway.

'Dot! It's me! Bobbie?'

'Who? Who is that?'

'Dot! It's me! Bobbie! How are you? I've been so worried about you!'

'Who?' They must have taken away her hearing aid.

439

'It's Bobbie! Your sister, Bobbie!'

'No, Bobbie's here with me. She's just gone into the kitchen to make a cup of tea.'

Bobbie sat, stunned. 'Dot!' she almost cried. 'Dot! What's the matter? This *is* Bobbie. I'm telephoning you from Juliet's.'

'I'm sorry. I really can't come now. I'm taking the lacrosse team to Godolphin in a minute. I shall miss the bus if I don't look sharp.' Dot gave a small yelp of laughter, but a very weak one by her normal standard.

'Oh, Dot! Please!' But the line was dead.

Bobbie sought her handkerchief in her sleeve. She couldn't bear hearing Dot like that, behaving in that peculiar way. Dear Dot, who had always been so bossy and reliable and quite equal to anything and anybody. Bobbie remembered how she had shouted out of the window at the drug dealer, telling him he should be ashamed of himself. What had happened to her? Had she lost her mind? She felt so helpless, stuck down here in this cottage, miles away from anyone she knew. If only they had allowed her to stay in London she could have asked her nice Italian neighbours to take her into the hospital to visit her sister. What use was she here when Dot needed her?

She felt a hand on her arm and looked up to see Rachel's concerned face.

'Mrs Fairweather, let me take you through to the sitting room. I've made you a nice cup of tea. Was your sister a bit, you know, confused? Don't worry. It'll be the anaesthetic and the post-op trauma, and being in hospital. You don't get any sleep, you know, on a ward. Give her a bit of time and she'll soon be back to her old self.'

'Do you think so? Do you really think so?' How kind this young woman was, and someone whom she had never even met before.

Bobbie allowed herself to be helped to her feet and gently guided to an armchair. Rachel put a mug of tea on a table by her side.

'Have you had any lunch? I thought not. I'm going to cut you a sandwich,' she said. 'A ham sandwich with proper butcher's ham. There's some in the fridge.'

'Thank you,' said Bobbie, weakly. She didn't feel in the least hungry. 'That would be very kind.'

'And afterwards I'll help you upstairs for a little lie-down. I'll be back later, so don't worry, and I'll give you my telephone number in case you need me.'

'Thank you,' said Bobbie again. She sipped her tea

obediently. Henry had disappeared but she noticed that her bag was now sitting on the kitchen table. She couldn't even remember now what it was she wanted it for.

Rachel wondered at Juliet going off and leaving her mother. She was such a nice old lady, and had been in such a state about her sister in hospital. The two old girls lived together, Juliet had told her, so of course they were close. It was frightening for Bobbie to think that her sister might have lost her marbles, you could under-stand that.

She hardly touched the sandwich and then Rachel helped her upstairs and onto her bed. She took off her shoes for her and fetched her a glass of water and put the radio where she could reach it. She just hoped that she would stay put until she came back to check on her after she'd done her afternoon job. Juliet had said to ring her if she was worried about anything, and she might do that if the old lady wasn't a bit steadier when she went back.

That afternoon Rachel was cleaning a holiday cottage in the next village, ready for a weekend let. She had to strip the beds and wash the sheets and empty the dishwasher, but thank goodness the last tenants had left it reasonably clean. They had done most of the washing up, even if there were two pans left to soak in the sink.

She had a routine she stuck to, a mental checklist, so that she did not forget anything, and she could do the work on autopilot. It was very quiet down here at the end of the lane, and even with the doors and windows open she couldn't hear a sound except the harsh cawing of rooks in the tall trees along the hedge, and the bleating of sheep from the field behind the cottage.

As she worked, Rachel went over what she had seen at the house in Shillington. So, it wasn't a lie, she thought. There really was a loft conversion, but now the doubts were creeping back. OK, maybe Dave really had been working there, but he wasn't, for sure, on the evening that Jodie went missing. He was somewhere else then, because he had asked Mike to give him an alibi and he had lied to her and to the police.

He said he didn't tell me the truth about doing work on the side, she thought, struggling to sort through the implications, because he didn't want to worry me. All right, I have to accept that. Then he told me and the police that he was working on the loft that night, and I know that's a lie. So he was somewhere else that he didn't want me to know about and didn't want them checking on.

Round and round it went in her head and all the time at the back of her mind Rachel knew that there was only one explanation. Dave worked late *some* evenings, but not on all the occasions that he said he was, and it was at those times that he saw the other woman.

The relief she had felt earlier had now not only evaporated but had been replaced by a more intense pain than before. She felt as if someone was driving a blunt instrument through her body below her ribs, and in a moment she would cave in, double up, and be hunched over for the rest of her days.

This morning she had told Dave about the holiday. She told him that she wasn't going with him, that she couldn't leave Pete on his own and neither could they force him to go with them. She had known it would end in a row. She had anticipated it. Dave had said that in that case they could scrap the whole thing, he wasn't going without her, and when she said that it wasn't fair on Jamie, he had hit the roof and said that it was Jamie that she should consider for once, and not always be pandering to Pete.

'If he wants to stay behind, then let him,' he shouted. 'He's old enough to be on his own. Jamie needs us to go away together, as a family.'

'That's not fair,' she had said, obstinately. 'You and Jamie will be surfing all day every day. You'll be fine together. You can just do boy things, not worry about me.'

'I want you to come. I hardly see you as it is,' he had said.

On and on, but she wouldn't listen because all the time a voice in her head was saying, 'He doesn't really want you. He's got someone else.' She wanted to provoke his anger. She didn't know why, but she wanted him to lose his temper, hit her even.

Eventually he had shouted, 'I don't understand you, Rachel. I don't know what you want, and I don't think you do either. Are you trying to drive me away? Are you? Because you're going the right bloody way about it!' He'd gone then, slamming the door, leaving his lunch box on the table. Although she was shaking, she had also felt triumphant, as if she had won.

She worked frantically through the cottage, mopping,

wiping, dragging the Hoover up the steep stairs. If I stop, she thought, I'll have to do something to silence this voice in my head, and I don't know what it will be. As she polished the glass, she looked out of the tiny cottage window to the gravel path below. She imagined falling, the swift rush of air, her forehead striking the sharp stones. Then there would be a different sort of pain and it would be a welcome relief, drowning out the voice in her head. You're mad, she told herself. Stop thinking things like that. But at the top of the steep flight of narrow stairs, with the heavy machine and its unwieldy hose in her hand, she nearly fell and only caught herself in time by grabbing the wooden handrail. An accident. That's what it would be. It would get her out of this situation. Someone else would have to take control of her life. She imagined lying calm and still in a smooth hospital bed in a silent ward. But she knew it wouldn't be like that. She'd got the boys to worry about, for one thing.

As she took the bin bag out to the dustbin, she heard her mobile telephone bleep. She had left it on the table in the cottage. Instantly, she knew it would be a message and what the message would be, and when she went back in and picked it up, she read, 'Working late 2nite.

Don't keep tea.' I was right, she thought triumphantly, I'm always right. I've been right all along.

She stood looking at the words on the screen, the plan already formed in her mind. Tonight she would catch him. Jamie was late at school for gym team, Pete was staying with a friend to share exam revision. She felt her stomach knot with a mixture of dread and excitement as she consulted her watch. She had an hour to spare before she drove to where Dave worked and parked outside to wait for him to leave. She would have to be careful that he didn't see her but she guessed that he would be careless because he suspected nothing. She would follow him and see where it was he went, and who he was going to meet. Soon she would know the truth.

Upstairs in Jasmine Cottage, Bobbie waited and waited. She got up to go to the bathroom, and then put on her shoes and combed her hair and consulted her watch. She could not remember what time Rachel said that she would come back but it was now late afternoon and she would very much like a cup of tea. She heard the telephone ringing twice but could not get through to the other bedroom to answer it in time. She went to the top of the stairs and looked down. There was no handrail for the first few steps and they were very steep and narrow. Although she felt sure that she could manage them she was suddenly afraid that on her own, and feeling unsteady, she might fall and create an awful nuisance for everyone. She wondered if she could go down on her bottom like a child, one step at a time, but it was getting down there to sit on the top step that was the problem. No, she had better stay put. Rachel would be back at any moment.

She went to the window and looked out. The school bus must have been through long ago and now there were several knots of older children in the road. Bobbie was reminded of the teenagers who sometimes sat on the low wall outside her house in London, annoying Dot as they tossed their fag ends into the garden and dropped their litter on the pavement. Bobbie couldn't admit to her that she loved to see them, the girls in their school uniforms with the waists of their skirts rolled up, shortening them to pelmet length to show off their legs, and their ties loose, and the boys with their shirts hanging out and their peculiar baggy trousers.

She watched as the teenagers sauntered off and then

there was nothing and no one about. The sunshine moved across the distant hills as if drawn by a finger, and then disappeared as it was swallowed by a cloud. Hills, woods, fields, gardens were all entirely empty. She longed for the noise of her London road which would be busy at this time of the day with people going home from work. Then an enormous tractor roared past, towing an even larger piece of agricultural machinery, making the cottage shake and rattling the window. A man, wearing headphones, sat closed off in the cab, nearly as high up as the bedroom window.

She consulted her watch again. Half past five. She wondered where Juliet was and if it had been her on the telephone. She had promised to ring when she and Gavin had found somewhere to stay. She hoped that they would enjoy their time together. After what Gavin had told her in the kitchen it had occurred to Bobbie that perhaps now that his wife had left him, he would want to marry Juliet. Perhaps it was that thought that had made Juliet so on edge and irritable. Bobbie understood that she wouldn't want to make a mistake. You were really more vulnerable to wounding love affairs when you were older and had lost the resilience of youth.

What Bobbie wished most for her daughter was the sort of love she had felt for Roddy, but maybe that was only possible when you were very young and idealistic. Expectations were different in middle age, of course, and perhaps the need for companionship was greater. From what she had seen of him, she had the feeling that Gavin was exactly that, a good companion.

He seemed to be the sort of man who liked the company of women, which was rather unusual in an Englishman, or at least those of her generation who had been brought up by stern nannies and then sent to single-sex boarding schools. No wonder most of them grew up so strange and awkward, as if they were of a different species. Poor Stephen, for instance, would have preferred an idealised woman. He was repelled by the workings of the female body. Menstruation, childbirth, breast feeding, the menopause made him feel quite sick. She had to keep them all from him.

Gavin looked to be rather a high maintenance sort of man. He would need a lot of entertaining, she could see that, and those linen shirts were the devil to iron. She tried to picture Juliet at the ironing board, but then wives were not expected to do that sort of chore any longer. Everything would be sent to the laundry, or maybe at Oxford there were college servants who saw to that kind of domestic detail.

There, she almost had them married already! The telephone rang again. This time Bobbie did not even try to get to it in time. She let it ring, and it echoed unanswered through the empty cottage, making her feel more lonely and helpless than ever.

She heard a car being driven rather fast, she thought, through a village where there must be a speed limit, and to her surprise it sounded as if it pulled up below her, outside the front door of the cottage. She heard the slam of a car door and then the sound of running feet and then from within the cottage she heard another door open and bang shut. It was Rachel, Bobbie thought, with relief, come back at last, as promised. A moment later, she heard her voice from downstairs.

'I'm here!' she called back, going out onto the landing. 'Upstairs! I didn't like to try to come down on my own.'

When Rachel appeared, running up the stairs to her, her face looked very strange and agitated and Bobbie knew instantly that something was wrong.

'What's the matter? Has something happened?'

Rachel stood on the top step holding her head in

her hands in an attitude of despair or grief, Bobbie didn't know which.

'What is it, my dear?' she cried, alarmed.

'I'm sorry, I'm sorry,' said Rachel in a peculiar, strangled voice. 'I'm so sorry to come here like this . . .'

'Well, I've been waiting for you, but it doesn't matter. I felt a little unsteady and didn't like to . . .' and then Bobbie realised that it wasn't about this at all, that there was something else much worse, much more serious.

'My dear. You must tell me. What is it? Is it one of your boys?'

'No, no. It's my husband.'

'What about him? Has he had an accident?'

'No!' Rachel almost shouted. She was walking to and fro now, between the bedroom and the landing, wringing her hands, rubbing her temples. Something reminded Bobbie of the war, of the shelters, of the cries of women half out of their minds with fear.

Something of those times came back to her. 'Calm down!' she said firmly. 'I can't help you if you keep pacing about like that. You must calm down. Stand still and take three deep breaths. I'm going to count. One, two, three. Now, three more. There, now keep breathing deeply and come and sit here on the bed and tell me what has happened.'

Despite speaking so confidently, Bobbie was surprised that Rachel did as she was told, almost like a child, and came and sat beside her and turned to her, her eyes so full of pain and fear that she dreaded what she was going to hear. I'm too old to be of any use to her, she thought, alarmed. What can I do if this is some kind of emergency? What use is an old lady like me? But the story that tumbled out, muddled and jumbled so that from time to time she had to stop Rachel and get her to explain again, was so familiar, so universal, that Bobbie felt herself gathering strength from the one thing she had to offer, all the accumulated wisdom of age and experience.

As Rachel talked, Bobbie took her hand and listened with an expression of such compassion and understanding that Rachel felt less frightened and despairing. This old lady whom she had only just met seemed closer to her then than anyone else she had ever known. She had never talked about herself like this before. She had always kept things hidden and it was like lifting a stone and finding the horrible crawling things beneath, but when Bobbie gently began to ask questions, making her repeat some of her story and tell of her terrible fears, remarkably she felt calmer. Somehow in the telling of it, the burden of what had happened seemed less great. I shouldn't have done it, she thought then. I shouldn't have told this poor old lady, with her white hair and her kind blue eyes. What can she do to help? I shouldn't have come here, upsetting her, when I'm supposed to be looking after her.

At last she had finished and they sat for a moment in silence and the little bedroom under the cottage eaves was filled with the golden light of the evening sun. Rachel, now much calmer, felt that strange detached sensation she had experienced before, as if she was watching the scene from a distance and as if it was happening to someone else.

Bobbie, in fact, was far from upset. Instead she felt a renewed mental vigour as she thought about what Rachel had told her.

'My poor, poor dear,' she said finally. 'What a time you've had. But I think that maybe I can be of some use. Talking to someone, having to explain from the beginning because they know nothing of the situation, can help clear the mind. But first of all, perhaps you would see me safely downstairs and we will both have a glass of sherry. It will do us good and settle our nerves. Do you think it would help if you told me a bit about this husband of yours? He's a good man, you say, and a good father. And you love him but you've always been frightened of losing him. Wasn't that what you said?' Suddenly Bobbie thought of Juliet that morning, snapping at Gavin out of a similar sort of fear. She'd lost him once and she couldn't bear the thought of setting herself up to lose him a second time. It was safer to keep him at arm's length.

As they talked, Rachel took Bobbie's elbow and helped her step by step down the crooked stairs, and led her to an armchair in the sitting room.

'Now tell me again what happened this afternoon. You say that you followed your husband from his work to a house in Martinstown, a village six miles from here, and that he parked in the drive, rang the bell and went inside, and that you are convinced that this is the home of a woman with whom he is having an affair. You say that you saw her briefly when she opened the door and that she was young and blonde.'

'Yes, yes,' said Rachel and her hands started to shake again as she poured a glass of sherry. Despite Bobbie's instructions she couldn't swallow a mouthful herself.

'But what makes you so sure that this woman isn't just another customer? Someone who he is doing work for?'

'Because he's been lying to me. I told you. I heard him on the telephone asking a friend of his to say he'd been with him on the evening that Jodie disappeared.'

Bobbie stopped to think. 'Hmm. Well, that's something I can't explain. But why haven't you asked him?'

Rachel almost cried. 'I couldn't do that! He's always saying I'm paranoid! He's always saying I don't trust him.'

'But he's right. You don't.'

'Yes, I do, or did, until this time.'

'So why does he say that to you?'

'Because there have been times when I've been upset about certain things.'

'So he *has* given you cause, in the past, to believe that he's lied to you?'

'No, not lied exactly, but I've suspected that he's been with other women.'

'And has he?'

'Well, no. Or at least he has managed to persuade me that he hadn't. Eventually.'

Bobbie thought for a long time and Rachel sat

gnawing at a finger and twisting her hair. Eventually Bobbie said, 'Rachel, I wonder what it is you really want.'

'What do you mean? I don't know. I can't think, not now.'

'You must. It's important.'

'All right. I want what everyone does. To have a happy home. For the boys.'

'And you want a faithful husband who loves you?'

'Of course!'

'Because it seems to me,' said Bobbie, 'that you don't have very much real evidence that Dave is having an affair. You say that he is loving and kind, but that lately you have been arguing more than usual, often because he accuses you, wrongly, you think, of being possessive or suspicious. You've put together some pieces of evidence and arrived at a story which flies in the face of the mass of proof that Dave is a good husband. You've done this because you are convinced that you are right about him – a sort of gut reaction, and based on a belief that wives generally do know, intuitively, when their husbands are being unfaithful.'

Rachel nodded.

'And so this afternoon you reached a crisis point,

when you followed your husband from his work to another woman's house, where you think he is, at this moment, making love to her.'

Rachel nodded again.

'And what now?'

'I don't know, I don't know.'

'Well, either you are right about him, in which case you have to decide if your marriage is over because your husband is unfaithful, or you are wrong, and then you have to ask if you are married to a man in whom you have no trust.'

'Don't, don't,' pleaded Rachel. 'I can't think of life without Dave. He's all I've got. Him and the boys.'

'But you must think about it, because unless you do, you'll just get carried along and this whole thing will grow out of your control. You will end up losing him anyway.'

'Control?' said Rachel. 'What kind of control have I got over it? It's not me who's lying or cheating!'

'It is you who are accusing your husband, though. Does he have any idea of your suspicions?'

'No! I've been really, really careful. I've been hoping, you see, that I was wrong.'

Have you, though? thought Bobbie.

'Why didn't you knock on the door this evening and confront him?'

'When it came to it, I didn't have the courage.'

'But then you would have known, wouldn't you, for sure?'

'Yeah. But what if I was wrong? What then?'

'Rachel, my dear. Unless you face this fear of yours, this suspicion, it's going to haunt the rest of your marriage and, whether you like it or not, affect your children's happiness now and in the future when they have relationships of their own. If Dave is being unfaithful, then you need to know and decide what to do about it, whether you can forgive him and whether your marriage can survive. If he's not, then you've got to ask what it is that makes you mistrust him so. Suspicion is a poisonous thing. It can infect a healthy relationship and kill it stone dead. You end up destroying what you want to save.' Rachel was staring at her as she spoke.

'Do you think it's all in my head?' she said. 'Is that what you're saying?'

'I don't know you,' said Bobbie, simply. 'I've no idea what you are really like, or your husband, or your marriage. All I'm doing is telling you how it seems to me.'

'I feel like running away, disappearing, just not being here. I'd do that if it wasn't for the boys.'

'But what about your feelings for him? You've never said that you love him. You said something about you couldn't think of life without him, but not that you loved him.'

'I'm too scared!' cried Rachel. 'I'm too terrified to think about that. He *made* me love him. He *made* me believe in him, and now he does this to me!'

'So far you've done this to yourself. Until you know for sure.'

'How can I find out? I thought I could go and knock on the door and see his face, but when it came to it, I couldn't. I'm too pathetic even to do that.'

'What time is it?' asked Bobbie suddenly.

Rachel looked at her watch. 'Nearly six o'clock.'

'What time will he be home?'

'Any time. Seven thirty. Eight o'clock. I've learned not to ask.' Her tone was bitter.

'Are your boys taken care of for the next half an hour or so?'

'Yes. Why?'

Bobbie was already getting to her feet. 'I'll go with you, Rachel. If you would like me to, of course. I'll go with you to this woman's house. It's an extraordinary thing to do, go knocking on her door, but if it will help, I'll do it for you.'

Rachel stared at her. 'You would? But I don't know that—'

'Come along. I need my stick and my bag, that's all. It's still quite warm and I have my cardigan on the back of this chair. Should you decide on the way that you don't want me to, then you can just bring me home again.'

Sitting beside Rachel in her old car, her feet resting on the papers and empty drinks cans that the boys left behind in the well of the passenger seat, Bobbie experienced her first real fear that she was being foolish. What on earth would Dot say if she could see her now? What did she think she was doing, interfering in this young woman's marriage? What would happen if Rachel was right in her suspicions and it was left to her to confirm that her husband was indeed having an affair?

Dear God, she thought. Let him have finished and gone by the time we get there, and if he's still there, let them not open the door. Anyone busy making illicit love would surely not come downstairs to answer a knock. But then Rachel would see that as evidence of guilt. Oh dear, what had she done? She must make an attempt to prepare Rachel for the worst.

'Men can have affairs without wanting to end their marriages, you know. They have affairs for lots of other reasons, but rarely because they don't love their wives.'

'How can you say that?' Rachel almost shouted and the car swerved. Bobbie closed her eyes. 'If you're married and you love someone, how can you do it to them?'

'Life isn't as simple as that, Rachel. People are more complicated.' She thought of Roddy. Until she met him she hadn't known what it was to be in love. She thought that she loved her husband, without knowing that the passion she later felt for Roddy even existed. After he had been killed and the future without him seemed utterly pointless, she had forced herself on an hourly, a daily, a weekly basis to pretend to Stephen that she loved him still, and eventually a miracle occurred and she found that she did, and that it wasn't a pretence.

'I'm just telling you, dear, that even if you find that Dave is unfaithful, it doesn't mean he doesn't want and love you. It doesn't necessarily mean that at all.'

'We're nearly there. The house is in this village. It's along here on the left. Look, his van is still there.'

Bobbie's heart sank as Rachel pulled up opposite a detached house set behind a privet hedge. In the drive was a white transit van.

'What am I to say?' she said, now feeling very apprehensive. 'I go to the door and ring the bell and then what do I say? I must have my story ready.' It's a bit late to be thinking of this, she told herself in Dot's voice.

'Anything. Ask the way somewhere. Pretend you've come to the wrong house.'

'I could say that I was walking past and felt faint and wondered if they'd be kind enough to give me a glass of water.'

'Say anything. It doesn't matter.'

Rachel got out and came round to Bobbie's door. 'Let me help you. Here's your stick. It's not very far to walk. Are you really sure you can do this? I'm not asking you to. You do know that, don't you?'

'Yes. It's entirely my own idea.' In for a penny, in for a pound. She always had had a foolhardy streak. Sometimes it led to a disaster of sorts and at other times, well, if she hadn't been reckless – thoughtless, almost – she would never have known Roddy.

It was an ordinary-looking post-war house with a short gravelled drive. Bobbie turned and watched Rachel go back to her car and get in and then she made her way slowly to the front door. 'Oakdene', she read, above the letter box. There was a brass knocker and white plastic bell. This is madness, she thought. Then she pushed the bell and also rapped the knocker and when the door opened some time later, she stepped inside.

Rachel saw Bobbie go in and waited, chewing a finger-nail. She felt physically sick and her heart was pounding so hard that she wondered if she might have a heart attack. Why had she allowed this to happen? Terrible doubts now crowded into her mind. What if she was wrong? How could Dave forgive her for doing this, using a stranger to check up on him? He would never believe that it hadn't been her idea. You're driving me away, that's what he'd said to her, and he was right. How could she expect him to go on loving her if she behaved towards him like this? Dear God, she thought, what have I done? She found her hand moving towards the ignition key as if she intended to turn on the engine and drive away, but she couldn't do that. She couldn't abandon Juliet's mother.

But wherever was she? Ten, then fifteen minutes went by. Some children walked slowly past with a yellow Labrador puppy on a lead. They looked in at her curiously, and then Rachel saw that the door of the house had opened and Mrs Fairweather was coming down the drive to the road, walking slowly and leaning on her stick. Rachel got out and went to meet her and helped her into the passenger seat. Neither of them spoke and the enormity of what lay between them made Rachel feel faint with apprehension.

Bobbie's face gave nothing away but when Rachel started the engine Bobbie looked across at her and said, 'Inside that house there is a blond-haired woman of about thirty, and a baby of six months, and the baby's grandmother. The young woman's husband is in the army and he is serving in Afghanistan. They moved into that house two months before he was posted abroad and amongst other things it requires rewiring. I made up some cock and bull story about staying with my daughter and going out for a little walk to look for a friend's house and getting the wrong address. I could see they thought I was quite batty, but they asked me if I would like to sit down and made me a cup of tea. I told them that my daughter was coming by to collect me from the top of the road in twenty minutes or so and I accepted the cup of tea. I didn't see your husband, but there was hammering and drilling coming from upstairs.

'Do you know what the young woman told me, Rachel? She said that her husband had found a very good electrician – someone who had been in his regiment and had been recommended by a friend. So there, my dear. Mission accomplished.' She looked across at Rachel whose face was very pale. She did not look as relieved as Bobbie might have hoped.

'What does it make me?' Rachel said in an anguished voice. 'What sort of wife does it make me? How could I have got all that stuff into my head? It makes me some kind of sicko, doesn't it?'

'Oh, Rachel, I'm not the one to advise you,' said Bobbie, anxiously. This was what she had feared, that however this escapade turned out, she had meddled with something larger and more complicated than she was equipped to deal with. 'There must be reasons for you to think these things, to get these ideas in your head. I'm sure we are all capable of being suspicious or jealous at times, but I suppose it's when it gets out of control that you realise you need help. I expect you could go to a counsellor or see your doctor. Therapy, that's the thing, isn't it?'

'I couldn't. I couldn't do that. I'm too ashamed. I don't want anyone to know.'

'I can understand that. Now you know the truth, you feel ashamed of believing in your suspicions, but you must remember how real they seemed to you at the time. You don't want this to happen again, do you? You don't want to be caught up in this web again?'

'Never. Never again. I don't know what to do to make it right now between me and Dave. He doesn't know, does he? He can't find out what I've been thinking, or about what happened this afternoon?'

'No. How could he? But he must be confused, mustn't he? He must have noticed that you've been behaving oddly towards him.'

'We should talk more, shouldn't we? He should have told me about doing this moonlighting. He shouldn't have kept it from me.'

'No. Perhaps you both need to change. Maybe he doesn't tell you things because he thinks you'll worry or be upset.'

'That's true. That's what he said. And I still don't

know why he lied about where he was on the evening Jodie was missing.'

'I think you must accept that he had his reasons, and trust him. Or else let him see how much it has distressed you and ask for an explanation. I expect that would be the best thing.'

'Yes.'

Bobbie closed her eyes. She suddenly felt very tired. She knew that openness and frankness between husband and wife was the doctrine preached today, while all her married life she and Stephen had never once discussed how they felt about each other, and been none the worse for it, in her view. How easy it was to give advice and yet how difficult to act upon it. She hoped with all her heart that Rachel would be able to rid herself of her demon. It was clear from what she said that she and Dave loved each other, but what a torment love could be.

Chapter Thirteen

LATER THAT WEEK, when Henry got back from work at lunchtime, he pushed his bicycle to the back of the house as usual to let himself in the scullery door. By now the postman should have finished his round and if Henry had a letter, it would be waiting for him on the mat in the hall. He could almost see it lying there, the bright blue envelope, and imagined how he would pick it up and carry it through to the kitchen where he would sit at the table before he slit it neatly open with a knife and carefully draw out the letter within.

He was just unlocking the door when he heard the side gate bang and Billy and Bingo came round the corner.

'Have you had your dinner yet, Henry?'

'No. It's early yet. I've only just got back.'

'I hoped I'd catch you. I've got some cold beef here.

From my lass. She brought me some this morning, more than I'll ever eat.' Billy was holding a plate covered in a tent of foil, and Bingo was hopping around it sniffing, his nose lifted, in a state of anticipation.

'What's she giving out cold beef for?'

'It's leftovers from the Hunt Supporters supper last night. You know she works evenings at the Coach and Horses. She was told she could take the leftovers along home with her.'

'You'd best come in then,' said Henry, opening the door, although it was the last thing he wanted, Billy there, if there was a letter on the mat. Billy was through the door like a shot, Bingo dancing round him.

'Got any bread?' he asked, looking round the kitchen. 'Makes a lovely sandwich, does cold beef, and I've only got a loaf in the freezer, see.'

'Aye,' said Henry, washing his hands at the sink. He had the feeling Billy intended to stay.

'Got any of them pickled onions of yours? Grand they'd be, along with a nice slice of beef.'

Henry dried his hands on the roller towel behind the door.

'They'll be in the larder,' he said. 'You have a look for they.'

While Billy was doing this, Henry swiftly opened the door to the hall. The mat was bare. There was no letter for him today. With a sinking heart he closed it again and fetched two plates from the draining board, and the loaf from the bread bin. The disappointment had taken his hunger away.

'You staying, then?' he asked.

'Yes, you old bugger. Share and share alike, eh?' Billy put down the jar of onions and went to the drawer for a fork.

Henry cut the bread and put two thick slices on each plate. Now Billy was struggling to open the jar. 'Here,' he said. 'You have a go.'

Henry picked it up in his enormous hand and with a swift turn released the lid. 'There.'

Billy took the foil off the plate and revealed thick brown slices of meat, edged with a frill of yellow fat. 'Ooh! Look at that. Lovely beef, that is.' He pulled off a shred and threw it towards Bingo who, quick as a flash, jumped in the air and caught it neatly.

As they ate, Billy talked, his mouth full, stopping only to pop in a whole glistening brown onion. Henry hardly listened. All he could think of was that it was now five days since he had sent his letter and still no reply. What did that mean? he wondered. Had Betty decided not to answer? Perhaps he had frightened her off with the suggestion that he should meet her. Maybe that was rushing things.

Billy was still going at it, hammer and tongs, when Bingo, head cocked, started to bark and scrabble at the inner door.

'What's that?' said Billy. 'Someone at the door, Henry. You've got a visitor, my son.'

But when Henry got up and opened the door, he saw that on the mat, slightly askew, lay the blue envelope of which he had almost given up hope, and a postcard with it.

'Was that the postman?' asked Billy. 'The lazy bugger. What sort of time is this to get your post? Remember when we were lads, Henry? Two deliveries a day there were then and two collections, and postie on a bicycle, too, not sitting on his arse in a van.'

Henry picked up the envelope and the card and brought them to the table.

'Well!' said Billy. 'Is it your birthday, lad? A letter and a postcard! It's not often you get a letter, is it? Who's that from, then?'

Henry took up the card and looked at it. On the

front was a view of heathery moorland, a rocky outcrop and two shaggy ponies standing head to tail under a sky of unlikely blue. He turned it over and looked at the signature. It was from Jessie. He would deal with this first before he took up the blue envelope.

'You got your reading glasses?' asked Billy, but Henry had already fetched them off the shelf by the cooker.

'Dear Henry,' he read out loud. 'Thought you would like to see where we were yesterday, up on the moor. Having a lovely time although weather is changeable. Hotel v. comfortable. Thank you for looking after Smokey. See you Thursday. All the best, Jessie. PS. Next time you should come too, you would enjoy the change.'

'That's nice,' said Billy. 'That's thoughtful, that is, sending you a card. She's never sent me one.'

'You've never done nothing for her,' retorted Henry. All the time he was thinking about the letter in the envelope. He turned it over in his hands. This time Betty had got his address right, of course. Mr Henry Streeter, 8 Green Lane. He didn't want to open it in front of Billy, but he couldn't bear to wait, either.

'Make us a cup of tea, Bill,' he said. 'Put the kettle on, will you, while I see what this is about.'

473

Taking up a knife, he slit open the envelope and drew out two closely written sheets.

Dear Cousin Henry,

I can't begin to tell you how pleased I was to get your letter. I wasn't at all sure that mine would find you, or that you would want to reply.

First of all I am truly sorry to hear about Fred. It must be a great loss to you, especially with you having been so close. As I said, I know what loneliness is and what it is to be alone in the world. Still, we have to keep smiling, don't we, and there is a silver lining to every dark cloud, if we look for it.

As to your mother and that dreadful night, yes, she and my mum spent the evening together. They'd been to the early evening show at the Empire Cinema on Green Street, off the Roman Road, and they'd seen a newsreel of the Berlin bombing. We'll catch it next, they said to one another, and then they walked home, to collect me from Nan, who was babysitting. The sirens went off about half past eight and there wasn't much warning given, so they ran for it, my mother carrying me

in her arms. It was cold and raining and a dark
night. By then they were very used to going down
the shelter at the tube station, they'd done it so
often.

They were halfway down the steps when there
was a terrible roar and people thought it was
bombs falling and started to press forward in a
panic. Down at the bottom a woman carrying a
baby slipped and fell and the people behind her
went down like ninepins, and they were still pushing from the top. Our mothers were just carried
on down in the crush, but Mum said she held on
tight to your mother's hand. She held on tight
right through until the end, when they both lost
consciousness. She said that your mother's last words
were of you and Fred, saying to tell you she loved
you. When we were pulled out, my mother and I
were taken to Whitechapel hospital where we
stayed for a day or two. It was a miracle that we
survived. Our nan had to go to St John's Church
opposite the station where the bodies had been
laid out, to look for your mother. She never got
over the shock of finding her there, but said that
she looked beautiful, with not a mark on her. She

is laid to rest in Tower Hamlet's Cemetery Park along with my mother, Nan and Grandad, so you don't have to think of her on her own. She has the family all around her and I have done what I can to keep her grave tended.

I think it would be a good idea to meet you and suggest that I come and fetch you off the train at Waterloo station. If you feel up to it we could go to Bethnal Green where there is a memorial tablet on the wall of the tube station, and after we could visit the cemetery. I know this is all a bit sudden for you to take in after all this time. It is a piece of your life that has been missing all these years.

I have a lovely photograph of you and Fred and your mother, taken on a day trip to the beach at Whitstable. She has her arms round the two of you and she is laughing and looks so young and carefree, just like a girl. Right little imps, you look, proper boys, but the three of you make a happy picture and it is something you might like to keep by you. I don't suppose, things turning out as they did, that you have many keepsakes.

Being retired, I am available to meet you any

day, but as you still work, perhaps a Saturday is best? Just let me know when and what time your train arrives and I will be there to meet you. I know what you look like, having seen you on the television. I'm sure you were the tall man, not the small, fat one who did all the talking.

Looking forward to hearing from you soon.

Fondest regards,

Your cousin,

Betty

PS. I am very glad to hear about the girl, back home safe and sound. Funny to think, it was her going missing that brought us together.

It took Henry a long time to read. He forgot about Billy and Bingo both sitting there, watching him, Billy silenced for once in his life. When he got to the end, he took up the first page and started again, while sound-less tears flowed down his cheeks and he brushed them hastily away.

'What is it, Henry?' asked Billy, at last. 'What is it? Are you all right, mate? Not bad news, is it?'

Bingo hopped over to lay his head in sympathy on

477

Henry's knee, all the better to keep his eye on the last piece of beef pushed temptingly to the side of his plate.

'There's something weird going on at home,' said Pete to Honor as they walked hand in hand to get a coffee in the town. They had just been let out of exams and had free time until after lunch.

'What sort of weird?' said Honor. 'Ordinary weird or weird weird? Is it still about you not going away on holiday?'

'Yeah, kind of. I dunno, though, it's more than that. It's like something going on between Mum and Dad.'

Honor sighed. Last night she'd had a telephone call from her mother in Spain, full of complaints about her father's record selfishness. She was weary of parent troubles.

'Dad seems to be trying really hard and Mum's always pushing him away, like she's hurt, or something. Over this holiday thing, he really wanted her to go away with him and Jamie, and she was so off about it. All that stuff about having to stay to look after me, that was all bollocks. She just didn't want to go, and she wouldn't even talk about it.'

'What does your dad say?'

'He gets arsey and then that makes it worse and Mum goes all silent. I don't hang around to listen. It does my head in because I can see it from both sides. I mean, he's cool about me staying. He reckons that your mum and dad, being doctors and stuff, will know the scene. He's not bothered about it.'

'What's with your mum, then?'

'She's always been like hyper about some things. She's always asking questions as if she doesn't trust Dad and me. She's all right with Jamie but it seems like she's trying to hang on to me as if I was a kid.'

'That's the eldest child syndrome. Mothers are always more protective about their firstborn and find it hard to let them go. I read that somewhere. She's had a funny life, too, hasn't she? All that about her mother dying and then in and out of children's homes. That's sure to make her a bit insecure or clingy, or something.'

'Yeah. I suppose so. I mean, my dad can be a wanker sometimes, but he so does love her, you can see that. It just does my head in that they don't seem to be able to get it together.'

'It's scary, isn't it, when you're old enough to be able to see your parents as people yet you don't want to know what goes on between them? I hate it when my mother

479

complains to me about Dad. I mean, it's not my business, is it? It's not like I'm one of her girlfriends who's going to take sides with her. So what's happening now?'

'I don't know exactly because I've been with you, but Jamie came to find me in break and said Mum's changed her mind. She's going on holiday with them now. He'd got this great grin on his face. You'd think Jamie doesn't mind about stuff because he's always, like, cheerful but he does, and he's been really pissed off about it. He can tell when Mum's unhappy, like the rest of us can.'

'So if your mum goes too, that gives us the whole time together?' Honor asked slyly.

'Yeah.'

'I love you.'

'I love you too. They're weird, though, aren't they? I don't know why they keep mucking each other about.'

'They're all the same. It stops them getting bored with each other, I expect.'

'We've still got an hour,' said Pete, checking his watch. 'Shall we go back to your house? We've got time.'

They grinned at each other and wheeled round, still holding hands, to walk in the opposite direction.

★   ★   ★

As Juliet and Gavin drove into the village, they saw a large white van parked outside Jasmine Cottage. It took a moment for the penny to drop.

'Oh God! What day is it?' cried Gavin, clutching his head.

'Thursday. I thought you'd left Sonia a message about not sending the van.'

'I did. She must have ignored it. The bloody, bloody cow.'

As they drew up they could see that the van doors were open and a man was standing inside passing colourful armfuls of loose clothing, suits and jackets and trousers, down to Henry, who was carrying them through the open front door of the cottage.

Gavin jumped out.

'I don't believe it!' he cried, peering into the van. 'All my clothes are here, just thrown in loose, and my books and filing cabinets – everything. I just don't believe it! Here, careful with that! That's vintage Paul Smith you're treading on!'

Juliet couldn't help laughing. You really had to hand it to Sonia. She didn't do things by halves.

'Where are you putting it all?' demanded Gavin as Henry went by with another bundle.

'Where I've been told,' said Henry gruffly. He didn't take to this man with his white jacket and hoity-toity manner.

Rachel came out of the cottage with some black plastic bags in her hand.

'Oh, hi, Juliet. You're back! Mrs Fairweather said as to put the clothes in the sitting room for now. She said they'll need sorting into what stays and what goes to the charity shop. Everything else is going in the garage.'

'Charity shop!' shouted Gavin, pushing past Henry into the cottage.

'Oh, Rachel,' said Juliet. 'I'm so sorry about this! Really, I had no idea that all this stuff was arriving here. It's too bad. Where's my mother? Is she all right?'

'She's fine. She's showing the man where to put the boxes.'

Juliet walked round the side of the cottage to where the wooden garage doors stood open. The back section was already half filled. Sonia had made a thorough job of clearing Gavin out of her life and, it seemed, into Hector Ballantyne's instead. Bobbie was standing inside, giving directions.

'Mother, I'm so sorry about this! Gavin thought he

had stopped Sonia sending the van, but she clearly takes no notice of him any more. How are you? Have you been all right on your own?'

'Juliet, my dear! Yes, perfectly all right, thank you. Rachel has been wonderful. It was a bit of a surprise when the man knocked on the door, but he was very insistent. I checked that he had the right address, and he assured me that it was a delivery for you, Juliet, so what was I to do? He wants to be paid in cash, by the way. Thank goodness Rachel was here to help, and then Henry came past on his bicycle. But how are you? And did you have a lovely time, you and Gavin?'

'Come inside and I'll tell you.'

The sitting room was swathed with heaps of Gavin's clothing, through which he now rootled, like a keen woman at a jumble sale, grumbling all the time as he did so.

'I thought the clothes had better come in here and the rest into the garage,' said Bobbie anxiously.

'Yes, Mother. You did exactly right. Gavin, do stop it. You look like someone trying to find their possessions after some natural disaster. An earthquake or something.'

'I don't know why you can't be a bit more sympathetic!' he complained, waving his hands around the room and towards the van outside the window. 'This is my whole life, just thrown here in a heap!'

'Are you moving in?' asked Bobbie, innocently.

'No, he isn't,' said Juliet, firmly. 'This is temporary storage, isn't it, Gavin? Tomorrow we're going to Oxford, Mother, to look for a flat, or at least Gavin is. I thought that you and I could go on to London on the train and see Aunt Dot in hospital and spend the night in Highgate. I expect there's post you'll want to look at. Would that be a good idea?'

'Oh, yes!' Bobbie looked delighted. 'I telephoned Dot this morning and she sounded so much better. Almost her old self. Her confused state of mind was because of the antibiotics, apparently.'

Gavin, who had rushed outside to check on the garage, reappeared looking hot and flustered and cast himself dramatically into an armchair.

'It's preposterous!' he cried. 'Outrageous! Thrown out in the street, and me the innocent party!'

'Oh, yes, Mother,' said Juliet calmly, taking a newspaper cutting out of her bag. 'Read this. It will bring you up to date with Gavin's situation.'

As Bobbie searched for her spectacles, Rachel put her head round the door. 'Would anyone like coffee? I'm making it for the van driver.'

'Oh, yes, please, Rachel. I think we could all do with a cup,' said Juliet, with some emphasis.

'Oh, my goodness,' said Bobbie when she had finished reading and put the cutting down in her lap. 'I'm dreadfully sorry, Gavin. How horrid to read such a thing in a newspaper. And you had no idea? Well, of course, you couldn't have.'

'None at all. Sonia has utterly deceived me,' he said in a piteous tone.

'Oh, Gavin, do stop it. Your pride is wounded, naturally, but you'll recover. You've got to muster some dignity.' Juliet was being very tough on him, thought Bobbie. 'What he minds very much,' she added, turning to Bobbie, 'is that this man Sonia has run off with is a Tory peer. It's a double betrayal, Gavin being a good Oxford socialist.' She seemed to be treating the whole thing as a bit of a joke. 'Sonia's taken the girls and gone off on holiday, with or without His Lordship, Gavin doesn't know.' She got up then and with a sudden affectionate gesture put her arms round his neck over the back of the chair where he was sitting. 'You poor old thing,' she said and he raised a hand to pat her arm. Somehow he made Bobbie think of an invalid, slumped like that. He only needed a tartan rug over his knees. And slumped was the word. All the chirpiness she had noted when she had first met him had quite evaporated.

'Mrs Fairweather,' said Gavin, turning to speak to her. 'Juliet's been absolutely wonderful through all of this. God only knows what I would have done without her.'

Bobbie didn't know quite what to say, so she murmured something and glanced at Juliet, and caught a flicker of satisfaction pass over her face. She's happy, Bobbie thought. Juliet's happy because he needs her for probably the first time.

Rachel banged the door open with the edge of the tray she was carrying and Gavin got up to help her. Amongst all the confusion of the piles of clothes there was nowhere to put it down, so they each took a mug and thanked her.

'The driver's finished unloading and wants to get on back,' she said, 'but he's waiting for his cash.'

'Bloody Sonia!' said Gavin, indignant again. 'It's an outrage, it really is!'

★   ★   ★

486

Rachel took her coffee out to the garage where Henry was rearranging the boxes to make room for Dr Ballantyne's car. She felt awkward about talking to him because although he glanced at her, he didn't stop what he was doing or acknowledge that she was standing there, watching.

'What a to-do, eh?' she said, nursing her mug. 'It seems like even Juliet didn't know all this stuff was arriving.' Henry did not respond. Why should he care, one way or the other? Rachel thought.

'Would you like a cup of coffee?' she asked. 'Or tea?'

'No, thanks. I shouldn't be here at all. I've got jobs to be getting on with.'

'You keep the gardens lovely,' persisted Rachel. 'I always notice the ones you look after.'

'Oh, aye.'

'Juliet told me that you don't come from round here, that you're a Londoner, like me.'

Henry stopped then and turned towards her. He took off his cap and wiped his brow.

'Aye,' he said.

There was a silence in which Rachel thought, I give up. He doesn't want this. Not from me, anyway. He prefers to be left alone.

'Came here as kids in the war. Me and Fred.'

'Yes. She said that. It's like history to me. To my generation, it seems that long ago, but I can imagine what it was like for your mum having to part with you boys. How she would have felt it.' As soon as she said it, Rachel wanted to scream out, no, no, I didn't mean to say that, but Henry didn't appear to take it badly.

He came over to where she was standing and said, 'Well, you would, wouldn't you? Having lads of your own.'

'Yes,' said Rachel, gratefully, and then summoning her courage because after all she had got this far, she went on, 'I always meant to say how sorry I was about Fred. You losing him like that. I always meant to drop you a note, or come round or something, but somehow I didn't like to. It was easier not to, if you know what I mean. But he was a lovely man, your brother. We all thought so. Me and Dave and the boys. He was a bit different, I know, but he was just so cheerful and smiling that you always felt better for seeing him.' There, she had done it. She felt her face grow hot and she bent down to rub at her ankle.

'Aye,' said Henry, but his tone was softer. There was a pause, and then he turned to close the garage doors.

'I'll be off then,' he said. 'There's nothing more for me to do here.'

As he cycled away, Henry wished that he'd said something in return. Now he thought back on it, the occasion seemed to demand more in the way of a response. Perhaps he should have said something about her boys, something on the lines of, 'They're grand lads, those boys of yours,' and he'd have meant it, too, but it was too late now. It was all very well to work out what he should have said after the event, but it counted as nothing if it didn't come to him at the time. She'd think he was a sour old bugger now, and she'd be right.

It was quite a push up the hill out of the village and he bent over his handlebars with the effort of it. He was going into the next village to get a few things for Jessie. A carton of milk and a loaf of bread, and a few rashers of bacon she'd need when she got back this afternoon because she'd have nothing in the house. He'd leave it in the kitchen along with a lettuce and some veg from the garden and a few eggs. He'd got her postcard in his shirt pocket. He could see the top of it if he glanced down. When he had first read it out to Billy, he hadn't really noticed what she had written, he was so taken up with what was waiting for him in the blue envelope from Betty, but later on when he had another read of it, it was the last line that struck him. The PS. It was written cramped at the bottom where there was no room left. 'Next time you should come too. You would enjoy the change.'

At first he wondered what she meant. For starters, she knew him too well to really think that he would enjoy a change, and he guessed it was a joke. Written down like that, you couldn't tell. Then when he had a think about it he started to wonder whether she was really suggesting that he booked a place on a coach trip and went gadding off somewhere, and after a bit, he thought, and why not? Perhaps Jessie was right and he would enjoy it. He'd had another look at the front of the card, at the photo of the ponies on the moor, and thought it would be grand to see a view like that, or to have another look at the sea, and walk along a beach, and it had been at the back of his mind ever since.

It had to take back place because he'd got Betty's letter to think about. He'd left that on the mantelpiece and when he got home he'd have another read of it. This morning he had only had the briefest opportunity to tell Mrs Fairweather that he had had a reply and promised that he would come round and show her later on.

'Is it good news, Henry?' she had asked, anxiously.

'You could say that,' he'd said, and she had clapped her hands together, she was that pleased.

He still couldn't believe it. He and Billy had gone over it line by line and Billy had been full of it. They'd both sat there wiping a tear away from their eyes. Billy knew, see. Billy knew what it had been like when they were kids. Henry didn't have to tell him anything about the Bettses and all the misery, and so he understood what it meant to Henry to have news of his mother after all these years and to know that he'd got a family and that he belonged somewhere.

'You were the lost boys, Henry,' Billy said. 'That's what me mam called you and Fred. The lost boys. She used to say she'd have had you come and live with us if we hadn't been eleven already in a cottage with an earth floor and a privy out the back.'

At the top of the hill, Henry stopped and sat for a few moments on the bench set there for those who wanted to catch their breath and admire the view. The village looked small from here, just a cluster of stone cottages and some newer houses where once there had been farms right there on the village street. The church tower rose up from the dark churchyard yews and behind it was the graveyard where Fred lay buried. Further on Henry could see the thatched roof of the pub and the tables set outside under umbrellas. His own road was hidden by a curve of the hill but he could see the allotments as orderly lines of green opposite where his house would be.

His eye travelled further out of the village to the top road and there on the brow of the hill was the Bettses' old farm, transformed now by new money and owned by horsey people moved out of London. The last time he'd been that way he'd heard children laughing in the garden and he'd seen a tree house in the oak at the edge of the paddock where they'd kept the dry cows.

Change could be a good thing, he thought as he got back on his bicycle. Things didn't always want to stay the same.

Rachel was in the kitchen making a cake when Cathy put her head round the door.

'It's only me. Can I come in? Are you busy?'

'No, come on in. I'm doing a bit of baking.'

'It smells lovely. I'm that famished what with the

breast-feeding that I could eat for Britain, and I had two Cornish pasties for breakfast. No wonder I look as if I'm still pregnant. Do you know someone asked me the other day when the baby was due!'

They both groaned and laughed.

'Well, you can't eat what I'm making, because it's still in the oven,' said Rachel and then held out her arms. 'Here, let me have Hope.'

Rachel took the baby and sat with her at the kitchen table while Cathy put the kettle on.

'I've come to tell you about the christening,' said Cathy. 'We've been to see the vicar and we've booked the first Sunday in September. It'll be during the morning service, like, so I had to come and check with you that that'll be all right, and for Dave and the lads. We want you all there. After, it'll be at the pub – sandwiches and that, and my mum's got the cake ordered.'

'That'll be lovely,' said Rachel, giving Hope her finger to hold. 'It's so kind of you, Cathy, to ask me. I can't really believe it.'

'Oh, stop it!' said Cathy. 'Don't start all that nonsense again. It's you I want, and that's that.' She poured hot water into two mugs of coffee and set them on the table.

'There are biscuits in the tin in the cupboard,' said Rachel, grinning. 'Not for me. I've got to be in a bikini in a few weeks.'

'You're going then?'

'Yeah. I decided that it wasn't fair on Dave. He didn't want to go without me and I suppose I should be glad of that.' She looked down at Hope and bent to kiss her dark downy head. 'Although I don't know that I'll enjoy it, I'll be so worried about leaving Pete.'

'He'll be fine!' said Cathy. 'He's a good lad. So things are better now between you and Dave? You look a lot happier.'

'Do I? Yeah, well, it came to a bit of head, actually, Cathy. I realised that I hadn't been fair on Dave. I'd been thinking things about him that turned out to be wrong.'

'What sort of things?' Cathy's broad face was full of interest and Rachel felt the old resistance to give anything away. 'Come on, Rachel, you can tell me.'

Yes, I can, Rachel decided. Cathy is a friend. I've got to trust her. She took a deep breath. 'I thought he was carrying on with someone else. Another woman. It was all the working late, and then I discovered that he lied to me and the police about where he was on the evening Jodie disappeared. It was that that made me suspicious and then everything else seemed to fall into place.'

'Oh, shit,' said Cathy. 'I'm really sorry. But it's not true, is it? It can't be.'

'No, I was wrong. I found out in time before I accused him of anything, thank God, but I did tell him I had to know why he had lied.'

'Yes?'

'He'd been doing some work for a woman whose husband is in the army in Afghanistan. He didn't want the police going round asking her questions because she's alone with a baby and sick with worry. If he was going to get into trouble for moonlighting he didn't want to get her involved, so he asked a mate from the rugby club to say he'd been there that evening. He had been doing the wiring for a loft conversion for him at the same time, you see. As soon as he told me it made sense. It's Dave all over, you see. He'd be protective like that. Anyway, as soon as he lied, he regretted it. He could see that it could get him into serious trouble, and then, thank goodness, Jodie turned up and the inquiry was dropped.'

'That was a relief all round then.'

'Yes. But it was just the beginning for me. I was so sure he was having an affair that I went nearly mad. I've been to the doctor, since, because I think I need some help to deal with these fears I get. He wanted to put me on anti-depressants but I said no. I'd rather have some other sort of help, so he's fixed up for me to see a therapist. I start next week.'

'Oh, Rachel. If only I'd known. If only you'd told me.'

'I felt too ashamed. I didn't want anyone to know. Just telling you this is quite a big thing for me.'

Cathy got up and came to put her arms round both Rachel and Hope. 'If only I'd known, love. You always seem so in control of everything. Mrs Perfect, I thought. It's quite a relief to hear you have problems like the rest of us. I like you all the better for it.'

'Thanks, Cathy.'

'Did I tell you I saw Marion yesterday? She's started action to try and get Jodie home. She hates her being away at that school. She really misses her. I know you don't like her much, but at heart she's a good mother. She loves her kids.'

'Yes, I know. I hope she gets her back. That's what Jodie needs most, to be with her mum. All kids do.

Now, I'm going to have to give Hope back to you. Those sponges need to come out of the oven.'

After Cathy had gone, Rachel waited for her opportunity. She saw Henry cross the road from the allotment just before teatime and she left him a few minutes to put his tools away and unlock his back door. On the counter, on a blue plate covered with clingfilm was the sponge cake that she had always intended to make him, yellow and springy and filled with raspberry jam.

She wasn't at all sure how it was going to be received, but it was now or never, and so she picked up the plate and left her own house and crossed the road. She had never opened Henry's gate or walked along his gravel path before. Her feet made a loud scrunching noise and when she turned the corner she saw that the back door stood open and Henry was sitting at his kitchen table. He looked sunk in thought and so absorbed that she nearly turned round and crept away, but she had come this far and she had better get it over with.

She knocked at the open door and he looked up suddenly and his face was so strange that she nearly backed away. She couldn't read the emotion that she saw there, but she knew that it was private and that Henry would not want her there, seeing him like that.

'I'm sorry,' she began. 'I just . . .' and she saw that on the table in front of him was a letter, several close-written pages on bright blue paper.

He said nothing and the silence was so oppressive that she had to begin again. 'Henry, I've brought you a sponge cake. I hoped you might enjoy it. I always meant to come over, like I told you this morning, and I feel really bad that I wasn't a better neighbour to you when you lost your brother.' Without crossing the threshold she reached inside and put the plate down on the draining board just inside the door, and turned to go.

'Come back,' said Henry. 'Come back. Come and sit here a minute. I've got something I'd like to show you.' He held out the letter. 'I know about you losing your mother and all. That old Mrs Fairweather at Jasmine Cottage told me. Come and read this here.'

Rachel went in and sat opposite Henry where he had pulled out a chair for her. She took up the letter. 'Are you sure?' she said, anxiously.

'You go ahead, lass.'

When she had finished she leant across and touched

his hand. 'I see now,' she said, her voice deliberately bright to hide her tears. 'I see how you were feeling. It's a lovely letter.'

'It's more than that,' said Henry. 'It's a bloody miracle.'

Later that evening after Bobbie had gone up to her room, Juliet came to sit on her bed and after preliminary chatter said, 'Ma, may I ask you what you think? About me and Gavin?'

'What about you?'

'Well, what you think of him, for a start.'

'Oh, Juliet, he's charming. I like him very much and I have to say I do feel sorry for him. Sonia has been very ruthless, hasn't she? Although, of course, I don't know the whole story.'

'Exactly. She has had a lot to put up with over the years, you know. Not that I'm defending what she's done.'

'He seems very fond of you. He told me so himself.'

'He did?' Juliet turned to look at her mother's face. 'Really?'

'Yes.'

'You see, he wants me to stay in England, to give up my job in New York and move back.'

'Goodness! And do you want to?'

'I don't know. Half of me wants to very much indeed because even after years of training myself not to, I find that I still love him.'

'I see.'

'It's far too soon, I know that. He's hardly had time to think straight with Sonia's drama playing itself out and his life in complete turmoil.'

'And the other half of you? The half that isn't so sure?'

'Well, my independence has been hard won, and I am quite content living on my own. Well, if not entirely happy, then anyway at peace, and I feel a real reluctance to put that at risk. But do you remember when you first looked round this cottage, what you said to me about Dr Ballantyne? You said something like, "Would he do for you?" I know you were half joking, but in fact I had thought exactly the same thing. You see, if I'm honest, I was still looking, Mother. I was still hoping that I might meet a man who would make up for me not having Gavin. It took only a look in Dr B's wardrobe to convince me that he wouldn't do, as you put it, and Gavin has since told me that he's very pedantic and dull, and has a bushy grey beard, but the point is, I feel there is a gap in my life, which I can't ignore. I used to think that maybe it's because I've never had children, but I realise that isn't true. I'm not one of those women who feel unfulfilled in that way. It's more that I want to share my life with someone. I want to have that sense of belonging to someone, and them to me. I suppose it's very old-fashioned, but I think it really does make a difference to have a partner in life and for life.'

Bobbie said nothing. She had the feeling that Juliet was less asking for her opinion than telling her what she had decided.

'If I say yes to Gavin, I know it's risky, but we have known one another and been friends for years, and I think that is the best possible position from which to start. I certainly don't want to marry him in a hurry, and goodness knows how long the divorce will take, so we'll just take it step by step and see how it goes.'

'But you're not letting him stay here? You seem adamant about that.'

'No, I'm not. I want to have this summer here as I planned, and get my research done and also spend time with you. He has to find somewhere to live in Oxford and I can go backwards and forwards quite easily while we get used to the idea of seeing more of each other. If it all works out then I will give in my notice and look for a job in Oxford.'

'Juliet, darling. I am very happy for you.'

'The other thing that I want to make clear to you is that I did feel very guilty when we were having an affair, years ago. I knew what damage I was doing to Sonia, but I wanted him more than I cared about her. I've always felt bad about that. However, I don't think I am at all the reason she has decided to leave him. He would never have left her for me, you know.'

Bobbie said nothing.

'No doubt she considers her Tory peer is a better bet. I never realised what an ambitious woman she is.'

'From what the paper said, that man has left his wife of forty years for Sonia,' said Bobbie. 'I wonder how she feels. It just goes on and on, doesn't it? The hurt people do to one another.'

Juliet looked at her mother sharply. Was this condemnation? She couldn't tell. It sounded more like an observation.

'What about the girls?' asked Bobbie. 'No one mentions them and surely they matter very much indeed.'

'Yes, of course they do, and that's the other thing. I want to take it slowly for their sakes. It won't be easy for them, and although I don't like babies or small children I do like teenagers very much indeed. I shall take a great deal of trouble over them, Ma, don't worry.' She patted her mother's hand. How old it looked, she thought, lying there on the sheet, snaked with blue veins, and how very familiar and dear. 'I shall have to go back to New York for another term, and I think that will be a good test of our relationship, won't it?' She stood up and went to the window and looked out. 'I couldn't live in a village like this, could you? Apart from the non-event of that missing child, nothing seems to happen. I'd die of boredom.'

Bobbie thought of Henry and the news of his letter that he had brought her that morning, and Rachel and her near disaster, and all that had been at stake yesterday and how many lives could have been changed for ever. Juliet had been too involved in her own drama to take much notice, but no, she didn't think it was boring. Not a bit of it. Rather the reverse.

SARAH CHALLIS

Footprints in the Sand

When Emily Kingsley arrives at the church for her eccentric Great-Aunt Mary's funeral, she is still grieving for her broken relationship with the vain, mean and unfaithful Ted, and has little sorrow to spare. At the wake afterwards, she is dismayed to learn the contents of Mary's will. Emily and her cousin Clemmie must go to Mali, where they are to travel by camel into the Sahara Desert to scatter her ashes.

Clemmie, fanciful and rootless, is thrilled at the chance of adventure. Emily is not. With immense reluctance, she agrees to travel to Mali, and find Timadjlalen, a place in the desert that no one has ever heard of. Why Mary chose it as her final resting place she cannot imagine, and the thought of a hot, pointless trip is almost too much to bear. But once Emily and Clemmie set foot on the Saharan sand, and begin to uncover Mary's sixty-year-old secret, they come to understand why they must complete her journey . . .

Praise for Sarah Challis:

'So perceptive . . . Brilliant' Rosamunde Pilcher

'The characters are well drawn and the story . . . moves at a gripping pace' *Daily Telegraph*

978 0 7553 2169 8

headline
review

SARAH CHALLIS

Jumping to Conclusions

Point to point jockey Jess Haddon has maintained a resolute silence about the identity of the father of her little daughter, Izzy. But that hasn't stopped the rumours swirling around their small Dorset village: Izzy's adoring grandmother Belinda is not the only one who believes Jess must have had a fling with charming Johnnie Bearsden before he moved to America with his wife and children.

Belinda is certain Jess's secret cannot be kept for ever. And when she discovers Johnnie is back in the area, she knows everything is about to change. Sooner or later the story must break, and when it does, there will surely be terrible consequences.

Filled with all Sarah Challis's warmth, drama and humour, and set against the ravishing English countryside, *Jumping to Conclusions* will run away with you from the first page.

'Her evocation of the English countryside is elegiac . . . a pleasure to read' *Oxford Times*

'Sarah Challis is becoming a novelist to be reckoned with' *Dorset Life*

978 0 7553 2166 7

headline
review